MICHAEL MORECI

BLACK STAR RENEGADES

ST. MARTIN'S GRIFFIN ❧ NEW YORK

For my family. Every single day, it's all for my family.

BLACK STAR RENEGADES. Copyright © 2017 by Michael Moreci. All rights reserved. Printed in the United States of America. For information, address St. Martin's Press, 175 Fifth Avenue, New York, N.Y. 10010.

www.stmartins.com

Excerpt from *We Are Mayhem* copyright © 2019 by Michael Moreci

The Library of Congress has cataloged the hardcover edition as follows:

Names: Moreci, Michael, author.
Title: Black star renegades / Michael Moreci.
Description: First edition. | New York : St. Martin's Press, 2018.
Identifiers: LCCN 2017037539 | ISBN 978-1-250-11784-7 (hardcover) | ISBN 978-1-250-11783-0 (ebook)
Subjects: LCSH: Space operas. | Science fiction.
Classification: LCC PS3613.071727 B57 2018 | DDC 813/.6—dc23
LC record available at https://lccn.loc.gov/2017037539

ISBN 978-1-250-19506-7 (trade paperback)

Our books may be purchased in bulk for promotional, educational, or business use. Please contact your local bookseller or the Macmillan Corporate and Premium Sales Department at 1-800-221-7945, extension 5442, or by email at MacmillanSpecialMarkets@macmillan.com.

First St. Martin's Griffin Edition: January 2019

10 9 8 7 6 5 4 3 2 1

PROLOGUE

Cade ran.

Warm blood poured out of his nose and over his lips, but he was too distracted to smear it away. He was running as fast as his legs would take him while his brother urged him to "keep going, keep going," even though, soon, there'd be nowhere left to go. Tristan was older, bigger, and stronger; he could have outpaced Cade and their pursuers with ease, but he stayed by his brother's side, pushing him ahead. Cade sucked in shallow gasps of air as he heard his own racing pulse pounding in his ears. Exhaustion nearly claimed Cade, twice, but Tristan wrapped his fist around the back of his brother's shirt, keeping him close, keeping him upright. He wouldn't let them quit, not with the Zeros on their heels. They'd left their best friend, Mig, behind, knocked unconscious by one of the Zero thugs. Cade knew he'd be fine, though. The Zeros weren't after Mig.

They were after Cade and Tristan.

The brothers followed the narrow, winding path that cut through the back alleys of the Kyysring outdoor bazaar. Tristan knocked over harvesting bulbs, crates of dried botho meat, and anything else that might slow down the maniacs chasing them. Cade cursed their decision to sneak out of the shelter, even though it was his idea. Mig was aching to get parts for the dasher bike he was trying to repair, and Cade was itching to break the claustrophobic mania brought on by the shelter's confinement. Still, it was Tristan's job to talk Cade out of his dumb ideas, and if he didn't think strolling through a crowded bazaar at midday was the dumbest of ideas, then he'd somehow gotten as judgment-impaired as his brother. Cade and Tristan both had targets on their backs, and until they could jack a starship that would shoot them to the other side of the galaxy, the shelter was the only place they were safe.

Cade tumbled around a corner, a half step behind Tristan's lead, even though they both knew what they'd find: a dead end. In the halcyon days before a ruthless gunrunning gang wanted them strung up in the town square, all of Kyysring had been their playground. They grew up on this planet and knew every inch of its market, inside and out. And that's why Cade knew being pegged by the Zeros in the bazaar was the worst thing that could happen. There'd be no escape this time. They'd been able to outrun the Zeros in the past, outmaneuver them, even outthink them. But the rabble pursuing them was eight strong, and all they had to do was shed some of their numbers to block off the few points of egress, and Cade and Tristan would be bottled in. That's exactly what they did.

"All right, all right," Tristan said as he hunched over and cupped his hands together. "If you jump right when I boost you up, you should be able to reach the top of the wall and climb over."

Cade shoved his brother upright. "Don't be an idiot," he said, winded. "I'm not leaving you."

"You'll do what I tell you to do," Tristan snapped, taking a parental tone. "I'm your—"

"You're my what? Not my dad, Tristan. You're my brother, and we stick togeth—"

"Oy!" a voice called from behind. Cade and Tristan turned to see four Zeros—led by their scrawny leader who scraped a pair of shock batons along the ground as he sauntered ahead—closing around them. "It's charming, you brothers having a spat over who is more eager to die. That decision is in the hands of The Zero, not either one of you punks."

Cade could almost smell the leader—Qwayg was his name— as he stalked toward them. He wore a loose-fitting tank top covered by a fur-lined jacket, and he had a tattoo of an elongated star sloppily applied over his right eye. Everything about him was coated in sickly grime.

"Leave my brother," Tristan said, stepping in front of Cade. "If The Zero wants to make an example, he can do so with just one of us."

Qwayg scoffed. "This isn't a negotiation, kiddo. You're worth more to The Zero alive, but he'll take ya dead all the same. Your parents cost him a lot of money by attracting Praxis to our planet. And because of that, we have to show what happens when someone interferes with Zero business."

"Our parents didn't bring Praxis here," Cade spat. "They weren't helping the Kaldorian uprising—they were aid workers, not freedom fighters. Everyone knows that."

"Too bad they aren't around to say so themselves"—Qwayg shrugged—"or pay the price themselves. Now—"

At his signal, Qwayg's lackeys raised their weapons: One was equipped with a shock baton while the other two packed snub-nosed outpost pistols.

"How's this going to go?" Qwayg smugly asked.

Cade, though, was focused less on the threat of lethal weapons bearing down on him and more on the strange man who'd entered the alleyway. He was standing a couple paces behind the Zeros, a three-foot wooden bo staff gripped in his right hand.

"Let them go," the man said, evenly. "Let them go and walk away from here while you still can."

Cade watched Qwayg turn around, slowly, the satisfied grin already disappearing from his face. "And who's this? Granpappy?"

The strange man took two steps forward, and Cade studied him in more detail. He was older than any of the Zeros and wore a tight-fitting tunic the color of rust. His tidy appearance and measured demeanor were, to say the least, oddities on Kyysring. Same for the weapon. Cade noticed that three immaculate blades studded the top of his staff, but it was still just a wooden stick with some sharp edges. While it was nice for this crazy person to intervene on his and Tristan's behalf, what Cade really hoped was that he could last long enough in a fight against the Zeros so they could escape.

"Those young men belong to me now, so I'll say this one more time," the man explained. "Leave them be and get out of here while I'm still willing to let you do so."

"You have any idea who we are?" Qwayg yelled. "We're emissaries of The Zero! We're—"

"Poor choice," the man said, and in that same instant, he twisted the center of his staff and it crackled to life. Cycling sparks of raw energy, dark blue and orange, crowned the top of the staff, contained by the protruding blades.

Capitalizing on the distraction his fiery staff provided, the man jumped on the offensive. He swung his weapon around, using the blunt end to knock the outpost pistol out of the hand of the nearest Zero. He then jabbed the same end of his staff into the Zero's torso, doubling her over. Cade was about to yell out a warning as the other pistol-armed Zero trained it on the man, but before a syllable could slip through Cade's lips, the man grabbed the doubled-over Zero and used her as a shield against the incoming fire. He then charged forward, still using the woman for protection, and when he neared the Zero who was shooting at him, he plunged his staff forward—close enough so the energy could jump from the weapon onto the man, sending him into a fit of electrified convulsions. Unconscious, he fell to the ground, and Cade could see the smoke wafting off his body.

The man dropped the woman and pointed his weapon ahead, waiting for the two remaining Zeros to make their move.

"This guy is *awesome*," Cade whispered to his brother. Tristan wasn't listening, though; he was staring at the scene in front of them in wonderment.

Qwayg tried pushing his last remaining ally forward, toward the man, but he wouldn't budge. "You know what?" he said as he dropped his baton. "This isn't even worth it. I'm out." He kept his arms raised in surrender as he crept by the strange man, who let the Zero pass.

"You'll have no such luck with me, Granpappy," Qwayg snarled as he held his batons forward, their ends pulsing with dull purple energy—nothing compared to his opponent's crackling weapon. "I've been trained by some of the nastiest fighters you'll ever know."

"That's very nice," the man said and launched into his attack. He wrapped his hands around the center of his staff, using both the charged and blunt ends to fight off Qwayg's baton strikes. Qwayg came at the man with fast and varied strikes, but the man, as far as Cade could tell, defended himself with ease. And the more attacks he defended, the more ferocious and frustrated Qwayg became; he started to grunt with each swing of his baton, while the man remained silent, his face a mask of impassivity.

Having tired of toying with Qwayg, the next time he came to attack, the man caught his batons on his staff; he spun his staff around, disarming Qwayg, and then, in a swift, fluid movement, he swept out Qwayg's legs and knocked him on his back, hard. Before Qwayg could so much as groan, the man had the charged end of his weapon pointed just above his face, daring him to move.

"Those boys are coming with me," the man said. "Do we have an understanding?"

"The Zeros don't surrender," Qwayg grunted. "We are the ruling pow—"

The man inched his weapon down the slightest bit, and the cycling energy leapt onto Qwayg's face, frying what few brain cells he possessed. By the time the man pulled his staff back, Qwayg was out cold.

The man then turned his attention to Cade and Tristan, neither of whom had moved while the Zeros were being dispatched. Tristan was still dumbstruck, and Cade was torn between satisfying his curiosity of finding out who this guy was and the urge to grab his brother and run.

"Don't be afraid," the man said. "I'm not here to hurt you, either of you."

"What . . . who are you?" Tristan muttered.

The man twisted his staff once more, and the energy that'd been pulsing at its head subsided. He walked closer to Cade and Tristan as he slung his weapon over his back.

"My name is Jorken, Ser Jorken. I am a Master Rai at the Well. Have you heard of the Well?"

"Nope," Cade sharply replied, even though he'd of course heard of the Well. Who hadn't? Defenders of galactic peace, spiritual warriors—all that stuff. But Cade wasn't sold on this Ser Jorken, and he wasn't going to give him what he wanted so easily. Especially when it seemed that the thing he wanted was him and Tristan, which was more than a little strange.

"You're a Master Rai. From the Well," Tristan said, still spellbound. "And that," he continued, craning his neck to espy the weapon strapped to Jorken's back, "is your shido."

"Excellent, you already know much," Jorken said. "That will serve you well."

"Serve us well for what?" Tristan asked.

Jorken smiled and leaned down so he could directly address both brothers. "For your training, Tristan Sura. And for your training, Cade Sura. You are to become Rai, like me, if you choose."

Cade and Tristan shared a glance; Tristan was still agape, while Cade shrugged at Jorken's offer. Unlike his brother, tragic events had aged Cade into skeptical pragmatism. Still, if the offer was real, Cade knew abandoning Kyysring for the Well would be a considerable upgrade. If nothing else, it would be nice to live in a place where he wasn't chased around by people trying to kill him.

"Does this mean we'll get to knock the snot out of some Praxis a-holes?" Cade asked.

"You live up to your reputation for possessing a unique fire," Jorken said with a laugh. "But that's not quite how we operate. You'll help people; you'll provide security, relief, whatever's needed to keep peace and justice alive throughout the galaxy. Much like your parents, in a way."

Tristan looked once more at Cade, and he already knew what his brother was going to say. "We go together, that's the only way," Tristan said. "If Cade isn't up for it, then the discussion ends here."

Jorken and Tristan's eyes trained on Cade, who wasted no time getting to the inevitable. "Anywhere beats this place," he said. "Let's go."

"I had a feeling this would work out just fine," Jorken said, and he led them through the alleyway, circumventing the downed Zero thugs as they passed.

They were walking through the artery leading them to the bazaar, teeming with people, when Cade broke the silence and their progress.

"Wait, I want to know something before we get too far," he said.

"Anything," Jorken replied.

"Why us? I mean, of all people, why did we get chosen for this?"

"It's simple," Jorken said, as he backed into the heart of the marketplace, leading the brothers to follow him. "I believe one of you may be destined to save the galaxy."

CHAPTER ONE

TEN YEARS LATER

The starship screamed through the sky, piercing the volatile upper atmosphere of the planet Quarry. Aerial detonations battered the assault cruiser, sending it careening off course and threatening to tear it in half. Inside the ship, the scanners were rendered useless, unable to predict the explosive squalls or chart a course to safety. The ship was flying blind through a neon-green-and-purple minefield, and Cade loved every second of it.

Cade's brother was less amused.

"I told you this was a bad idea," Tristan said, his arms folded over his chest as he expressed his disapproval from the copilot's seat.

"Did you?" Cade replied, feigning sincerity. "I must have missed that."

A nearby eruption on the port side rocked the starship. Tristan groaned. "Just try not to get us killed."

Visiting Quarry hadn't always been such a dangerous proposition. There was a time when it was a thriving planet and active member of the Galactic Alliance; its commitment to open trade brought its native spices to the farthest reaches of the galaxy and, with them, a small piece of Quarrian culture. But that was before the Praxis kingdom used the small planet to show the rest of the galaxy what, exactly, it was capable of.

Still, there was a way to reach the surface without incurring the wrath of the combustible atmosphere. Cade and Tristan, in fact, had a detailed flight plan that would have guided them to a small sliver of airspace that wasn't exploding. It was a hard-won map, learned through the trial and error of previous pilots, some giving their lives to find the one slice of sky that wasn't certain death.

They were nowhere near that sliver right now.

While Cade's penchant for taking unnecessary risks was well-documented—the Well literally had a file detailing his recklessness—he felt that his reasoning for abandoning the mandated "safe" plan was justified. After all, his and Tristan's pilgrimage was meant to be a clandestine one, and Cade knew how thorough the watchful eye of Praxis tended to be; if the ruthless kingdom was going to monitor any part of Quarry, wouldn't it be looking at the one safe place to land?

Plus, Cade happily admitted to himself, the opportunity to fly his ship—which he'd named the *Horizon Dawn*, for no other reason than it sounded cool—through Quarry's fabled sky of doom was too good to pass up. Cade just wished they'd get through it already. It felt like an eternity since their starship had plunged into this thunderous, life-threatening turbulence, and Cade was beginning to think that maybe, just maybe, this was a bad idea after all. He acknowledged the white-knuckle grip he had on the stick, which belied his cavalier attitude. But then, as if the galaxy was in a wish-fulfilling mood, the ship began to settle. Cade waited, expecting something horrible to happen to compensate for the galaxy's generosity, and when it didn't, he breathed a sigh of relief. Even the sensors righted themselves, detecting the small amount of light that the nearest moon managed to capture from the flickering sun and deflect to the planetary surface.

"You see?" Cade said, turning toward Tristan and flashing a playful grin. "I told you there was nothing to worry about."

"You're the only person I know who can provoke death with a smile," Tristan replied, unable to hold back a smile of his own. Cade knew that his brother enjoyed the thrill of doing things that you weren't supposed to do, even though he couldn't indulge in them like his brother.

"And what's that supposed to mean?"

Tristan leaned toward Cade and spoke quietly, sharing a secret that no one was around to hear. "You're a good pilot, little brother. But you're not *that* good."

Cade shot his brother a wounded look. "I can't believe you'd say that. After all, I'm not doing this for me, I'm doing this for y—"

Suddenly, the ship's warning array bellowed to life.

"You were saying?" Tristan yelled over the alarm. He swiped through the control panel's notifications, trying to determine the problem. "There's some kind of pressure building in front of us, it's about to—"

Although the viewport was coated with a gossamer residue, a gift from the atmosphere's strange chemical makeup, Cade couldn't mistake what the electronic screaming and Tristan's truncated warning was all about: A neon-green fireball, large enough to incinerate the entire starship, had burst in the sky ahead and was thundering directly toward them.

Cade jammed the stick to the left, sending them barreling out of the raging fire's path. His reaction to the explosion was instant, but its proximity left no possibility for a clean escape. As the *Dawn* jerked to the side, the fireball tore across its underbelly, violently whipsawing the craft. Cade flared the ship's stabilizers as he fought the stick, which was bucking out of his grip. The dashboard spat out one damage report after another.

"Yeah, yeah, yeah," Cade muttered, muting the shrill sensors. He already knew what the most pressing damage was and, at the moment, had no interest in hearing about the functionality of the ice machine or anything else. The rear propulsion engine had been clipped, and unless Cade found a way to compensate for it, and fast, the *Dawn* was going to drop out of the Quarrian sky in a spinning free fall.

"Cade," Tristan said, trying his very best to stifle the frustration that Cade knew was simmering within him. "We really, really need to stabilize the ship."

At the moment, Cade knew that the only thing that would stabilize the *Dawn* would be the surface—and only after several bounces.

"I'm. Working. On. It."

That pesky surface. Cade reminded himself that he had no idea when they'd get out of this minefield and, when they finally did, how close they'd be to the ground. That made it a little hard to plot a landing that wouldn't leave parts of them spread across half the planet.

Cade fired what remained of the thrusters at full throttle and was treated to a final burst that pushed the ship in the opposite direction of its spin. That, combined with the stabilizers being stretched to their maximum limits, worked to bring an end to the *Dawn*'s spinning. Metal shrieked and groaned as the ship fought against its own momentum until, finally, it came back under control. The ship was still free-falling, though, and Cade knew he didn't have a whole lot of time to solve this problem.

Meanwhile, Tristan unbuckled his restraints and carefully got up from his seat.

"What do you think you're doing?" Cade asked, agitated.

"I actually read that damage report, Cade. Our landing gear is stuck. I know it seems futile to fix that, but I figure it's best to have it working—just in case."

Tristan clambered out of the cockpit just as the *Dawn* began to violently stutter. Cade looked through the muddy viewport and watched as the ship, at last, escaped from the minefield for good. Below, the moon's soft light did a poor job of providing surface visibility, but Cade got a good enough eyeful to know he didn't have all day to figure out how to get out of this mess. Opaque darkness began to gain clarity as the ship hurtled closer to the ground, revealing a long, indistinct swath of brown and green. Cade gripped the stick and pulled back, hard, though it was of no use; gravity had the ship tightly in its grasp, and what was left of the thrusters was already screaming.

Cade had an idea. It was crazy, he knew that, but crazy was a big improvement over certain death. Turning to the dashboard's control panel, he worked his fingers over the ship's status report, getting a comprehensive picture of its vital functions. In front of him, Quarry's topography began to take shape: canyons, river-beds, and valleys, every stitch of it barren. It was a wasteland just waiting to become Cade and Tristan's final resting place.

All of the ship's essential operations were functional, kind of, except for the rear propulsion engine, which was exactly what Cade anticipated. With a couple of taps on the control panel's touch screen and a double confirmation that this was *really* what he wanted to do, Cade disabled every other engine. The *Dawn* groaned like an aggrieved power generator being terminated against its will, and what little bit of resistance the thrusters had offered against the free fall stopped.

Cade's beloved *Horizon Dawn* was now dropping from the sky. And starting to spin again.

Behind him, Cade heard the cockpit door slam open; using whatever parts of the ship he could grab on to for purchase,

Tristan climbed back into the copilot's seat and slapped his harness home.

"What happened to the engines?" he gasped, winded from the exertion of moving about the turbulent starship.

Cade could feel the heat accumulating at the front of the ship, the atmosphere's friction causing flames to spark around its nose. Ahead, a forest populated by black, dead trees rose from the ground like a line of jagged teeth protruding from the maw of a hideous beast. It couldn't have been placed in a more perfect spot.

"The engines?" Cade absentmindedly replied as he mentally ran the numbers calculating the ship's rate of descent and their distance to the forest. "Oh, yeah. I killed the engines."

"You what?!" Tristan howled.

Cade shot open the emergency flaps and fired the reverse thruster to get the ship better angled for its approach. He then called up the engine's manual-override screen. "You got the landing gear down, right?" He had to yell now over the noise of the ship melting around him.

"Yes, but that was when I thought you were going to avoid crashing!"

Cade ignored his brother's comment as he prepared to punch a maximum burn to all engines, grinning at this moment of unbridled lunacy.

The very tops of the trees came blistering into view, looking charred and awful. Cade still felt that a hideous monster was just waiting to loose itself from the ground and swallow the *Dawn* whole. But it wouldn't like the taste of what he was going to do next. He jammed his finger into the control panel's override command, sending maximum thrust bursting out of each of the ship's engines.

The *Dawn* heaved against its own momentum, pasting both Cade and Tristan to the back of their seats. A hostile swaying motion seized control of the ship, rocking it in every direction as if it were trapped in an ocean current, while the engines, over-whelmed by the sudden jolt of power, tried to find their level. They were still plummeting to the ground at a terrifying rate, but at least now they were flying forward. Cade just had to land before the full power burned out the engines for good. That would be bad. If those engines failed, the landing would be a lot less horizontal than he would've hoped for. People might even say he crashed.

As the ship fishtailed through its landing vector, Cade engaged the landing vanes—hoping they wouldn't be torn off the ship—and braced for impact with the forest below.

"Cade! We're coming in too hot!" Tristan yelled as he clutched the safety belts that ran over his chest.

"You think?!" Cade snapped.

The ship pounded into the forest, exploding a copse of brittle trees as it went. Metal screeched and screamed as the ship slammed into one tree after another—but it also began to slow. Cade wrenched the stick back—prolonging the time he had to rely on the rear engine to keep the ship stable—and let the path of destruction be the ship's natural brake. A large tree struck the viewport, splintering the reinforced, shielded glass into a multitude of pieces. The stick rattled so intensely in Cade's hands that it caused his entire body to tremble, and he accepted the fact that the ship's current conditions—too much velocity, too little stability—were probably the best he was going to get.

As the *Dawn* smashed nose-first into the ground, a mountain of dirt exploded over the viewport. Blinded, Cade could only hope there wasn't a ravine ahead, or a drop-off that flung them straight over the side of a cliff. But as the ship skidded across the ground, leaving another swath of pulverized trees in its wake, Cade realized their flight was at an end. His two modest goals had now been satisfied: get the ship on the ground; get it to stop while still in one piece. With an exasperated groan and a cathartic hiss, the ship finally came to a halt.

Cade released the stick, expecting to find his grip impressed upon the metal; his body shivered as his muscles released the pent-up tension. After all that chaos, the ship was now silent, eerily so, and Cade couldn't resist shattering it with a victorious howl.

"You're a lunatic," Tristan said, throwing off his safety straps. "And just because you brought this thing down in one piece, don't get it in your head that this landing is anything to brag about."

Cade rose from the pilot's seat and took a few cautious steps away from it. He was unconvinced that the ship wasn't a sneeze away from splitting in half. Still, he couldn't help meeting his brother with an ear-to-ear grin. "One day, they'll tell stories about this landing."

"Oh, I'm sure they will. Cautionary tales are the best way to learn."

With a casual swipe of his hand, Cade waved his brother off and headed to the rear of the cockpit. There, fit snugly into a frame molded to its exact size specifications, was the ship's remote drone unit. Or, as Cade called him: Duke. Across the galaxy, being bestowed with the title of "duke" was a mark of nobility. It signified bravery, manners, and kindness. The *Horizon Dawn*'s drone possessed none of these qualities. Mouthy and insubordinate, Duke never met a task he could do without resistance or complaint, but Cade knew two things: One, because Duke was connected directly to the *Dawn*, no one had a better handle on the condition of the ship in real time; and, two, Cade also could trust the old drone to follow orders and get the ship in working order. Probably.

"Wakey, wakey, Duke," Cade sang. "Time to earn your keep."

Cade activated Duke's control panel, and his mechanical body began to wheeze and whir. Like the *Dawn* itself, Duke was a fossil when it came to drone evolution; drones now were far more advanced and came with way better tech, more features, and seamlessly fluid body movements. Plus, whoever did the programming on the updated models had ironed out the kinks that caused older units, like Duke, to evolve into cagey old tin cans with sour attitudes.

When Duke laboriously stepped out of his housing, he sounded like he was going to take the wall of the ship with him. His boxy, bulky limbs released themselves of his casing with noticeable exertion, and when he finally was free, there was a pregnant pause before he spread out his broad shoulders and chest. His oval eyes glowed a soft yellow. Duke was a good head taller than Cade, painted black, with long arms that hung stiffly at his sides. If Cade didn't know Duke, he might be intimidated by him.

"Greetings, Cade Sura," Duke said as he came fully online. "How may I be of service? It seems that the ship has—oh, my. I take it that you fought a battle and lost, Mr. Sura. How dreadful."

"Knock it off, Duke. The flight logs are already in that brain piece of yours," Cade said. "Just have the *Dawn* ready to fly by the time we get back."

"Judging by the damage, I take it you'll return in four months?"

"You have four hours, and I don't want to hear any excuses. Also, set a security perimeter around the ship; if anyone or anything breaches it, let us know immediately."

"I will kill it."

"No. Absolutely not," Tristan ordered, poking his head in. "We have no idea if there's anything out there besides Praxis forces, and I don't want you shooting up any locals."

Duke's voice box rattled, his equivalent of a sigh. "Fine, be that way. I will instead play hide-and-deactivated should guests arrive.

You Rai have fun out there, and try not to get captured and or killed."

Although Duke got on Cade's nerves with his "can't do" insolence, Cade had a soft spot for the cantankerous drone. At least it had some personality. His tolerance of Duke—after all, wiping his memory banks would take five seconds—ran parallel to the loyalty he felt for his ship. Sure, most other ships in the Well's fleet were sleeker, faster, even sturdier, but Cade didn't waste time thinking about that. The *Horizon Dawn* was his, and if all it had going for it was attitude enough to stand out from the pack, that was fine by him.

Cade patted Duke on the shoulder as he walked toward the ship's exit. Tristan was waiting for him there.

"You know, I was thinking," Cade said as he caught up to Tristan. "On the way back, let's take the easy way."

Cade was certain he and Tristan were going to be swarmed by a Praxis combat legion at any moment. They strode on a path from the crash site that, even as it zigged and zagged all over the place, Tristan swore led right to the Quarrian spire. Cade darted his eyes to the sky with every other step, checking, even though they had good aerial coverage. But Cade wasn't about to leave anything to chance, especially when one glimpse from a Praxis scout drone was all it would take to ruin his and Tristan's party before it even started. The trees were packed so densely together— something Cade hadn't noticed on their descent to the surface, as he was too busy trying not to die—that their twisted and gnarled branches had grown into one another, creating a natural canopy.

Seeing the scorched limbs intertwined as they were, Cade imagined how horrifying Praxis's invasion of Quarry must have been. One minute the planet and its inhabitants were getting along as they always had, and the next a fleet of warships came along and the biggest one sucked the energy out of their star. This was before Praxis transformed into the galactic kingdom, before anyone knew they had such designs or technological capabilities. But the entire galaxy found out both in one awful swoop.

Cade was just a kid when all this happened, so he only knew the story through history texts and the recollections of others. From what he learned, the obliteration of Quarry's star was so sudden and so unbelievable that the myriad races living on the planet barely had time to process what was happening and respond. The death toll was staggering, as those who didn't have the resources to escape, or simply failed to escape in time, faced the agony of life—or lack thereof—on a planet that was quickly freezing and losing oxygen.

Quarry's government did all it could to respond from their provisional home in orbit around the planet, ultimately firing a series of atomic accelerator missiles at its lifeless star in the hopes of bringing it back to life. The payload succeeded, sort of. It resuscitated the sun to a fraction of its former power, but it also ignited the planet's atmosphere, sheathing it in the layer of explosions that Cade recently discovered was even worse than he'd been told. The result was a planet covered in a veritable minefield and habitable only to the most resilient species.

The trees that hung over Cade's head were one such species that couldn't survive the extremities the planet was forced to endure. For some reason, Cade couldn't shake the idea that somehow they knew that, and their last act was to embrace one another as their existence came to an end. While there were still some withering plants and shrubs on the ground generating the planet's breathable air, Cade realized how badly he underestimated what Praxis had done to this planet. Back home at the

Well, people described Quarry as a wasteland, but that didn't suffice. No new life would ever thrive here. No one would ever call Quarry home again. This planet wasn't barren like a desert; it was dead. And Praxis had killed it.

After mile upon mile of pushing ahead through the dead forest, Cade had to stop. Though he didn't want to admit it, the crash landing left him more than a little beaten up. He was sore and bruised, and the effort it took to keep his body moving wore him out. Breathing became a chore. The acrid smell of chemical refuse in the air competed with the whiffs of putrid compost Cade caught from the ground to see which could torch his olfactory senses first. The eggheads back at the Well assured him that Quarry's air was breathable—and now Cade couldn't wait to ream them out for not explaining that "breathable" air could still hurt like he was swallowing shards of glass every time he sucked it into his lungs.

"Cade!" Tristan beckoned from up ahead. But Cade couldn't answer. With one hand planted against a tree, Cade was doubled over, trying to catch his breath. Trying, and failing, to will himself to keep going.

Cade heard his brother yell again, but this time he detected concern in his voice. When Cade looked up he saw Tristan rushing toward him. "Cade!" he yelled again, and when he got to Cade's side he put one hand on his back and another on his chest, as if he were going to pump his lungs like an accordion. Tristan wasn't at all affected by Quarry's air, which made Cade irrationally annoyed.

"I know," Tristan said. "I know. This air is definitely worse than anyone thought. Just try to calm down; relax and it'll get better. Breathe."

Tristan was right. But, that was Tristan's thing: He knew what to do in any given situation. Not only did Tristan possess the rare combination of genuine bravery and strength, he was able to instill the same in others. Anyone who fought alongside him knew Tristan was just as committed to making himself the best person he could be as he was to inspiring others to do the same. Tristan, by his presence alone, made everyone around him better. Even his brother, which was no easy task. But now, now it was time to find out just how good—how special—Tristan was. Was he a savior, or an unintentional charlatan?

Not coincidentally, that question could only be answered on the one planet that the galaxy's tyrannical kingdom forbade everyone else from even *thinking* about. Never mind the aerial bombs that surrounded Quarry; Praxis was all over this planet. Their drones, in the skies and on the ground, were sure to be positioned between Cade and Tristan and their goal. It was just a matter of how robust of a force awaited them.

When each breath became less painful than the one before it, Cade was able to stand upright again. And he was more than ready to finish their mission so they could get off this rock and never look back.

"Come on," Tristan said, helping guide Cade through his first shaky steps forward. "You're going to want to see this."

Cade shadowed a few steps behind his older brother, who was taking, by his standards, a leisurely pace. They followed a path that rose along a steady incline until it resolved itself into a ridge just a few feet ahead.

"It's right over here," Tristan said, and Cade detected something in his voice that he hadn't heard from his brother in years: excitement. He was taken back to when they were just a couple of street kids on Kyysring, chasing after one another as they stole their way through the planet's bazaar. Life changed when they left their native world, and growing up, for Tristan, meant more responsibility, more pressure, and, in Cade's opinion, impossible expectations. Cade could only watch with a hint of mournfulness as the rambunctious boy he once knew turned into the serious and determined man who was supposed to shoulder the fate of the galaxy. Cade admired his brother and he believed in him more than anyone could possibly understand, but a big part of him still thought of Tristan as a grubby kid, constrained by nothing and answering to no one. He found himself missing those days more and more, and he wondered if Tristan did, too.

Cade inched his way toward the ridge, the path's incline rising to what felt like a straight upward trek. Tristan eagerly waved him forward. "All right, all right!" Cade said as he steadied himself. "I'm coming!"

The trees were less dense here, breaking up the overhead canopy. Hazy beams of moonlight poked through, providing Quarry with a soft glow that was like a blistering sunrise compared to the darkness of the forest Cade had just trudged through. Tristan grabbed Cade's elbow, yanking him to the ridge's crest. When he got there, Cade stopped dead in his tracks. He blinked hard as if trying to focus his eyes, and his jaw dropped. There, in the distance, was the spire.

Cade expected big. He was prepared for big. But the spire was so colossal that Cade questioned whether it could even be real. It was like a thing of myth come to life. Gray and auburn rock twisted, turned, and entwined into one another on its upward march, forming the spire's daunting exterior. Its immensity implied invulnerability, an assurance that no cataclysmic event would compromise its integrity, no ruthless kingdom would breach its walls. That spire would stand, always.

"Well . . . crap," Cade breathlessly said. "We don't have to go to the top, do we?"

Tristan rolled his eyes but then smiled. "That, little brother, is where our destiny awaits."

That's a stretch, Cade thought, but he nodded along anyway.

Cade knew the legend of the Quarry spire inside and out, how, many generations ago—so many there was no evidence of any of this taking place, casting more than a little bit of doubt over the whole thing—a great warrior named Wu-Xia single-handedly brought peace to a war-torn galaxy. If the legend was true, Wu-Xia was so profoundly distraught by the endless wars and hopelessness that consumed every star system that he retreated to the spire and vowed to stay there, meditating in solitude, until he could discover a way to bring peace to all worlds. He entered the tower with little food or water, humbly asking the Quarrian people to pray for his continued strength. Many committed themselves to his request, praying daily for Wu-Xia's return, even though, weeks after his ascent into the spire, most others assumed he was dead.

Wu-Xia had been gone for months, through two Quarrian seasons, when he stepped through the snow-covered mouth of the spire and rejoined the world. And he wasn't alone. At his side was a weapon, forged of materials no one—not even Wu-Xia's most fervent doubters—could identify. Wu-Xia claimed that the weapon materialized before him when his spiritual odyssey plunged him deeper than he'd ever been into the fabric that bound the entire galaxy together. Its name, Wu-Xia declared, was the Rokura.

Conveniently, no details existed of what the Rokura could actually do. Shoot lasers? Cast plagues on planets? Transform despots into cute baby bothos? No one had the slightest clue. The legend only boasted of Wu-Xia's power, Rokura in hand, to destroy or cow the dark forces of the galaxy and deliver peace wherever there was none. In short order, any wide-scale aggressions ceased, and things were pretty much okay after that.

Years passed, and with the galaxy no longer in jeopardy, Wu-Xia declared that it was time for "the corporeal phase of his life to come to an end." Which, as far as Cade was concerned, was a nice way to say that he decided to take a one-way rocket to the beyond. But before he did, there was one final duty for him to perform: He had to return the Rokura to the spire. It would remain there, he told the people, and could only be removed when the galaxy's peace was once again threatened by a great darkness. Then someone worthy of the mantle would rise to take the weapon. "They will be the best of all people, the 'Paragon,'" Wu-Xia said, his final words before disappearing into the spire forever.

And now, here were Cade and Tristan, on a mission to sneak into the spire under Praxis's nose to see if Tristan could accomplish what no one had been able to do in recorded history: remove the Rokura from its stasis. The Masters and other Rai at the Well seemed to think he could, and they were the experts. While the Well safeguarded peace throughout the galaxy, its primary function was to spiritually and physically train potential Paragons. For generations, its Masters adhered to Wu-Xia's principles and remained vigilant for the time when an evil so comprehensive, so unrelenting, would arise and threaten the galaxy's long-standing peace.

Praxis was that darkness.

Tristan was the light.

And Cade? Cade was his ride to Quarry so Tristan could grab the Rokura and blast every last vestige of Praxis into a black hole of the Rokura's making. Assuming it could do something as cool as that. Cade knew his role in this mission, so when his brother said things like "that's where *our* destiny awaits," he knew it was where *Tristan*'s destiny awaited. Retrieving the Rokura wasn't a game of chance; plenty of Rai had tried to remove it from its stasis, but none had succeeded. Not ever. And since Wu-Xia's time, of course, war and peace had come and gone, and the galaxy had had to muddle on without the Paragon. But this time was different.

Praxis was different.

Other would-be empires had risen and fallen, but they'd crumbled under their own weight or been stalemated by other powers. And usually most weren't what you'd call "evil," but Praxis was staking its claim to be the worst of the worst—building its power slowly, quietly, until it suddenly burst out everywhere in the galaxy, not just looking to rule, but to lay waste to whole systems in a thirst for resources. Its crippling of Quarry and its sun at the start of their push cemented that they were looking to do what no empire had done in millennia: rule it all. And Praxis would tolerate no saviors rising on their watch.

Getting Tristan to the Rokura, though, was worth whatever consequences Cade, Tristan, and the Well would face should the mission go wrong and they were detected. Praxis had grown so powerful that not even the Well and its elite Rai had a chance at defeating the evil kingdom. The Rokura was the only chance the galaxy had left.

"All right, we didn't come here to stand around and take in the view," Cade said, even though he had to shake off a feeling of awe when seeing the spire. He unsheathed his shido—a three-foot steel staff studded with four blades protruding horizontally out from its head—and held it close to his side. "Let's go have some fun."

CHAPTER TWO

T hat's a lot of drones."

Cade ducked behind the decaying monument that kept them hidden from the drones' sight and handed the field scanner back to Tristan. They were positioned about a mile from the spire's entrance in what had once been, according to Tristan, the burial grounds for the long-disbanded Quarrian Regal Guard. Huge, broken statues and other ceremonial edifices, reaching as high as twenty feet in the air, littered the grounds. The guard consisted solely of Quarrian nobility, all of whom dedicated themselves to safeguarding the Rokura after Wu-Xia embarked on his spiritual afterlife journey . . . thing. The Quarrian—who pretty much looked like humans save for their scarlet skin and the three braided tails that grew from the back of their heads—protected the spire for generations until one of their own spearheaded an internal coup in an attempt to claim the Rokura for himself. The mutiny was foiled, but seeing themselves tainted and unfit to serve the Rokura, the members disbanded and the Regal Guard was no more. All that remained were these monuments, ravaged by war and time.

Actually, that wasn't all—there were also the Heemahs, a race of creatures who, for whatever reason, called the burial grounds their home. They somehow came to the conclusion that Cade and Tristan were the most interesting things they'd ever seen in their lives, and they'd been shuffling alongside them, eyeballing them, even sniffing them, since the brothers entered the grounds. Cade knew they were harmless, and he was proud of how well he'd been able to keep his cool—but as they were surveying the spire's entrance, he felt one picking through his hair for bugs.

He slapped the Heemah's hand away and pointed angrily in its face. The Heemah, hunched over as it stood upright on its squat hind legs, looked at Cade curiously, not comprehending why he wouldn't want it looking for dinner in his scalp. With its leathery blue skin, fiery orange eyes, and patches of coarse hair popping up all over its body, it was one of the grossest creatures Cade had ever laid eyes on.

"Cade," Tristan said, interrupting his attempt to scold the Heemah, "will you focus, please?"

Cade wagged his finger one last time at the Heemah then turned back to Tristan; not a single one of those beasts was paying *him* any attention.

"There's only two alpha drones, right?" Tristan asked.

"As far as I saw, yeah. I doubt they'd station more inside; the alphas' job is to spot intruders and alert their Praxis overlords."

"Exactly. But alphas are the only ones who have the comms range to transmit an alert back to the Praxis fleet. So, they're the priority. We can take care of the sentry drones once the alphas are out of commission."

Cade raised an eyebrow at Tristan. He took back the field scanner, lifted it to his eyes, and studied the scene in front of the spire once more. He saw exactly what he'd seen five minutes ago: two alpha drones surrounded by thirty-five sentry drones, broken into seven squads of five. Now, Cade had no problem shredding a squad of drones. He relished the opportunity, in fact. The problem was that there was no way he and Tristan would be able to slice, dice, and bash their way through that many sentries before an alpha could send an alert back to its fleet, which happened in, oh, the blink of an eye. Cade truly loathed the alphas. They were identical to the sentry model in nearly every way: Coated in Praxis black and red, they both had broad shoulders that stabilized the weight of the reinforced, boxy armor that hung down to cover their torsos. Where they differed was in their cylindrical heads; in the alpha, there was an optical lens that could transmit visual data via high-frequency streams, making them the galaxy's most proficient tattletales.

"Yep, nothing's changed. The alphas are still guarded by a swarm of sentries who, I'm just assuming, are going to get in our way."

"We need to do something about that, then," Tristan replied, a hint of sly satisfaction in his voice. Cade knew he already had a plan, but he was going to make Cade work for it. Tristan loved giving him learning exercises he never asked for.

Cade groaned. "Okay. Our best bet is to somehow distract the sentries. Or at least some of them. *Most* of them."

"Agreed."

"I can use my impact detonator, but even if I threw it away from the spire's entrance, an explosion would probably be reason enough for the alphas to signal Praxis."

"Agreed again."

Cade rolled his eyes. "I don't know. Any distraction we manufacture will set off the alphas, and that's it. We're done for."

"Then maybe we don't manufacture one."

"What do you mean?" Even though his brother's unwanted

tutelage irked him, Cade enjoyed seeing his mind at work. No one could strategize like Tristan, and watching him assess a situation and problem-solve never got old.

"I mean we don't manufacture a distraction," Tristan said, thumbing toward a group of Heemahs. "We use a natural one that's already at our disposal."

Cade looked at the scavengers—three of them—that Tristan had pointed toward. They were currently engaged in testing a patch of dirt for edibility.

"You can't be serious. There's no way we can trust these things. How are they even going to do whatever it is that you want them to do?"

"Leave that to me," Tristan said, smiling.

"Oh, you're a Heemah whisperer now?"

Tristan crouched down, preparing to stealthily move between the monuments. It was unlikely that the drones could spot them at this distance, but it wasn't worth taking an unnecessary risk. No, they had to be cautious so, at this crucial moment, they could put their entire mission in the hands of the stupid Heemahs.

"I think I can get them to listen," Tristan said as he stepped away. "Trust me."

Of course, Tristan was right about the first part. Even without the simple language of the Heemahs at his disposal, Tristan was able to rally the beasts the same way he was able to rally so many other species around the galaxy. It was what he did. Cade could see him assuring the Heemahs that he and Cade were on Quarry to fight against Praxis, knowing that even the most primitive life-forms hated the fascist kingdom. He organized all twenty Heemahs into a pack, and he sent that pack rushing out of the burial grounds right toward the drones. More than once, Cade's doubt in Tristan's planning was proven wrong, but sending Heemahs on a stampede was ridiculous.

There wasn't much of a gap between where the burial grounds ended and where the drones were positioned. Cade and Tristan stayed a few steps behind the Heemahs, remaining hidden.

"I hope you're not setting these things up for a bloodbath," Cade said.

"Engaging indigenous life-forms isn't one of the drones' directives," Tristan replied. "They won't know what to do."

Cade was still nervous; if the sentries drew their B-18 blaster rifles and opened fire on the Heemahs, that would doubtless set off the alphas and elicit a knee-jerk response from Praxis. There was no way the *Dawn* was airworthy yet, which meant there'd be no escape; Tristan and Cade might as well make good use of the burial grounds and start digging their own graves.

As the Heemahs broke through the final line of monuments, they let out a painful howl that Cade assumed was supposed to be a battle cry but sounded more like a feral air horn. But, as Tristan predicted, the drones didn't respond, since the Heemahs didn't register as a threat; Praxis couldn't risk their primary objective—to guard the spire's entrance—being compromised by drones scattered away from their post, hunting down whatever life-forms registered on their scanners. So, at least for a moment, they were inactive. They clearly saw the Heemahs charging right toward them, but they didn't care.

The Heemahs lowered their shoulders and charged through the enemy line, knocking sentries clean off their feet. Sentries from untouched squads came to help their mates off the ground and were also bulldozed by Heemahs, who were running wild through what was once the drones' carefully arranged security wall. Now it was beautiful, beautiful chaos.

Cade and Tristan flanked the far side and positioned them-selves behind the alphas without being detected. There was a small window for them to slip into the temple unnoticed; they could get in, grab the Rokura, and not think twice about what-ever drones stood between them and their ship. But that window, Cade knew, was slammed shut once he saw both the alphas light the electric blades on their quanta staffs and move into attack position. The Heemahs were about to be slaughtered.

Tristan inched forward, and Cade grabbed his arm.

"Tristan, don't," Cade said, knowing there was no way he'd change his brother's mind. Even if the justification for the Heemahs' deaths was his opportunity to retrieve the weapon that would bring peace to the galaxy, he couldn't turn his back on anyone in danger.

Tristan, having already taken a few steps toward the fracas, didn't bother with words. He shot his brother a look that said "You should know better" and continued on his way.

Cade followed a few paces behind Tristan, providing backup Cade knew he wouldn't need. Ahead, the Heemahs were still busying themselves with keeping the sentries down, almost like they were making a sport out of it. They didn't notice the crack-ling sound of the ignited quanta staffs or the aggressive shift in the alphas' stances; thankfully, the alphas moved slowly and methodically, providing Tristan with just enough time to reach the nearest one right before it brained an oblivious Heemah.

In one fluid and fast movement, Tristan used his shido to smash the closer alpha's quanta staff out of its hands and, with the drone defenseless and caught off guard, he swiped an upper-cut blow that knocked its head clean off its shoulders. Its oval dome landed with a clank right at Cade's feet. One down, he notched, but as Cade assessed the situation and saw how far away the other alpha was, he realized they were screwed. A good ten feet separated Tristan and the remaining alpha, and the drone would soon turn its ocular lens on him. It would register the intrusion, transmit, and Tristan and Cade would maybe have a matter of minutes to climb the spire, figure out how to free the Rokura, fix their ship, and get off this planet. "Un-effing-likely" was Cade's official assessment.

Cade sprinted toward the alpha, even though he knew he wouldn't reach it in time. But he didn't have to.

As the drone's head turned, Tristan activated his shido and blue-and-orange energy began to pour off the weapon's head. He launched the shido like a spear, and it whistled across the air until it smashed through the alpha's optical lens. The alpha stumbled around, its flailing arms trying to grab the object that was sticking out of its faceplate, but it was done for. Its head discharged a couple of electric bursts before the drone collapsed to the ground, its hefty weight kicking up a cloud of dirt and debris.

Cade changed course and rushed to Tristan's side. "See? I'm not the only one who makes reckless decisions that—"

"Hush. We're not clear yet," Tristan said.

Cade was about to query his brother about how he'd enjoy walking back home should he be told to "hush" again, when he realized what was going on:

The sentries had recovered.

While their single-minded programming allowed them to be easily duped, it was that same programming that helped them quickly recover. They were coded to do one thing, and that one thing was their objective. Now they were focused on Cade and Tristan.

The sentries clicked and beeped, telling each other, Cade assumed, to "kill these idiots." Any Heemah that still charged were downed by the butt of a blaster rifle, making a nice, clear space for the drones to fire at will on their targets.

"Ah, damn it," Cade grumbled.

Cade felt the pressure of a whole lot of B-18s trained on the parts of himself that he'd grown accustomed to keeping in one piece. He liked his organs. He needed them.

"Okay, here's what we do," Tristan said as, instinctually, he and Cade backed into each other. "You give me your shido, and I'll get you an opening to get into the temple."

"To do *what*?!" Cade burst.

"Cade, you can do this, you can—"

The sound of the Heemahs' feral cry. The sound of blaster fire.

Cade hadn't noticed, and apparently neither had the sentries, but the Heemahs had regrouped and were back on the offensive. But not just mindlessly charging as they had before. They were aggressively attacking the sentries and displaying strength and agility Cade would've never assumed they were capable of. And because they were already so close to the drones, the Heemahs could prevent them, at least for a time, from being able to get clean shots off. The mangy beasts tore off sentry limbs, pounced and chewed through faceplates, and battered their metal bodies with ferocious strength.

The unbridled violence made Cade smile. "On second thought, I like these nutcases."

With the sentries distracted, Cade got to work thinning their numbers. As he rushed forward, Cade ignited his shido, and, like Tristan's, crackling energy burst from its head. Most Rai, including Tristan, held their ignited shidos at the base of the weapon, using it almost like a spear. Cade, though, kept his hands centrally positioned, allowing him to make faster, compact strikes using either the electrified blades at the top or the reinforced boka wood at the bottom to pound his enemies. The combination served him well; he reached the sentries and, using a quick series of strikes, he was able to cut off the power supply in the neck of one drone, tear through the back of another, and—after a near blaster-fire miss—shatter the head of another. Tristan, meanwhile, was a whirlwind. Once he retrieved his shido from the alpha's head, he struck with remarkable efficiency, destroying every sentry in his path.

Tristan broke off to the right—heading to where the Heemahs were least concentrated and the sentries were regrouping—which meant Cade was to break left. When they first began their training at the Well, the Masters marveled at how Cade and Tristan could predict each other's movements and act seamlessly as one, as if they shared a supernatural bond. But Cade knew there was nothing inexplicable about the depths of their relationship. All he had to do was think back on their nights on Kyysring, when they were cold, hungry, and scared, when the only thing in the galaxy they had was each other. He remembered the promises they'd made, that they'd get through the worst and make it someplace better. That was their bond—to survive, together, always. So when Tristan went right, Cade instinctively knew that the play was to divide and conquer and ensure their backs were never exposed.

Cade had easy pickings. He finished off drones that'd been mangled by the Heemahs and short-circuited others. All the while, he kept an eye on Tristan; no matter how many times they sparred together, how many times he watched Tristan train the Well's youngest recruits, Cade couldn't stop himself from marveling at his brother's preternatural fighting skills. Most people misunderstood why Tristan was so good at beating the snot out of everyone, but Cade knew the answer as clear as day. It wasn't Tristan's speed, strength, or reflexes that made him so unique. Nor was it his fighting style, which was as graceful as a silent dance. The secret to Tristan's success came down to one simple ability that no one else recognized: Tristan could see the future.

No one would believe Cade if he said that out loud, but it was true—in its own way. Be it human, drone, or an alien from some backward planet no one had ever heard of, Tristan always knew what his opponents were going to do before they did it, maybe even before they thought it. Cade watched as Tristan found himself surrounded by four sentries, three armed with B-18s while the fourth wielded a quanta staff. Any other Rai, including himself, would be dead. But Tristan? Tristan knew that the sentry at his eleven o'clock would fire first, so he kicked the side of the rifle just as it fired, sending the blast into the sentry at his seven. The sentry behind Tristan charged with his staff, and Tristan sidestepped it and took the staff right out of its hands. Seamlessly. He then flung the staff at the sentry at his three; the staff driving right into the sentry's head and knocking it off its feet. The sentry at his eleven fired again, and Tristan in turn used the sentry who had attacked with its staff as a shield. He shoved the shield sentry forward, where it collided with the sentry that'd been firing its B-18 and landed on top of it. Never one for showy displays, Tristan walked to the pinned sentry and, using his shido, smoothly dispatched it.

And like that, the battle was over.

All that remained was the sound of dying electric sparks as the sentries powered down for good. Cade and Tristan were surrounded by nothing more than a metal scrap heap.

"I guess we don't have to worry about sneaking back out," Cade said.

Tristan smiled halfheartedly, then gestured ahead, calling Cade's attention back in the direction of the burial grounds. There, he saw that the Heemahs were gathered in a circle—silent, all of them—their heads lowered to the ground. Cade followed Tristan closer, and he recognized what was happening: Centered in the circle of Heemahs was one of their brethren, lying lifelessly on its back. Cade stepped closer and saw charred skin on the Heemah's chest, the unmistakable wound of blaster fire. Tristan bowed his head, joining the Heemahs in their mourning.

Cade had always been troubled by death, more than Tristan, more than any Rai. Though he and Tristan both experienced the traumatic permanence of death—and at a very young age—Tristan was well-adjusted enough to acknowledge the tragedy and move on. He had to; all the Rai did. They faced death so often, caused it even, that dwelling on it would probably cripple the lot of them. Cade knew he was supposed to be more . . . mature, he supposed, and fortify himself with the acceptance of death as part of life, but he couldn't. He looked at these Heemahs and couldn't help but wonder if any of them were related to the one who'd been killed. Maybe they'd been friends.

"Should we say something?" Cade whispered into Tristan's ear. "I don't know what they believe in, or what they pray to, but I feel we owe them—I don't know—some kind of comfort. I feel bad."

Tristan turned to Cade and clasped his hand on his brother's shoulder. "It's okay," Tristan assured him. "Let them wish their deceased into a peaceful afterlife."

When the moment was over, the Heemahs turned to Cade and Tristan. For a moment, Cade was nervous they were going to redirect their outrage at losing one of their own toward its cause: Tristan and Cade's meddling. It was their fault, after all, that the Heemahs had gotten involved in something that wasn't their problem. Cade knew he'd be more than upset if the roles were reversed.

"I am sorry for your loss," Tristan said, stepping forward. "Your mate, like all of you, fought bravely."

The centermost Heemah nodded, then grunted in a way that sounded like it accepted Tristan's condolences. It pointed sharply at Tristan, then it raised its arm and pointed toward the sky. The other Heemahs followed and did the same thing until they were all standing, silently, pointing upward.

"Come on," Tristan said, pulling Cade away. "We should go."

As he walked away, he realized that the Heemahs weren't pointing to the sky to say their friend had gone there. They were pointing to the spire. He turned back and saw the Heemahs hadn't moved; they were all standing as they had been, watching Cade and Tristan go as they kept their fingers directed toward the Rokura.

Even they knew what was going to happen next.

The spire's sanctum was located in the center of the structure, and though he and Tristan were just starting their ascent, Cade was already compelled to complain about having such a long way to walk.

A winding staircase, carved out of the spire's own rock, wrapped up and around, probably to the very top. Cade couldn't tell, as the perspective from the bottom to the top eclipsed before it could give a clear view of the peak. At least they didn't have to drag their butts all the way to the top, Cade thought. That would take forever. Luckily, the trek up the staircase wasn't without interesting things to look at. All the way up, rooms were dug into the spire, set right into the rock, which was a marvel unto itself. And each room was adorned with spiritual talismans, artifacts, and paintings that, as far as Cade could tell, told the story of the Quarrian race's history. It was a good thing all that stuff was inside the spire: Its interior was probably the only place that had survived Praxis's assault and the subsequent fallout intact.

"Do you ever think about it?" Cade asked as he Tristan stopped to take a break on a platform between stairs. Cade sat with his legs dangling over the edge; they were on fire, sore from all the climbing. "I mean *really* think about it?"

"About what?" Tristan stood next to Cade on the platform, eyes scanning everything, eager to move.

"About what we're going to eat when we get back home," Cade sharply replied. "About becoming the Paragon, idiot."

"Of course I do, all the time." Tristan sighed then looked up, as if he were being cautious so the Rokura wouldn't hear him.

Cade groaned. He hated having to wrench opinions out of his brother. Somewhere along the path to becoming the most perfect person ever, Tristan had concluded that the best way to satisfy the most people was to keep his opinions to himself. That way, there'd be nothing about him to disagree with or disapprove of.

"And what do you think about when you think about being the Paragon, *Tristan*?"

"I don't know. I mean, I think . . ." Tristan paused as his brow beetled in thought. "I think I won't be able to solve all the galaxy's problems."

Cade screwed up his face into a full "Huh?" so Tristan continued: "Look, I don't know how Wu-Xia brought peace to the galaxy. I have no clue. Neither does Master Jorken or the Well High Council or anyone else. But I'm willing to bet he didn't do it alone. If I claim the Rokura, then, sure, I suppose that grants me some kind of authority to lead—but a leader is useless without people unified behind him. Praxis can be defeated, I know they can, but only if the galaxy unites and fights as one."

"Oh, sure," Cade said. "Because the galaxy is just looking for a reason to put aside its differences and start getting along."

"They'll get it together, I know it."

"Yeah, when a messiah tells them to," Cade sardonically replied.

Tristan tousled his brother's already unruly hair. "Your fake cynicism doesn't impress anyone."

Cade swatted Tristan's hand away and fixed his hair. "And your unrelenting optimism makes people uncomfortable. You know that, right?"

"I do, but they come around. Goodness always wins out."

"Ugh. You can't even stop yourself."

"Oh, come on," Tristan said. "I was joking."

Tristan pulled Cade up, ending their break. "Let's go, little brother," he said. "We're almost there." Cade looked at his brother and felt the need to say something. Something important. Soon, things would never be the same for them again. Tristan was about to be vaulted into a new life, and Cade would continue to just be Cade. It was as if Cade were standing on a hangar platform, watching his brother board a ship that would take him somewhere he could never go. The idea filled Cade with a sense of loss, of mourning. But before Tristan departed, Cade wanted to somehow capture this moment and hold it so he could think back, fondly, on the last time when he and Tristan were a pair. Just like they always had been.

The words didn't come, though, and Cade continued their climb, following one step behind his brother.

Tristan was right; they weren't far. A few turns of the staircase was all that remained before they spotted glyphs, ancient and rendered unreadable by time, that marked the entrance to the Rokura's sanctum.

All the Masters had told Cade and Tristan the same thing, that it was impossible to describe the chamber where the Rokura was locked in its stasis. Master Jorken said that thinking about it was like trying to remember a dream, and Cade rolled his eyes. He thought it was code for "I'm too old to remember." But he was wrong.

They stepped inside the sanctum, which was much larger than any of the other chambers they'd passed on the way up the spire. And unlike those other chambers, this one wasn't adorned in any way whatsoever. It was just a cavern given shape by black walls that were slightly obscured by a thin layer of red-tinted mist that hovered eerily throughout the space. The patches of mist swirled slowly, like little universes holding their planets in orbit. And who knows, Cade thought, in this weird place, maybe they were.

"Echo!" Cade yelled, but the only response he received in return was a scowl from Tristan.

They continued to take cautious steps forward, and Cade felt the atmosphere change all around him. It was cold, so much so that Cade clasped the outer layer of his tunic shut and huddled into it for warmth. But it wasn't just that. Cade got the sense that there was a presence in the room with him, something he couldn't touch or see, but he could detect it all around him. He tried to laugh about the idea of the Rokura's magical spirit controlling its surrounding climate and setting the mood so it could haunt anyone who dared breach its sanctum. But as much as Cade wanted to make light of what he was experiencing, he had a hard time drawing upon his usual levity. What was happening was real. Cade could feel the presence of the Rokura envelope him, and he felt awed because of it.

"This is not what I expected," Cade said.

Tristan shushed him. "Concentrate," he said. "Something's happening."

They took another step forward, and suddenly the cavern began to glow. Chrysthums—floating orbs ranging in size from just a few inches in circumference to nearly two feet—bathed the surrounding area in soft blue-tinted light from their luminous core. Cade reached out to touch one that was floating in front of him; as he made contact with its translucent exterior, light met his fingertips and its glow carried warmth right into his core. It soothed him, and he wondered if that's what the chrysthums were there, in this special place, to do.

Tristan squeezed Cade's shoulder, and Cade turned to see many of the chrysthums organized into a single-file row. The orbs formed a line along a stone path that rose out of the cavern's ground and up; Cade's gaze followed the chrysthums to where the path ended at a floating platform.

"I take it they want us to follow," Cade said.

"I would say so," Tristan replied.

Silently, Cade and Tristan walked the chrysthum path. With every step, Cade felt anxiety welling within him. He knew people took him as cavalier, and he didn't blame them, because most of the time he acted cavalier. He was reckless, rebellious, and tended to make light of too many serious situations. But, Cade would argue, his shortcomings weren't *all* his fault. The Well barely let him do anything. When a civil war broke out on Durang, the Well sent in all their Rai, except for Cade. Someone, they'd told him, had to help the Masters protect their home in case of attack—even though that hadn't happened since *never*. When a trade blockade threatened to strangle Sulac, Tristan led a team of Rai to solve the problem, and, even though his brother petitioned for Cade to accompany him, the Masters wouldn't budge. Cade was excluded like this all the time, and, yeah, it made him pissed and bored. Because the fact was, despite superficial appearances, Cade cared. He cared about the galaxy's strife, and he wanted to fulfill his duty as a Rai and be an agent of peace and justice. He cared about the planets being trampled by Praxis, the families and homes being torn apart as the kingdom spread its cancer from one end of the galaxy to the next. He cared about his brother, and as proud of him as he was, he was afraid for what might happen if Tristan became the Paragon. How enemies would target him. How allies would use him. Things were about to change in a way no one—not Cade, not Tristan, not the Masters—understood, and Cade couldn't shake the nagging feeling that these changes weren't all going to be good.

But there was no turning back. The Masters were counting on them; the galaxy was counting on them. As Cade and Tristan stepped onto the platform, uncertainty jabbed Cade in his gut. His instinct was to grab his brother and run, to forget all about the Rokura and leave while they still could. Cade knew that wouldn't happen—especially when he looked straight ahead and there, not ten feet away from them, was the weapon that had the power to change the course of the entire galaxy.

The Rokura.

Cade froze, his glance locked on the object suspended in space, bathed in a soft light that had no source, hovering just above eye level. He didn't know what he had expected; he spent years conceptualizing the Rokura as a legend, not an object that actually existed. Examining it, Cade noticed nothing outstanding about the Rokura. His own shido, like all shidos, was a replication of its design. Though no one knew what kind of power the Rokura might contain—speculation abounded—its outward appearance was purposefully identical to Cade's weapon. Long ago, the Masters decided to train all Rai to be proficient with a Rokura knockoff, making it their primary weapon. That way, when the Paragon arrived, he or she would be prepared to wield his or her birthright.

"What are you waiting for?" Tristan asked. Cade craned his neck to see his brother still standing at the top of the platform, watching him. "Grab it."

"Yeah, no thanks. Cleaning up the galaxy is going to be *your* problem." Cade laughed, wiggling his fingers like some kind of spell. "You and your magical weapon."

If Cade was honest with himself, he'd cop to having moments in which he considered what it'd be like to try to pull the Rokura from its stasis. It's not like that was something he had the chance to do every day. While the actual moment would be nice, what came after was so terrifying that it didn't justify the chance he'd be taking simply by putting his hands on the weapon. If he tried to pull the Rokura out and it failed to budge, well, it would be just another reminder that Cade wasn't good enough. Wasn't good enough to be the Paragon, wasn't as good as his brother. It would be the galaxy telling him he was stuck in second place— second place of two. Or—and this is where things got truly awful—if he removed the Rokura, he'd become the savior for countless people on numerous worlds. Cade could not imagine a worse scenario for himself or the galactic population. So he preferred path three: Don't get involved.

Tristan walked a circle around Cade. "Look—I'm perfectly aware of what I probably am. And even if I am the Chosen One, I'm not comfortable finding out until you've taken your chance. You trained your body, mind, and soul for this moment, just like me, and I won't take it from you."

Cade rolled his eyes. He knew Tristan wouldn't relent. Once he got his mind set on something—especially if he considered it "the right thing to do"—there was no talking him out of it. Cade knew to save himself a lot of time and annoyance by just doing what his brother wanted him to do. And it wasn't like he had anything to lose; there was no chance the Rokura—after denying so many of Cade's betters—was going to end up in his possession.

Cade took a deep breath and reached his hand toward the Rokura. He expected nothing. He'd grab the Rokura, give it a tug, say "oh, well," and be done with it.

But that's not what happened.

The moment Cade's hand made contact with the Rokura, he felt the weapon surge a jolt of energy throughout his entire body. It didn't hurt, nor did it cause the least discomfort. The feeling, though, was real, and with it came a very unusual discovery: The Rokura was *alive*.

As its energy coursed through Cade, he could feel all his fears being allayed. His concerns over the fate of the galaxy in its struggle against Praxis, for Tristan's well-being, even for his own future—they were all laid bare and stripped away. In the absence of fear, Cade was free to focus on that which he wanted most: to be a person of his own. Maybe it was a juvenile desire, maybe it was trite, but Cade spent his life surrounded by people—his fellow Rai—who were doing what they were meant to do and living the life they wanted. While Cade wasn't jealous, he also recognized his lack of personal satisfaction. Since as far back as Cade could remember, he was just kinda *there*, just gliding along on the stream of life, going wherever it took him without having much of a say in where he was taken. Sure, tragedy robbed him and Tristan of the luxury of having all that many options, but at least Tristan had been dropped into something meaningful. He had found his destiny, and Cade was stuck living in its shadow.

Cade looked up, and he saw his right hand wrapped around the Rokura's hilt. It looked otherworldly, like it was some other hand not connected to his body. For a moment, no longer than a beat of his heart, Cade thought the weapon was about to break free, and his instinct was to tear his hand away. But the Rokura wouldn't let him. The stasis field tightened as its light was swallowed by an invading darkness that brought a sense of urgent fear. Cade winced. His vision went dark, like the chrysthums had all been snuffed out, and he was on the platform alone, captured by the Rokura. The weapon pushed a horrible omen into his mind, like death and disease and pure evil all balled into one. It horrified Cade, sickened him, and though he couldn't understand what it meant, he knew that the Rokura was trying to convey something vital to Cade—that something terrible was coming.

Finally, the Rokura released Cade, sending him tumbling backward. He had dropped to one knee and was panting when Tristan reached his side.

"Cade!" Tristan yelled, propping his brother up. "What happened? Are you okay?"

Catching his breath, Cade got uneasily to his feet. "I'm fine, I . . . I'm just a little unnerved," he said. "I saw . . ."

"What?"

"I don't know. I don't think it liked me very much."

"Well, come on," Tristan said, leading Cade back toward the path. "Let's get you out of the spire so you can get some fresh—"

Cade jerked his hand out of Tristan's grasp. "Don't be stupid. You are going to do what we came here to do. Besides, I'm not climbing up and down those stairs again."

Tristan looked back at the Rokura, then caught Cade's eyes and nodded. For once, Cade thought, my brother isn't going to argue with me.

As Tristan approached the Rokura, Cade's mind drifted into wondering about what just happened. He felt like he'd forged some sort of bond with the Rokura, and in the brief flash of time he spent connected with it, it told him the one thing he was afraid to tell himself: that he should, and *could*, be a better person. No one expected much of Cade, not the Masters at the Well, not even his fellow Rai. He knew this, but he winced at the realization that all his shortcomings were manifesting their destiny, not his own. There was a deep-seated desire within Cade, one he kept stuffed way down deep out of fear of what it might mean for his future, his relationship with his brother, and his place in the universe. . . .

Screw the Well.

He never, ever said it aloud, and even the thought of such rebellion—like real rebellion, not just showing off in fight training or something similarly juvenile—shot a shiver up his spine. It also made Cade realize a truth that really hurt. The Well didn't value him. Sure, they trained him and he was trusted with the occasional low-risk responsibility or mission, but he was more or less just hanging around in the background watching everyone else do things of real consequence. He was an outsider and always would be. So why stick around? Well, there was fear, for one thing. As in, leaving the Well and going . . . wherever scared him to death. If there was one thing he knew about the galaxy, it was that it was a harsh, unforgiving place. Which brought him to the practical considerations involved with leaving the only home he'd known since he was thirteen years old: He had no coin, no ship of his own, and was trained to do one specific thing—be a Rai—that didn't have the most transferable skill set. And, there was no one around to help him. Voicing even the idea of abandoning his position would make every single person he was close to—who all happened to be Rai and Masters—look at him like a foot had started growing out of his forehead. To them, being a Rai was the greatest thing ever all the time because, unlike Cade, they were allowed to do cool stuff. So if Cade ever mustered the courage to embark on this endeavor, he'd do so without so much as an understanding ear. And, worse still, he'd do it without his brother. That's where his motivation to leave went from difficult to inconceivable in the past. But now, for the first time in his life, things might be different. Tristan would be gone, out saving the galaxy. While that happened, Cade could sit at the Well and lament his loneliness, or he could change. He could stop being selfish, stop being foolish, and, most important of all, stop being angry about his lot in life. The Rokura gave Cade the confidence to walk the path that he knew was eventual, not because he wasn't good enough to be at the Well, but because he could do better elsewhere.

But there was that moment of darkness as well. A vision of pure hopelessness had erupted in his mind, one of pain and suffering. Cade couldn't make sense of anything the weapon was trying to convey to him, but he knew it terrified him. He'd have to remember to discuss it with Tristan, whatever it was, because Cade couldn't shake the feeling that it was something his brother needed to know.

As thoughts of the dark vision pecked at his mind, Cade's focus shifted to Tristan just as he was about to grab the Rokura. Tristan's eyes were intensely locked on the weapon, and as his hand drew nearer and nearer, Cade swore he could feel the room start to murmur. Just a soft tremble that carried through the floor and hummed at Cade's feet. Cade exhaled, and he saw a plume of his own breath dissipate in front of him.

The chamber had gotten colder.

The murmuring was growing stronger.

Something was happening.

And whatever that something was, it went into overdrive the moment Tristan made contact with the Rokura.

A violent shudder quaked the platform, making the ground beneath Cade's feet feel like it was being pumped by a hydraulics system gone haywire. Cade tried to steady his footing as the seismic shifts threw his body back and forth and side to side, making it nearly impossible to go anywhere. But he couldn't just stand there like an idiot and wait to be thrown off the platform. He had to run. He had to get his brother and get out of that chamber, out of the spire even, as fast as possible.

Cade looked ahead at Tristan, whose grip was still tight on the Rokura's hilt. Another tremor rocked the chamber, and Tristan's knees buckled beneath him. Cade could see that his face was locked in what seemed like intense agony; there was no telling if Tristan could get free of the weapon even if he tried.

Still, Cade had to do something. This, he feared, was what the dark vision was trying to tell him—that Tristan's contact with the Rokura would have the opposite effect of what everyone assumed. Cade tried to run to his brother, but he barely made it three feet before the ground around him cleaved, opening a chasm between himself and Tristan. Cade was knocked off his feet, but he'd be damned if anything—be it a hole in the floor or a magical weapon—was going to stop him from getting to his brother.

Cade heard rock breaking loose from the walls and the ceiling, and he knew it was only a matter of time before this whole chamber came crashing down. Having placed enough room between himself and the chasm, Cade was ready to try to vault over it when he heard Tristan howl in pain. He was still glued to the staff, even as stalactites began to harpoon from the ceiling and drive into the ground. Cade dove out of the way just in time to dodge one of the spears, and when he rolled to his feet he saw chrysthums being split and erupting all around him. It was only a matter of time, Cade recognized, before it was him and Tristan getting split in half—or worse.

"Tristan!" Cade yelled. "Tristan! We have to get out of here!"

But as Cade tried again to rush to his brother, Tristan shot him a look that stopped him in his tracks. Cade anticipated agony, even suffering, in his brother's face. Instead, he saw a newfound poise and control. Tristan radiated *power*. "It's okay," he yelled, his words sounding far, far away. "It's almost over."

As Tristan's final word floated from his mouth, a crash of lightning burst from the top of the Rokura. Three bolts of light shot out from the weapon, and a thunderous explosion echoed throughout the cavern. The room went completely white.

When the blinding light finally dissipated, Cade's eyes focused on Tristan—and the legendary weapon he held in his hands. He was lowering it down, slowly and ceremoniously; his eyes were fixed on it, filled with awe and certainty. Cade immediately recognized that Tristan knew exactly what to do.

"You . . ." Cade stammered. "You're really him. The Chosen One. You're the Paragon."

Tristan smiled and walked steadily to his brother; he leapt over the chasm between them with hardly any effort.

"We're going to save the galaxy, Cade," Tristan said, standing tall over his brother. "You and I. Together."

They'd made a pact when they were kids, a simple promise to

each other. After they lost everything in their world that they knew and loved, after living on the streets and feeling broken enough to enter the orphanage, they'd huddle together at night and dream of traversing space, protecting people from the galaxy's darkness. The same darkness that took their parents. The sky held infinite stars, and each night they'd renew their promise on a new star: Wherever they went, whatever happened, they'd do it together. Even when the Well took them away from Kyysring, they held fast to their word. Together they'd endured more adversity than they deserved, and together they'd continue to face, unflinching, whatever the galaxy had in store for them.

"Brothers," Cade said, grasping Tristan's shoulder. He started to laugh and cry a little bit—tears of relief and joy at the same time.

"Broth—" Tristan began to reply, but was cut short by the fluorescent black spear that was sticking out of his chest. He spat blood, convulsed once, and the light fled from his eyes.

Cade grappled his brother's crumpling body, a "NO!" bursting from his lips.

Tristan was the only family Cade had in the entire galaxy.

Tristan was the Paragon.

Tristan was dead.

CHAPTER THREE

They both hit the ground, Tristan's blood staining Cade's tunic a dark crimson as it gushed out.

In the moments that followed, when the entire world went silent, Cade could hear his brother's final, labored breaths. Muffled, distant. Cade slumped to Tristan's side, though he was unable to speak a single word; they were deep in an ancient spire, miles from their ship, and on a planet that was so very far from home. Cade couldn't even find the words to lie to his dying brother that everything was going to be okay. And he certainly couldn't say good-bye.

Cade fixed his eyes on Tristan's, hoping that, somehow, if he held his gaze, he could keep his brother with him. But it wasn't possible. Tristan faded, and Cade knew his dying expression would be seared in his memory for as long as he lived. There wasn't anger; he didn't fight against the coming darkness, nor did he seem afraid of it. Cade saw sadness in his brother's eyes, like he harbored some great regret that would never be atoned for.

"I'm . . ." he said, gasping. "I'm sorry."

Cade shook his head, trying to deny what was happening. But it was no use. Tristan closed his eyes, and then he was gone.

Cade wanted to scream. He wanted to cry and beg for Tristan to return. He felt frightened, confused, and alone—only he wasn't. Someone had stabbed Tristan from behind.

Someone else was in the chamber.

Quickly, Cade grabbed his shido and raised it above his head with both hands, blocking a downward strike from a blade that glinted in the light cast by the few remaining chrysthums. The glowing black blade pushed down so hard on Cade's shido that it buckled his body backward. Cade gritted his teeth; he tried to make out the assassin, but the cavern's darkness consumed the being. All he could see was the blade—tarnished by his brother's blood—bearing down on him. Cade could almost feel the weapon's intensity pressing into his face. He was caught off guard, overpowered, and quite possibly overmatched—which meant he'd have to be creative if he wanted to get out of this cavern alive.

He'd have to fight dirty.

"RRRAAHHH!" Cade shoved his attacker's blade to the side, allowing him just enough time to grab a rock from the rubble that surrounded him. Right as the menacing figure recovered for another attack, Cade nailed the shadow with the rock, interrupting its movement. He rolled right, dodging the blade's awkward lunge as the assassin lost his footing.

Cade sprang to his feet and took a defensive position. As he did, the remaining chrysthums' glow renewed, shining more brilliantly than ever before. With their light, Cade was finally able to see the coward that had sprung from the darkness and murdered his brother from behind. Before him stood a hulking figure covered in black armor with gold scales, replete with a horned helmet and a bronze mask sculpted with a facial expression of pure hatred. Cade had never seen anything like it before, but what was most alarming was the assassin's weapon. From day one at the Well, Cade had been taught, in no uncertain terms, that shidos were rare weapons used only by Rai.

Yet here was the assassin, shido in hand, crackling with vicious black energy.

Fury welling inside Cade, he ignited his own shido, bringing its blue-and-orange glow to life. Cade had every intention of driving it through the assassin's heart.

"I don't know where you come from, but wherever it is, you're *never* going to see it again." Cade's words shot like daggers from his mouth; he could feel his pulse racing, his heart thumping in his chest, and he couldn't tell if he was being driven more by fear or rage. Maybe both in equal parts. "This cavern will be the last thing you see—no—check that. My face will be the last thing you see, right before you take your last breath."

The assassin scoffed, his voice a hollow rasp behind the mask. "Such strong words, little Rai. But your only hope's guts are on the floor, and you are no threat to anyone."

"Such convincing threats coming from someone who murders people from behind."

"Lay down your weapon, and I'll make your death a painless and noble one."

Cade's blood ran cold. He'd been walking a circle opposite the assassin, and he stopped dead in his tracks. If fear and rage had been fighting for dominance within Cade, rage had just taken over. Blinding, furious rage. "You'll make my death a noble one? *Noble?* Like you did to MY BROTHER?!"

Cade ran and leapt, thrusting his shido down on his enemy, who met the strike with ease. The two parried, Cade on the offensive with short, controlled stabs from the sharp end of his weapon and jabs from the blunt end. His enemy was strong; Cade could tell that his defense was effortless and, because of that, his attacks weren't going to get through. Patterned, strategic moves were never Cade's strong suit, anyway. Master Jorken had been the first to recognize that Cade was at his best when he deployed a more "free-spirited" fighting style—or so he called it. Sometimes, as Jorken said, proficiency is best countered with unpredictability. Which was a nice way of saying that Cade should do what he did best: make it up as he went.

As the pair sidestepped the rubble that surrounded them, Cade could feel the assassin trying to shift their entanglement so he was the one controlling the tempo. Cade refused to let that happen. He let his natural style take over, varying his strikes—their location and degree of force—so the assassin was too preoccupied with riposting Cade's wild movements to mount his own attack. Shido met shido until Cade delivered a quick sequence of slashes and sideswipes that created a brief opening. Cade flicked the bottom of his weapon up, batting off the assassin's mask and busting his face; the man staggered back, and in a paired movement Cade swung around and swiped his shido's electrified blade across the assassin's guts, slicing against his armor's golden scales.

It should have been a crippling, if not fatal, blow. Only it wasn't. The strike hadn't come close to cutting through the assassin's armor.

"Surprised?" the assassin taunted. Cade could see his face now; the man was much older than he anticipated. A coarse white beard—slowly turning red from the blood that seeped out of his wound—covered his cheeks and neck; deep wrinkles splintered outward from his eyes, and a condescending smirk stretched across his lips. " 'There's nothing as strong as a shido's blade. And we Rai are the only ones who wield this sacred weapon,' " came a singsong voice from his cruel lips. "That's still the bedtime story the Masters tell you, correct? Seems like there're a lot of things they're hiding from you. Things they don't want you to know."

"You bastard," Cade spat. "Your mask was just the start—I'll take the rest of your armor piece by piece if I have to."

Mocking Cade with a chuckle, the assassin removed the rest of his headgear and tossed it to the side. "You just try."

Cade leapt at the assassin again, who was ready for his attack. He lunged with his blade forward, bearing his momentum into the movement—something Jorken had yelled at him many times never to do. The assassin sidestepped, but not before letting Cade's forward motion plow right into his shido's hilt. Cade heard the crunch of his nose and felt hot blood pour from his nostrils before he registered the pain blooming in his face. Wounded and off-balance, Cade expected the assassin to cut his feet out from under him, but he didn't. The huge, armored man stood his ground, waiting. Provoking Cade to attack again.

Cade smeared the blood on the sleeve of his tunic and drew a deep, ragged breath. He deliberately kept his eyes off Tristan's body and focused on the weapon in his hands. It was part of him; it was an extension of his own self. And he had to be calm for his shido to do its work. That is what he'd been trained to do, but he knew it was all a lie. He couldn't defeat the assassin; he couldn't even cut him. Which meant he had a new objective: escape. Get past the assassin, get the Rokura, and get off Quarry while he still could. Because whoever this lunatic was, Cade couldn't let him get his hands on the Rokura. He couldn't let the weapon of alleged limitless power go wild in the galaxy. As much as he craved vengeance, he couldn't let his brother's birthright fall into the hands of some psycho who probably had grand dreams of despotism—or worse. That wasn't happening.

Cade's eyes flicked to the Rokura lying on the ground just a few paces behind the assassin. It had rolled out of Tristan's grip, but his hand was open and outstretched, like he was still reaching for the weapon. And then Cade launched himself at the monster before him. Toe-to-toe, blades flashing in the chrysthums' light and clanging as they met, the fighters seemed evenly matched. Cade suspected that the assassin was just toying with him, trying to prove his superiority by showing how easily he could take whatever Cade offered.

And the moment Cade felt an ounce of weariness, the assassin—with what seemed like preternatural recognition— went on the offensive. He was fast for his age, and his strength pushed Cade back on his heels. The assassin's shido locked with Cade's; he leaned in close, close enough for Cade to feel the heat of his breath and see the fury in his eyes. This man, whoever he was, was as good as any Master at the Well, but his technique was so much fiercer, a graceful rage flowing through every stroke. He may have wielded the weapon of the Rai and fought like one, but he was no Rai.

"You're not leaving here with the Rokura, *boy*," the assassin spat.

The tide was turning. Cade knew that once the assassin took control of the battle's tempo, there'd be no going back. He'd wear Cade down, create an opening, and then kill him and take the Rokura.

Cade was determined to not let any of that happen.

The assassin continued to press his weight and strength against Cade, and Cade continued to lose ground. The muscles in his arms were beginning to slacken; his knees burned from resisting someone much stronger than him. Something was going to give, and soon.

"It's not your fault," the assassin grunted. "You've been lied to and made to fight in a war you don't even understand. But it will all be over soon."

Cade had only one chance, one counter he had to execute if he wanted to make it out of the cavern alive. Moving as fast as he could, Cade spun away, disentangling his weapon in the process. He hoped the assassin's own momentum would work against him, that he'd stumble forward and lose balance. And in that narrow window when the assassin was defenseless, Cade could knock him down, maybe brain him, and pray that the armor keeping out a killing strike would also keep the man on the ground long enough for Cade to grab the Rokura and run.

But when Cade turned to strike, the assassin was waiting; he'd barely lost his composure. Cade, though, was already wildly plunging forward. The assassin swatted Cade aside easily, using just one hand to do it; with his other hand, he removed a small knife that was tucked behind his chest plating. Cade knew what was going to happen, but he couldn't move his body before the assassin drove the knife into his thigh, twisting it as it tore through his muscle.

Cade cried out in anguish, but his scream was stopped when he was punched in his mouth by the assassin's armored fist. He was struck again, then again, and when he made a feeble attempt to fight back with his shido, the assassin knocked it out of his hand and then pushed him to the ground.

Though disorientated, Cade tried to stand, but it was useless; his wounded leg couldn't support his weight. His only option was to use upper-body strength to drag the rest of him along, though there was nowhere for him to go.

"You fight well enough for a little Rai," Cade heard the assassin say as he crept behind him. "But I have a mission to complete, and I will not disappoint my master."

Cade spat blood, then he felt a sharp pain dig into his midsection as the assassin kicked him in his ribs; that was his way of asking Cade to turn over. He pointed his shido directly into Cade's face, the tip of its black blade hovering directly between his eyes; Cade could see the dried blood, Tristan's blood, and it filled him with a renewed, but hollow, fury. He shoved the assassin's shido out of his face, only to be met with it once again.

"Your brother died quietly. Why can't you?"

Suddenly, out of the corner of his eye, Cade caught a flash from a chrysthum as it started to glow. He glanced over at it, as well as he could, and noticed what was directly below it: the Rokura, just out of his reach.

The assassin followed Cade's line of sight and spotted the Rokura as well. "As if you could wield such power," he said. "Accept your defeat and make this easier on yourself."

The assassin's warning was hollow; after all, it's not like he could kill Cade twice. Okay, he could torture Cade and make his one death as terrible as possible, but dead was still dead. And while going for the Rokura didn't make any sense—Cade had no idea how to unlock its supposed power, and using it just as a shido was pretty much pointless—Cade couldn't resist.

Though it felt like fire was ripping through his thigh, Cade willed his wounded leg to move. He kicked the assassin in his knee, catching him off guard. The large man staggered backward, and, using his good leg, Cade swept the assassin's ankle, knocking him to the ground. With precious few moments to act, Cade dove for the Rokura and grabbed it.

He was rewarded with pain. Like being electrified, stabbed, and burned, Cade's body—every inch of it—erupted with agony.

When Cade grabbed the Rokura before, it played nice with him; it even tried to warn him, Cade realized now, of the masked lunatic waiting for Tristan to claim the weapon so he could make his move. But now—now it rejected Cade. Now it wasn't in the safety of its stasis. The Rokura was free, and its instinct must have been to protect itself from whomever came near, because the moment Cade came into contact with it, his mind was punctured with stabbing pain. The Rokura was not only fighting him, but it was letting Cade know that he had no business trying to use the weapon. He was not the Paragon, and the pain of that message being conveyed was unbearable.

"And what are you going to do with that thing?" the assassin yelled over Cade's screaming. "Look at you—it's killing you just to hold it."

The Rokura continued to resist as the assassin drew nearer. In just a few paces he'd be on top of Cade, close enough to aid the mystical weapon's efforts to kill him. Still, Cade couldn't let go. That weapon was the only hope he had.

"Come on!" Cade yelled, slapping the Rokura with his free hand and hoping for it to respond. "Do something!"

As the assassin stood over him, biding his time, Cade pleaded with the Rokura, trying to will it to action. Cade pointed the weapon at the assassin, urging lasers, fire, a stiff breeze, *anything*, to come out. Nothing happened.

The assassin laughed, a low belly laugh up from deep inside his armor. "It's a shame your Masters told you so little. Your brother wouldn't be dead, and you wouldn't be joining him."

Cade gripped the Rokura tightly, absorbing the pain it caused him. In a flash, his life came into focus. Anger over being stuck in a pointless rut; shame that he didn't have the guts to do anything about it. Fury over his brother's death raged inside of him, and he felt more alone than he ever had in his entire life. Despair threatened all.

And then, out of nothing, he felt a twin flame inside him, a rage that matched his own. A mutual grief, a shared fear of being misused and alone in the world. Nothing was happening as it was supposed to, and millennia of plans had been wrecked in an instant. It was all gone in the blink of an eye, and none of what was lost would ever come back.

"I hope that means we're on the same side," Cade prayed, hoping the Rokura was open to suggestion. Because as the assassin's shido came down on him, Cade flashed one thought and one thought alone:

Revenge. We need to take revenge on the coward who murdered my brother. Who murdered the Paragon.

The Rokura agreed.

Light sparked off the Rokura's tip, just like Cade's own shido, just like described by legend. But this light burned white, it burned brighter. The light was *more*.

Blistering heat surged through the weapon, scorching Cade's hand; even though they both wanted the same thing—to make the man who murdered the Paragon pay—Cade got the sense the weapon wasn't happy about being wielded by someone unworthy of its power.

But neither the Rokura's feelings nor Cade's melting hand mattered. Not in this moment. The assassin screamed as he threw all his strength and weight into driving his shido down on Cade, but it was of no consequence. He was frozen, painfully, exactly where he was. "You're not the Chosen One!" he yelled. "You can't use the Rokura!"

As if to only prove him wrong, a single beam of energy burst from the Rokura and enveloped itself around the assassin. It lifted him in the air, and as he hovered there, his armor began to disintegrate, piece by piece, until the entire carapace was gone. His body trembled uncontrollably, and Cade could see the agonizing pain in his face; the assassin wanted to scream, but his jaw was locked shut. Then, just as his armor had, the assassin's flesh began to disintegrate, revealing tissue, muscle, then eventually bone.

Cade tore his gaze away from the gruesomeness in front of him only to be exposed to the damage the Rokura had inflicted on his hand. All Cade could feel was burning, white-hot pain, but what he saw was different: His flesh had blackened from the wrist to his fingertips, not like it was burned but like it was dead. Like the vitality of everything in his hand—from flesh to muscle to bone—had the life drained out of it. The torment was no more unbearable than it had been before he laid eyes on the actual effects, but Cade's revulsion at what was happening to his own body lumped in his throat.

A cascade of light caught Cade's eye, and he turned in time to see the last remaining bits of the assassin's corporeal existence flash out of sight. Cade was horrified by the gratuitous display, but his response meant nothing. The Rokura was in control now, and it was much, much too late for anything to be undone.

In an instant, all the Rokura's light extinguished and the cavern was dark again. Cade lay on the ground taking short, shallow breaths. He couldn't move. The shock of what had just happened—so unreal, so awful—gripped him tightly. The assassin was just *gone*. Obliterated. What kind of weapon was this?

And his hand—Cade couldn't forget his hand. The fading trauma of the assassin's death was replaced by a searing pain, but it wasn't confined to his hand. It was in his arm, his chest, his entire being, like a poison coursing through his veins. Cade was terrified to look, even though he already knew. He lifted his arm and saw the lifeless hand. Cade couldn't even move it an inch. Still, the pain was so intense that it brought Cade to the brink of unconsciousness, which he was ready to welcome.

Then the cavern began to violently shake, just like it did when Tristan had taken hold of the Rokura. Chunks of rock smashed on the ground all around him, and Cade knew that if he wanted to live, he had to muster the energy to get on his feet and run.

Cade couldn't remember how he found the platform that protruded out from the spire about halfway between the ground and the Rokura's sanctum. It took every ounce of his energy—and tolerance for pain—to hobble even that far. He stumbled onto the jutting rock and lost his footing; he fell to the ground and he knew he wouldn't be able to get back up. His hand was dead. His leg had been stabbed, his face busted, and he was pretty sure the assassin cracked a few of his ribs with his boot. Cade was physically and emotionally spent, and this was as far as he could go.

Lying on his back, he fought unconsciousness. He pressed his wrist comms device to his face, thankful it was on his left wrist and not his right, activating it. He could only hope that Duke was listening.

"Duke," Cade mouthed, but all that came out was a raspy murmur. Cade could hear his labored breathing, could feel the darkness closing in every time he blinked. "Duke," he said, this time more coherently. "Lock on to me, Duke. I need . . . I need . . ."

Cade drifted. As he did, his thoughts were of Tristan and the lifeless body he'd been forced to leave behind. He had tried to take his brother with him, but it was no use. Cade could hardly drag him an inch without collapsing. The best he could do was take his shido and make a promise, a solemn oath, to use it just as Tristan would have.

But then Cade remembered that Tristan's shido wasn't his weapon anymore—the Rokura was, and Cade brought that with him as well, even though part of him believed leaving it in the cavern to be buried under a mountain of rubble might be for the best. How could Wu-Xia, master of peace, bring something so monstrous to life? How could this be Tristan's birthright? Something had to be wrong, and whether it was with the Rokura or the legend that surrounded it, Cade didn't know. But this was no instrument of peace. Unless peace meant the wanton destruction of everything and everyone that stood in its way. Sure, Cade had no problem imagining how a Paragon could use the Rokura to effortlessly smooth out the galaxy's problems, from the Galactic Fringe to the Inner Cluster of planets, in the blink of an eye. All he or she had to do was demonstrate the weapon's atrocious might, and every superpower, every rogue state, every backwater planet that no one bothered to even put on a star chart would tremble in fear. But that person would be no better than Praxis. Praxis offered order through fear, not peace. It demanded obedience by training a blaster—or a magical weapon, or technology that could obliterate a sun, take your pick—on the heads of the entire galaxy.

Cade could be wrong, though. After all, if Wu-Xia really was a totalitarian warlord and not an apotheosis of peace, there was no way his reputation would have survived unblemished, regardless of how powerful he had been. And despite what had happened in the spire, Cade didn't know what the Rokura was capable of when placed in proper hands. Cade wasn't meant to wield the Rokura, and of all the things racing through his mind, *that* he was certain of.

If the problem wasn't with the Rokura, and if the legend of Wu-Xia held true, that left Cade with only one option: The problem was with him. The Rokura didn't want him, and, truth be told, he didn't want it in return. Still, something had to be done with the damn thing. It was too powerful to be left to bounce around the galaxy, and as much as Cade tried, his mind was fading too fast for him to come up with an idea of what should be done.

Darkness consumed him. The edges of his vision blurred, and just before he faded away, Cade thought he saw the outline of a ship hovering in the sky above him. But any conclusions of what that might mean failed to materialize as his thoughts remained fixed on the Rokura and how he didn't want to touch it. He didn't want to see it.

He wanted nothing to do with it ever again.

CHAPTER FOUR

Praxis found him.

Cade startled awake to the sound of a homing alarm. The blaring siren pierced his brain, and he had to scan his surroundings twice to realize that he was in the *Horizon Dawn*'s cockpit, seated in the pilot's chair. He had no idea how he'd gotten there, as the last thing he could remember was desperately calling for Duke to come scoop him up before death's grip got to him first. Now Cade was yelling for Duke again, but nothing came out of his throat but a dehydrated, raspy gasp. It was great that the mouthy drone had saved him, but how did he let them get into this mess? Cade pinched the bridge of his nose, focusing his vision so he could study the nav system; as far as he could tell, the ship was free-floating in space just outside of Quarry. No wonder they'd been found.

Putting together the pieces that connected Cade being trapped outside the spire to being back in his starship would have to wait. At the moment, he had to figure out how he was going to lose the four Praxis Intruders—and who knows how many more were waiting outside of his scanner's range—that were closing in on him, fast. Cade couldn't help but curse Duke once more, even though it didn't help his situation in the least. It just made him feel better.

Evasive maneuvers were imperative, but when Cade went to grab the stick, nothing happened. He looked down, and then he remembered: His hand was dead, thanks to the Rokura. Instead of a palm and five digits, all Cade had was a blackened paw that couldn't grip a cup of water let alone maneuver the *Dawn* through a dogfight. Looking at it, Cade felt the pain and the agony all over again, and for a moment he felt physically ill when he remembered that the ancient weapon was somewhere on the ship. It was probably just waiting for its next chance to do something unimaginably terrible.

Survival odds were dwindling fast. Down to his left hand, Cade gripped the stick and hoped he'd be able to at least come close to matching his normal proficiency. Considering the *Dawn*'s temperamental flight controls, he wasn't optimistic. Plus, he'd have to alternate his left hand between plotting a course for a mass jump that would get them free and clear of this mess while evading Intruder fire once they got in range. Which just happened.

More alarms. Cade was really tired of hearing his ship scream at him, so he allotted himself a quick second to jam his right claw against the control panel and silence all alerts. He knew he was in deep trouble, *again;* he didn't need a soundtrack for it. Right now he needed to focus and find a way to not be blown to space dust. Assuming there was one.

The *Dawn*'s nose slammed downward and shot back up as proton fire from overhead battered the ship. Cade caught the briefest glimpse of the oblong vessel as it hurtled past, its stubby wings remarkably deceptive in cloaking its offensive capacity. You'd think wings that short wouldn't be able to hold much firepower but, as usual, Praxis found a way to innovate their capacity to kill to perfection.

Cade studied his scanner and identified the Praxis vessel as a scout-class Intruder, which didn't come as a surprise. Typical Praxis offensive protocol called for a scout to race ahead of its squad and lay down cover fire to get a sense of its enemy's defensive capacity. In this case, the scout had to have been overjoyed by what it discovered: There were no defenses. Cade didn't have the dexterity, or even the warning time, to remotely man his ship's gunner and offer a return salvo that would at least let the Intruder know someone was on board, and that someone didn't appreciate being shot at. As he glanced at the damage report scrolling—and scrolling—across the control panel, Cade remembered the shape the *Dawn* was in. It would have been more concise for the ship to generate a report of what *wasn't* off-line, malfunctioning, or inoperable. All Cade could make of the report was that he was hurtling through the cold, harsh vacuum of space in a vessel held together by luck and whatever nuts and bolts had the temerity to hold on.

There was no time for screwing around if Cade wanted to survive, which meant he needed help. Even if doing so would tear the tissue off his raw throat, Cade had to scream and get Duke's attention. If Duke could manage the gunner hull and keep the Intruders at bay for just a few minutes, Cade might be able to get them to a jump lane and rocket them far, far away from here. It was his only chance, and a slim one at that.

Just as Cade opened his mouth to howl for his insolent drone, the cockpit door slid open. Duke lumbered in and, without saying a word, brought the *Dawn*'s heavy artillery system online. The drone had some nerve, Cade grimaced. Taking on four Intruders in this rickety scrap heap was insanity. They needed to defend and flee, not engage in a suicide run.

"Duke!" Cade yelled, feeling every syllable lacerate his throat.

"I ought to repurpose you for industrial waste cleanup. Where have you been?!"

Duke looked askance at Cade, and his yellow eyes darkened. "Where have I been? Where do you think?" the drone erupted. "I was attending to your brother!"

Cade felt his chest sink as the air rushed out of his lungs. It was impossible, he thought. He saw the spear—the shido—pierce through Tristan's chest. He felt the life wither from his brother's body. But then again, did he? How could he know for sure? And the shido—maybe it missed anything vital. Maybe Cade had made the worst mistake of his life by leaving Tristan behind. And that's when the real terror sunk in, when Cade's mind flashed an image of Tristan, barely holding on to his life as he clawed his way out of the spire. All the while wondering where his brother had gone.

"How—how is he?" Cade softly asked.

Duke continued to work the artillery system as the Intruders moved into attack formation and started racing toward the ship. There wasn't much time.

"He's not well, Cade. And he's certainly not happy with you."

"With me? Why?"

Duke gripped the edges of the weapons array as he dropped his head, shaking it in what Cade took to be disgust. Contempt, even. "Maybe because you left him to die. Is that reason enough?"

"I . . ." Cade stammered, but no other words would come. What could he say? That he didn't mean to? That was the coldest comfort there ever was. "Sorry I left you for dead," wasn't an apology you could come back from. Still, Cade couldn't shake the feeling that this was all wrong, and he didn't like it. It wasn't bad enough that he'd lost his hand, been cowed by the Rokura, and lost his brother: Now his brother had somehow returned, and Cade was made to bear the weight of giving up on the one person in the galaxy who would never, ever give up on him.

More alarms blared, and Cade punched the control panel hard, cracking the screen. "I said turn off!" he yelled, but the alarms kept blaring.

Enemy fire was incoming. Cade took hold of the stick and spun the ship hard starboard. He drove the ship down, avoiding Intruder proton blasts, but he knew they'd be locking on his tail within moments.

"The heavy artillery is inoperable," Duke said, a hint of bitter resignation in his voice. "Maybe if the ship hadn't been trashed during landing, we would have the chance to mount a defense."

Cade was going to kill Duke. Decommission, scrap, and have his parts melted down. But not now. Now, he still needed his help.

"You shouldn't have been bothering with it in the first place!" Cade barked. "Now get in the gunner hull and spray defensive fire while I—"

The *Dawn*'s radar exploded as, out of nowhere, a Praxis warship and a dozen more Intruders dropped on top of Cade's position.

Cade gasped. He rose from his seat and, wide-eyed, he could see the fleet through his viewport; the busted glass splintered Praxis's numbers from a dozen to a hundred, though it didn't matter. They were dead either way.

Watching the Intruders and the massive warship descend upon him, Cade felt like he was losing his mind. There was no way— no *way*—for a fleet to jump on top of them the way they did. Even with coordinates, mass jumping was never that precise.

"Incinerator missile fired from the warship," Duke said. "We have . . . seconds."

Cade could see the missile heading his way, like a star streaking through the sky. And all he could do was stand by Duke's side and accept his fate. Cade closed his eyes, shutting out the death that was hurtling toward him, and thought it best to go peacefully. He could scream and yell and curse destiny, condemn the Well, but it wouldn't change a thing. This was happening. But as Cade shut his eyes for the final time, an image projected inside his head:

Tristan.

His brother was on the ship, and he was still alive. Maybe Cade was ready to die, but he wouldn't resign his brother to death a second time. He failed him once; he wouldn't do it again.

Cade dropped back into his seat and gripped the stick. He drove the ship to port, feeling it resist the sudden, sharp movement.

"Duke, get to the gunner! Go for the Intruders. If we can destroy enough between us and the incinerator missiles, we might be able to shake them off!"

But Duke didn't move. His focus remained locked on the viewport, and Cade was about to scream for him to move when he saw what Duke was mesmerized by. The incinerator missile had multiplied by three, and they were all racing toward the *Dawn*. The lead missile seemed no more than a breath away from impact.

Cade drove the ship down as hard and as fast as he could. He tried to voice his rejection of the situation, his utter refusal to allow this to happen, but no sound escaped his lips. Just a silent scream, then everything went white.

Cade's eyes shot open and he choked for air like he'd been drowning. His torso propelled forward, sitting Cade upright. His lungs heaved as his eyes struggled to bring his surroundings into focus. Cade's memory rushed fragmented images across his mind—the Intruders roaring toward him, the incoming incinerator missiles, the scorching white light, and even a glimpse of his own body, reduced to bones. The recollection felt distant, though.

Like a dream.

Cade sunk into himself. He couldn't shake how real Tristan's presence seemed. In the dream he was alive, and Cade felt his presence so strongly that the sensation lingered into his waking life. But as the world around him gained clarity, Cade recognized the truth: Tristan was gone, forever, his body buried in a ruined spire on a planet that no one would ever be able to reach. The realization washed over Cade, and it was like losing his brother all over again.

Cade clutched his chest, and he was startled by the knowledge that he *could* clutch his chest. Cade looked down and, with no small amount of shock, saw that his deceased extremity was gone. Someone had given him a new hand, an implant that Cade assumed was supposed to be a seamless replacement for what he'd lost. But it wasn't. The skin tone was a shade off, and the hairs poking through the latticework of skin cells on the back of his hand were slightly coarser than they had been. As Cade examined his new body part with an uneasy eye, he felt disquieted by its presence; a dull pain circulated from his wrist to his fingertips, like an echo of his gruesome encounter with the Rokura. His instinct, fleeting, was to claw and gnaw at the wrist and get the thing removed. It felt too unnatural, and in the moment, Cade would just as soon go back to the lifeless stump rather than have some foreign host agitating him from within.

He let his body fall back, and he felt his head hit a soft pillow. A bed—Cade was in a bed, though he didn't care where the bed was or how he got there. Not now. Instead, Cade shoved the pillow over his face and screamed. Hot tears formed in his eyes, and he screamed and screamed until he ran out of breath. He didn't even want to go on the mission to Quarry and, now, because of it, Tristan was dead and Cade . . . Cade was left with what? He didn't even have anyone to notify of Tristan's death. His parents were gone, and his only real friend, Mig, wanted nothing to do with him. Sucking in musky air through the filter of the pillow, Cade figured that the best he could hope for was oblivion. If he did nothing, then nothing terrible would happen and he could eventually fade into the fabric of the universe and live in anonymity on some planet deep in the Galactic Fringe.

It was a nice thought, but one he couldn't sustain for long, not even in his darkest moment.

Cade might be a pain in most everyone's side, he might not take things seriously, and he tended to follow his own set of rules—but he was no coward. While he could ditch the Well with a smile on his face as he left the Masters and Rai to suck on his ship's fumes, Cade couldn't abandon the responsibility he owed his brother. Having experienced the Rokura's sheer insanity, Cade knew that if Tristan wasn't going to wield it, then no one should. Which meant Cade had to find a way to destroy it and its terrible purpose—assuming that was even possible. Slowly, Cade pulled the pillow down from his face.

He wasn't on a starcruiser, that much he could tell. There was no grav system tugging at his core, adding just enough heft to his body mass to remind him that he was connected to the ground only by the grace of artificial gravity. He took a long, deep breath and got a good whiff of antiseptic, industrial-grade cleaning products, and urine. That alone was enough to tell him that he was in a medical facility. With that conclusion drawn, the rest of the room began to take shape around him. A half-dozen monitors blipped and beeped in disharmony at his bedside, aligned just over his shoulders in a tidy row. Just outside his door, a wellness drone wheeled back and forth, rehearsing the delivery of a troubling diagnosis in the chipper voice modulation all doc bots were packaged with. If Cade could fling something at the drone to get its attention and order it to get lost, he would. But there was nothing nearby except his comms device, and that had been buzzing with so many alerts that he didn't want to even look at it. Cade narrowed his eyes like he was fighting back a headache. He had to slow things down. He was in a med center, and it was safe to assume it wasn't a Praxis facility, which meant he hadn't been captured. The memory of crawling out of the spire came to him, how he desperately called Duke to rescue him. Cade put aside what a low point in his life that was—putting his life in Duke's hands—and he struggled to recall what happened after that. But there was nothing. Just blackness between then and now. And there was no telling how large the gap between the two was or what happened to him in that time.

That's when Cade's heart dropped. The Rokura. His head whipped around the room, searching, like the galaxy's most powerful weapon would be propped in the corner as if it were a broom.

Terrific, Cade thought. I lost the thing already.

In a panic, Cade tried to bolt out of bed, only to have his body fiercely reject his movement. Everywhere hurt. From his skin to his muscles, all the way down to his bones and even his teeth, he felt bruised, sore, and tired. As quickly as he popped up, he slumped right back down. If this was his permanent condition, he didn't want to ever move again. It was like the first time he'd gotten drunk off cheap root whiskey back on Kyysring with Mig. As he debated which side of the bed it was best to vomit off of, he pleaded for mercy from the universe, vowing to never drink again.

"It's the stem blast," someone said from behind Cade. For a second, Cade thought maybe it was the universe come to answer his plea, but he'd recognize that gravelly voice anywhere. He knew it was Ser Jorken.

Cade shifted his head just enough to see Jorken coming around the foot of his bed. Jorken was a tall, bulky man who always seemed to wear a sour expression, even though it belied his pleasant disposition. Every Master at the Well was charged with mentoring young Rai through their training and spiritual development, and whether by chance or design—Cade didn't know—Jorken drew Cade. And whatever happy countenance Jorken might have had in him prior was ground to dust by Cade and his antics. But, to be fair, it was the intensity of their relationship that drew them together. Jorken was like a father to Cade, and it was very unusual for a Master and a Rai to get that close. Most Masters had sparring rods up their butts, and the relationship they forged with their wards rarely grew beyond a rigid mentorship. What Cade and Jorken shared was parsecs beyond that, and Cade knew he would never have made it through the Well's rigors without Jorken's guidance.

"Your injuries were so extensive that the doctors figured it would be best to give you a comprehensive refresher. Plus, they were able to give you that new hand while you were under. The effects will wear off in, oh, about an hour by my watch."

"How long was I out for?" Cade asked, his voice dry and raspy.

"Just over two days," Jorken said, handing Cade a small cup of water. "Take some, but go slow."

A single drop of water met Cade's lips, and he felt like he'd been plunged into a spring on the cooling shores of Ohan, the paradisiacal planet. The water soothed his mouth and throat; he even felt it cool his insides as it slid into his belly. Cade drank down the entire cup, greedily, never knowing water could taste so amazing.

"Now," Jorken said, drawing nearer as his eyes examined Cade's face, "let me get a good look at you."

Cade withdrew from Jorken's gaze, which made him feel uneasy. "What? Why? I'm fine," Cade said. "Just a little banged up."

Jorken's scowl upturned into a proud, endearing smile. "Oh, I'd say you're more than fine, Cade. *You're the Paragon.*"

Cade blinked hard, three times, and on the third blink he held his eyes shut in what had to have looked like a pained squint. He knew Jorken had said words, and Cade knew what each of those words meant, but he couldn't make sense of them in the order they were delivered. Although Jorken had no sense of humor—though his wry observations could be funny in their blunt honesty—Cade assumed that his Master had to be messing with him, and he almost let out a self-deprecating laugh. But then he considered the circumstances: Cade was unconscious when Duke landed them on Ticus, the Well's home planet, and when he was carted out of the ship, he wasn't alone. The Rokura was on him. And who could possess the Rokura other than the Paragon? Nobody. And since Duke knew nothing of what happened inside the spire, he couldn't contradict everyone's natural conclusion: Cade holds the Rokura. Therefore, Cade is the Paragon.

Things keep getting better and better, Cade thought.

Cade's immediate impulse was to correct Jorken, to end this madness right then and there. But he stopped himself. If he copped to being a fraud, the Masters would yank the Rokura from his hands—forcibly, if need be—and they'd have a brand-new reason to argue and squabble among themselves over what best to do with it. There would be tribunals and closed-door meetings, open debates and latent animosity. The weapon would languish in their possession, as their inability to compromise, conceive a plan, and act would corrode the opportunity staring them in the face. Worse than that, though, was when they finally did put the Rokura to use, the consequences would be unimaginable. Because they'd never listen to Cade. No matter how deeply in horrifying detail he described his ordeal with the Rokura, no matter how hard he pleaded his case, knowing what its power could do to the galaxy, they'd never dare destroy it. If there was one thing all the Masters shared in common, it was desperation. They *needed* the Rokura, and Cade wondered if it was more to restore a balance of power to the galaxy or to justify their own existences. Either way, Cade would be damned if he was going to let the Masters step in and screw up his plans. If that meant lying to every single person at the Well until he could make his escape, so be it.

"I'm sorry to beam like this," Jorken continued when Cade failed to respond. "I know that Tristan didn't make the trip back, so I can only assume . . . I can only assume the worst, I'm afraid."

Cade sighed and rubbed his hand, his new hand, over his face and was reminded of what had happened to him in the spire. His hand was dead and gone, yet here he was with a brand-new hand and five digits, moving and touching just like the real thing. Only they weren't, Cade ruefully acknowledged. And the presence of this replacement felt like a reminder of what the Rokura was capable of and what it would do if Cade stepped out of line again. Not only that, but Cade felt like the weapon was assaulting him from afar, reminding him of how incomplete he was. When Cade left Tristan behind in the spire, he left part of himself as well— part of his spirit, part of his heart. That, like his hand, was gone forever, and any substitution would only serve to remind him of how much he was missing.

"It was . . ." Cade struggled to find the words, to find any suitable way to express how he was feeling. He knew it was impossible. "I can't believe he's gone. He's all I had. He's the only family—"

Jorken squeezed Cade's fake hand. "You have me," he said.

Cade smiled, gently, hoping that his expression conveyed the gratitude he felt for his Master. It was nice to know there was someone in the galaxy who still cared about him—someone, maybe more important, he could still trust.

"We need to talk about what happened in the spire," Cade said, angling closer to Jorken. "About what happened to Tristan."

For a moment, Jorken furrowed his brow as if Cade wanting to talk about his dead brother was an oddity. But he quickly snapped back into focus, lending Cade his sympathetic ear. "What of it?"

"There was a man in the spire with us. We didn't even know he was there until . . . until it was too late. The spire was dark, and it all happened so fast. He just . . . he came out of nowhere."

"And this is the man who killed Tristan? And ruined your hand?" Jorken asked. "One of the Praxis drones must have detected you, and it—"

"No, you don't understand," Cade interrupted. "This man, he was there *before* we got there—like he was waiting."

Jorken flinched. *"Waiting?"*

"That's not all. He wore this . . . this armor, this indestructible black armor. He was powerful, and fast. And *mean*. And whoever this guy was, whatever he was—he had a shido."

Jorken's face remained impassive, much to Cade's surprise. He expected shock, even disbelief. Instead, Jorken steepled his fingers in front of his face, and Cade could almost hear the gears in his head turning as he choose his next words very carefully.

"Cade, what I'm going to tell you is something only top members of the Well know. But, being that you are what you are now, nothing will be kept secret from you. Not anymore."

Cade nodded along, wondering just how many secrets there were to reveal to him. And who gave the Masters the right to keep things secret in the first place?

"You encountered what's known as a Fatebreaker."

"I'm sorry—a what?"

"Put simply? They are the personal killing force of Praxis's Supreme Queen—Ga Halle herself. Whether she's in the mood for a political assassination, or a revenge murder, or she just wants to send a message to anyone who dares oppose her will, the Fatebreakers carry out her command. They operate only in the darkest corners of the world, and they leave no trace or witnesses to their deplorable acts."

Cade propped himself up, carefully, and shook his head. He couldn't decide what was more unbelievable: that an entire force of these Fatebreakers existed, or that the Masters had kept their existence totally hidden. "But he had a shido. He fought like a Rai. How is that even possible? And why do it?"

Jorken sighed. "We don't know. Maybe to taunt us? Maybe to rival us? One thing I do know is that you were lucky to leave that spire with your life. How did you manage to survive?"

"What do you mean 'How did I survive?'" Cade replied, feigning arrogance at being asked such a question. He was the Paragon, after all. Yet beneath the display, Cade concealed paranoia and doubt. Was Jorken suspicious of what really happened in the spire? "I used the Rokura to blast that murderous thug into oblivion."

"Of course," Jorken replied, a hint of hesitation in his voice. "I don't know why I even asked that. I suppose I'm still getting used to . . . well, what you've become. May I advise something, though?"

"You're still my Master," Cade said, shifting into a smile. "Giving me guidance is your job."

Jorken tried to smile in return, but it wouldn't come. Instead, a shadow fell across his face. "Be cautious using the weapon. Until you learn to master it, it could be very dangerous—even for you."

"I'll keep that in mind," Cade said, sarcastically. "Speaking of the Rokura—where is it?"

"Your ship's drone is a stubborn one," Jorken said as he stood up. "He refused to hand it over to anyone but you, so we agreed to let him watch over it in the Masters' inner sanctum. It works out well, as we Masters agree that no human hand should touch it. Other than yours, of course."

"I hope you're keeping an eye on him," Cade said. "I wouldn't put it past him to try making off with it so he can sell the thing."

"He's being guarded at all times, and only select individuals even know the Rokura is there. Or that you're the Paragon. We figured it's best to keep this quiet until you're back on your feet and we all take the time to say our good-byes to your brother.

"Now it's late and you need to rest. Is there anything I can do for you before I go?"

Was there anything Cade needed? Cade had to chuckle at the question and fight back the urge to tell Jorken to get comfortable. There were plenty of things Cade needed, like, for instance, he needed to unburden his soul of the terrible guilt he felt over Tristan's death. If one of them had to die, there was no question Cade was the one who should have gone, not the savior of the entire galaxy. But here he was, alive and sort of well, with the most powerful weapon known to all sentient life his to control. And his plan? To plunge it into the heart of a burning sun—or something equally dramatic—the first chance he got. Cade needed to explain to Jorken how wrong they all might be about Wu-Xia and the Rokura, and how, if in the wrong hands, it was a means to terror, not peace. He wanted someone to understand why he had to destroy the thing, even though he knew no one possibly could. When the Masters discovered Cade wasn't the Paragon, he'd again be just some reckless screw-up whose opinion held no value; he'd be discredited and cast aside the moment he confessed what really happened in the spire. And if he did manage to complete his mission of destroying what everyone believed was their one chance for galactic peace, his name would be demonized until the very last human took its very last breath. So, did Cade need anything? Yeah, one or two things. But he wasn't going to get any of them.

"I'm good," Cade said, bottling up all his anxiety, guilt, and dread. "Just need to rest."

"Have someone notify me when you're discharged, and I'll come for you. There's a memorial service for Tristan tomorrow at dusk. We wanted to wait until you could attend. Cardinal Master Teeg will oversee the procession himself, and we'll make sure Tristan gets the send-off he deserves."

Cade looked at Jorken, holding back the emotions that were

building up inside of him. Jorken started to leave, but then he stopped himself. He held on to the doorframe, physically preventing himself from exiting.

"I know I shouldn't say this, Cade, but on a personal note, I couldn't be more gratified by what's happened to you. I've always known there was something special about you, that a destiny awaited that none of us could predict, and it turns out I was right." Jorken looked at Cade, smiling and withholding tears of his own. "You've made me proud, my boy."

Cade smiled in return, even though he knew soon enough he was going to break Jorken's heart.

Jorken left, and Cade stretched his neck to see him walk down the med center's corridor and disappear around a corner. The moment he was out of sight, Cade fought against his pain—which was, as Jorken promised, beginning to reduce—and stepped out of bed. He refused to stay in the med center for another second. He needed to be free, he needed to be where no one could find him, talk to him, even look at him. His clothes had been cleaned and were folded on a chair in the corner, and he assumed the *Horizon Dawn* was docked in its usual bay. If there was one thing growing up as a teenager at the Well had taught him, it was how to sneak off and back on to Ticus without a single person noticing. It might have been Cade's greatest skill as a Rai.

The Masters would advise him to meditate, to withdraw within himself and find his center, Cade reminded himself as he yanked his tunic over his head. They'd tell him that peace would come with focus.

But Cade didn't need focus. And he especially didn't hope for the harmony he couldn't find when his brother was still with him. Cade needed a drink.

CHAPTER FIVE

Ticus's three moons shone brightly in the southern sky as twilight fell over the planet. Cade gave the serene sky a long look before hopping into the *Horizon Dawn* to make his getaway. Beyond those moons, countless stars and their many systems. Some, like Ticus, were still free; others had fallen to Praxis annexation, and others still, like Quarry, had been conquered by the evil kingdom, their stars shining a little dimmer than they had before. Word of the Rokura's retrieval, and Cade's ascension, would soon be reaching all of them, free and annexed, and they'd all be looking to Cade to do things he could not: protect them. Free them. Put an end to Praxis's reign of fear and violent control. What they really needed was a time machine so they could all go back and stop Praxis's reign before it even started. There was a window in which the Well, the Galactic Alliance, and every responsible planet could have taken measures to halt Praxis's transition from an irksome star system to a totalitarian kingdom. But they all blew it. They either failed to take Praxis threat seriously—despite the crystal-clear writing on the wall—or they poor-mouthed their available resources and ability to fight a war, or, like the Well, they couldn't agree on a course of action and did nothing, secretly hoping that the problem would just go away. Their negligence, in whatever form it took, played no small role in getting them to where they were today—desperate for one single, solitary person with a magical weapon to come along and save their asses.

Cade tried not to bother himself with thoughts of the galaxy's fate now that its lone chance for salvation—Tristan—was buried beneath a metric ton of rubble back on Quarry. He sat with his feet kicked up in the pilot seat of his beloved *Horizon Dawn*, eyes closed, hands resting on his chest. He felt comforted to be in his ship, the one place he could truly call home. Technically, it belonged to the Well, but come tomorrow night, after Tristan's service ended and the Rokura was back in Cade's possession, the ship would be all his as he sailed away from Ticus one final time. What was a little theft when it came to saving the galaxy from the very thing that was supposed to set it free? If the Well was the galaxy's protector, then it had no higher calling than to provide Cade with a ship so he could see his mission through to the end.

Or maybe that was just Cade's justification for stealing his ship from under the Well's nose. The *Dawn* was a little worse for wear, but as far as Cade could tell, it was still spaceworthy. At least for now. Saying he didn't foresee any problems arising with his ship in the very near future greatly downplayed his level of concern. Cade wouldn't have been surprised if the *Dawn*'s operations ceased altogether and he was left to float through space in a useless tin can. He just hoped it didn't come to that.

An alert sounded and Cade jumped. Even though he was safely back home and the secret of his "role" as the Paragon was at least still sort of safe, Cade couldn't shake the feeling that everyone in the galaxy was after him. Some to enlist him, others to kill him. For now, the alarm coming from his ship was only the proximity alarm, telling him he was nearing his destination. "Get ahold of yourself, Sura," he whispered as he took control of the ship and entered his landing vector.

With the autopilot switched off, the blackout shutters that covered the *Dawn*'s viewport automatically raised. Through the splintered glass, Cade caught an eyeful of Aria, Ticus's orange-tinted moon.

Thousands upon thousands of points of light spread across the diminutive orb, the mark of the multitudinous agricultural companies that occupied the surface. Greenhouses, water reclaimers, harvesting bulbs, and other necessities for cultivating kerbis crisscrossed the entire moon, blanketing it in active, and lucrative, industry. Although kerbis was native to Aria—the only location in the galaxy it was native to, as far as anyone knew—not enough of it grew naturally to satiate the galaxy's demand. Hence, the need for farmers and botanists to occupy the moon and keep that little plant growing fast and strong. The leafy herb had more uses than Cade could list, from medicinal to culinary to being a rudimentary energy source. Cade even heard rumor that if you let the plant dry out, crumbled it into tiny bits, and then smoked it, it served a recreational purpose. Not that he knew anything about that. Not at all.

The best thing about Aria, though, was its liquor. If Cade knew one thing about the moon's botanists, laborers, and farmers—and he probably only did know one thing about them—it's that they loved to drink. The number of bars ran second only to greenhouses, although very few of them welcomed visitors from Ticus. And for good reason. After all, not everyone shared the Well's principles of keeping and enforcing peace by stocking a well-trained and well-armed military force. Some believed that the most effective path to peace was through diplomacy and nonviolent resistance. Although Cade thought this view of the galaxy was naive and uninformed—while it's true he didn't get off Ticus all that much, he'd seen enough to know that some people simply could not be bargained with—he respected freedom of speech and opinions, even if he disagreed. The Well tried its best to be a reactionary state, providing relief and offering diplomacy first when possible, but there was always the underlying knowledge that they could, and would, resolve any galactic conflict through their Rai, fighter squadrons, or ground troops. Most of the people on Aria happened to stand firm against these methods, which meant Cade had to play nice. After all, he didn't sneak off Ticus to engage in political debate; he came for booze—which was strictly forbidden by the buzzkills who ran the Well.

Cade stepped off his ship and breathed in air so thick and musty he was convinced he could catch it between his fingers and it would leave an oily residue behind. He crisscrossed a path between harvesting bulbs quietly churning a dim orange glow, the only light to be found in the dark, and empty, kerbis field. A farming drone expended a series of curious chimes and beeps as Cade passed it by, no doubt assessing the stranger in its fields; Cade had made it a point to dock in a secluded spot, another precaution against drawing attention. Dropping a signature Well cruiser that looked like it had just gotten out of a dogfight into Aria's public port wasn't the kind of subtlety Cade was after. He knew the proprietor of the field he parked on, and he knew where to leave the fee for doing so. Since trouble was attracted to Cade like a magnet, he figured dropping some coin to help him keep a low profile was a wise investment.

Just beyond the kerbis field, the glow of one of Aria's public centers began to take shape—the lights of the squat buildings, the din of the denizens crowding between the narrow corridors that separated the small trading kiosks, food counters, and public houses were just beyond Cade's grasp. But only one establishment had any value to Cade. He stepped through the final row of sweet-smelling kerbis—trying his best to look inconspicuous—and spotted his destination straight ahead:

The Gray Ghost.

There was nothing remarkable about the Ghost other than its reputation. Its exterior was crafted from reinforced blown glass—salvaged, likely, from nearby greenhouses—and its inside was a public house like any other. But there was one exception: The proprietors didn't care who they slung drinks to, including the occasional wayward denizen from the Well. Other establishments tended to let their politics get in the way of a good time, and that generally spelled trouble of one kind or another. Cade could handle trouble, but he had no interest in the grief he'd be slapped with once word of his indulgence got back to the Masters. All he wanted was to unwind with a couple of quiet drinks alone and then stumble back to his ship so he could pass out on its rock-hard drop-down bed.

But the moment Cade walked in, he knew the possibility of a peaceful drink had been taken out back and executed with a single, merciless shot from a sidewinder.

He grumbled the worst curse he could conceive to himself.

Cade slumped at the door and surveyed the crowd. It was packed with a dozen different species from around the galaxy, people who worked the kerbis fields in one way or another. Cade spied their dirt-encrusted hands, sun-beaten skin, and their lean, trim bodies; he breathed in a rich organic smell, like wet dirt mixed with the faintest whiff of compost. Keeping up the supply to meet the kerbis demand was no small task, and the reward was whatever liquor places like the Ghost managed to concoct throughout the day. The locals, though, weren't Cade's problem. That distinction was reserved for the crass, arrogant jerks of the Well's Omega Squadron.

They had positioned themselves in the middle of the Ghost—all sixteen of them—spreading their numbers across three tables that were covered by empty beer mugs. Terrific, Cade thought as his jaw clenched.

Cade couldn't turn back. If he shuffled back to his ship now, he'd have nothing in his belly but defeat, and that wasn't what he came to Aria for. He came for booze, so he'd have to hope to be lucky enough to avoid detection until he could find a dark corner to disappear into.

Four steps into the Ghost, Cade wondered why he'd been stupid enough to think luck was going to be by his side.

"Whoa ho ho!" a voice bellowed at Cade's side. "The almighty Chosen One walks among us!"

Cade shot a glance over his shoulder, knowing who he'd find: Elko, Omega's knuckle-dragger prime, standing just a few feet away from him.

"And he's gracing me with his glare," Elko added. "I thank ye, O regal one."

Cade should have known. "Select individuals know about the Rokura" Jorken had said, but secrets on the Well were as secure as water poured into a colander.

Having no other choice, Cade chewed the few steps between him and Elko, closing the distance between them. No one was looking in their direction, not yet, and Cade wanted to keep it that way. The last thing he wanted was a scene.

"I'm not royalty, genius," Cade said. "And I have no interest in entertaining whatever you're trying to provoke. So why don't I just buy you a drink and we consider that the price of you leaving me alone?"

Cade tried to turn toward the bar, but his movement was interrupted by Elko's mitt as it grabbed him by the shoulder and spun him back around. Elko straightened his slouched posture and rose even higher over Cade, who realized it was hard to appreciate a man's size until he's towering over you. Elko was an

Azzal, and his remarkable size was rare, even for his species. He stood a good foot taller than Cade, with shoulders so wide it looked like he could collapse them around Cade and absorb his body. He was so big, in fact, that the cockpit of his Echo-class starfighter had to be modified to accommodate his bulk. Like all Omega pilots, he had Omega's sigil tattooed into the side of his head—two symmetrical wings that morphed into fangs, bisected by a rising star—the ink spreading across the three gills that ran across his narrow scalp. Elko was one of two nonhumans in Omega Squadron, and while Cade didn't want to say he looked like a giant fish—that was considered offensive—the fact was that Elko looked like a giant fish. He had gills and scales, ashen-gray skin, eyelids that blinked from left to right, and webbed fingers. All pretty clear signs of marine life. Cade just had to make the slightest mention of Elko resembling something that came from the water, and he'd get a fight started right then and there.

"So tell me, all powerful one, what do you and your Masters plan on doing with this weapon? Are we going to continue to sit around and let Praxis take over more systems, or are you finally going to let Omega Squadron put its boots up their asses?"

"Oh," Cade said, feigning surprise, "I didn't know you and your squadron could defeat Praxis all on your own. Please, don't let me stop you. I'll just kick back and wait for you to finish."

Elko snarled, and Cade could smell the alcohol on his breath. "We've been waiting a long time for this, Sura. Too long. Your Masters keep us in check because—why? They don't want to start an all-out war, right? That's what they always say. But war's *already here*. They're too afraid to fight back because they think we'll lose. So instead, their strategy is to let Praxis press its boots on the galaxy's throat, just as long as they do it gently. But I'll tell you what: I'd rather die fighting than live under someone else's heel. There's a whole lot of us who aren't going to let your cowardly Masters stand in our way for much longer. We're going to fight back."

Cade studied Elko, considering what to say. There was a lot of truth in his words, because the Well was, arguably, complicit in Praxis's rise. At first, the Masters didn't take Praxis's aggressions seriously; then, they attributed the burgeoning kingdom's growth to fringe fanaticism; then, they discounted Praxis's growing might. By the time the Masters realized what Praxis had become, it was too late. The kingdom was already born. But Elko's insights ended there, and they were balanced by just as much stupidity. "You know, Elko, you're right. The Well has problems. The Masters screwed up more than once, and had a lot of people and planets been smarter, we wouldn't even be in this mess. But we are, and I know the Masters are doing what they can to help. You've been there; you've seen it. We've quelled interplanetary conflicts that saved thousands of lives, we've broken Praxis blockades and delivered relief to starving people—to families and children. If you think you and whatever other angry idiots you've surrounded yourself with can actually make a stand against Praxis, you're dead wrong. Praxis will eat you for lunch, and when they find out where you came from, they'll suck the life from our sun just to prove their point."

Somehow, another drink materialized in Elko's hand. He took a long, sloppy swig, wiped the foam off his mouth with the back of his hand, then shook it off so the residue splashed in Cade's face. Cade upturned his lip, but decided to let the offense slide. With any luck, that'd be the end of his conversation with Elko.

"Just like the rest," Elko grumbled. "Nothing but pitiful excuses. Guess that answers the question of whether you're with us or not."

"See you around, Elko," Cade said, and turned once more toward the bar. He wanted a drink more than ever.

"Yeah, walk away, Mr. Paragon," Elko mocked from behind

Cade's back. "Mr. Powerful. So powerful. So powerful you couldn't even save your own brother."

Cade stopped dead in his tracks and took a long, deep breath. He could just keep walking, he could get a drink and forget all about Elko. If he were a better person, one who was in control of his impulses, he could absolutely do that. But Cade was Cade, and while he generally couldn't care less what people thought of him, insulting his brother—his *dead* brother—was an entirely different thing. That slimy fish-face was lucky he didn't have the Rokura on him, because blasting Elko into complete and utter nothingness didn't sound like such a bad idea. But Cade was armed with nothing but his brother's shido, and he couldn't already break the promise he'd made to use it only for noble purposes. That meant he'd have to settle this thing the old-fashioned way. He turned, slowly, and shot a cold, hard glance at the other members of Omega Squadron. They were either looking away or shaking their heads, conceding that Elko had gone too far. It was their way of saying that should Cade go after Elko, they weren't going to jump in. That was exactly what Cade was looking for.

"Get real, Sura," Elko said. "We all know there's nothing you can—"

Cade didn't want to hear one more word come out of Elko's stupid mouth. He whipped around, led by his fist, and landed a right hook across Elko's face. He felt the squishy impact on his knuckles as flesh met flesh, and, as weird as it was, he was glad for the padding. Cade had thrown his entire body into the punch, which resulted in a wild, unorthodox strike. He knew better than to hurl his weight into a punch, but he wasn't in the mood for controlling himself. Cade's emotions were leading him, and right now, his emotions told him to attack like a wild animal, so that's what he did. And it worked. His punch landed squarely, much to Cade's surprise. What came as even more of a surprise was when

Cade realized that his punch, the one he directed all his strength into, had budged Elko maybe an inch back on his heels.

"Well . . . *crap*," Cade said as Elko glared furiously at him. He bared his chiseled, gray teeth and took three shallow breaths before unleashing a wet, gargled roar. His "MMMRR-RAAAAWWW!" echoed throughout the entire bar, and Cade could only watch as he raised his webbed right hand, which looked like it could suction the skin right off Cade's face. And who knows? Maybe that's exactly what he would have done had the one person who had the power to stop him not intervened.

"STUPID MEN!" a voice yelled from across the bar, sounding less like a comment and more like a command. As in, "Stupid men, stop being stupid." Whatever it was, it worked, and Elko froze his hand mid-plunge.

Cade turned to see Kira Sen stomping toward him, her fluffy Mohawk—a single row of hair set in dreadlocks—bouncing with every step she took. "Ah, great," he heard Elko grumble, and he glanced over to see Elko dusting himself off as he tried to stand at attention.

Kira stood between Cade and Elko, alternating her perturbed glance between both of them. Nobody in the entire bar said a single word until she reached her verdict.

"You said something dumb, Elko," she said.

Elko immediately went on the defensive. "I did not! He came in and—"

Kira shoved her hand in front of Elko's face, and he immediately shut up. She then turned her attention to Cade, keeping her hand in place to maintain Elko's silence.

"Cade, I apologize for whatever Elko did or said. Best I can tell, he was exposed to too much radion as a child. He's lucky he's such a skilled pilot, otherwise he'd probably be digging ditches somewhere. And poorly at that."

Cade gave a cavalier shrug, trying to conceal his deep, deep relief. "It's cool," Cade said. "I mean, I had the whole thing under control. But I appreciate you stopping him."

"Sure you did," Kira said, shooting Cade a patronizing smile. "Elko, go join your squadron. Cade, I'm buying you a drink."

"No, you don't have to. I mean, I'm—"

"That wasn't an offer," Kira said, turning back to face Cade— she had already started heading toward her own table in the back corner of the bar. "It was a command. Now come on; you're having a drink with me."

Kira Sen was, without question, the Well's best pilot. Just ask her, and she'd say so herself. She formed Omega Squadron, hand-selecting its members and training them to fly and fight exactly the way she did. And like all of them, she had the squadron's sigil tattooed on the right side of her shaved head, though it was often obscured by the dreads falling from her Mohawk. Cade eyed her and considered her vaunted—and insane—reputation and had to remind himself that she was only a few years older than he was, even though her accomplishments made it seem like she was a grizzled combat veteran. He also had to remind himself to keep his attraction in check. Sure, she had full lips and mysterious gray eyes, and while her tendency to be abrasive and brash could be really irritating, it was also really sexy. Kira was loaded with contradictions like this, and it drove Cade nuts. More than once he pondered how much he admired her for carving out her own niche at the Well while he flailed around aimlessly, but he also hated her for it. He *should* hate Kira, because she got to do all the cool stuff he was sidelined from, and she did it her own way. There was no one else like Kira, and being alone with her sprung an idea in Cade's head, but he immediately shot it down. Cade was smart enough to know that if he even intimated flirting with her, he'd probably end up flat on his back. And not in a good way.

"Two shots of root!" Kira yelled as Cade took the chair opposite her.

"Oh, okay. We're going right for shots?"

"I'm sorry," Kira said, pouting her lip. "Did you want something different? Maybe a floral concoction?"

Cade rolled his eyes and took the shot as it was dropped in front of him. "This is fine."

"A toast!" Kira yelled, hoisting her shot glass to the sky. "To the person who, apparently, is going to liberate the entire galaxy." Kira lifted her glass to her lips, but before she kicked back her shot of root, she looked at Cade and winked. "But no pressure."

Cade tossed the root into his mouth and tried to endure its unique, fiery burn as it coated his throat. Balanced with other ingredients—like mash, hops, or some kind of sweetener—root could be okay. Not great, but an improvement over its raw form, which tasted like rocket fuel combined with its own afterburner. Cade tried not to wince like he'd just been fed the stuff that made his ship go, but he couldn't contain his body's involuntary revulsion. His eyes burst open and he emphatically shook his head "no," as if rejecting what had already happened would somehow make things better. Luckily for him, he saw that Kira was having the same reaction, though she was better at forcing it back. At least he wasn't losing face as he torched his insides.

Kira pounded her empty glass on the table, twice, then held it up above her head. "Another round!" she yelled.

"I thought you commanded me for *one* drink," Cade said.

"Shut up," Kira replied. "You just lost your brother. I'm not going to let you sit here alone and wallow. It brings the whole place down."

A second round was dropped in front of them. The bartender must have known not to leave Kira waiting.

"So," Kira said, spinning her first empty drink glass clockwise on the table. "What's your plan?"

Cade slouched back in his chair. "Come on, I left Ticus so I didn't have to talk about . . . anything."

"Oh, what? You want to talk about the grim things that I can tell are on your mind instead? This is the fun part: You're going to have those Praxis dogs kneeling before you in terror. You don't want to indulge, at least a little bit, in how awesome that's going to be?"

"Assuming that's how any of this works."

"You don't know?"

"Kira, I just spent the last fifty-some hours in a medical coma. I'm lucky I didn't crash into an asteroid on my way here."

"If it was me who pulled that weapon, we'd already be storming Praxis wherever they are and wherever they go."

"And I'm assuming you have a foolproof plan for crushing the Praxis kingdom? I mean, who doesn't?"

Kira stopped spinning her glass and glanced at Cade with a look on her face that was entirely lacking in humor. Even by Kira's standards. "Yeah, actually, maybe I do. And maybe I'll pull it off."

"Careful now," Cade said with a playful smile, trying to bring back some levity. "You're starting to sound like the Rising Suns."

Kira scoffed. "Is that so wrong?"

Cade paused. He knew the Well's official line: The Rising Suns were a terrorist group that didn't diminish any of the galaxy's turmoil; they only contributed to it. They bombed Praxis outposts; they sought the weakest links in their supply lines and decimated them; they even started inspiring copycats who launched guerrilla attacks that compromised Praxis occupations. It was true that when the Rising Suns struck, Praxis responded by doubling down—their efforts, their cruelty, their suffocating presence. But there was no telling the intangible gains the Rising Suns were responsible for. Did their presence cause Praxis to second-guess themselves? Would showing Praxis's vulnerability give entire systems the confidence to fight back? Cade privately wondered about these things, knowing the ostracism he'd be treated to if he voiced any of these questions. Still, even with Kira, he figured it best to tread lightly when it came to appearing to side with denounced terrorists.

"Well," he said, "they're pretty much the opposite of what the Rai stand for. We're meant to be peacekeepers, not aggressors. The Rising Suns tend to only make our job harder. They attack, and then we have to clean up their mess."

"You mean you have to assuage Praxis so they don't do something atrocious."

Cade tried to counter with something but instead froze. There were times when the control panel on Cade's ship caught a glitch, and the screen would blink again and again until the system righted itself. Cade's face, as he tried to think of a way to counter Kira's statement, was that blinking screen.

"Face it, Cade. The Rising Suns are out there doing something, and we're not. End of story."

"Well, I'm sorry not everyone is obsessed with annihilating Praxis like it's personal, Kira."

Cade awkwardly groaned. He wished he could take all the words he just said and shove them right back inside his mouth. Everyone at the Well was dedicated to fighting Praxis, even if their methods for doing so tended to be unpopular. But no one had Kira's fanaticism. No one was as dogged in pursuit of inflicting pain and misery on Praxis. She trained like she was still learning the ropes; she was the first one to volunteer for any mission, and she was so headstrong in her tactics and methods that her superiors had no choice but to let her have her own rogue squadron. No one could contain her, and the Well couldn't afford to lose someone as gifted as she was, so they gave her what she needed. They let her operate however she wanted and surround herself with people who, if they were lucky, could keep up.

What caught most people's attention, though, was the way Kira fought. She went after Praxis like she had a vendetta, though no one knew why. And no one dared ask. Or comment on it.

"Look, Kira, I—"

Kira raised her glass and looked at Cade with a smile; he couldn't tell if it was forced or not. Either way, she was letting him off the hook.

"To Praxis's downfall," she said, and Cade joined her in the toast. The second helping of root did not go down any easier than the first. In fact, it might have been worse.

"So," Kira said, waving her empty glass in the air for the bartender to see. "Do I need a reason?"

"A reason for what?" Cade asked, still wincing from the drink.

"To want Praxis buried yesterday."

"For the way you go at it? Yeah, you kinda do."

Kira spun the glass on the table, nodding her head to whatever train of thought was going on in her mind. "I'll make you a deal: I'll tell you why I want to see everything Praxis burned to the ground, and you promise to let me be there when you do . . . whatever it is you end up doing."

Cade pursed his lips as if considering her offer. A third round was placed in front of him. He was the one to initiate the toasting ritual this time, and he used the liquid fire to bury any mixed feelings he had about agreeing to give Kira something he knew he never could. The urge to know her story overrode his guilt, and he reasoned that whatever she told him didn't matter anyway; he was long gone by the next moons.

"You got yourself a deal," Cade said, raising his empty glass to be seen. His equilibrium shifted with the sudden movement, and he felt his eyes roll before snapping back into focus. Cade wasn't much of a drinker, and he certainly wasn't one to match Kira.

"First, put your glass down. You're embarrassing yourself,"

Kira said as she raised her own. "And if you tell *anyone* about this, I'll—"

Cade raised a stiff hand to his brow and shot a lazy salute.

"On my honor."

Kira rolled her eyes and sighed. "This is a bad idea."

"Too late now," Cade smiled. "Spill."

Another round appeared. Cade decided it was best to take a breather even as Kira raised hers, staring wistfully inside. She took a breath, then downed her fourth shot—or at least her fourth with Cade.

"You ever hear of Lehara?"

"Nope," Cade replied. He took a sip of his shot and realized the grievous mistake he'd made. It was just as bad in small doses. Kira noticed and shook her head at his stupidity.

"It's a small agricultural moon in the Latos system, buried deep in the Galactic Fringe. It's like Aria, except more rural and way poorer. Nobody demands what they have to offer the way, say, kerbis is demanded. Nobody except for Praxis.

"See, the interesting thing about Lehara is that it's part of a cluster. Lots of moons nearby, lots of planets. Latos is a dense system, and it's strategically located. You can get to more than a few systems fast and easy from there. Praxis recognized this, and they made it a point to establish a stronghold there, as they're wont to do."

"Yeah," Cade agreed. "They sure like having a thorough presence."

"That they do," Kira said venomously. "That they do."

Kira raised her glass for another drink and continued. "Anyway, I was part of a squadron that was called to Lehara because we'd heard negotiations between the Leharans and Praxis had taken a, well . . . let's call it a bloody turn. Now, keep in mind this was one of my very first assignments. I didn't have a say in what happened or how things were handled. I was just along for the fight, and all I knew was that Praxis wanted to position their stronghold on Lehara for no reason other than that's where they picked, and they weren't taking no for an answer.

"So, you had Praxis with their boots on the ground, and then you had the Leharan people, who were these pacifists and spiritualists. A little weird but, you know, they weren't bothering anybody, so who cares? All they wanted was to be left alone, but Praxis wouldn't have it. They'd picked Lehara, and even when other moons stepped up and offered Praxis the real estate for their base, Praxis still wouldn't budge. Those bastards would. Not. Budge."

Kira paused and threw back her drink. Cade, dreading where this story was headed, did the same.

"We . . . we didn't get there in time. My commander, Shepard, had us stop on the way to check on some supply run that was supposedly being disrupted. I can't even remember what it was that we were doing, but it was a waste of a stop. He never took the Lehara situation seriously, and everyone knew it. But he learned. When we touched down on Lehara, he learned *exactly* how seriously he should have taken things."

Kira sighed and was quiet for a moment.

"Nazine gas," she resumed. "It attacks your nervous system, and the first thing it does is paralyze you. So by the time it spreads to your organs, you're completely and utterly helpless to do anything to save yourself as it erodes your body from the inside out. Praxis used this on Lehara, but not indiscriminately—no. They rounded up the women. They rounded up the children. And *then* they used it.

"We landed on a platform overlooking a massive cloot field, and it was like Praxis knew that's where we'd drop. Because the first thing we saw, the very first thing, were the bodies. All these bodies stretched out for . . . for who knows how long. Dead women and children. A dead crop field. We were lucky that the gas had dissipated by the time we arrived, otherwise we would've been right there with them."

Kira bit her bottom lip and stared at something over Cade's shoulder. Cade opened his mouth to say something, knowing how banal even his best-placed words would be. He was thankful that Kira stopped him and continued her story.

"Why do something like this, you might ask? I've been at this for ten years now, and I could only come up with one conclusion: Because that's the kind of messed up thing Praxis does. Granted, I heard Ga Halle held a tribunal and had the Praxian soldiers who used the gas executed, but I don't buy it. And even if she did, so what? They still built their stronghold on Lehara, right in the shadow of the atrocity they were responsible for. So, are they really *that* bothered by what happened?"

Kira leaned in close, and Cade felt beckoned to do the same. He could smell the root on her breath, and he liked it. Something stirred within his gut; the mixture of the root swirling inside of him, the intensity of Kira's story, and being this close to her was making his hands shake. He was swimming deep—too deep—and he knew he'd better start paddling back to shore before he embarked any further into uncharted waters.

"Does that answer your question? I saw something on Lehara that I never, ever want to see again. That's why I do what I do, and I challenge Praxis to try and stop me."

Cade raised his glass to take a drink, only to realize it was empty. Kira called for another round. As she did, Cade studied her, just as he had been studying her during her entire recollection. There could be a lot of ways to describe Cade—underachiever, troublemaker, undisciplined. But for all his flaws, there were still a few things Cade had going for him. One such thing, salient to this moment with Kira, was his prowess as an accomplished liar. He could talk his way out of just about any situation, he could connive and cajole to get things he wanted, and, because of that, he could detect his own kind. While the root coming off Kira's breath was potent, what was just as potent was the sliver of phoniness behind her story. It was all true, every word of it, and it was tragic. Kira's rendition of it was perfect. But that was her tell. It was *too* perfect. Kira was good, Cade gave her that, but not good enough to kid a kidder. And Cade had just enough drinks in him to call her on it.

"I believe you," he said. "I believe every word you just said."

Kira arched a curious eyebrow. "That's . . . an odd response. Thanks, I guess?"

"Now, look. I don't want to say that what you experienced on Lehara doesn't give you your, um . . . intense drive. It's a story, and it helps make you *you*. But it's not *the* story."

Another round appeared, and Kira immediately lifted her glass. She looked impassively at Cade, and he wondered when she'd splash her root right in his face. But, instead, she smiled. A devilish smile.

"You're smarter than you look, Sura."

Relieved, Cade raised his glass to match Kira's. "Yeah, well, I don't look all that great, so that's not hard."

"True."

"Screw you."

Kira downed her root without so much as batting an eye. She was beyond that. She thumped down her glass, then upturned her lip into a sly smile. "In your dreams."

Cade polished off his drink, trying to remember how many this made. Five? Twenty? He'd lost count. The only thing he knew for certain was that he wasn't paddling back to shore like he should have been. He was way, way out in the deep, and there was a massive wave rising from the depths, cresting right in front of his face. It was about to crash on top of him, and there wasn't a thing he could do about it.

The rest of the night was a complete blur.

CHAPTER SIX

Cade woke up on the floor of the *Horizon Dawn* with a dry mouth, a sore nose, and pounding pain in his head. It was as if his skull had shrunk overnight and it was now squeezing his brain like a vice. He peeled himself off the grimy metal, even as his stomach, which churned with every move he made, implored him to stay put. Dry blood was caked under his nose, and it was sensitive to his touch. It wasn't broken, which was a relief, though it was swollen enough so that every breath he took was paired with a sibilant hiss. He sounded, and felt, like a tire running out of air.

As he got to his feet, he nearly smashed his head on the drop-down bed protruding out from the ship's wall just above him. Great, he thought. I managed to pull out the bed but still wound up on the floor. But then came the moment of curiosity as Cade realized there was a strange body lying in his bed. He should have been alarmed, or at least concerned, by the sight of a slender, arched back crowding his sight at eye level, but he just didn't have it in him. He was too tired and sore to get worked up about anything.

Agitation, though—agitation he could muster. And that's what he felt when the back uncurled, and Cade realized he'd been staring at Kira.

"Morning, sunshine," she said as she stretched out, dressed in a tank top that hung loosely from her slight shoulders down to her underpants.

"Is it?" Cade grumbled. "I hardly know where we are, let alone when."

"Don't tell me you don't remember last night," Kira said as she leaned down and caressed Cade's cheek while shooting him a tender smile. "And how special it was for both of us."

Regret and dread vied for dominance within Cade, overworking his already frayed nerves. And then there was Kira, wearing much too little, distracting every thought that got started in his mind. The last thing he needed was to get entangled with her or anyone, and no one, especially Kira, deserved to be his cure for loneliness. Still, while the practical and sensitive half of Cade's brain laid out all the reasons why sleeping with Kira had been a bad idea, the cruder half of his brain was excited by the very same bad idea. As he looked at her, dumbfounded, he tried to summon at least a hazy recollection of the previous night from his mind. But there was nothing there.

"Did we, um . . ."

Kira stopped her caress and slapped Cade, not gently, across his face, breaking his stupor.

"Please. You could hardly walk back to your ship, let alone try to coax me into this wonderful bed of yours. And this is assuming I would even entertain the idea."

Cade vigorously rubbed his eyes as Kira jumped down from the bed and started getting dressed. Her explanation was a lot more probable than what he'd previously thought. And yet, despite all his hang-ups, Cade couldn't help but feel a little crestfallen.

"So, what happened, then?" Cade asked. "I remember being at the bar. I remember us having drinks. *A lot* of drinks. And then . . . and then, then there's a patch of nothing in my brain."

"Well, first, the bar closed, as bars tend to do. When that happened, you were too blasted to make it back to your own ship, so I had to haul your sorry ass all the way back."

Cade groaned in embarrassment. "Okay, but my nose. How did I bust my nose?"

"Uh, you fell trying to get inside," Kira said. "I had to carry you in like a wee little baby."

"Shut. Up. You did not."

"Okay, maybe not like a baby, but I did have to drag you up the ramp."

There were other questions in need of asking about the hours that were lost from his memory, but Cade had had enough humiliation for one morning. Besides, he had to get back to Ticus and clean himself up before Tristan's service. He managed to stand up, swaying a little in the process, and to keep down all the root that he felt swirling around inside of him.

Kira bent down to grab her flight jacket, and Cade spotted the beginnings of a scar dug into her chest, just below her shoulder. He didn't mean to gawk at it, but it caught his attention. Kira had always been an enigma to him, and here was this thing on her that had to have a story. He wondered how it happened, but he knew better than to ask.

"My eyes are up here," Kira said. Cade snapped out of his staring and spun around, away from Kira. The too-fast movement threatened to erupt his insides right out of him.

"Sorry," Cade mumbled as he turned his back on Kira and started to get dressed. "My mind's not even here yet."

Silence captured the ship, only to be interrupted by an incoming comms. Cade threw on his tunic and spotted Kira at the comms portal.

"No!" he yelled, quick and panicked. "I know what that call is about, and I don't even want to deal with it."

"Facing things that make you uncomfortable is good for you," Kira said, her finger hovering over the button that would accept the transmission. "Builds character."

"Kira," Cade warned.

"I think you should," Kira replied as she dropped her finger on the pad.

Before Cade could lob every curse he knew at Kira, a pixilated face of a man began to take shape just above his head. Before it came fully into view, Cade recognized the stiff posture and could identify the stern throat-clearing rasp that belonged to only one man: Cardinal Master Teeg.

"Cade Soora," Teeg intoned in his Galibad accent. "We've been looking for you."

"Well, you found me," Cade replied, hoping to end all inquiry into his whereabouts right there and then.

"You're weren't in the hauspital; you weren't in your quarters. Where were you?"

Behind Teeg's projection, Kira pantomimed drinking straight from a liquor bottle, followed by wobbling with her eyes crossed. Cade choked back a growl and focused instead on Teeg. "Just, you know . . . taking some time alone. After everything, I needed some time by myself."

Teeg's purple face—marked by traditional Galibad tribal markings stitched onto his cheeks—pressed closer in the comms projector, and his eyes sharply narrowed. Despite the image's graininess brought on by a poor connection, Cade easily picked up on the dissatisfaction in Teeg's expression. It wasn't uncommon to Cade. Once, long ago, Cade imagined that the Cardinal Master position would be filled by a wise, soulful individual who shepherded everyone's noble mission at the Well with delicacy and grace. That wasn't how Teeg operated. He didn't capture the role of Cardinal Master by being everyone's kindly grandpa; like most leaders, Teeg manipulated and connived his way up the Well's ladder, primarily motivated by his desire to get himself to the top. Now he was there, having seemingly forgotten why he was climbing in the first place, and everyone had to deal with a leader whose vision didn't extend beyond the bridge of his nose.

"Were you on Aria?" Teeg pointedly asked.

"Aria?" Cade said as he stuck out his lower lip and shook his head. "Nope. I haven't been here—there. I haven't been there."

"Regardless, myself and the other Masters would like you to come to the sanctum for . . . questioning."

"Questioning?" Cade asked, careful not to show his indignation. "About what?"

"Details of your trip to Quarry, of course. Standard for this kind of situation."

"Standard? There's never been a Paragon before. Ever. How can . . . whatever it is that you're talking about be standard?"

Teeg puffed out an agitated breath. "Are you disobeying the chain of command—once again?"

"No, sir," Cade said sheepishly after drawing a deep breath. He knew there was no use in arguing, and no point. Neither side of the discussion cared what the other had to say, but it was only Cade who recognized that.

"Then we will see you at the sanctum directly after your brother's funeral."

Teeg faded in the projector, glaring at Cade as his image disappeared. Cade couldn't have been happier to see a digital person vanish.

With Teeg gone, Cade got to work weighing his options while he absentmindedly straightened his wrinkled tunic. He knew what was happening: The Masters didn't believe he was the Paragon, and this sanctum meeting was likely their way to withhold the Rokura once they officially recorded credible doubt. Cade loathed being stuck in the middle of the Well's bureaucracy. If there was one thing the Masters excelled at, it was getting in the way of themselves and everyone around them. Cade would sooner evacuate himself out of an airlock before he got his hands that kind of dirty. In fact, had Kira not been on his ship with him, this would be a fine time to disappear and forget he had anything to do with any magical weapon.

"Don't let him talk to you like that," Kira said.

Cade looked at Kira and, as his attention diverted away from his thoughts, he realized he was no longer patting the wrinkles out of his tunic; he was gripping the fabric hard, at his chest, his hands clenched in a white-knuckle grip. "Oh, that's just how Teeg is," Cade said as he slowly let go of his tunic. "It's, you know . . . it's fine."

"No, it is not fine," Kira snapped. "If Papa Teeg talked to me like that he'd be eating his meals through a straw for a long time."

"Well, I don't beat up old people."

Cade walked toward the cockpit, but Kira blocked his way. "You're the Paragon, Cade. And even if you weren't—let's just *say*—no one should treat you that way. It's not right, and you should know that."

"Thanks," Cade softly said, even though what he wanted to say was that he didn't care. He appreciated Kira's support, but he didn't care about what Teeg had to say or Kira's take on it. Tristan was dead, and all Cade wanted was to be *gone*.

Kira cleared the path for Cade but called him back before he could get to his ship's controls.

"So, hey—my squad all left last night," Kira said, breaking the discomfort between them. "Mind if I hitch a ride back to the Well?"

"Sure, sure, of course," Cade said, feeling the night's exploits suddenly bubble up inside of him. "I'm just gonna puke really fast."

"Approaching fighter-class vessel, what is your clearance code? I repeat: Approaching fighter-class vessel, what is your clearance code?"

Cade thumbed through the control panel's many menus and submenus, growling as he tried to burrow through the security firewalls and nab his landing code. Duke had these things memorized, which gave Cade just another reason to curse the salty old drone.

"Fighter vessel, if you do not respond we will consider you a hostile vessel and execute defensive measures. Meaning—we will shoot you out of the sky."

"All right, all right!" Cade barked into the comms receiver. "I'm getting it!"

"What's the problem in here?" Kira asked as she stormed into the cockpit.

"Just Rao being uptight as usual," Cade said. "He can see this hunk of junk on the monitor by now—what does he think we're capable of doing? And isn't visual confirmation enough?"

"Move," Kira said, elbowing Cade aside as she spoke into the comms. "Rao, this is Commander Kira Sen. Clearance code NH-JX-one-one-oh-nine."

There was a pause and Cade rolled his eyes. Rao Ursa, Rothanian chief of Ticus's Watcher Corps, loved his dramatic effect.

"Verified, Commander Sen. Welcome back, sir."

"What's with the aggressive security, chief?" Kira asked.

"He takes his job too seriously," Cade whispered, and Kira shushed him quiet.

"We picked up a few unusual signatures just out of range," Rao replied. "I'm sure it's just a passing meteor shower or some kind of floating debris, but you can never be too careful."

"Understood," Kira replied, her voice authoritative. "Maintain your vigilance, chief."

"Aye, aye, commander."

Kira plopped into the copilot's chair. "Need me to bring us down, too?" she asked, and Cade groaned. It was the dozenth time she'd offered to drive during the short trip from Aria.

Cade took control of the *Horizon Dawn* and began his descent, breaking through the planet's thin layer of clouds and mist to reveal Ticus's snowcapped mountain range and, just below its peaks, the massive temple that anchored his home.

The Floating Temple—so named because on days when cloud coverage was low, the temple seemed to magically float in the air—was carved out of one of Ticus's highest mountains a long, long time ago. Cade didn't have a clue when it was built; no one did. Its first appearance in the historical records cataloged the six months Wu-Xia spent there, meditating before his final battle. The only age Cade could stick to the temple was "crazy old," and it certainly looked the part. Its four exterior columns were so weathered by time that their once-intricate reliefs—capturing, as far as anyone could guess, the temple's history—had been all but smoothed away. Still, the mighty columns managed to hold up the protruding awning that distinguished the temple's entrance. The awning, like the columns, had seen better days; although, while the awning was also starting to erode one chunk of stone at a time, an epic frieze—fashioned to its western face and depicting the battle between Ser Ukosa and the Faceless Four—defied the odds and held on.

After Wu-Xia's death, warriors from across the galaxy traveled to the temple seeking spiritual guidance, focus, and inner peace, just as Wu-Xia had. Over time, what had once been an obscure temple for a small order of monks became the nexus for people, inspired by Wu-Xia, who wanted to make themselves worthy to claim the Rokura. Tristan was the first person to yank the mystical weapon from its stasis: Every Paragon-hopeful before him, and there was no telling how many, had failed. Still, the widespread failure to remove the Rokura didn't deter more and more warriors—from nearly every race and planet—from flocking to Ticus. With all these galactic badasses under one roof, they decided to make a pact: Even if they couldn't seize the Rokura, they'd remain committed to Wu-Xia's ideal of the spiritual warrior, the Rai, and uphold the peace he'd established by crushing any jerk or band of jerks—and there always seemed to be plenty—who threatened to disrupt the galaxy's harmony.

With that agreement, the Well was born, and though Cade joked that its standards must have eroded over time—Cade was part of the club, after all—it had stood for countless years as the galaxy's defender of peace.

Stretching out wide across the mountains—with the Floating Temple as its nucleus—was the architecture of the Well as it was now, replete with armories, launch bays, and training dojos. The Well maintained an army of ground troops and some of the best pilots in the galaxy; it was a coalition of men and women who believed that the path to peace required relentless vigilance. Though it was only in recent years that the Masters allowed their corps of peacekeepers to expand and include people who weren't totally on board with the whole "spiritual warrior" thing. Cade understood why that might not make sense to some people. It was a little hokey even when he thought about it.

As Cade approached his landing platform, he eyed the dojo where he and Tristan had trained to become Rai. They learned to balance inward calm with controlled fighting techniques; they learned selflessness, justice, and how to come to terms with the inevitable results of battle. And now, on the dojo's rooftop, his fellow Rai were preparing for Tristan's memorial. All the time he spent with Tristan gazing out at the tremendous sweep of unobstructed space from the training dojo's rooftop came rushing back to Cade. In his mind's eye, he could see the stars and distant worlds that were so clearly visible from the dojo's roof, and Cade remembered hearing someone say how the vastness of the cosmos made the lives of everyone beneath seem small in context. Cade didn't buy that, though, especially not today. Tristan's absence was felt just as profoundly as extinguishing one of those stars in the sky. Maybe even more, Cade considered, as he fought the urge to turn his ship around and flee. The idea of ceremonially saying good-bye to his brother was unbearable, and Cade struggled to find one good reason to put himself through such torture.

But the roaring of the Well's alarms—never heard outside of testing—snapped Cade's impulse to flee right out of him. In impulse's place was panic—panic and terror.

Kira leapt out of her seat and shot Cade a terrified look that mirrored his own.

"Call up your scanners," she said. "And patch us through to Rao."

"The scanner has nothing beyond navigation," Cade said. "And . . . oh man. The comms are jammed."

"Turn this ship around," Kira said, her voice steady. "I need visual on what's happening."

Cade did as he was told, though he knew what he was going to find. He knew they would come for him; he just didn't think it'd be so soon. With the *Dawn* flipped to what had been its stern position, Cade spotted a scene that was every bit as bad as he imagined:

A fleet of Praxis ships was invading Ticus's airspace.

Cade's heart dropped into his guts. "Oh, *no*," he said.

"Get us on the ground, Cade. *Now!*"

Cade hesitated. He couldn't take his eyes off the Praxis drop ship and six Intruders that were accelerating toward his home. It wasn't enough for a full assault, especially when considering the battery Praxis could have sent; if they really wanted to end their silent truce and eradicate the Well, Cade reasoned, they'd have sent warships and dozens of Intruders. Praxis wasn't trying to destroy the Well; they wanted to infiltrate it. Which he knew meant only one thing: They were coming for the Rokura. Through all the years of conflict, Praxis never had the audacity to launch any kind of assault against Ticus and the Well. Despite the oppression the rotten kingdom spread throughout the galaxy, Praxis masked their true motivation—to become the galaxy's ruling fascist regime—under the guise of delivering order from chaos. Those who resisted order as defined by Praxis's rigorous definition of the term were branded terrorists and outlaws and were dealt with as seen fit. The Well, for whatever it was worth, had always stood somewhere in between. Praxian leaders were smart enough to know that any direct conflict with the Well would undermine their alleged devotion to peace, and that's why the two sides were locked at silent odds. Praxis had too much to lose by symbolically incinerating peace, and the Well couldn't even dream of mounting an effective large-scale assault against the galaxy's oppressor. The best either could do was work against each other in the shadows. Until now, that is.

"Cade!" Kira yelled, grabbing his attention. "Let's move!"

Cade flipped the *Dawn* back around and zipped them to the landing platform. As the ship descended, Cade armed himself with Tristan's shido and an antique sidewinder that he kept stashed in a storage compartment. The *Dawn* touched down with a thud, and when Cade stepped out of the ship, the first thing he saw was Duke being dragged away by two Masters.

"Hey!" he yelled, running after Duke. His voice was drowned out by the rolling alarm, so he yelled, louder, once more, "HEY!"

Duke turned at the sound of Cade's voice and lumbered his boxy body toward him, the Masters each a step behind. He had the Rokura held tightly in his grip.

"Have you fried a circuit, Duke?" Cade asked. "What are you doing out here—and with that thing, no less?"

"I'll have you know I've been waiting for your return, enjoying the company of the two charming Masters you see behind me."

"He insisted on waiting for you," Nu Kan, the Ohanian Master, said. His counterpart, a Hesbonian named Plar, was observing his people's annual vow of silence and didn't say a word. Cade never felt so fortunate for such a silly ritual; though Plar and Nu Kan were skilled Masters, they each had the charisma of a sack of rocks. The less they said, the better.

"There've been people wanting to visit the Rokura," Duke said. "Wanting to *see* it."

Cade arched an eyebrow, and before he could say a word, Duke grabbed Cade by the back of his head and pulled him close.

"Be cautious of who you trust, Cade Sura."

When Cade pulled back, he expected Duke to make some kind of snide remark that offset his warning, but he didn't. Instead, Duke held out the weapon for him to take while Nu Kan and Plar waited, filled with obvious anticipation, for Cade to make his move. Reluctantly, Cade grabbed the Rokura; he was relieved nothing terrible happened when he wrapped his fingers around the hilt. At least not yet.

"Okay, then," Cade said, feigning command. "Nu Kan and Plar, get back to the other Masters. Tell them I'm on my way." Cade paused, watching over Duke's shoulder as the Masters ran out of earshot. "Duke, go find us a ship that's in better shape than the *Dawn*—one that could actually get us through this mess. We need to get out of here, immediately."

"Whoa, whoa, whoa, whoa," Kira said, coming up behind Cade. "Did I hear you correctly? Because for a second it sounded like you said you were leaving."

Cade grasped Duke by his shoulders and pushed him ahead,

demanding that he go. He turned back to Kira, who looked ready to knock him out and take the Rokura for herself. "Kira, I don't have time to explain a million things to you. Go round up your squadron and do what you need to do. I'm going to do the same."

Kira got in Cade's face, pinning him against the wall without laying a hand on him. Sweat rolled down his back as he took a stuttered breath. Everything was literally crashing down around him. There was no telling what Praxis would do to him if captured; there was no telling what the evil kingdom would do to the galaxy if it got its hands on the Rokura. He should have left it behind on Quarry; he should have escaped with it instead of running off for a pity party on Aria. But he didn't, and now everything was on the precipice of somehow being even more disastrous than it already was.

"There's going to be Praxis boots on the ground in a matter of minutes, and you're holding the strongest weapon in the galaxy in your hands. What you need to do is obliterate every last one of them without hesitation or mercy."

"You have no idea what you're even talking about," Cade yelled. "Now get in the sky and get to defending our—"

Kira grabbed Cade's tunic and shoved him against the wall of the landing bay. "You listen to me and you listen good: I know you, Cade Sura. Yeah, I *know* you. And while I'm not entirely sure what happened in the spire or to your brother, I'm certain that there's *no way* you're the Paragon. So you either start kicking Praxis ass right here, right now and prove me wrong, or you tell me what's really going on."

Cade froze, torn between wanting to unburden himself of the truth and terrified of the judgment he'd be subject to if he did.

"Do something!" Kira said, throwing her body weight into the grip she had on him.

"What? You want me to say it? Is that it?" Cade said, pushing Kira away from him.

"Cade," Kira spat through clenched teeth as she released her hold and took a step back. *"Damn it."*

"My brother was the Paragon," Cade said, tossing the Rokura on the ground between Kira and himself. "He pulled the Rokura from its stasis, then some lunatic murdered him. I killed that lunatic, and now the weapon is mine to deal with. I'm nothing, okay? I'm nobody."

Kira shook her head, and Cade could see her recalibrating her resolve. "No," she said, then she picked the Rokura off the ground and shoved it in Cade's chest. "You're the person everyone *thinks* is the Paragon, which is good enough. Now come on, we've got to get you out of here."

Cade, realizing he had no other choice, followed Kira to the landing bay's opening. She stopped at its edge and peeked her head out to check for enemies as she slammed a charge into her sidewinder.

"I don't understand. What are we doing?" Cade stammered.

"Cade, if you die—if the *Paragon* dies—any hope we have of finally taking the fight to Praxis dies, too. The Masters will be more lost than they are now, and everything we've been fighting for will be gone. The Well will fall, the galaxy will crumble, and I'm not going to live in a world that sucks that bad. So you're going to follow me, you're going to do exactly what I tell you to do, and maybe, by some miracle, we can get out of here alive."

Cade nodded vigorously, bolstered by Kira's confidence and grit. "All right, okay. So, how do we do this?"

"One step at a time, that's how. Step one: We get to my ship."

"Are you crazy? Your ship is on the opposite platform; we'll pass half a dozen on our way to it."

"Those ships are garbage, and this isn't a discussion. We're getting to my ship, and that's that. Now come on."

Intruders pounded the surface with proton fire as they executed uncontested flybys over Ticus. Cade and Kira ran from the landing platform with their heads ducked down, but Cade still saw the Floating Temple get blasted by consecutive hits that erupted on its facade. Slabs of rock tumbled to the ground, and the ancient temple, its structure compromised, began to buckle under its own weight. The grinding of rock against rock was unmistakable as the top half of the temple depressed into its lower component. Cade stopped, struck by the enormity of what was happening all around him, and he was fortunate to have done so. As Kira turned around, presumably to tell him to move his butt, he heard a powerful whirring overhead—the sound of dual turbine propellers, unmistakably belonging to the massive wings of a Praxis drop ship. He grabbed Kira and dove into the adjacent dojo just as the drop ship descended on their position. They landed on the ground, hard, and neither said a word. They didn't even breathe as their eyes remained fixed on the ceiling above them, wondering if the drop ship had spotted them or not.

Their curiosity was sated when four Praxis gunners—armed with automatic E-9 tri-blasters and protected by AI-enhanced armor, painted Praxis black and red, that formed to their body and made them very difficult to hit with conventional blasters—crashed through the dojo's ceiling.

"Go!" Kira yelled, hopping to her feet and drawing her sidewinder. "Take cover and keep them pushed back."

Ignoring Kira's orders, Cade rushed the gunners, wanting to get to them before they got their bearings. His charging sprint turned into a slide as one of the gunners raised his blaster to fire; Cade slid beneath the gunner's weapon and sliced the Rokura's blade across his legs. The cut went right through his armor and dropped him to the ground. A firm punch to the back of his head rendered him unconscious.

Kira ducked behind a wooden training dummy, taking fire from an approaching gunner. She returned fire, but the gunner's armor kept reshaping itself—based on all the information it self-compiled, such as blaster type, distance, and aim—to deflect each blast. Cade drew Tristan's shido, ignited it, and threw it at the gunner, plunging the weapon directly into his back. The blow drove him to the ground. But, the moment he fell, the dojo was pounded by an aerial assault that shook the ground, violently jostling everyone in the room. Cade was thrown from his feet, and as he got back up, he heard Kira yell out behind him.

"On your left!" she said, and Cade spotted a gunner with his E-9 trained on him from just a few feet away. The gunner fired, and the Rokura, without any input from Cade, jolted outward in his hand and absorbed the blast. Cade and the gunner both paused, in awe of what the Rokura had done and unsure what to do next as the energy from the blast danced at the weapon's head. They both found out in a flash, as the energy shot back at the gunner, knocking him through the dojo wall.

"Oh, so *now* you want to help me," Cade said to the Rokura, a little annoyed about it.

Cade heard a blast, and he turned to see the final gunner being electrocuted behind him. In a fit of spasms, the gunner dropped to her knees then face-planted on the floor.

Kira, blaster held up, joined Cade as they took a moment to admire their work. "If you shoot their armor's AI control panel, they fry," Kira said. "It's on their right wrist. I liked your move with the Rokura, by the way. Maybe you're not so hopeless after all."

"Who said anything about being hopeless?" Cade asked as he ripped his shido out of the gunner's back.

"Hm. I guess I was just drawing my own conclusions."

Cade grunted. "So, still plan on getting to your ship?"

"No, Cade, let's just stick around here and hope for the best."

Cade followed Kira to the edge of the dojo and surveyed the scene outside. What had started as a small-scale invasion had turned into an all-out battle. The scent of cinders and ash wafted in the air. In the time since they left the landing bay, drop ships had dispersed dozens of gunners and sentry drones over the area, and Cade couldn't even count the number of Intruders that dotted the sky, spraying proton fire as they roared overhead. Rao and his squad, positioned in the cannon towers spread across the Well, repelled the Intruder attacks with all the firepower they had available, but they were overmatched. Until a full fleet of Echoes were able to take to the sky and engage the Intruders, they would continue to rain down destruction on the Well.

"I truly detest these jerks," Kira said as she punched a fresh charge into her sidewinder.

"Come on," Cade said, leading them out of the dojo. Their first step was met with debris pouring down on them from above. Cade looked up with a sour grimace. "We'll worry about dismantling the Praxis fleet once we're out of here."

Cade and Kira hugged the side of the dojo as they pushed forward. Just ahead, covering the area between where they were and where they needed to be, Rai and ground troopers met the enemy gunners and sentries before they could reach any of the Well's structures. While they appeared to be doing a good job of keeping them back, there was no telling what kind of numbers awaited in drop ships that might still be making their approach or what it would take, other than retrieving the Rokura, to make Praxis leave. But like Kira said, one step at a time. The problem was that Kira's "step one" now included a trip through a veritable battlefield. Because there was no getting around it—the only way out was through. Gripping the Rokura, Cade hoped it was going to behave more like it did in the dojo and less like it did in the spire. It better, Cade thought, because he couldn't stomach the idea of anyone else dying when, seemingly, this crazy weapon could've done something to stop it. But Cade felt something in the Rokura, and maybe he was crazy, but he got the impression that as repulsed as it was by being commanded by him, it loathed the idea of serving some other nobody even more. Cade was the devil the Rokura knew, and having won the battle of two evils, he was confident that the Rokura, at the very least, wasn't going to try to kill him. It might even help him. On its own terms, of course, but Cade could live with that. He was about to turn to Kira and tell her to follow his— and the Rokura's—lead, when she shoved him out of her way and fired off a single blast from her sidewinder. Cade turned in time to see a sentry, just coming up the stone pathway toward their position, take Kira's blast directly to its chest and fall to the ground.

"I know what you're thinking, Cade, and yeah, there's a lot of enemies between us and my ship. But that's just a bonus, because we're going to take out every single one that stands in our way. You got me?"

Cade nodded and together they closed in on the battle. As they did, Cade's attention became attuned to the screams he heard— screams that cut through the blaster fire and explosions. He tried to pinpoint the source of the agonized cries, but the battle, from a distance, was too chaotic. It wasn't until he and Kira reached a raised platform just outside the bloody fray that he saw what was happening.

Fatebreakers, four of them, cut a line straight through the battle, mowing down everyone—Rai and troopers alike—in their path.

From the middle of the battlefield, one of them spotted Cade— their leader, Cade assumed, judging by the red Mohawk that ran down his helmet—and from his position in the middle of the battlefield, he pointed his shido directly at him.

"We need to run," Cade gasped.

CHAPTER SEVEN

B ut there was nowhere to go.

Cade turned and darted back the way they came, but he halted in his tracks after just a few steps. An Intruder rocketed overhead, unleashing a punishing assault on the dojo's already brittle facade and rooftop. Slabs of the building's exterior erupted and avalanched to the ground, obstructing the only path that could lead Cade and Kira back the way they came. Cade supposed they could dig their way through, but not before any one of the Fatebreakers got to them first.

No, the only way to go was forward. Cade went to grab Kira's hand to pull her along with him, but even she was frozen by what she was seeing.

"Cade—what *are* those things?" Kira asked.

"Oh, just some old friends of mine. They like to call themselves the Fatebreakers, apparently," Cade said, feeling the leader's eyes burning a hole through him. "They're Ga Halle's secret murder squad. One of them killed Tristan and tried his best to kill me as well."

"That . . . complicates things," Kira replied.

"Just a little."

"Okay," Kira said, drawing a deep breath, and the situation, in. "What do we do?"

They couldn't just stand there, Cade knew that much. Ticus was being blasted to bits, and if the Well fell—if Cade fell—the most powerful weapon in the galaxy would be captured and delivered into the hands of a tyrant. So, Cade had to do *something*. He knew the things he couldn't do: He couldn't run, couldn't hide, and he couldn't even fathom fighting back. Taking on a lone Fatebreaker was one thing; taking on a group was something else entirely. Something like suicide. That left Cade with only one course of action: He had to turn the tables on his enemies. The Fatebreakers took Cade, and the Well, by surprise; now it was Cade's turn to return the favor.

"Look, I have an idea, but I'm going to need you to deny all of your instincts to make it work."

"Meaning what?" Kira said.

"Meaning you're going to run through that battle as fast as you can, and you're not going to kill anybody. For real. No killing."

Kira eyed Cade skeptically. "And what are you going to do?" she scoffed.

"What I always do," Cade sighed. "Something stupid."

Cade jumped into the fray alongside the Well ground troopers and his fellow Rai and, working as a collective unit, they over-powered Praxis's ground-assault battery. The sentries were hardly a match, and even the gunners, with their AI armor, couldn't withstand the Rais' elite fighting skills. As Echoes took to the skies and repelled Intruders, the infrastructure of the

Well—or what was left of it—got the defense it needed. Things seemed to be going well, except Cade knew what was really happening. Praxis didn't care about crippling the Well or even winning this fight. All that mattered was getting the Fatebreakers in and giving them space to hunt down the Rokura. Everything else—the skirmishes happening on the ground and in the air—was just window dressing.

Cade weaved through the battle. His goal wasn't to dismantle drones or down gunners; he needed spectacle. He needed a distraction. Wasting as little time as possible, Cade navigated the fracas with his sights set on reaching the Fatebreakers. He dodged an overhead attack from a sentry's quanta staff, then crushed its head with the Rokura. When a power gunner, armed with a compression pike, came charging at Cade, he unholstered his sidewinder, set it to maximum charge, and shot out a chunk of the ground. The gunner, unable to slow his momentum before he hit the hole in the ground, stumbled forward, and Cade sliced the Rokura right through him. Cade watched the gunner fall, and when he turned his attention forward again, he saw all the heads of those around him turning his way. By now, everyone from the Well and Praxis both knew who Cade was, or at least they thought they did. Catching the Paragon in action—and Cade had to admit, his contributions so far were pretty slick—was an attention-grabbing moment. This was exactly what he wanted, even if the second part of his plan—what needed to happen once he had all eyes on him—scared the crap out of him. But at least he was off to a promising start: The Paragon was here, so everyone make way.

And make way they did. A lane cleared directly in front of Cade, and at the end of that lane his real adversaries awaited. Four Fatebreakers, covered by bloodstained black-and-gold armor, were no more than fifteen yards away, catching their breath as they readied themselves for a fight.

Fury began to overwhelm fear. As Cade stared at his four enemies, all he could see was one: the monster that killed his brother. His first thought was to abandon his plan and turn the Rokura loose on all four Fatebreakers, forgetting about the consequences. With grim satisfaction, he'd watch them all obliterate from time and space, and he'd let the remaining Praxis forces flee with a poignant message to deliver to their leader: Do *not* mess with the Paragon. But Cade wasn't eager about taking that kind of chance. Just because the Rokura might be willing to save his life didn't mean it was ready to eradicate his enemies because he said so. If Cade banked on that happening and lost, and the Rokura was taken from him, the consequences would be bad, to say the least. Twilight would fall on the galaxy, and maybe not just figuratively. Cade's only recourse was to stick to his plan, even if, in terms of how crazy the plan was, it outpaced counting on the Rokura by only the slightest margin.

With a saunter in his step, Cade strolled toward the Fatebreakers. He held the Rokura tightly in his right hand, hoping it didn't do anything unexpected. The lead Fatebreaker wiped the blood off his shido and stepped forward to meet Cade. When they reached a few paces beyond striking distance, they stopped, and Cade began to wonder why this person wasn't trembling at the sight of the Rokura. Instead of fear, he displayed reverence. The Fatebreaker bowed toward Cade, and the other three did the same.

"Oh, good," Cade said, feeling relieved. "You're going to surrender."

"The bow was for the Rokura, not *you*, you shit," the leader sneered, his words crackling like wood in a fire.

"Nice mouth you have on you," Cade replied, needing to keep the Fatebreaker at bay. "I don't remember your friend—you know, the one I wiped out back on Quarry—being so crude. And speaking of your friend, which one of you wants to see him first?"

The leader released an exasperated breath. He then removed his helmet and placed it on the ground next to him. Like the Fatebreaker Cade encountered before, this one too was an older man. He had thinning blond hair and soft wrinkles woven across his face. His soft blue eyes hinted at a man with more compassion than Cade assumed a brutal killer would possess, and that belied the viciousness of his words. "I'm going to say this once and only once, so please listen carefully: Deliver us the Rokura, or we will kill you, right here, right now. You will surely get to some of us, but not all. And those remaining will reduce your temple and bases to ash before plunging this planet into eternal darkness."

Cade nodded, acting like he was considering his enemy's threat. "That's an attractive offer, and very specific. I have a response for you, but I want to make sure *you* listen carefully. Are you ready?"

With half a smile on his face, the leader nodded.

"You're gross, and nobody here is intimidated by a word that comes out of your gross mouth."

As if that was the answer he expected, the leader let out a disappointed sigh as he picked up his helmet and put it back on. "So be it," he said and dropped into a fighting position, knees bent, shido directed forward. The other three Fatebreakers did the same and began to encroach on Cade. Had he not detected the sound of a whirring engine coming from just over the ridge, Cade would have assumed he was moments away from death. But this was just where the fun part began.

"Your master is going to be disappointed," Cade said, aiming the Rokura directly at the lead Fatebreaker, "because you've forced me to unleash my magic."

Now it was the leader's turn to flinch. "Magic?" he asked, his voice conveying equal parts confusion and exasperation. "What are you even talking about?"

"What am I talking about?" Cade asked as he raised his left hand and pantomimed a sidewinder's dual blasters, using his pinkie and pointer fingers as barrels and his thumb as the trigger. "I'm talking about *this*."

Cade dropped his thumb and the exact moment he did, proton fire erupted through the mountain's mist, directly at the Fatebreakers.

The blasts sent them scrambling; one blast only narrowly missed one of its targets, landing so close it propelled a Fatebreaker ten feet in the air, spinning him hard into a pile of the Floating Temple's rubble. Yet somehow, despite the assault coming from overhead, the lead Fatebreaker was undaunted, refusing to run for cover as the others had. He charged Cade, leaping off his feet and bringing his shido down on him. Cade, not expecting such determination, was caught off guard and barely moved in time to avoid the strike. He dove to his right, and by the time he turned back around, the leader was on him, swinging his shido directly at Cade's head. Cade raised the Rokura in time to defend himself, but the Fatebreaker pushed him back, pressing their faces together.

"You should have used the Rokura to obliterate everyone in your path. Why haven't you?"

Cade, grunting under the leader's strength, rolled out from their locked position. The leader stumbled forward, just a few steps, but quickly regained his footing. "Because that kind of response is *crazy*," Cade said, pacing backward to put some distance between them. "When someone disagrees with Praxis, you take away their sun, or you subject their planet to a military occupation. That's *not* a healthy way to solve problems."

"Galactic order is a zero-sum game, but no one has the courage to embrace that. No one except Ga Halle. Come with us, obey my master, and we can bring the galaxy peace at last."

"Peace? It sounds a lot more like domination to me."

The leader shrugged. "As if you can have one without the other."

Behind Cade, two other Fatebreakers regained their poise and started to close in. A circle was beginning to form around him. "If you really think you can kill your way to peace," Cade said, "all you're going to have is a bunch of dead people everywhere you go. Now, if you'll excuse me, my ride's here."

Cade took off running as fast as he could toward the mountain's edge. The Fatebreakers pursued, but hesitantly; it seemed like Cade had nowhere to go. But as he neared the edge of the mountain—and the fatal drop one step past it—a starship materialized through the mist, laying down suppressive fire that screamed past Cade's head.

"Watch it!" he yelled, though he knew Kira couldn't hear him from her seat in the cannon's hull.

The *Rubicon*, Kira's custom-made ship that she had constructed over the skeleton of an industrial junker vessel, came into full view. Its oval shape—like an egg turned on its side—was unlike any other in the Well's fleet, or any fleet; at its rear, making the ship even more distinct, was an oversized transparent cockpit shielding—a detail that captured Kira's boldness. She said the shielding was to give her better range of visualization, but anyone who knew her understood it was there so her enemies could see her in the moment just before she blew them out of the sky.

When Cade was just steps away from the *Rubicon*, its body flipped on its side while the cockpit remained static. The entry hatch dropped down and Cade leapt; he hit the platform with a thud, but he was safely on board. As the *Rubicon* pulled up and away, Cade locked his sights on the Fatebreakers until the entry hatch closed. He had a feeling he hadn't seen the last of them.

Cade was dusting himself off when Kira grabbed him and pulled him toward the gunner hull.

"You survived. Good," she said. "But, so we're clear, the next time you make me turn my ship over to the AI's controls, it will be the last thing you do."

"You know, you might be a *little* too attached to your ship. And, thanks."

"Don't thank me yet," Kira said, strapping a comms device to Cade's head. "You think you can manage the cannon?"

Cade, exaggerating his offense, replied, "Yes, Kira, I think I can manage the cannon. Why?"

"Because I'm taking control of this ship," Kira said, heading toward the cockpit. "We still have a dogfight to punch through if we want to mass jump out of here."

The sky above Ticus burned with war. Under Kira's deft controls, the *Rubicon* maneuvered gracefully through the aerial battlefield even as debris from unfortunate starfighters clogged the known flight corridors. The area beyond was punctuated by streams of crisscrossing proton fire, leaving the *Rubicon* with no option but to punch right through the battle. Cade, now positioned in the ship's cannon seat at the bottom of the ship, heard Kira's voice crackle through his headset. "We're going in," was all she said, and before Cade could respond, the *Rubicon* dropped sharply and then, just as quickly as it'd dropped, rose again and accelerated full throttle toward the heat of the battle.

As the ship stabilized, Cade caught an eyeful that explained where Kira was taking them, and why. He gasped. Just ahead, Intruders and Echoes exchanged proton volleys, the Intruders executing protective patterns around a Praxis warship that was making its slow descent toward Ticus. With its array of heavy artillery weaponry, Cade and Kira both knew that if allowed to park over their planet, it would deliver enough firepower to decimate whatever remained of the Well within minutes.

"Focus your fire on the Intruders," Kira ordered. "I'll hit the warship with vapor torpedoes as we pass."

"Aye, aye," Cade responded, even though he knew they should have been clearing a path to make their mass jump and get as far away from Ticus as possible. It was the tougher choice—fleeing—but it was also the safer one. They needed to get out and take the Rokura with them.

But safe choices weren't exactly Cade's or Kira's thing. Even though they didn't speak it, they both knew they couldn't leave the Well to ruin.

Kira banked the *Rubicon* to port just as an Intruder cut off their approach with a burst of proton blasts. Cade spun around in his 360-degree cannon chair and returned fire, narrowly missing. As the Intruder turned to make its second attack approach, Kira dropped the *Rubicon* into a downward spiral and broke for the warship. The Intruder followed, and Cade was anxiously waiting for it to get back into range when he heard Kara yell, "We've got company!"

Ahead, two more Intruders streaked toward their direction, firing as they came. Cade's cannon hull hummed as the Intruders' proton fire deflected off the *Rubicon*'s shields. He whipped his cannon around, returning fire that, at the very least, would impair them from getting off such clean shots. The Intruders, in response to Cade's fire, both banked, firing wild shots that failed to connect with the *Rubicon*.

"Shields are holding, but we're down to sixty-four percent," Kira informed Cade through the headset.

As they neared the warship, Cade got a closer look at its artillery; "overkill" was the only word that came to mind. Even on something known as a *warship*, the destructive capacity was hard to comprehend. Its cannons were focused on crisscrossing Echoes that swarmed the ship's vicinity, while torpedoes poked out of launch tubes across the exterior, a warning to anyone who dared to come close. Like Kira. Cade, for a moment, felt a kind of grim awe in the face of the warship; he'd never been this close to one before, and he could hardly process how massive it was. It was black as midnight with red streaks that looked like smears of its enemies' blood; its helix shape allowed it to be covered in offensive weaponry, so no angle was safe from its assault. Cade's chest tightened as he couldn't help but imagine what kind of damage the warship's artillery could inflict.

"Just out of curiosity, how much shield do we need to withstand a hit from that warship?" Cade asked.

"If a torpedo gets us, every inch of the *Rubicon*, us included, will be space dust."

"Oh," Cade said, just as the *Rubicon* accelerated toward the warship. As it did, Cade's targeting sensors began to whir. He turned and spotted the three Intruders they'd tangled with already, unified and flying toward his position in an attack pattern. Cade locked his targeting sights on the lead Intruder's triangular-shaped cockpit, but its pilot spun right, avoiding the attack. Its two counterparts followed as they closed the gap between themselves and the *Rubicon*.

The ship jostled again as antifighter proton missiles—longer range than the warship's cannons, though less potent—erupted around them. Kira, with smooth adroitness, dodged each missile, positioning the *Rubicon* to return fire. Cade spun to follow the three Intruders as they came around for a frontal attack, continuing to fire as they did, and he saw a single torpedo launch from the *Rubicon*'s starboard battery. The torpedo, timed perfectly, soared through the nettles of Intruders and Echoes ahead and nailed the warship's antifighter turret.

"Woooo!" Cade yelled. "Great shot!"

"There're about a dozen more on that ship," Kira responded. "So let's not celebrate victory just yet. Now, what about those three Intruders that've been hounding us?"

"Coming around for another pass, port side."

"I've got them," Kira said, pulling the ship to the left and putting it on a direct course for the incoming Intruders. "Focus on the center fighter; I'll take care of the other two."

In Cade's experience, Intruder ships were heavily armored and, given the distance between his ship and the Intruder he had in his sights, breaking through its shields and landing a fatal strike was nearly impossible. But, Cade also knew that just because he couldn't destroy the Intruder, that didn't mean he couldn't disable it and get it off the playing field.

With its aerodynamic design, Intruders relied on compact wings that protruded from their sides and rose up and in, nearly meeting at their tips. Cade focused his fire on those wings—less protected by the ship's shield generator, but harder to hit.

The opposing sides raced toward each other, exchanging fire as they neared.

"How are the shields holding up?" Cade asked as he jabbed at the dual fire buttons beneath his thumbs.

"Fifty-six percent!" Kira yelled back. "But we need these ships out of our way if we're going to be able to make a clean run at that warship. Now blast that Intruder out of the sky already!"

The space between the *Rubicon* and the oncoming enemies was razor-thin, and the Intruders were not going to back down. It was counter to their conditioning as pilots, Cade and Kira both knew that. They'd sooner crash into an enemy than retreat. With precious time left, Cade rattled off as many shots as he could, and he buried nearly every one of them in the Intruder's wings. The ship careened off into space.

"Got him!" Cade yelled. "Whatever you were going to do—" Cade couldn't get the words out, as he saw the remaining two Intruders angling directly toward the *Rubicon*. They were on a collision course, and there was no time to pull out.

The *Rubicon* didn't need to pull out, though. A split second before impact, the *Rubicon* flipped back on its axis, flattening out. The oncoming Intruders were left with no time to respond to this sudden change of position; Cade whipped around to see them smash into each other—erupting into one gloriously fiery mass—as the *Rubicon* continued forward, unscathed.

"Can I 'wooo' now?" Cade asked. "Because that deserves a 'wooo.'"

"You may 'wooo.'"

"WOOOO," Cade yelled, fueled by the exhilaration of coming within a hair of dying and escaping. He was getting used to the feeling.

Kira snapped the ship's body back into its upward position and dove toward the warship. Exposed and in range, the *Rubicon* was blanketed in suppressive fire from antifighter turrets, turboprotons, and heavy artillery cannons. Kira banked and broke, dodging strike after strike with precision Cade had never seen before. But for every cannon blast she evaded, a proton clipped their hull, or antifighter spray came close to penetrating the cockpit.

"Shields at twenty-nine percent!" Kira yelled, the frustration coming through her voice. She fully expected to be able to single-handedly take down a Praxis warship, even though that wild determination—which was no stranger to Cade—was more likely to get them killed. He just hoped Kira understood that, too.

Cade surveyed their situation: They were coming close to the warship and could soon drop below to its underside and make a few effective strikes, but none that would bring the ship down. And that was assuming they'd even get *that* far, which was becoming more and more unlikely.

"Kira, we're not going to make it!"

"Yes. We. Are," Kira snapped, and Cade could almost hear the tightening of her jaw muscles through his comms.

A proton battered the bottom quadrant of the ship, just above Cade. The hull throttled, and Cade was thrown from his seat and flipped head over heels. As he got to his feet, he saw it—the Intruder ship whose wings he'd clipped, floating in space. It gave him an idea.

Cade rushed to the cockpit. "I've got it," he told Kira, whose concentration was so intense she barely registered his presence.

"Got what? And why aren't you returning fire?!"

Cade slid into the copilot's seat and swiveled toward Kira. "Because we're getting *hammered* out here, and we need to pull out."

"Not a chance," Kira said, her focus still locked on evading the warship's relentless barrage.

"Kira!" Cade yelled, turning her around by her shoulder. "We can't make it, not like this. But I have an idea that will get us through. Trust me."

Kira hesitated a moment, then went back to the controls. She pushed a raging breath through her clenched jaw then twisted the *Rubicon* out of the warship's range.

"This better be brilliant," she said the moment they were clear.

"This ship—it was built over a junk cruiser, right?"

"A Balenian reclamation vessel, actually. Which, yes, is a junk ship."

"Does it still have the cargo arm?"

Kira gazed at him warily. "It does. Why?"

"Because," Cade replied, smiling, "we're going to pick up some junk."

"I don't know who's the bigger idiot. You for coming up with this idea or me for following it," Kira said as the *Rubicon* flew toward the Praxis warship once again. This time, though, was different.

Following Cade's instructions, Kira returned to the downed Intruder and, using the *Rubicon*'s cargo arm, positioned it directly in front of her own ship so it worked as a cloak. With the *Rubicon* flipped downward, it was just narrow enough to hide, unseen, behind the Intruder. And now they were approaching the Praxis warship, acting like they were coming in for a landing due to battle damage. They scrambled the Intruder's comms so no messages from the pilot could transmit; Cade and Kira would just have to hope that no one in the warship's landing bay got suspicious about one of their fighter vessels coming in dark.

What they didn't anticipate was being spotted from behind.

A blast smashed into the *Rubicon*'s stern, catching Cade and Kira off guard and reducing the ship's shields to 12 percent.

"Great, we've got incoming!" Cade yelled.

Kira and Cade turned to see two Intruder ships quickly approaching from the rear.

"No way," Kira said. "No, no way."

Cade, though it made him sweat, couldn't argue with Kira's decision to accelerate forward rather than retreat. They were nearly at the warship's command bridge, which was embedded in the center of its hulking mass. They would never get a shot like this again.

Another blast drove into the *Rubicon*, then another. "Take the cannon," Kira ordered. "If we can't fly this thing into their command bridge, then I'm going to torpedo it there."

Cade darted out of the cockpit but halted before he reached the door. It took a minute for Kira's proposal to sink in. "Is that . . . is that safe?"

"Go!" Kira barked as the *Rubicon*'s control panel announced that shields were below 10 percent.

Cade hopped in the cannon and rattled off wild shots in the direction of the Intruders. Anything, he figured, to keep them off their tail for just a few more seconds. It seemed to be working, until three more Intruders approached and joined the other two. "Uh . . . Kira?"

"I see them," Kira replied through the comms. "Torpedoes are hot—hold on!"

Kira threw the ship's power to the rear engine, firing maximum reverse thrust to the *Rubicon*. As the ship hurled back, Kira launched a series of torpedoes—Cade had no idea how many—that smashed into the downed Intruder and erupted at nearly point-blank range. The *Rubicon* careened backward, spinning out of control as a result of the explosion; the dummy Intruder was reduced to nothing more than a ball of fiery wreckage, but it was a fiery ball of wreckage that was racing toward the warship. Kira stabilized the *Rubicon* just in time for her and Cade to see that massive fireball smash directly into the warship's command bridge. The impact sent a rippling power surge throughout the warship, and it went completely dark before it began to slowly fall through space.

This time, it was Kira's turn to cheer.

"WOOO!" she yelled. "Take *that*!"

Cade rushed back to the cockpit. He had his own choice words for the Praxis fleet, but they were cut off by the sound of enemy fire making impact with the *Rubicon*. Kira and Cade refocused in time to see a half-dozen Intruders bearing down on their position.

"We should go," Cade said as Kira, sharing his opinion, dropped back into the pilot's seat.

"Setting a course to mass jump to the Fringe," Kira said. "Any preference?"

"Yeah, out of here," Cade said as another strike drove into the *Rubicon*'s backside. And with that strike came the last thing Cade and Kira wanted to hear:

"Shields are now zero percent. Shields are now inoperable," came the tinny control-panel voice.

"Now you see why I hate the AI?" Kira said as she punched coordinates into the mass-jump drive. "All right, coordinates set, let's—"

Another blast struck the *Rubicon*, this time with more profound impact and a thunderous booming sound. An alarm sounded.

Cade surveyed the scene and saw the Intruder fleet closing in fast. Their attacks would only become more severe and proficient. "Kira, we need to jump—now!"

Kira frantically worked the control panel. "Yeah, well, tell that to the drive and its damaged core."

"Kira, don't even say that! Don't tell me we're stuck here!"

"Hush," Kira said as she studied the information in front of her, assessing as quickly as she could. "Okay . . . good. We can jump, we just won't make it to the Fringe. I'm programming the AI to take us as far as we can go."

Cade looked up to see a proton blast race overhead, missing the cockpit by inches.

"Making jump to the Kyysring system," the control panel announced.

"Kyysring?!" Cade erupted. "No—no. Take us *anywhere* but Kyys—"

Cade's protestations were too late. The galaxy in view began to ripple and distort, and within a fraction of a second, the *Rubicon* was gone.

CHAPTER EIGHT

Everything was in its right place.

In the privacy of her Sutra Room, Ga Halle floated on a hoverdisc, meditating on recent events. Four small torches, one in each corner of the room, provided the only light, and the reinforced walls were sure to smother the din of the surrounding ship before a single decibel could penetrate her sacred chamber. The silence was uninterrupted; the serenity absolute.

She knew calm. She knew peace.

Ga Halle considered the might of the Praxis kingdom—*her* kingdom, built through the determination and audacity of her will—and found comfort in the order it had brought to the galaxy. Some systems still stood opposed to Praxis, but dissent would soon be a thing of the past. The Rising Suns would be rooted out; those who incited rebellion in any system would be made a public example of. Praxis had invaded Ticus at last, and it would only be a matter of time before every Rai and every Master was battered and broken. And while Ga Halle planned on taking unimaginable joy exposing the Well's fraudulent spiritualism and defeating its vaunted Rai, Ticus's end was a footnote in her motivation for sacking her rival's planet. The Praxis kingdom was spread comfortably throughout the galaxy, with numerous systems under annexation and possessing a fleet large enough to dwarf even the unification of those opposed. It couldn't be defeated. Even with their efforts to prevent a bloody galactic war and interrupt further annexations, the Well was nothing more than a nuisance that was closer to a relief brigade than the galactic guardians it claimed to be, and the only thing that had prevented Ga Halle from decimating it before was perception. Had Praxis, without provocation, launched a preemptive strike on Ticus, it would create martyrs, and martyrs make for rebellion.

But that reasoning didn't matter anymore. Nothing mattered the way it once had. The Rokura had been released at long last, and no one could prevent the Praxis queen—a self-appointed role, and the first ever known to Praxis—from claiming what was rightfully hers. When she did, the galaxy would see Ticus—and the Well, specifically—fall, and they'd bear witness to Ga Halle, wielding the Rokura, as the one responsible for bringing them to heel. And no one, not one person in the entire galaxy, would dare utter one word in opposition about it.

Ga Halle knew calm. She knew peace.

This vision of a future sure to come helped bring Ga Halle as close as she could to inner tranquility. For years, she prepared herself, in body, mind, and spirit, and she would prove herself worthy of the coveted mantle that should have been hers years ago. As her body rested under the spell of her meditation, the world around her went dark. She could no longer sense the engine's rhythmic hum or even feel her legs resting on the hover-disc. Ga Halle felt close to transcending her body, but then she'd remember—the parts of her that weren't her own. How her left arm, part of her chest, and the side of her face had been scorched off her body and replaced with flesh and bone that, even after all these years, felt like an invasive presence. How half of her body—a body she'd persistently cultivated throughout her life, physically and spiritually—was forever trapped in a containment suit that pulsed dark blue waves of antimatter over its indestructible exterior, preventing any more of her from being lost. It reminded her of her greatest loss and suffering. It reminded her of her need for justice.

It reminded her of her *rage*.

Ga Halle didn't have to look at the apparatus grafted to her body to visualize it in her mind's eye. That, and how she got it, were forever burned in her memory. The suit rose from her waist, covering most of her rib cage before fitting snugly over her left arm, wrapping around her neck, and plating the bottom half of her jaw. It kept her body—what was left of it—contained. It kept her alive. There'd been a time, at the urging of her medical team, that Ga Halle also donned plating over the scarring that veined over her mouth, across her cheek, and through her eye, like a lattice of ravines that'd been scored into her flesh. The remembrance of her scars brought back pain that gave way to agony much deeper than any physical discomfort. Still, she had no desire to cover her scars like they were something to be ashamed of, when the opposite was true. The scars—and the hurt that still lingered—made Ga Halle strong. They ensured that she never, ever lost focus of her purpose.

The containment suit, choking her body, tore Ga Halle out of her reverie and assured her that she'd have no peace, nor transcendence, until she righted the wrong from so long ago. Until she had the power to control the fate of the galaxy in her hands.

And as the door to her Sutra Room opened, she knew that peace was delayed once again.

Ortzo, her chief Fatebreaker, entered the chamber, quietly and alone, and Ga Halle could tell by the apprehension in his gait that he'd failed his mission.

"My queen," he said, taking a knee as Ga Halle turned to face him, still positioned on her hoverdisc. "We've returned from Ticus. Your instincts were correct: They were caught completely unprepared in anticipation of services for the fallen Rai. Our aerial forces were able to deliver tremendous damage to the Well's infrastructure while our ground squads—"

"Buildings rise and fall. Soldiers die and new ones are recruited. Neither make for victory that is absolute," Ga Halle said as she lowered the hoverdisc and stepped off. She bent her body downward so her face was inches away from Ortzo's. Purposefully, so he felt the cold lifelessness of her touch, Ga Halle grasped his shoulder with her left hand. "You know what I'm concerned with, so tell me—what of the Rokura?"

Ortzo inhaled a shaky breath. "I take full responsibility, my queen."

Ga Halle unfurled her dark red tunic, revealing both her slender body and the shido she kept holstered at her side. She drew it, swiftly, and Ortzo flinched. But Ga Halle merely held it out, examining it as if there were a single nook or crevice that she wasn't already intimately aware of.

"This weapon," she said, pacing, "is nothing more than an imitation of something greater. When placed in capable hands, it is no doubt dangerous. But it will never, *ever* be anything more than a reminder that something infinitely more powerful is out there, ready to make you bow before it."

Ga Halle stopped and looked up, remembering. "Praxis was forced to bow once before, and I've committed my life to ensuring we never bow again."

Ortzo, seeing what he thought to be his cue, removed his shido, and pointed it toward his own abdomen. A clean horizontal swipe would spill his insides all over the Sutra Room's floor.

"Before I depart, I'd like to point out one . . . irregularity that I noticed when confronting the boy who holds the Rokura."

Ga Halle eyed Ortzo, considering his fate. "Go on," she said, then turned her back to Ortzo as ceremony dictated.

"Myself and the other Fatebreakers, we had him cornered but . . . he never used the weapon. I advanced on him, and still he made no overtures to turn the Rokura on me."

Ga Halle turned her head, an eyebrow cocked in curiosity. "What are you saying?"

"My queen, none of us know what the Rokura is capable of, not in fact. But this . . . this *boy*, he didn't do anything with it. In fact, he needed the aid of some kind of modified transport vehicle to escape. Which leads me to believe he either doesn't know how to use it—"

"Or it's not his to use."

"Yes, my queen."

Ga Halle paused, then turned to face Ortzo.

"How do we find him?"

"The ship he escaped in, our Intruders reported that it was damaged before making its mass jump. He couldn't have gone far."

Using her shido, Ga Halle slowly pushed Ortzo's shido away from his body. Ortzo blinked. "Rise, Ortzo," she said, and Ortzo did as she commanded.

"I'm holding you responsible for finding him. Use every ship. Pay every spy, enlist any gunrunner and pirate, do whatever it takes. Just find me this boy before the Rokura is taken off his hands by someone *else*."

"I will redeem myself."

Ga Halle returned to her hoverdisc and her meditating position. She turned her back on Ortzo, then floated away. "You'd better," she said, and Ortzo moved to leave her alone once again. "I want that boy, and the weapon, brought before me with haste."

CHAPTER NINE

The Kyysring spaceport bustled with activity as undocumented goods—illegal in one way or another, in one system or many—changed hands between smugglers, arms dealers, diplomats, mercenaries, ambassadors, and anyone else who wanted something they weren't supposed to have. The *Rubicon*, its engines pushed to their limit to compensate for the damaged jump drive, landed with a rumbling groan. Cade's disposition wasn't all that different as he stepped off the ship and onto his home planet for the first time in years. The spaceport was exactly as he remembered it: crowded and grimy with a feeling of dread mixed with exhilaration, like a gambler's high, permeating the air. Everywhere he looked, it was nothing but scams, hustle, and exploitation. The swindlers sold goods out of small stands, repurposed proton caches, or, in some special cases, the sweaty palms of their hands; the hustlers identified newcomers and cornered them into a game of "chance"; the desperate tried to do anything to get away with whatever they could. And these were the small-timers, Cade reminded himself. The bona fide crooks and cheats of Kyysring were comfortably nestled in the city, going about their business without having to worry about those pesky nuisances of life, like laws or paying taxes. Not on Kyysring. Everyone here did as they wanted; let the chips fall where they may. As long as you didn't interfere with the planet's criminal economy—and some did, do-gooders who thought they could "clean up" Kyysring; roaming marauders who possessed either the stupidity or the arrogance to think they could consolidate the entire illegitimate enterprise under their personal control—there wasn't a single prohibition that stood between someone's desire and its fulfillment. And that, Cade had seen firsthand, led to a lot of happy people, but it created even more broken ones. Cade learned, at a young age, that Kyysring was not for the faint of heart. This place deteriorated everyone in time; it was entropy accelerated, and Cade didn't care to spend any more time here than he absolutely had to.

"So, what are we doing here?" Kira asked as she set the *Rubicon*'s security protocols and then followed Cade off the ship. "You going to mope the entire time, or are we going to get our act together and figure out what to do next?"

Cade slid into a beat-up jacket Kira had given him, which fit loosely enough to conceal both the Rokura and the shido that he kept crisscrossed over his back. They'd changed clothes while awaiting landing clearance from Kyysring's central terminal, meaning they had to wait until their "docking levy" transacted. Cade abandoned his tunic, and Kira ditched her pilot jumpsuit. Both gave them away as coming from the Well, which marked them as authority figures. If there was one thing that the people of Kyysring unanimously rejected, it was authority in any shape or form. Plus, it was best to avoid recognition in general, given what Cade was masquerading as. There was no telling what kind of bounty Praxis would put on their heads, assuming they hadn't already. Kira comfortably wore a leather jacket and cargo pants, and Cade was relieved to ditch his tunic in exchange for a pair of dusty gray khakis and a collared shirt, though he couldn't help but crack a smile over Kira's possession of men's clothing. She must have sensed a wisecrack coming and stopped Cade dead in his tracks with a rigid finger pointed right in his face. He'd just have to let this one go.

"I'm not moping," Cade said, trying to conceal his moping. "I just don't like this place, okay? So let's fix the ship and get—"

"Yes, yessss, this ship," came a slurred voice from behind Cade and Kira. Cade didn't have to turn to know what he was hearing— a foul, bottom-feeding Sloos coming their way.

The Sloos lurched toward them, dragging the hunch on his back; he had a wide, bog-green flat face dotted with small features and tufts of hair that seemed like they'd been yanked out from beneath his skin. With his wet lisp, he continued. "Thish is some marvel of engineering you have here. The ownersh of this port, they charge you forty coin per day but do nothing to protect your property. What with the likesh you find around here, you never know what could happen. Now, if you'd like to discussh shervicess me and my men offer, we—"

Without bothering to turn her attention to the conniving creature, Kira unholstered her sidewinder and stuck it in the Sloos's face.

"Or we can talk about thish another time."

Kira jammed the weapon back in her holster as the Sloos hobbled off in the opposite direction.

"Get used to it," Cade dryly said as he and Kira continued down the spaceport's walkway, which led them to the city center. "Everyone here is looking for someone to dupe, rob, or who knows what."

"Thanks for the tip, grandpa, but I know all about this place, which is why I figure it might not be the worst thing that we ended up here."

Cade raised an eyebrow. "Totally, because, you know, we could've ended up parked on a lava geyser on F'Som. That would be mildly worse. Or marooned in the Darklands—that for sure would be worse. So, yeah, I guess from a certain point of view, landing in the galaxy's armpit isn't so bad."

Kira pulled back the dreads of her Mohawk, tugging on their ends. "Do I really have to explain this to you?" she asked, letting out a deep breath. "Cade, if you somehow didn't believe we were at war before, well, now it's literally exploded all over our doorstep. Praxis's attack on our home wasn't an isolated incident. They've opened a door, and now there's no going back. If they don't finish off the Well, and soon, they'll look weak in front of the entire galaxy. We have only one choice—"

Cade grabbed Kira by her arm, shoving them both into a nearby corner of the spaceport. "Kira, I know you think you get what this place is all about, but let me make something crystal clear: You can fire off whatever words you want against Praxis in the safety of the Well, but you can't talk like that here. People on this rock, they want nothing to do with Praxis, war, rebellion, or any of the other bothodung you're spouting. Trust me, they don't tolerate *anyone* who threatens to bring Praxis to their backyard. They'll either kill you or turn you over to whatever crime lord is closest. Maybe both."

"First of all," Kira said, shaking off Cade's grasp, "grab me like that again, and I'll feed your face to a ranglin. Second, the degenerates around here are as worrisome to me as a cloudy day."

"Well, congratulations, Kira. You're not afraid. But that doesn't mean you need to be dumb. Praxis has ears *everywhere*."

"You really don't get it, do you, Cade? Praxis is going to reduce the Well to cinders and ashes, and then they're going to rule the entire galaxy. Not a single system will be safe. Do you believe me or not?"

"It doesn't matter what I believe; nobody *cares* what I believe."

"I do," Kira said, without a hint of facetiousness in her tone. "I care."

Cade blinked. He wasn't used to votes of confidence, and he felt a pang of remorse for thinking Kira was just another person who was going to steamroll over him with no regard for his thoughts or opinions. He released his grip on her arm, sorry that he'd overreacted.

"I believe you," Cade said. "There's no doubt Praxis is going to go back to Ticus and finish what they started, and there's not a thing the Well can do to stop them. But what you're talking about, going up against Praxis . . . Look, I hate them as much as anyone, but we don't have the numbers, the firepower, or the organization to stop them."

"You're right, we don't have the conventional means to make a stand against Praxis. But what if I told you we don't need *any* of those things?"

Cade took a step back. "What are you talking about?"

From day one of Praxis's ascension, not a single star system had been able to make the evil kingdom so much as flinch. Part of that was chalked up to Praxis's judicious selection, especially in its earliest days, of weaker opponents, but that didn't change the fact that the kingdom was able to roll into systems and give its leaders a blunt choice: annex or else. There were four occasions when Praxis showed the entire galaxy what "or else" meant: First on Quarry, then Maqis, Romu, and Tor-Five. These four planets—these bold, stupid planets—refused to bow to Praxis, and their failure to receive the invading empire with total acquiescence was considered an act of sedition, and sedition meant war. While the forces of these noncompliant planets fought with every ounce of their strength, utilizing every resource they had, it always ended the same: in darkness. The Praxis *War Hammer* came, drained the energy from the nearest life-giving star, and left behind an entire race of refugees who had no choice but to flee their dying planet. It was only a matter of time now, as Cade and Kira both understood, before the *War Hammer* came to Ticus. Only when it did, annexation wouldn't be an option.

"I'm talking about making Praxis look vulnerable," Kira said. "I'm talking about hurting them the way they've hurt so many others."

At the end of the spaceport, Cade and Kira crossed beneath a pair of massive stone hands protruding from the ground, each holding a power blade that met at the center of the monument— some kind of bothodung ode to free enterprise—that marked the entrance to Kyysring's densely packed city center. Night was falling as Cade and Kira walked inside, and that meant the planetoid's pledge to fulfill its promise of anything-goes proclivities was about to be ratcheted up to the nth degree. Beyond this urban space, not a single inch of Kyysring was worth even thinking about; the landscape was sun-beaten and punishingly hot, making for an arid topography that was uninhabitable. What made Kyysring worth its placement on the stellar map was its fortuitous location directly between a bustling strand of Inner Cluster metropolises and a pocket of industrial planets on the Galactic Fringe. Back in the dark ages before mass jumping was equipped standard in every ship, being a strategic waypoint made Kyysring as valuable as its commodity-rich neighbors. After all, what good are commodities if they can't get anywhere? By the time improvements in mass-jumping drove Kyysring's layover value into the dirt, it didn't matter. The crafty planetoid—and the ruthless profiteers who ran it—had already capitalized on its ingress and egress by building a shadow economy that centered on the laundering and movement of illegal goods. While the galactic community turned its attention away from Kyysring, assuming the obsolescence of its purpose would also spell the end of the seedy planetoid, it thrived. The services the kings of Kyysring offered attracted a type of person to its shores, and those people saw opportunity; a lot could happen in a place that all the right people had forgotten about. And all these years later, like it or not, the galaxy kind of needed Kyysring—it needed consolidated, localized debauchery, so long as it was contained—even though no one was thrilled to admit it.

"Okay, look," Kira continued. "Everyone knows the *War Hammer* is impenetrable, right? No one who's gone up against it has so much as made a dent; and I'll tell you what—the Maqins had some heavy-duty firepower in their arsenal."

"Never mind the fact that weapons can't damage it," Cade said. "That thing can park right up against a star and somehow be totally fine. That's *insane*. How are you going to blow something up that can stand up to the heat of a star?"

"Well, here's the thing: We don't have to blow it up. We're going to make it blow itself up."

"Riiiiight," Cade said with a chuckle. "Of course we are."

"Don't do that," Kira said as a Boxton, reeking of root, lumbered between her and Cade, its floppy ears dangling down at its waist. "Don't dismiss me when you haven't even heard what I have to say. Don't be like the Masters."

"All right, all right," Cade replied, trying to sound apologetic without apologizing. "Let's have it. What's this plan of yours?"

They continued into the city, and Cade caught a whiff of panka dough frying in seedling oil from a food cart just ahead. It smelled like his childhood. Just beyond the spaceport, the city opened up to a marketplace of vendors offering all matter of counterfeit technology, knock-off products, and services that were, to say the least, frowned upon by polite company. Stout buildings demarcated the urban space from the nothingness beyond and defined the city's ins and outs; thick concrete walls with exposed piping characterized the architecture, which was no more than utilitarian. Cade knew every inch of this place, every corridor, every blind alley. He knew which doors to never enter. For a brief moment, he felt comforted by the familiarity, but he knew better than to let nostalgia distract him from his purpose. He still had the Rokura strapped to his back, which might as well be a bull's-eye inviting any takers to come after him.

"I'll make this as straightforward as possible," Kira said. "When the *War Hammer* comes to destroy a system's star, it's not sucking up all its energy like a vacuum. I don't care how badass the *War Hammer* is, you shove a sun inside of it without any means of containing it, bad things will happen. It has to control the influx of its energy so it can be contained—very precisely, very carefully. That's just the way it is."

"Yeah, that sounds about right. But—and no offense—but how do you know all this?"

"I know because I know."

Cade looked at Kira, whose face projected the definitive period she'd slapped on her statement. There'd be no more talk of how she knew what she knew.

"Okeydoke," Cade said. "So then what?"

"Well, since we can't damage the *War Hammer*, we have to do the next best thing: mess with its siphoning process *while* it's siphoning."

Cade faced Kira, his interest piqued. Her plan wasn't nearly as crazy as he expected. "Wait," he said. "This is actually making sense."

"Oh, thanks, Cade. Because that's the only thing this plan's been waiting for: your validation."

Cade shrugged. "I'm here to help."

"Look, what we need to do is bomb the *star*, not the *War Hammer*. If we can get an energy accelerator into the star at the point of siphoning, it will create a surge that overloads the *War Hammer*'s intake process. We do that, and that thing erupts from the inside out. We're talking about a mega explosion here—bye-bye to Praxis's greatest weapon."

"Okay, but you'd need to get right up on the *War Hammer*'s backside to drop the accelerator in the exact right spot. Praxis probably won't let that happen."

Kira shot Cade an arrogant smile. "You do know you're look-ing at the best pilot in the fleet, right?"

Cade rolled his eyes. "And this device of yours, the accelerator—you have it, I hope?"

"Well, see, that's the problem," Kira said, rubbing the back of her neck. "I don't. I have the accelerator part, and it's ready. But there's no way to shield it enough from a star's heat so it doesn't melt before it gets close enough to detonate. It's just . . . it's so frustrating. And I've talked to everyone; nobody knows how to get that close to a star."

"Nobody except Praxis," Cade said ruefully.

"Nobody except Praxis."

Cade wanted to trust Kira. This was the first plan he'd ever heard that had a legit shot at breaking the illusion that Praxis was invincible. For as long as Cade could remember, the king-dom managed to stomp around the galaxy doing as they pleased because everyone seemed to figure that was just how things went. But take out the *War Hammer* and suddenly Praxis ain't so tough. And who knew what could happen from that point? The psychology was simple: One kid busts the bully's nose and sud-denly even the weakest kid on the playground isn't getting pushed around anymore. But the nagging voice in his head—the voice of fear or reason, Cade couldn't tell—told him that the risk was too great. Yes, the solution to Kira's heat-shielding problem was out there. It had to be, otherwise the *War Hammer* would never be able to hang out next to a star as it stole its energy and, that being the case, there'd be no problem to begin with. And it's not like Cade was enthusiastic about destroying the Rokura based on his belief that it was a weapon of destruction and not salvation. Because what if, whoops, he was wrong? Even if he was right, he'd be condemning himself to a life of hiding on some forsaken planet, always looking over his shoulder until the day some lunatic caught up with him and let him know how grateful the galaxy was that he robbed them of their only hope.

Cade was beginning to miss the days when no one expected a thing from him.

"Cade, I know what you're thinking, and I get it," Kira said. "I'm afraid, too. I am. But this is our chance. This is our *only* chance to make a difference. And that's why I'm saying that being in this place might be, I don't know, fate."

"Don't even talk to me about fate," Cade grumbled.

"Okay, not fate. It's the opposite, in fact, because we're not sitting around waiting for the solution to drop into our laps. We can make the solution ourselves."

"Kira, take a look around," Cade snapped. "You are surrounded by nothing but criminals—"

Kira interrupted, raising her voice above Cade's. "Who've been to every corner of the galaxy and back. *Someone* has to know how Praxis shields the *War Hammer*, and if we can just find that one—"

"You're talking about people who can't be trusted and have no interest, none, in helping you. Or anyone else that isn't themselves."

Cade stopped and realized he'd been yelling. He felt his chest as it swelled and contracted in rapid bursts. The discussion had gotten too personal—Kyysring made it personal; the Rokura and the albatross it was to Cade made it personal. Kira couldn't have understood any of this, though, and as he scanned the crowd to make sure they hadn't caught unwanted attention, he felt disappointment in himself for lashing out at her.

Kira stepped close to Cade and brought her voice down to a conciliatory hush. "What are we going to do then, Cade? Just sit back and watch Praxis destroy our home and seize total control of the galaxy? Unless you've magically become the Paragon in the past five minutes, my plan is all we have."

"That's low," Cade said.

"I don't mean it to be, but it's the truth. You want to be pissed about fate?" Kira asked, impassioned. "Then be pissed that we allowed the idea of the Paragon to control all of our fates. We sat around like idiots, myself included, when we should have been working to save *ourselves*."

Since Tristan's death, Cade found himself wishing, desperately, to see him one last time. He dreamed of his brother; he had him in his thoughts all the time. Memories of things he said, memories of the moments they shared, memories, simply, of what he looked like. All things that, he knew, would fade in time. But if he had one last moment with him, one last memory he could freeze in amber and know to hang on to because he knew it'd be their last, he felt like that could see him through the wilderness he was lost in. All he wanted was to ask Tristan what do. His brother always had the answers. He always knew where to direct the both of them. And now, when Cade needed him most, he was gone. His final words came to mind: Tristan had apologized. Cade couldn't understand what he could possibly be sorry for, but now he understood: He knew he was leaving Cade alone, and in his final moment, all he had on his mind was Cade's well-being, knowing that he couldn't guide him any longer. Knowing that, for the first time, Cade would be on his own.

Cade couldn't run. In everything they'd been through together, Tristan never had them hide. He never made them abandon their courage. Cade refused to go against his brother's example now.

"All right," Cade said, resolved.

"All right? All right what?"

"That thing you said about us saving ourselves? Tristan said the same thing. He agreed, completely."

"Sooooo . . ." Kira said, tilting her head so her smiling face crowded Cade's vision.

"Don't be cute, it's unbecoming."

Kira clapped her hands like she was smashing their discussion. It was over; the decision was made. Now it was time to get to work. "All right, then. So, who can we find to help get this thing made? A smuggler? A disgraced Praxis soldier willing to trade some secrets? What's on the menu around here?"

Cade scanned the area, considering all the paths open to them. There was no shortage of unscrupulous options all around, but only one provided Cade with at least a little bit of confidence.

"We want someone who knows how to make things, someone who has an eye on getting a leg up on everyone else," he said. He then turned down a narrow alleyway where a trio of zep addicts were roasting botho meat over a flame that roared out of the bottom half of what was once a service drone. "If you want to find people trying to outdo each other with crazy tech, there's only one place to go."

"And where's that?" Kira asked.

Cade stopped and looked back over his shoulder at Kira. "The drone fighting pit."

The galactic consensus on drone modification was clear: The practice was immoral, cruel, and, therefore, forbidden. Even though the decision to outlaw customization was driven by a philosophical premise, the Galactic Alliance spent an unusually small amount of time passing an official ban. To be fair, the Alliance's deliberation was buoyed by an overwhelming majority of sentient, drone-owning beings from across the galaxy who all agreed that, over time, drones unquestionably developed their own personalities. They had their own likes and dislikes, their own sense of humor, and in some cases their own prejudices, much to most people's chagrin, against alien cultures. All of which defied their programming and demonstrated the capacity to become individuals, bringing into question the very idea of sentience. As such, the manufacturing of drones—from companion drones to stellarbots—continued unabated; but once they were activated for the first time—their "birth" date—any further modification, save necessary repairs or routine updates, was illegal.

Except on Kyysring.

The drone fighting pit was exactly as advertised—it was a pit. Dug into the reserve of the planetoid's softest minerals, the oval fighting ring descended deep into the ground, while an arena expanded upward and out from its center. The grandstand's seating pods were stacked in staggered columns all the way up to where the vestibule and its fortified walls separated the arena from the outside world. The place smelled of grease and, strangely, of blood, both of which commingled with the zep smoke that wafted overhead. Cade closed his arms tightly at his sides and let his wrist rub nonchalantly against the sidewinder that was holstered on his waist. He felt it important to make sure it was still there.

When Cade and Kira entered the arena, the final match of the undercard was getting under way. On one side of the oval pit stood an older model alpha drone, upgraded so that it was now equipped with a shield welded to its right forearm and a ten-inch blade grafted to its left. Protruding from its protective helmet was a tightly bunched collection of wires, grounded in the drone's central nervous system located in its spine. Cade assumed these wires enabled more advanced enhancements like speed, reflexes, and battle readiness. The drone would need all the help it could get, as its opponent, a Nootharian service drone that'd undergone such extensive modifications Cade could barely discern its original frame, waited on the opposite side of the oval. Over-laying the Nootharian's body was a cache of weapons that could have jump-started a small militia—very little was for-bidden in the drone pit—including a personal shield genera-tor, and even, if Cade was seeing things correctly, a cloaking device.

"I kind of want that Nootharian drone," Cade said.

Kira shot him a sidelong glance. "This is disgusting."

And she was right. But Cade couldn't help but feel a small amount of exhilaration being in the drone fighting pit. Forbid-den to minors—especially poor orphans—the pit tantalized Cade and Tristan, their adolescent imaginations running wild on the possibilities of what happened beyond the giant steel doors that kept them locked out. Because, really, when you stripped away the morality of it all—which didn't mean all that much to a couple of kids—what remained was robots fighting each other. And that was awesome. Of all the illicit things they wit-nessed and heard about on Kyysring, they couldn't imagine anything that would truly shock them. But then there was the pit, taunting them with its promise of robot warfare.

Cade and Kira found an empty pod just as the betting opened. The pod's gaming screen turned on, beckoning them to lay a wager. All around them, the near-capacity crowd roared as the lowlifes and crooks made their bets, then immediately lobbed taunts and jeers at their opponent. Cade moved to get his own wager in the mix, but Kira stopped him.

"No," Kira said, blocking Cade's coin from the intake slot. "We're not doing this."

"You want to blend in?" Cade asked, gently moving Kira's hand away. "Well, this is how you blend in on Kyysring."

Kira acquiesced with a grunt, and Cade dropped a fifty coin on the Nootharian drone.

An air horn boomed throughout the arena, bringing the crowd

to a roar as the match began. The Nootharian quickly went on the offensive, firing a series of concussive blasts at the alpha drone, which it blocked easily with its shield. With incredible speed, the alpha ran to the pit wall, leapt sideways onto it, and used it as leverage to propel itself toward the Nootharian. It rocketed past the Nootharian, who was too slow to respond, and used its blade to pierce through its shielding and slice off a considerable portion of its weapons array. The crowd exclaimed at the maneuver and the turn of events; they had a real match on their hands.

"What, exactly, are we looking for in this place?" Kira asked, making no attempt to mask her contempt.

"The . . . *thing* we're looking to build—we need someone who can think outside the box. Someone who is willing to take risks that are, well, some may call them unconventional, others may say illegal. . . ."

The alpha attempted to launch itself at the Nootharian again, but this time it was ready; its forearm broke off into a spinning propeller that sliced off the alpha's blade just as it was about to strike. The blow silenced the crowd, who, regardless of their wagers, had grown invested in an underdog victory. Cade spotted a lavender-skinned Nootharian in the front row with his arms raised, presumably the drone's creator, arrogantly calling for the crowd's cheers.

"And you really think we can trust one of these unconventional risk-takers?"

"On Kyysring, with the right amount of coin," Cade said, just as the Nootharian ripped off the alpha's head, "you can buy anything you need. And we just doubled ours."

Two fifty coins in hand, Cade stepped out of the pod and joined the throng of people heading upward.

"Hey! Where are you going?" Kira yelled after him.

"To get us a drink. Remember? Blending in?"

———

In the main concourse, Cade shuffled his way forward, sandwiched between a pair of guffawing Toofars and an amphibious Arkly. The Toofars communicated through a series of guttural sounds that, to Cade, sounded like "ar ar ar" repeated over and over, but to them was a complex language. When the one closest to Cade got a little too worked up about what he was "ar"-ing about, he threw out his arms and shoved Cade onto the Arkly, who was none too happy about their collision. Arklys conveyed their moods by the changing colors of their scales. Though Cade had never seen one in person before, he had to figure that her scales going from a neutral soft gray to seamless black wasn't indicative of her being amused. Cade smiled, awkwardly, and her scales only got darker.

The line was going nowhere fast, and Cade didn't want to leave Kira on her own for too long. Not because he was worried about her safety, but because he didn't trust her to stay out of trouble. Kira didn't suffer fools lightly, and the pit was crammed full of fools. Inebriated ones, at that. Plus, no shot of root was worth missing the main event, a spectacle he'd practically waited his entire life to see.

Cade sidestepped his way out of the mass of people—holding his arms straight above his head as he went so any contact he made was understood as purely incidental—and onto the concourse ramp leading back to the pits. He turned down an empty corridor that he hoped was a connective artery that would avoid the crowds and lead him back to his pod. It was completely empty, or at least it had been when he entered. But then he heard his name, first and last, echoing off the walls, and it was such an unexpected thing that he assumed he was just hearing things. His name echoed again, and Cade understood that it was no illusion.

Somebody was behind him, and that somebody knew who he was.

Cade stopped and considered his best defense: He had a sidewinder at his side and a shido and the Rokura strapped to his back. The latter would take some doing to get free, and, if Cade was being honest with himself—and now was an ideal time to do so—he had to admit he was a slow draw with a sidewinder. Still, it was the surest bet he had to put up some kind of fight. And a fight, he was certain, was what waited for him the moment he turned around. It was just a matter of who it was going to be with. The old-ass Fatebreaker he encountered on Ticus? A bounty hunter? Some Praxis loyalist out to do his overlords a favor? Cade fretted how many people would do anything to get their hands on the Rokura as he whipped around, drawing his sidewinder. But the moment he turned, he knew he didn't need his weapon. That's not what kind of fight this was going to be.

"Hello, Cade Sura," the scarred, portly man said. "How's life pretending to be the Paragon treating you?"

Cade stammered. Here was a man he never thought he'd see again: Valis Portnoy, infomerchant.

"Valis," Cade finally said. "It's . . . good to see you."

"Hmmm, I'm sure," Valis replied. "Come, come closer. We have much to discuss."

Cade tore his eyes off Valis to assess the stone-faced guards that stood a step behind him, one over each shoulder. They weren't holding any weapons, though Cade easily identified the shock rifles under their cloaks. It was fair to assume both were very, very quick draws.

That didn't matter, though, because Valis was the real threat, and Cade had no choice but to start walking straight toward the most dangerous man on Kyysring.

CHAPTER TEN

Oh, don't look at me like I just killed your pet meesema, Cade. I haven't told anyone what I know."

Cade hadn't laid eyes on Valis since he was a kid, yet the info-merchant looked remarkably the same. If someone would have asked him, in those intervening years, where he figured Valis was, Cade would've assumed he was dead. Not that he wished it, but he figured all the games Valis played and the people he manipulated had to catch up with him at some point. Infomerchanting—collecting dirt, trading secrets, dealing in blackmail with the casualness of brushing your teeth—wasn't a career known for its longevity. Still, somehow, Valis managed to survive and, judging by his looks and the muscle he could keep on payroll, thrive. He stayed one step ahead of everyone, and Cade feared, with dread settling like a stone in his gut, Valis was half a dozen steps ahead of him.

"Who said anything about me pretending?" Cade asked, trying to shove a noble tone from his mouth, one that took umbrage against Valis's accusation. "Who would dare?"

"Please," Valis replied. "You may be surrounded by magical-thinking fools at the Well, but it's no mystery to me what happened when you and your brother went to retrieve the Rokura. Making sense of information and events is what I do."

Cade groaned. He knew there was no dodging Valis's conclusion. Valis knew, and that's all there was to it. It was just a matter of what he planned on doing with his knowledge.

"So what do you want, then? You know I can't pay for your silence, and I wouldn't trust you not to sell me out if I could."

"Well, *someone*'s grown curt," Valis snapped. His brow furrowed, calling attention to the scar tissue that formed over his left eye socket, where an eye used to be. Rumor was he lost the eye after trading information to a gang of gunrunners who were supplying arms to an insurgency against Praxis on Tor-Five. It might have been the only time Valis didn't come out on top of a dangerous situation. "I never, ever double-cross anyone. That's bad business."

"Well excuse *me*, Valis," Cade said. "I didn't know you were so sensitive about your conduct for extortion."

Valis sighed and eyed Cade up and down. "You look like your father, but you've got the fire of your mother. Wasn't the Well supposed to straighten you out?"

"I guess it didn't take," Cade said. And, with such pointedness that it made Valis's guards gesture toward their rifles, he added, "And don't talk about my parents."

Valis casually gestured for his guards to ease, then turned back to Cade. "Understood. I know it's a difficult subject for you. But I do want to give my condolences for the loss of your brother. I don't know if you were aware, but Tristan and I crossed paths just a few years ago. He helped me out of a . . . a misunderstanding, let's call it. He was one of the good ones, and I know he'll be missed."

"Yeah, and you also know he was supposed to be the Paragon, not me. Which gets us back to my question: What do you want?"

Valis began to stroll down the corridor, and Cade walked by his side.

"It's so generous of you to offer, Caderick—"

"Cade. *Nobody* calls me Caderick. Are you trying to piss me off?"

"A little. But I just want to wish you luck. Listen, I wouldn't dream of selling you out to Praxis. Those beasts have done nothing but make my business harder and harder. Every time I turn around there's new laws, new restrictions, new curfews. I swear, if their mission is to make the galaxy a boring place, well, bravo. They're doing splendid job of taking all our fun away."

"Yeah, Valis, that's really what's at stake here. Good times."

Valis waved him off. "Oh, you know what I mean."

Cade stopped and let Valis take a few steps away from him. He turned around, his reptilian smile as intimidating as ever. Cade knew there was an angle in this meeting, somewhere, and he didn't have the patience to entertain Valis's gab as they circled around the point. "I appreciate the sentiment, Valis, but I should get going. Thanks for the kind words about Tristan; that was nice of you."

"Yes, yes, of course. And, again, I wish you all the luck in the world. I hope you fare better than our previous Paragon."

And there it was. Cade had just turned to leave and was stopped with one foot suspended in the air. He could keep his momentum going, he knew this, and leave Valis and his trap behind. But Cade wasn't dumb. He'd been caught in Valis's trap since he first called his name.

"What do you mean, 'previous Paragon'?" Cade asked, holding back the urge to grab Valis by his silky robe and scream "Tellmetellmetellme!" in his face until he spilled what he knew.

Now was the time for Valis to start his performance. He threw a flat hand against his chest, his face awash in a combination of being stunned that Cade didn't know this information and mortified that he'd slipped. Cade felt like he should applaud such theatrics.

"You mean—you didn't *know*?" Valis asked. "Oh, my, the things your Masters don't tell you."

Cade shook his head, gingerly, as he considered that Valis might be lying in order to get what he wanted. Nobody laid a trap like a crafty infomerchant, and Valis was the craftiest. "There's no way. No. Way. How can that even be possible? Everyone would know."

"You're right, Cade. If a Paragon popped up fifteen years ago and screwed up so badly that he went into hiding, I'm certain the Masters would have been very forthright about the matter. I mean, what an ideal way for the Chosen One to behave."

"Okay, then who is this mystery person? Where did he go?" Cade knew he had to press Valis for verifying details, but he also knew this was how Valis's game was played. He'd dangled the carrot for Cade to see; now it was time he brandished his stick— and it would cost Cade a price not to be lashed with it.

"Well now, I'd say the answer to that question is where things get interesting. Very interesting, indeed."

"I'm going to ask you for the third and final time, Valis: What. Do. You. Want?"

Valis's expression changed: Gone was the shadowy lizard, and in its place was what Cade might actually consider to be a human being. Valis seemed serious, he seemed intent, but Cade couldn't decide if it was a moment of authenticity or another layer of subterfuge.

"I want to see Praxis burn," Valis said, his voice deep and dark. "I want to see their ships, their bases, their flags in flames from one end of this galaxy to the next. Whether you like it or not, Cade Sura, fate has thrust you into a fight that's larger than you even know. The galaxy calls to you, and you must play your role in service to the Rokura, whatever role that may be."

Cade studied Valis, staring into his one good eye, expecting him to flinch. But the infomerchant didn't, not for one second.

"And you think I'll discover what my role is by finding this former Paragon?" Cade asked.

"Yes," Valis answered. "I do."

The decision to pursue Valis's path, Cade knew, had already been made. If there was a living, breathing Paragon out there, Cade had no choice but to track him down.

"Okay then," Cade said. "Now tell me who this Paragon is and how I find him."

"I'm afraid I can't tell you the former, as I think it's better that you find out for yourself who he is. But the latter, I can do."

"Whatever," Cade said, knowing he had to take what Valis was willing to give him. "Let's have it."

"Mithlador. He moves around a lot, but you can find him on Mithlador at the moment."

Wonderful, Cade thought. Mithlador. A barely habitable planet on the Galactic Fringe that was known for its aggressive hostility toward outsiders. All Cade had to do was fly a ship he didn't have to a planet nobody could land on. Still, the possibility of another Paragon was better than anything he had, including Kira's plan to make a suicidal run straight at the *War Hammer* and deliver a bomb they couldn't make. Because if this Paragon was out there, Cade was saved. *Everyone* was saved. All Cade had to do was deliver him the Rokura, point him toward the Praxis kingdom, and let him do the rest.

"Now don't go getting yourself killed," Valis said, his tone righting itself as he and his bodyguards walked away. "The galaxy needs you."

Cade grimaced. There went another person he was soon to disappoint.

Cade returned to his pod in a daze. He still had doubts about the authenticity of Valis's claim, even though he knew he had no option but to pursue the one person in the galaxy who could fix everything that had gone terribly, terribly wrong. He looked at Kira with a pang of shame already settling over him; somewhere along the way, he'd have to ditch her, which he wasn't happy about. She wouldn't follow him to Mithlador, though, not while she was resolutely committed to seeing her plans through. Kira was the only person Cade knew who was strong and brave enough to have a unique vision and live it out. But while she was convinced of her path, he was just as convinced of his: Going after this former Paragon, whoever he was, was the only way to put the Rokura in safe hands and maybe even make its prophecy of peace a reality. Cade just wished he hadn't made a promise that, now, he was forced to break. And he wished Kira wouldn't hate him for what he had to do.

"Where's the drinks?" Kira asked as Cade took his seat next to her.

"The drinks?"

"Yeah, the ones you left to go and get. Remember?"

"Yeah, right. Too crowded."

Kira snapped her fingers in front of Cade's eyes. "Hey, you in there?"

Cade blinked and pulled himself out of his reverie. "Yeah, yeah. Sorry. I'm just tired, I guess."

"Well, snap out of it. Something you'll never see again is happening right in front of your eyes. Take a look."

When Cade saw what Kira was talking about, his jaw dropped.

"Is that . . . wait. What is a Qel doing here?"

"I'd say it's getting ready to tear its opponent in half," Kira commented.

Cade couldn't take his eyes off what he was seeing. Qels were the stuff of legend; actually, he thought, check that. They *would* be the stuff of legend if more than a handful of people in the galaxy knew they existed. Because the Well had schooled them on galactic cultures, Cade and Kira knew what they were looking at when they saw the Qel. Otherwise, they, like the entire audience in the pit, would think they were seeing just another modified drone. The Qels were indeed drones, technically, but if they were capable of half the things Cade had heard they could do, that classification hardly fit. Superdrone would be more appropriate. They were strong, fast, agile, and smart, programmed with artificial intelligence that was parsecs beyond the technology that any other system possessed. And that programming was specifically tailored to make them perfect and unstoppable warriors. More drone than drone, more human than human.

Strangely, though, Qels didn't look like vicious killing machines. As Cade eyed the one in the fighting pit, he was awed by what he saw. The Qel was tall, reaching well over six feet, Cade figured, and it was surprisingly svelte, especially where its torso narrowed before connecting to its hips. Colored in a mixture of olive green and obsidian, the Qel stood with a slight hunch in its posture, its gangly arms stretching below its pelvis. Its chest was double armored, Cade could see, though most of its housing was said to be impenetrable. When the Qel craned its neck in Cade's direction, he finally got a good look at its face—which stirred a little bit of fright inside of him. The Qel had a rectangular voice box that protruded out from its face and, above that, two oblong, red glowing eyes. While the Qel's body didn't scream "murder machine," its face certainly didn't invite people to want to be on its bad side. Cade knew he sure wouldn't.

For some reason, this Qel had also been provided with an

overlay that made it seem like it'd been modified with homemade tech. It had propulsive boosters attached to its feet, a weapons system on its right arm, and a control panel / targeting system at the ready on his forehead—but Cade knew it was all for show. Qels had no need for homemade modifications. They required no help in doing what they were made to do.

"How'd this thing even get here?" Cade asked.

"Look, you know what it is, and I know what it is," Kira said as she leaned in close and lowered her voice. "But do you think the knuckle-draggers around here know what we know?"

Cade smiled as he realized what Kira was getting at. She was right: The Qels were created with one purpose—to guard the royal palace of Eris and annihilate any threat that dared oppose the throne. A dwarf planet on the cusp of the Galactic Fringe, Eris's isolationism dated back at least a millennium. They didn't participate in the Galactic Alliance, and it was rare, nearly inconceivable, for Erisians to leave their home world, permanently or otherwise. How a Qel—manufactured to be a security slave to a planet with tightly shut borders—made its way from Eris to Kyysring was unimaginable. But here it was.

"You want to hear something that will take your mind from blown to obliterated?" Kira asked.

"We're not at obliterated now?"

"That Qel you're looking at—that, as far as I can tell, is a model four."

Cade shook his head. "No way. I'd heard Eris was up to model six. Which would mean . . ."

". . . that all the fours are dead. Apparently," Kira said, gesturing toward the Qel no more than forty yards away, "at least one is not."

"This gets weirder and weirder. I'm dying to know who registered him in the fight. Someone has to be bankrolling this thing. But how?"

Kira threw up her arms, surrendering to the mystery. "All I know is, that souped-up manhunter droid is about to get whooped. You can throw a Praxis annihilator in there, and I'd still push coin on the Qel."

Cade looked over to the manhunter drone, the Qel's opponent, whom he failed to even consider in his wonderment over the Qel. It stood no chance. Studying the manhunter, Cade could barely count the numerous modifications that encumbered its slender frame, from weapons to shielding to devices Cade wasn't even familiar with. And that was all in addition to the manhunter's stock programming, which was already equipped with the necessary skills to track and capture the worst fugitives across the galaxy. Cade now understood why this match was the main event: As much as the denizens of Kyysring loved to gamble, they enjoyed the occasional bloodbath just as much. And this was going to be a bloodbath all right. Just not the way people expected.

The gaming screen set the manhunter odds at 3:2; the Qel, listed as "custom drone" was set at 20:1. Kira pushed five hundred coin on the Qel. Noticing this, Cade threw Kira a surprised look.

"What?" she asked, innocently. "We can buy anything we need, right?"

Cade smiled. He was rubbing off on her.

The air horn boomed, signaling the start of the match. The crowd rose to its feet, the promise of an easy payoff and bearing witness to a lopsided victory unifying them for the first time all evening.

The combatants circled each other cautiously; the manhunter wasn't as cocky and therefore not as rash as the Nootharian had been in the previous match. Though it didn't know what it was up against, the manhunter knew better than to underestimate any opponent. In fact, it was that uncertainty that made the drone slow to act. Manhunters were programmed with extensive knowledge of humans, aliens, and drones throughout the galaxy, and they acted according to this knowledge. Doubtless, this manhunter had no supporting data on the adversary that circled slowly around him. Still, Cade knew that particular disadvantage was the least of the manhunter's problems.

As the manhunter and the Qel continued their showdown, the crowd grew restless. Stuffed with booze and zep, many shouted their disapproval and urged the fighting to begin. Obscenities were lobbed, then empty liquor bottles. Cade looked at Kira, sharing an exasperated groan.

"Another happy day on Kyysring," he said.

Maybe in response to the crowd's restlessness, the manhunter finally made its move and seized the crowd's anticipation. The entire audience, save Cade and Kira, roared as the manhunter shot an electroaxe out from the apparatus on its right arm and brought it down, mightily, on the Qel. With little effort, the Qel dodged the attack, weaving to its right. The manhunter, committed to its offensive strategy, continued to take swipes at the Qel; each attack was met with equal fluidity of movement from the Qel, until finally it decided to stop toying with its enemy. As the manhunter brought the electroaxe down for an overhead strike, the Qel held his ground. It clamped both its hands directly over the manhunter's, halting the electroaxe's descent. As they remained locked in this static position—the Qel gripped on the manhunter, who was struggling to break free—an astonished awe fell over the crowd. They knew something crazy was about to go down.

With no more than a tug from his forearms, the Qel tore the electroaxe from the manhunter's hands, taking its arm modification apparatus with him. The manhunter stumbled back and, from a compartment in its own chest, it removed a single barrel X-19 sentry pistol, but, anticipating this move, the Qel rolled into a somersault just as a shot was fired. The Qel leapt out of his roll toward the manhunter; before the drone could raise its pistol and have it pointed at its opponent, who was coming on *fast*, the Qel descended on it, bringing its fist down on the manhunter's face. The crunching sound hushed the crowd. The hoots and hollers, the stomping feet and clanging root bottles, all of it stopped. If the Qel had their interest before, now it had their attention. Because when the manhunter snapped its head back into position, the bottom half of its face was missing. Cade spotted it on the nearby ground, a small oval piece of metal glinting in the light cast from overhead.

Desperation set in for the manhunter. Meanwhile, the Qel, if Cade was hearing correctly, sounded like it was laughing. Which Cade found odd. It seemed to be enjoying the grisly blood sport, or maybe it just delighted in the thrill of victory. Either way, its joviality was more than a little unnerving.

The manhunter fired off one last wild shot from its pistol before the Qel knocked it from its hand. The combatants were in close quarters now, the Qel not giving the manhunter space or time to regroup. It tried to draw another weapon, this time from an apparatus on its leg, but the Qel kicked the manhunter at its knee joint, cleanly breaking it in two, then crushed its hand in its own. The manhunter dropped to its belly and was reduced to crawling away from the Qel, pulling its body with its one good arm toward its electroaxe. Abandoning all pretense, the Qel shoved off his modifications that, if anything, encumbered its natural abilities.

Just as the manhunter reached the electroaxe, the Qel snatched the weapon from its grasp. The manhunter was defeated, and the Qel had no interest in toying with it. It rose the electroaxe to the sky and plunged it into the manhunter's backside, through its powering unit, efficiently ending the manhunter and the match.

The arena was silent. Knowing his home planet all too well, Cade figured they were about to cheer or riot. Cade was glad and relieved when they chose the former, erupting in wild applause.

They all lost money—except Kira, who was collecting her coins—but the brutal thrill of what they'd just witnessed compensated for lost wages.

"Take your prize!" Cade heard a nearby Galibadan shout, the words gurgling through the two curved tusks that protruded outward from near his mouth. "Take your prize!" he repeated, and within moments, the yell became a chant. "Take your prize! Take your prize!" bellowed throughout the arena.

Kira leaned over to Cade, yelling in his ear so she could be heard. "Should I even ask?"

Cade drew a breath, then explained how it was customary for a winning combatant in the main event to take the head of its victim.

"Great," Kira intoned. "Now I feel even worse about winning money off this."

When the Qel failed to respond to the audience's insistence, Cade thought it was for dramatic effect. But as it stood at the pit's exit, the Qel gave the crowd one last surprise: It scanned the entire audience, and every single person waited for this mystery drone to do something. And it did: It delivered an affirming double thumbs-up into the air. It was possibly the weirdest thing Cade had ever seen.

Pandemonium ensued. If there was one thing the denizens of Kyysring shared in common—other than being scumbags and lowlifes—it was their devotion to upholding the customs of the drone fighting pit. These were traditions that went back years, and they were tied to the essential character of Kyysring itself. Taking an opponent's head, as a mark of victory in illegal battle, was the period on the sentence that said "Kyysring doesn't follow *your* rules." Bucking that statement—a statement that explicitly warned every galactic system to keep their law and order to themselves—was one of the few insults that anyone on Kyysring could suffer.

But, as indignant as the crowd was, based on what they'd witnessed of the Qel's fight, they knew not to take their aggressions too far. The way out of the oval pit led straight to the grandstand, and the aggrieved audience in the Qel's path all parted to make a clear lane for his exit.

All except one person.

A man around Cade's age joined the Qel midway through his walk up the ramp that led to the arena's exit. Cade only caught a glimpse of him—short and lean with a head full of unruly curly hair—in profile, but it was enough. Cade elbowed his way through the crowd ahead, trying to get a clearer look at the Qel's companion. Cade kept his eyes on him, not wanting to lose sight of him for a moment. But just as this man and the Qel were about to leave, the man turned his face to look back at the crowd, and at the exact second, a burly Nootharian stepped directly in Cade's field of vision, blocking him completely. A series of "boos" rattled through the crowd, and Cade looked up to see the source of the jeers: The Qel's companion was plastered on the overhead projector so the entire crowd could know who he was.

Except Cade already knew.

"Hey!" Kira yelled, crisscrossing through the people that stood between her and Cade. "Where do you think you're going?"

Cade's gaze remained fixed on the projector screen, even though the image of the Qel's companion had been replaced with a message telling everyone the fights were over, so get out.

Kira jostled Cade's right shoulder, catching his attention. "You with me?"

"Yeah," Cade responded, his voice cracking as he gave his head a sobering shake. "Just thought I saw someone I used to know."

"And?" Kira asked as both of them turned and joined the sea of people who'd begun to shuffle out of the arena.

"And nothing," Cade said, turning his head one last time to scan the other side of the arena. All he saw there was a bunch of drunk spectators leaving the pits. "It wasn't who I thought it was."

There was no peace and quiet to be had on Kyysring, not even in the spaceport. Not even in the middle of the night.

Wrapped in a blanket on the *Rubicon*'s cold floor, Cade's mind went back and forth: Should he or shouldn't he? Should he or shouldn't he? As tired as he was, his Rai training let him keep his mind awake while his body drifted into a restful state. Which was useful on the occasional lengthy mission he was allowed to go on but a pain in the ass when he couldn't turn the skill off and let the sweet embrace of sleep take away all of his problems. As much as he convinced himself it was the right thing to do, Cade was conflicted about abandoning Kira. They'd been through a lot in a short amount of time, and that made leaving her feel personal. Plotting to destroy the Rokura was one thing; the galaxy was just a faceless mass, and Cade hadn't even met, like, 99 percent of it. But sneaking off like a thief in the night and rejecting Kira and her plan—which he still believed would work if she somehow found the shielding material—was hurtful. She'd never let him leave, though. The only useful thing about the Rokura, in Kira's mind, was that it helped her put her plan in motion. Otherwise, the weapon and all the mystical, magical suppositions it was laden with weren't even worth her time. And as torn as Cade was about going his own way, it's not like the option Valis presented to him was any less of a sure thing than Kira's plan. If this former Paragon actually existed, Cade harbored some serious questions about his character. After all, this was someone who, allegedly, either screwed up so badly that the mantle was taken from him, or who decided to give it up. At least Cade had an excuse for freaking out—being the Paragon wasn't his destiny. But the Rokura was this guy's birthright, and if he had blown it, who knew what he had to offer all these years later?

Still, Cade had to know. Even if this alleged Paragon turned out to be a total washout, maybe he could at least reinforce Cade's decision to destroy the Rokura. Cade reminded himself that torching the Rokura wasn't just about unburdening himself of its hold over him; it was about ensuring it never, ever fell into the wrong hands. Like Praxis's. And if this Paragon wasn't going to take the weapon from Cade, then he must have a good reason why not. Cade could only assume that it would have something to do with him realizing that the Rokura didn't live up to its hype, but he had to know for sure. What did this person know about the Rokura that scared him away from his destiny?

So, Cade waited. With his eyes shut, he waited for Kira to drift off to sleep on her bunk. When he knew she was out cold, he crept out of the ship and into the humid night air that hung over the spaceport like a dampened sieve filtering every breath of air he took. He could only hope that he was making the right choice.

Unlike so many planets—thanks to Praxis's rabid need for control—there was no curfew or docking regulations on Kyysring. Visitors came and went for dealings that were, for the most part, unplanned, unpredictable, and unfriendly. And in their downtime, these pillars of the galactic community bided their time by indulging in Kyysring's vice-happy nightlife. When Cade arrived back at the city center, he was quickly overwhelmed by the sights and sounds all around him. Having spent most of his adolescent years in the shelter—which was locked down by nightfall—Cade never had the chance to know Kyysring after hours, and he felt almost claustrophobic in the face of the frenzied vitality that was totally unique from anything he'd ever known. If the Well was a place of tranquility, Kyysring was its antithesis. From one corner to the next, the district bustled with countless species from any number of systems. On Kyysring, no-body cared about class, rank, or race; all that mattered was taking care of business and indulging in good times, which were becoming more and more scarce under Praxis's oppressive watch. Wide-eyed, Cade walked the city's narrow streets, which were aglow with the sheen from neon lights and filled with the sound of bellowing promoters who enticed passersby into their establishments with offers of who-knows-what. The energy—which Cade understood was aided by plenty of root—kept the crowd moving and ensured Kyysring never, ever rested.

"Lonely?" a scantily clad, blue-skinned Roshan whispered in Cade's ear as her orange and silver claws placed a flyer in his hands. "You don't have to be."

Cade let out an awkward, juvenile laugh as he shuffled away. He crumbled up the flyer, knowing it was best not to even look, not to even *know*, and tossed it over his shoulder. He surveyed his surroundings, making sure he wasn't being followed. The last thing he needed was another ghost of Kyysring creeping up on him the way Valis did in the fighting pit. On a nearby corner, Cade eyed a man examining a firebrand rifle—outlawed in nearly every system for the part it played in the Gesling massacre—before settling on his purchase. It was one of a half dozen that a fur-covered Lokany was selling out of a crate. Nearby, Cade spotted a zep deal. Elsewhere, he saw a man pick another man's wallet. Any other Rai would've jumped in and, regardless of how stupid it was, done something noble. But Cade was too much of a pragmatist. Because, really, what was he going to do? Tell everyone on the planet he was very disappointed in them? There was a reason why the Galactic Alliance and its upright allies turned a blind eye to Kyysring. After all, there were only so many resources you could expend saving people from themselves. And it's not like Cade had room to talk—he was about to break at least three Galactic Alliance laws, and his justification was probably similar to the lawbreakers he saw all around him: You do what you gotta do.

Careful no one was watching him, Cade worked his way through the crowded main drag and ducked into an alleyway just past the Koga Club, the most notorious gambling house in the galaxy. At the end of the tight, dark alley, he came to a large corrugated door—twenty feet high and at least the same across, made of reinforced steel—that was sealed with a magnetic lock. Cade was glad to see the lock still in place; with any luck, what was on the other side of the door was still there as well.

Cade kicked open a small sewage cover that stuck out just above ground. Below the cover, though, wasn't a drainage pipe; instead, there was a keypad. Cade was amazed that he still remembered the code. Though Cade also remembered the cheat code for infinite lives in his favorite childhood video game, so maybe hording useless information was simply a gift he'd been born with.

He punched in the numbers and winced at the sound of the door as it rolled aside, thumping and rattling as it went.

"Shhhh," Cade whispered to the door, but it wouldn't listen.

Cade smiled as he stepped inside the private launchpad and caught sight of the starjumper that was parked there. It looked like it hadn't been touched since he was a kid. Cade was taken back to all the times he, Tristan, and Mig smuggled their way onto this vintage ship and took turns manning the captain and cannon chairs. They shared a fantasy of abandoning Kyysring and embarking on adventures as pirates of the stars, until Krag—a cranky old Boxton who had a mechanical right arm and was missing his left ear—chased them away and warned them to never return. Late nights in the shelter, Cade, Tristan, and Mig relived their adventures in the starjumper, all longing for the day they assumed would never come, the day they'd have the means to make real adventures of their own.

But in all the times Cade boarded the starjumper, he never dreamed of actually flying it. He assumed it didn't even work. Now he prayed that it would.

Starjumpers, which were no longer manufactured due to their penchant for occasionally erupting into flames during takeoff, had two unique features: First was its vertical takeoff, made possible by its propulsive thrust system—which was designed after supply rocket vessels—and the cause of its pesky takeoff fires. Second was its exterior powering unit, which allowed easier access to the ship's most common repairs. Cade worked at the powering unit as quickly and quietly as he could, using whatever knowledge he had to hot-wire its engine.

After a few mistakenly crossed wires—one that started a small fire dangerously close to the fuel line—Cade spliced the right combination of power cords together and a spark popped within the control panel followed by a whirring noise at the starjumper's nose. Cade popped his head out from the rear and watched as the ship's lights flickered on and its systems came online. The starjumper was alive.

Cade had to suppress a victorious hoot for fear of waking Krag, but that didn't diminish his excitement as his childhood fantasy was coming true right before his eyes.

Unfortunately, none of Cade's fantasies had him staring down the barrel of a rusty tempest rifle. That pleasure was reserved for his reality.

"Goin' somewhere?" Krag grumbled as he spat a gooey wad of yellow phlegm at Cade's feet.

Life is full of surprises, Cade bitterly thought, the least of which wasn't Krag catching him, but the fact that Krag was still alive. Boxtons weren't exactly known for having a passionate regard for their health and hygiene. They drank to excess, rarely bathed, and with the time saved from not bathing, they drank some more. And Krag, by all appearances, was a sterling example of his species' disregard for self-preservation. Cade could see the oil and dirt caked in his olive-green skin; he could smell the decay on his breath. His sweat-stained clothes hung loosely on his frame, run gaunt by years of hard living. While Cade wasn't too concerned about Krag's welfare, he was worried about how little Krag valued the continuation of anyone else's life, especially when considering how well he regarded his own. Training his rifle on Cade wasn't just for show; he would splatter Cade all over the hangar and then probably just let nature take its course with his remains.

"I know this looks bad," Cade started, "but I need this ship for official Galactic Alliance business—"

"Galaxy politics don't mean squat to me, boy. You're a thief trespassin' on ma property, and I don't like that."

Krag took two steps forward, using his rifle to shove Cade back against the ship.

"Hey, hey, come on," Cade said as he threw his arms in the air. "You know me. Me and my brother, we used to break in here and play with this ship all the time. Remember?"

Krag squinted at Cade, and a low rumbling noise came from his throat. It seemed like he was either thinking or about to fall asleep.

"That might be familiar," Krag admitted.

Cade let out a giant sigh of relief. "See? I wasn't stealing your ship, I was just reliving old times and—"

"It's familiar," Krag grunted, "but that don't mean Ah care."

"A trade—how about a trade?" Cade nervously blurted, feeling a bead of sweat roll down the side of his face. "I have a rare, very valuable weapon. I bet that someone with your connections can make a lot of coin off it."

"Ain't interested," Krag replied, and Cade wondered if anything would make the old credit launderer happy. Other than watching Cade bleed out on the floor of his hangar.

"Let me just show it to you," Cade said, slowly reaching over his shoulder to grab his shido. "I think, once you see it—"

"Move that ahrm another inch, and it'll be the first part of you ta go."

"Just take a look, it might change your—"

"You just achin' to do this the hard way, ain't you boy?" Krag said, and Cade could see the glint in his eye that telegraphed what was going to happen next. Cade redirected his hand away from his shido and thought to swat the rifle and make errant any shot Krag fired. But Cade hardly had time to finish his thought before he heard blaster fire echo throughout the hangar. Electrical currents jolted Krag, and his body spasmed uncontrollably before he drunkenly swayed on the balls of his feet and then dropped, facedown, on the ground.

Cade looked up from Krag's unconscious body and saw Kira standing just a few paces in front of him, sidewinder in hand.

"You know, for a brief moment, you had me convinced that you're not a total idiot."

"The performance of a lifetime," Cade said. "How are you here? How did you know I—"

"The *Rubicon*'s security system," Kira said, holstering her weapon. "I set it as protection against him being touched, sneezed on, even looked at funny while we're on this foul planet."

"Wait—the *Rubicon* is a guy?"

"You got a problem with that? What, every pilot bro in the galaxy can pretend that his ship is some obedient shrew, but one woman makes her ship a guy and—"

"Okay, okay—no judgment from me."

Cade took a long look at Kira, who folded her arms across her chest, waiting. He knew he had to say something, but he also knew that a half-assed apology wouldn't cut it.

"Look," Cade said, kicking away Krag's rifle, just in case. "I didn't want to leave you, but—"

"But what? You assumed I wouldn't listen to you because you have some sob story about no one at the Well taking you seriously?"

Cade swallowed his uneasiness down hard. "Well, kinda."

"Seriously, Cade, do you really think you're the *only* person the Masters disregard?"

"Oh, please," Cade said with a smirk. "You're the rock star of the Well. Don't even try to act like you understand how the Masters treat me."

Kira shook her head, pitying Cade. "No, Cade. No. You hear me because I'm loud, but the Masters, or my commanders, have no interest in dealing with me or anyone else in my squadron. I've told them my idea for the bomb, I've told them over and over again, and they've never so much as given it a second thought. I'm just a blunt instrument to them—they point me in a direction and tell me which bad guys to fight. That's all they'll ever see me as."

Cade broke his lips apart to speak, but he couldn't grasp the words to say. All that came out was a frustrated sigh; even so many miles away from Ticus, the Masters still had a way of making Cade feel like garbage. "I didn't know, Kira. I just thought that if I tried to tell you the reason why I was leaving, you wouldn't let me go."

"Try me."

Shame burned Cade's ears, but he divulged everything—his meeting with Valis, the other Paragon, Mithlador, and his plan to either rid himself of the Rokura or destroy it. Cade noticed Kira's disposition shift from agitation to exasperation; hearing his story, she seemed to pity him more and, hopefully, wanted to punch him less.

"Look, I can't stop you from going. You're an adult and you can make your own decisions," Kira said. "But I would be doing a disservice to, well, the *entire galaxy* if I didn't try to convince you not to do this. And it's not because I don't believe what this infomerchant told you, but because your plan is terrible."

Cade smirked. "Um, it's not that much worse than hedging our bets on a bomb that, most likely, is impossible to build. My plan at least has a weapon; it just needs the right user."

"Oooooh, now I get it," Kira said, hamming up her sarcasm. "So, let me get this straight: This Paragon, whoever he is, refused his calling back when things were decent in the galaxy, but now—but *now*—when we're on the brink of being taken over by a totalitarian regime, he's going to hop into his role with open arms?"

Cade was quiet. "I hadn't thought about it that way."

"Yeah, Cade, there's a lot you're not thinking about."

"What's that supposed to mean?" Cade asked with a cocked eyebrow.

Kira sighed and rubbed her forehead. "It means if you dump the Rokura, you'll never get revenge against whoever's responsible for Tristan's death."

"You have no idea what you're talking about," Cade said, his voice shaking. He didn't want to talk about what happened in the spire; he didn't want to *think* about what happened in the spire. "I got my revenge for Tristan—the Fatebreaker who killed him is dead. I *killed* him."

"Yeah?" Kira said, stepping into Cade's face. "And what about the person who put the Fatebreaker there?"

Cade's blood went cold, and he became overwhelmed with anger and anxiety. Anger over what happened; anxiety over how it happened. Because he knew, somewhere in the back of his mind, he knew. He just wasn't prepared to face the truth Kira was throwing in his face.

"Finally sinking in?" Kira continued, pacing around Cade. "Your trip to Quarry, it wasn't broadcasted to the galaxy, Cade. It wasn't even shared with everyone at the Well. Only a few people knew where you were going and what for. You said the Fatebreaker was *waiting* for you. Well, how do you think he got there?" Kira stopped in front of Cade, drilling her finger into his chest with every word. "You. Were. Sold. *Out.*"

Cade turned his back on Kira and smothered his face in his hands. His chest burst with every stuttered breath, and he felt burning hot tears forming at the corners of his eyes. The hangar began to spin, and Cade reached out to brace himself on the starjumper's wing. But his hand slowly wrapped into a fist.

"GAAAAHH," he bellowed as he brought his fist down on the grimy, dusty metal again and again, shouting his pain and anger until he exhausted himself.

Even with his eyes closed, he felt Kira taking cautious steps toward him. She clasped her hand on Cade's bicep and slowly pulled him away from the starjumper. "I'm sorry, Cade, I really am," she said. "You are going through some terrible, crazy stuff right now, and the last thing you need is for things to get worse. But I know that, when everything is at its worst, it's hard to think straight. And I just, I thought you should know."

Cade nodded, solemnly. "Don't feel bad, really. I think I knew this, I just didn't want to—I couldn't, you know? Not yet."

"Trust me," Kira said. "I know all about life giving you a whole lot of unfairness all at once."

Truth and honesty, as virtuous as they were, weren't always good things. There was a reason why people, Cade included, clung to denial like it was the last escape pod on a burning starship: It did a fine job keeping things going exactly as they were, allowing you to whistle a tune to the beat of "everything's A-okay" as the days, months, even years rolled on by. But every so often uncomfortable impasses presented themselves, and Cade knew he was at such an impasse. He had to be honest, and about everything. His role at the Well. Tristan's death. The Masters' secrecy and what it meant. For the first time in his adult life, he was responsible for figuring out what to do next and knowing that, whatever decision he made, he was responsible for the outcome.

"Look," Kira said, interrupting Cade's reverie, "if you think unloading the Rokura is what you need to do, I'm not going to stand in your way. It's bad enough you've had to deal with that thing this long. If you just want to get rid of it, for real, I get it."

Cade stopped his pacing—realized, in fact, that he had been pacing—and he shoved aside all the anguish and garbage that was weighing him down, and, with all of it cleared from his view, he knew exactly what he was going to do. His eyes shot open wide as the idea popped into his mind.

"I know how to make your bomb," he said.

Kira shook her head; Cade could tell she had the impression he was just trying to be nice. "Look, Cade, it's fine. I know it's crazy, and, you know, I can figure it out. It won't be the first time I've had to go it on my own."

"I'm serious. I know how we can do this."

"Don't mess with me, Cade," Kira said, her brows knitted together.

"I'm not, I swear. Look, remember back at the pit, how you thought I'd recognized someone?" Cade asked.

"Yeah, of course I do. But, Cade, before you get ahead of yourself, we need to make a pact, right here, right now.

"First of all, we need to stop acting the way the Well expects us to. We're a light-year away from Ticus, so you're not the screw-up and I'm not the loose cannon. Okay? Second, whatever we're doing here, it's not going to work without trust. That's how Omega works. Each and every one of us knows that we have each other's back, no matter what. Didn't you learn that with the Rai?"

"Not so much," Cade said, an uncomfortable grimace on his face, "I wasn't really part of that whole thing. They . . . they kind of left me out. Of everything."

Kira nodded, understanding. Cade got the impression she was used to taking in strays. "We can do this, Cade. You and I. But I need to know if you're in or if you're out. There's no in-between."

"I'm in," Cade said without hesitation. "I want to be part of this."

Kira ran her tongue along the inside of her mouth as she eyeballed Cade, sizing him up.

"What?" Cade asked. "There's not some weird Omega initiation that I have to do, right?"

"That depends. Tell me about this person from the pit. What's the deal?"

"I know him. His name's Mig, and he's a liar, a thief, and a professional instigator."

Kira scoffed. "Great. Sounds like he's made for this place."

"I wouldn't tell him that, but, yeah, pretty much. He's my best friend. Or he *was*, at least."

"And?" Kira asked, leading Cade to his point.

"Mig, no joke, is the best engineer in the galaxy. He's a genius. You want to know who can somehow enlist a Qel for the greatest con on a planet built on cons? Mig, that's who. If there's one person who knows where to get that bomb of yours shielded and figure out how to finish making it, he's the one. I have no doubt in my mind."

Kira eyed Cade skeptically. "But there's a catch."

Cade laughed uncomfortably. "I said Mig and I used to be friends, but that doesn't quite capture our relationship."

"Meaning?"

"Meaning he hates my guts, and he made it very clear that if he saw me again, he'd be, let's say, unhappy about it."

"How unhappy?" Kira asked, her face preemptively tightening in a wince as she prepared for the worst.

"So unhappy," Cade said, "that he promised to kill me."

CHAPTER ELEVEN

Dotax's snow-covered islands clung to one another in an endless ocean that was frozen to its very depths. Despite the solid ice surface that connected each landmass, the Dotaxians sculpted bridges carved of frozen rock that tethered each island to one other. The Dotaxian faith forbade anyone from walking on the ice for fear of upsetting the underworld spirits that were trapped below. Violators of this law were sentenced to the "black walk," a ritual that had been with the Dotaxians since their beginnings. A nomadic people, the Dotaxians' mobility was conditionally forced upon them; they moved to stay off the dark side of the planet, which was frigid enough to kill even the heartiest Dotaxian. The black walk sent offenders in the opposite direction of his or her tribe, and they were never heard from again.

This sacred custom was overlooked for one group and for one reason—the Dotaxian Royal Guard, when engaging in combat with an invading force. An invading force such as the Fatebreakers from Praxis. The encounter, though, was less combat and more slaughter.

The Praxis light cruiser dropped out of the overcast sky directly above the Dotaxian camp. It hovered just above the surface, near enough so six Fatebreakers could leap from its open hatch and immediately challenge the oncoming Royal Guardsmen.

Ortzo led the charge, meeting the head Guardsman himself while his men grappled with the others. The Guardsman spewed words in an unintelligible language at Ortzo, but they didn't matter. In battle, it was all the same—the enemy threatened, cursed, then eventually begged. And Ortzo had no mind for words that didn't bring him closer to his goal of recovering the Rokura and delivering it to Ga Halle. He knew what was at stake, for Praxis, for the galaxy, and for himself, and that blinded him to any other considerations. There'd be no sympathy, no patience, no mercy until the Rokura was in the hands of his master.

The Guardsman swung his broadsword down on Ortzo, an unconventional opening parry, but Ortzo predicted that the Guardsman was trying to knock him off his feet, figuring he hadn't established proper traction on the snow-covered ground. Ortzo and his Fatebreakers knew exactly what they were getting into on Dotax and prepared accordingly; the metal spikes on the bottom of their boots dug deep into the ground, giving them mobility equal to, if not better than, the Guardsmen.

Ortzo blocked the Guardsman's strike with his shido, then, bringing his arms downward in a half circle, dug the broadsword into the ground. Before the Guardsman could recover, Ortzo swiped his shido across the Guardsman's face, knocking away his pristine white helmet and opening a gash from his cheek diagonally to his forehead. Blood trickled into his eyes, and as they reflexively squinted, Ortzo slammed his shido into the Guardsman's gut, doubling him over. The Guardsman gasped for air and tried to raise his sword in defense, but Ortzo kicked it out of his hands, sending it skittering across the ice.

With the Guardsman at his mercy, Ortzo grabbed him by his head, turned him around, and thrust his shido to his throat. The blade pierced the very top of his skin, drawing a trickle of blood, but went no farther.

"People of Dotax!" Ortzo yelled. As he did, he could sense the hush coming over the area as all eyes darted to the captured head Guardsman. Ortzo, surveying the scene, saw five bloody guardsmen on the ground around him. His fellow Fatebreakers were unharmed.

"You are hereby called upon to serve the Praxis kingdom, the galaxy's ruling power, and, therefore, *your* ruling power. There are fugitives on the loose in this system or one very, very close by. They are traitors to Praxis, and anyone who harbors or aids these individuals will also be branded as traitors and delivered a fate worse than death.

"Now," Ortzo continued, scanning the crowd to make sure he had their full attention, "I'm going to ask you this question once and only once: Have these traitors been to Dotax?"

The Guardsman laughed in Ortzo's grasp. "You are not our ruler, Praxis scum. We'll never bow to you."

Ortzo shook his head ruefully. "I thought you'd say that." With minimal effort, Ortzo jabbed the shido into the Guardsman's throat; blood erupted from the wound, and Ortzo dropped him to the ground. Any head Guardsman who failed to repel an enemy's attack was sentenced to the black walk, this Ortzo knew. As he looked down on the Guardsmen, the once immaculate white ground beneath him turning crimson, Ortzo figured he was doing his fellow warrior a favor.

"Who else needs to be made an example of?" Ortzo bellowed. "Who else—"

"Enough!" a voice yelled out from the crowd. Ortzo looked over and spotted an older man, a Dotaxian Elder, pushing his way through the crowd. "No more bloodshed. No more death. I will answer your query."

Ortzo walked toward the Elder, dragging his shido in the snow as he went, cleaning off the blood.

"Answer then, Elder."

The Elder stood with his chest puffed out and spoke to Ortzo in a commanding, confident voice. "There have been no visitors to our world. We've harbored no one, traitor or otherwise. This is the truth."

Ortzo examined the Elder, waiting for his mien to crack, even a little. If he was lying, he was remarkably good at it.

"I know your people are primitive," Ortzo said, "but you have short-range vessels. You have means of communication. Should these traitors arrive, you are to notify the nearest Praxis fleet *immediately*."

"Very well," the Elder replied. "Now go, all of you. Let us attend to our dead and continue on with our journey."

Ortzo scoffed. "Old man, journeys require destinations. You're just running from death."

The Elder leaned his body and looked Ortzo dead in his eyes. "So are *you*."

Ortzo knew the Dotaxian death ritual: Bodies were wrapped in lubricated linen and pushed out onto the ice, an offering to the underworld gods. Keeping his gaze locked with the Elder's, Ortzo ordered the bodies of the fallen Guardsmen to be burned.

"Remember this as a warning," Ortzo said. Then, pointing his shido to the Elder, he added, "And a lesson."

Ortzo and the other Fatebreakers boarded their light cruiser and it shot off into the sky, leaving the Dotaxian people to watch them go, through the rising embers and smoke from the burning bodies of their Guardsmen.

In the cockpit of the cruiser, Ortzo asked Shira, the pilot, what the next system along the *Rubicon*'s potential trajectory was.

"Karif-Four or Kyysring, either are possible," Shira said.

Ortzo considered. Karif-Four was a barren desert, sparsely populated by a subhuman species. But Kyysring, that miserable pit of disorder, seemed appropriate.

"Get us to Kyysring," Ortzo commanded. "Waste no time in doing it."

CHAPTER TWELVE

At twelve stories tall, the Koga Club dwarfed Kyysring's sky-line, protruding from the ground in all its phallic glory—there was no way the likeness was unintentional, Cade was convinced—and easily visible from anywhere in the city. From its top floor, as advertised, gamblers could drink in the entirety of Kyysring's cityscape and beyond, for whatever that was worth. Even from its best view, Kyysring would never be guilty of leaving a favorable impression on anyone with working eyesight. Beyond the city center and its patchwork architecture that looked ready to tilt over with a strong enough breeze, there was the spaceport to the south and nothing but miles and miles of wasteland in every other direction. That was it. Perched above it all, on six reinforced stilts, the disk-shaped casino looked like a giant arachnid plotting its attack. Funny, Cade thought, that Kyysring's biggest building appeared to be ready to destroy the city or defecate on it. As he double-checked the charges in his rusty old sidewinder, he understood the difficulty in deciding which option was even worth the effort.

"What's with that sidewinder of yours?" Kira asked as she concealed her own sidewinder in the back of her pants. They were positioned across the street from the Koga, huddled behind a watering hole's six-foot-tall garish neon sign. "Does it actually fire, or do you just threaten people with tetanus?"

"Why don't you stand over there," Cade said, gesturing to a spot just a few paces ahead, "and I'll test it."

Kira nodded and grinned, pleasantly. "Nice one. Sometimes I think there might be hope for you yet."

"Gee, thanks."

"Provided you don't totally screw this thing up. So this buddy of your, this Mig?" Kira asked, sharpening her focus. "You sure that's him inside?"

"Mig lived with my family when we were kids; there was a time when he was just as much my brother as Tristan. Believe me, I'd spot that runt anywhere."

Kira clicked her tongue and eyed the sidewinder. "That thing works, for real? Something tells me you might be needing it pretty soon."

Cade rolled his eyes. He studied the Koga from where they stood, allowing himself a moment of hesitation before charging inside. The Koga was exactly like the drone fighting pit—forbidden to minors, mysterious—but without the luster. It was the apex of Kyysring's desperation and exploitation—people riding their last bit of coin pushed through the casino's double doors thinking they had nothing left to lose, but the Koga had the power to strip anyone of their notion of what rock bottom truly was. Theft, gunrunning, and all manner of garden-variety crime—these were nothing compared to the horrors committed by the kings of Koga as they forced their debtors to do their dark biddings. The way they changed people, the way they pushed them into doing things they never could, or would, until they were broken shells of something resembling human beings. Cade was hard on Kyysring, but the Koga was something different; one false move in that casino could spell very, very bad things for him and Kira. But, Cade thought with a grin, it's not like Cade or Kira were known for making false moves.

No, they'd be totally fine.

"Come on," he said, a hint of bitter resignation in his voice as he stepped into the street and toward the Koga. "Let's dive into this terrible place and meet another person who wants to kill me."

Entering the Koga's lobby was more or less like walking into the galaxy's biggest zep party. People huffed that stuff down like prohibition was about to hit Kyysring at sunup. They smoked it out of pipes, they smoked it out of joints, some people even smoked it out of elaborate vases that had to be wheeled alongside of them in carts. The fumes mingled at the ceiling like a ghostly presence, manufacturing an odor Cade couldn't quite find a word to describe. Acrid? Rotten? Blegh? Whatever the word, the point was that the combination of the many zep varieties circulating through the room didn't smell all that tasty, but it did make for one happy atmosphere.

The lobby's gaming area was where the casual gamblers were corralled, and for their own good; the stakes rose with each floor, all the way to the top—which is exactly where Cade and Kira were headed. They nudged their way through the overcrowded room, trying to catch the attention of many glassy eyes so they could excuse their way through with as little friction as possible. The elevator bank was set in the back wall, and any conversation Cade or Kira tried to initiate along the way was smothered by the dinging and whirring of seizure-inducing slot machines. People kept their eyes on the screens in front of them, smoking their smokes, drinking their drinks, and pouring coin after coin into the slots. Sometimes they blinked. As Cade shimmied and shuffled through the room, he tried to determine what the decor was trying to capture. A tawdry kingdom, he guessed? The lobby was stuffed with faux opulence, from the walls that were trimmed in shimmering gold to the massive overhead chandelier encrusted by rare gems—so hilariously fake—the size of Cade's fist. It couldn't be any gaudier, but Cade understood that it was all part of the show. You have to be motivated to gamble away your money, and dropping coin into a trash can doesn't have quite the same effect as dropping it into a palace, however ridiculous the palace may be.

When they finally boarded an elevator car and the sliding door cut them off from the lobby's dizzying cacophony, Cade figured Kira would have at least one biting remark about what they'd just passed through. But she was silent. Standing a step behind her in the elevator as it crawled upward, Cade could see the tension in her body. Her shoulders were elevated and narrowed inward; her back was awkwardly arched; and she kept one hand on her sidewinder, tapping on its butt. Kira was nervous, and Cade understood why. While she'd been in plenty of fights before, those battles all had clearly drawn lines: There were good guys and bad guys, and it was nearly impossible to confuse who was who. But what they were about to get into felt much more amorphous, as anything could happen. There was no telling who Mig's allies were or how the crowd might respond to a couple of outsiders causing a problem with one of their own. How would the pit bosses react to their customers being bothered and, more important, distracted from shelling out more coin? What if they were recognized for who they really were? This was the exact kind of situation the Masters preached to stay out of: Never engage in a conflict where you could be outnumbered, pinned down, and without an exit. Potentially, the Koga's top floor offered all three.

"It was my dad's," Cade said as the wall panel lit, indicating they'd finally reached the second floor.

"What?" Kira replied, a little surprised, like she'd forgotten Cade was in the elevator with her.

"You asked about the old sidewinder I carry. It belonged to my dad. Which is weird, because he hated violence. Total pacifist. But he carried this one just for the statement, I think. If you wanted to protect your family on Kyysring, you had to let people know you were prepared to back up that promise."

Kira turned to face Cade, examining him as if the questions she had in her mind were somehow written on his body. "I always wondered about that. How *did* you and Tristan wind up in this dump?"

"Well," Cade said, squinting his right eye as he tried to conjure the best entry point for what was essentially his life's story, "I guess the simplest answer is that my parents were aid workers, and this is where their lives took them."

"Aid workers? On Kyysring?"

Cade snorted. "As strange as it sounds, my parents discovered that it's easier to get relief to people by making creative partnerships with pirates and smugglers rather than navigating the Galactic Alliance's bureaucracy."

"No, that doesn't sound strange," Kira sighed. "That actually sounds pretty accurate."

Kira spun back to check their progress and, seeing they'd only reached the fourth floor, kicked the elevator door. "Is someone literally pulling us to the roof?"

"Kyysring ingenuity at work." Cade shrugged.

"All right," Kira said, facing Cade again, "since we're clearly going nowhere fast, I want more answers. Let's just dive right into the deep end. You ready?" Kira asked.

"I'm currently scanning the elevator for an escape hatch. What do you think?"

"What happened to your parents?"

"Next."

"How did your parents die?"

"*Next.*"

"Who killed your parents?"

Cade looked up at Kira, feeling like she'd cut him to the quick. She hadn't, as there was nothing really wrong with what she'd asked; maybe inappropriate, but this was Kira, so all things were relative. Still, Cade couldn't help feeling that he'd been wounded. There were chambers in Cade's mind that he worked hard to keep closed. Closed from himself and especially closed to others. He used these chambers to store things that he couldn't forget but didn't want to think about anymore. Things like his true thoughts about the Well and his role within it, or the grief he'd felt since Tristan's death. It'd been a long time since Cade had burrowed into the deep dark of these mental tunnels and pried open the first chamber he'd ever constructed: the chamber that stored the details of his parents' deaths.

"I-I don't know," Cade stammered, though he couldn't even convince himself of his uncertainty. Sure, he could recite the official report the Kyysring port officials had written up for him—he still had it memorized, even after all these years—but he knew it was all a lie. There was no accident, no "systems malfunction that triggered a catastrophic event." It was Praxis. Praxis killed Cade's parents.

"I told you my parents were aid workers; that's what they did— it was who they were," Cade said, steeling himself as he slowly pulled aside the rusted, heavy chamber door. "One day, pretty much like any other day, they went off to do their work. But they never came home again.

"They had an appointment to meet some Kaldorian smugglers who had been helping my folks get supplies off Kyysring and delivered wherever they were needed. A meeting like that would last a few hours. My mom and dad would jet out of Kyysring's orbit, board one of their partners' ships, and they'd be right back. But then nighttime came. Then the next morning. I was terrified even as Tristan tried to convince me that everything was going to be all right. But I knew nothing was all right, and he did, too.

"A few terrible days went by until finally our neighbor sat Tristan and me down and told us that the Kaldorian ship had exploded. Nobody knew why, because everyone on board was dead."

Cade paused as he realized that his hands were balled into tight fists, so tight the muscles were beginning to spasm. The chamber had been blown wide open, and Cade couldn't shove its contents back inside even if he tried. Instead he allowed the release to happen as the intensity of the moment rolled off his face like warmth from a glass. He continued:

"The Kyysring port authority—yeah, whatever that's worth— said it was some kind of hull breach that led to a bunch of other things and led to the explosion. A nearly impossible chain of events, they said. But then, a few days later, we heard some rumors. The Kaldorians were apparently in the heat of an uprising against Praxis back on their home planet, and all Kaldorian ships were being targeted across the galaxy to make sure supplies couldn't reach the freedom fighters on the ground.

"The Kaldorian ship in the sky above Kyysring, the one my parents were delivering aid supplies to—it didn't erupt in some kind of freak accident. It was attacked, and it was Praxis cannons that tore that ship apart. The kingdom was so pissed that someone would dare stand up to them, it went around destroying whatever ship it caught in its sites, just because. And *that* is why my mom and dad never came home again."

The rhythmic humming of the elevator as it willed its way upward was the only sound occupying the intimate space shared by Cade and Kira. Cade had told this story very few times in his life, and when he did, he was met, always, with pity. People apologized for something that, obviously, they weren't responsible for; they'd comment on how terrible everything that'd happened was, and that'd be that. But the look on Kira's face—it was different. And it wasn't that she wasn't affected by Cade's loss; it's that she didn't offer any kind of put-on sadness. It was more genuine. It was real.

"Well, what happened then? I mean, you and Tristan were still practically kids. Who took care of you?"

"Took care of us? Kira, this place tried to eat us alive. After the Kaldorian ship explosion, Praxis started sticking its nose in Kyysring's business, assuming—wrongly—that my parents had been funneling supplies to the Kaldorian insurgency and that others might do the same. Praxis being here stopped the usual way of things for a while, and people didn't like that. And, somehow, they got it in their heads that killing Tristan and me would make things better."

"Can I ask one more question?"

Cade snorted. "Do I have a say in the matter?"

"It's probably a tough question to answer. But, I'm just curious why you aren't raging at Praxis. I mean, they killed your parents. How are you not furious and dedicating every second of your life to plotting a bloody revenge?"

"Like you?" Cade asked, dryly.

Kira smirked. "Nice try; this is about you. Come on, for real, why aren't you more mad? Why aren't you determined to tear their kingdom apart, piece by piece, for what they did to you?"

"I was furious—I *am* furious. But . . ." Cade paused and ran his hands over his face. He felt the stubble growing along his cheeks and what seemed like wrinkles etched into his skin. It would make sense if he had developed wrinkles; he felt like he'd aged years in the past few days. "I spent a lot of time, *a lot of time*, trying to track down the Praxis ship that was responsible for killing my parents. But there was nothing. No records, no witnesses, and no one—not a single person, not even Praxis defectors—who would divulge a single useful thing to me. It was hopeless. I knew I'd never find out who issued the order to fire on the Kaldorian ship, and I knew there was nothing I could do to hurt the Praxis kingdom. Not by myself."

And with that acknowledgment, Cade felt an urgent need to slam his mental chamber shut and bury it deep once more. He'd never come to terms with losing his parents, but what still raked hot coals over his heart was the fact that he couldn't do a thing about it. Cade couldn't save his parents nor could he avenge them. He felt shame, he felt disappointment, and he didn't know how to cope with either.

Kira swung her dreads away from her face and wrapped him in a stare from her soft blue eyes. "But what if you could?" she asked.

"Could what?"

"Could hurt the Praxis kingdom. How would you do it?"

Cade lowered his head, considering, but it only took a moment to get to his conclusion. He looked back up at Kira, now with a sly smile breaking across his face. "I'd make a bomb," Cade said. "I'd make a bomb, and I'd use it to destroy Praxis as much as they destroyed me."

"Well, there you go," Kira said as the elevator chimed, notifying them that they'd reached their destination.

The door shuddered opened—finally—revealing the high-stakes room at the very top of the Koga Club.

"Wow," Kira said as they stepped off the elevator. "This is *nice*."

So different was the high-stakes room from the lobby that it felt less like they'd gone to another floor and more like they'd traveled to a different planet. Maybe that was the reason it took so long to get there. Where the casino's opening salvo couldn't have been any more crass, crude, and obnoxious, the top floor was subdued and, dare Cade say it, dignified. The place was still jam-packed with criminals and cheats, but at least they were of a more refined stock. Floor-to-ceiling windows covered the exterior wall, and the ceiling opened to a glass dome that, because the room was so dimly lit, gave a stirring view of a blanket of stars, twinkling planets, and a purple-and-orange nebula that looked like a giant bruise in the universe. Cade didn't want to admit it to himself, but the fact was that he kind of enjoyed this place. He had no delusions about being surrounded by people doing things they weren't supposed to be doing. People gambled with stolen money; they were accompanied by illegal companion drones; they carried volatile weapons that were outlawed across half the galaxy. But that was the appeal. He kind of liked the allure of danger and the implicit promise of trouble for those who were looking for it, and even for those who weren't. The Well's rigidity did Cade no favors when it came to him fitting in; everyone was always training, meditating, working out, or training to work out while meditating. It was hard, for Cade at least, to operate at such a high level of discipline. And while the Kyysring casino was the pendulum swinging from one extreme to another, Cade still welcomed the sweet world of lower standards.

"Well, what now?" Kira asked.

"We mingle," Cade answered with his most charming of smiles.

Cade took the first step into the room, and Kira followed closely behind. How well they blended in, Cade understood, was in direct proportion to how well they avoided trouble; standing by the elevators like a couple of squares clocking everything going on *might* have given them away. There were at least a hundred people inside, so it was doubtful that everyone knew each other, but it was best not to draw unwanted attention and have people already asking who Cade and Kira were and wondering why they were there. The room wasn't closed to the general public, not officially, but it was clear that a certain type of clientele wasn't welcome here. And when it came to the Koga Club, you were smart not to go where you weren't welcome.

"When I spotted Mig, he seemed pretty cozy at the tatow table that's straight ahead, near the back of the room. He's got his winnings from the fighting pit, so he's probably not going anywhere soon."

"He's alone?"

Cade made a weighing gesture with his two hands, then shrugged his shoulders. "Don't know. I didn't see the Qel, but at the same time, where else would it be? That's the thing, we need to watch Mig without *watching* Mig and find out what his status is around here. Because if he's a beloved figure—which I doubt—and I get into a confrontation with him, we don't want the entire room turning on us."

"And we can't just wait him out?"

"He could be here for like twelve hours, and I don't want to be on this planet for twelve more minutes. Besides, with Praxis having Ticus in its sights and doubtless on our tails, we don't have all day to sit around and wait for Mig."

Cade led them to a wellington table where there was room for them both to sit. He tossed some coin onto the purple felt table, betting that one of the spinning die would land on a knight.

"Okay, so we're basically trying to see who, if anyone, is going to jump in when you and your former pal get into a fight."

"Um, well," Cade said, watching the die spin in the clear oscillator. "Yeah, pretty much."

Kira shook her head; the die tumbled out, and two of the six landed with the knight facing up. For a moment, just one brief moment, Cade felt like his luck was starting to change.

"What did you do to this guy, anyway, that you two hate each other so much?" Kira asked.

"Whoa, whoa," Cade said, collecting his winnings. "I don't hate Mig. He hates *me*."

"Ah, I see. So it's one of those 'I didn't do anything wrong; the other person's feelings are totally unjustified' situations. Gotcha."

"No, not at all. Well, yes—sort of. I messed up, but Mig put me in a bad spot. And he could stand to be a little more understanding about the whole thing."

Cade tossed another bet, this time on the pirate. He looked over at Kira, who shot him an expectant look.

"Okay," she said. "Are you going to tell me what you did?"

"Yeah, *friend*," said a voice coming from behind Cade. It was accompanied by the feeling of a sidewinder's barrel digging into Cade's back. "Why don't you tell your girlfriend what happened between us?"

Cade groaned. He swore to himself and slowly turned around. There was Mig, as expected. It was the closest they'd been to each other in two years, but Mig still looked the same. The crazy tufts of black hair sprouting all over his head, those thick horn-rimmed glasses, and that ever-present sneer that called attention to the unseen chip that claimed residence on his shoulder.

"Hey, Mig," Cade said as they met eye to eye. "We were just talking about you."

"Don't let me interrupt," Mig said with a fake-gracious smile. "Go on."

"Nah," Cade said, casual as he could be with a blaster poking into his gut. "Digging up the past gets you nothing but dirty."

"I said '*Go on*,'" Mig stressed, pushing his sidewinder farther into Cade's belly.

"You little—" Cade said, but stopped himself. He smiled though his jaw was clenched. "Okay, Mig. I'll explain why you're sooooo mad at me.

"It's really simple: The Well sent me to Ragnar on a scouting assignment. Mig was there running some kind of . . . what was it? Selling faulty exhumation equipment to archaeologists?"

"No, no. See? You can't even get the basics right," Mig said, turning to Kira. "Sorry to be rude, but I haven't gotten your name yet."

"I'm Kira," Kira said with an amused smile. Cade couldn't tell if it was fake or not. "It's nice to meet you, Mig."

Mig took Kira's hand and kissed it. "It's nice to meet you as well. And the equipment I sold was fine. Now, Cade, if you would—continue on with the version of this story that you probably concocted on one of your long nights doing *nothing* as a Rai."

Cade could feel his nostrils flair as he let out a deep, hostile breath. "You're pushing it, Mig."

"I'll push what I want," Mig replied, jamming his sidewinder into Cade's belly to prove his point.

"Anyway," Cade continued, "when we were kids, Mig and I always said we'd get a cargo ship and go into some kind of transport business. Nothing big, nothing that would catch Praxis's attention. Just enough to get by and have no one on our backs. Well, on Ragnar, Mig decided that he'd take it upon himself to fulfill a promise we made when we were *children*, and he got his hands on a cargo ship. Not knowing it was a diplomatic vessel, my loose lips got it confiscated by the Alliance. Which was an ac-ci-dent."

"Mig had to flee Ragnar," Cade grudgingly conceded, "because the Galactic Alliance put a warrant out for his arrest."

"And it still is a live warrant to this day, all because of you," Mig added.

"Dang," Kira said. "You messed up, Cade. I mean, if it were me, I don't think I'd want to kill you, but I would want to hurt you. Even more than usual."

Cade shot a displeased look at Kira, and she winked in return.

"It's hurt me, it really has," Mig said to Kira, fake tenderness in his voice.

"Oh, screw you, Mig. This whole thing with this ship isn't even why you're mad. You're pissed, still, that Tristan and I left Kyysring for the Well. Every fight we've had since then, it's really about *that*."

"This again?!" Mig said, his voice getting heated. "How many times do I have to tell you that I'm over that?"

"Sure," Cade said, getting off his stool and pushing Mig back a half step. "You keep telling yourself that."

Cade knew Mig wasn't going to kill him. This whole situation was turning into more of an annoyance than anything else, and the only reason Cade was practicing delicacy was because he needed Mig. Mig knew how to push his buttons, though, and he knew, better than anyone, how to start trouble. But that didn't change the fact that Cade was bigger than him, and a trained fighter, and if Mig jammed that sidewinder in his stomach one more time, he was liable to shove it up Mig's ass.

Yet that's exactly what he did. Responding to Cade's resistance, Mig again pushed his sidewinder, this time with more force, into Cade's abdomen. Cade sucked in a deep breath between his teeth and shoved down the urge to knock Mig out, but it wasn't easy. He could see the taunting in Mig's eyes; there was no doubt that Mig was wise to Cade wanting something, and that gave him the power to push whatever boundaries he felt like pushing. Cade knew Mig better than anyone; he'd seen him use his sharp wit to play people like a conductor orchestrates a symphony. Mig's parents were a couple of degenerate zep addicts who didn't care if their only son lived or died, which meant that the only real parents he ever had were Cade's mom and dad. He spent most of his adolescence undersized and underdeveloped in what was probably the worst place in the galaxy to be either, as there was no sympathy for the weak on Kyysring. Cade knew how rough it had been for him when he and Tristan—Mig's only family, friends, and protectors—left, and Cade was tormented by guilt over it. Still, he didn't have time to argue over who was mad at whom and for what, and he was in no mood to have a lethal weapon pointed at him. Again.

"Seriously, Mig? What are you going to do?" Cade asked as he squared up against Mig, standing a head taller than him. "You're not going to kill me, so let's just cut to the point."

Mig smiled a devilish smile. "You're right, I'm not going to kill you. But I am going to settle our score."

"Is that so?" Cade said, pushing Mig's sidewinder away from his body. "You and what army?"

"That one," Mig said, his eyes leading to over Cade's shoulder. Cade turned and reacted with a start when he saw the Qel hovering over him like it'd appeared out of nowhere. Suddenly, the game had changed.

"I figure you owe me a ship," Mig said. "You must have gotten here somehow. Well, that somehow belongs to me now."

"Uh, no," Kira said, stepping toward Mig. "That ship is mine, and it will *not* be used to settle your little love spat."

Mig responded, calling attention to the Qel, but Cade had tuned him out. He was looking around the room, curious why every single set of eyes was locked directly on him. They weren't following the debate between Kira and Mig, and they didn't seem the least interested in the Qel. It was solely Cade, and he couldn't understand why—not until his eyes drifted up, catching sight of the massive projector screen that hung in the center of the room.

There, Cade saw his face slapped on a typical bounty transmission and posted for the entire room to see. "Typical," though, wasn't quite a fitting word, because there was nothing typical about the bounty being offered by the Praxis kingdom for his capture: ten coin fourthed, which was basically enough for someone to buy their own private planetoid.

And if the call for anyone in the galaxy with a firearm to make a run at Cade didn't sufficiently spice up his evening, the transmission also had a nice addendum attached to it, spilling the beans that Cade was the Paragon and that the bounty wasn't complete unless the Rokura, and Cade's accomplices, were also captured.

"Oh *no*," Cade said as he stumbled backward and bumped into the Qel.

The Qel looked down at Cade, its face expressionless. "Mig wanted you to know that I can throw you through the dome up there," it said in a gruff male voice, indicating the ceiling.

"You know what?" Cade asked. "That doesn't sound like a bad idea right about now."

Kira and Mig were still bickering over the finer points of ownership and debt when Cade grabbed them both by their shoulder. "Guys," Cade said, his wavering voice drowned out by Kira and Mig's increasingly heated argument. So he yelled, "GUYS!"

Both Kira and Mig stopped mid-sentence, and they both realized, at the same time, that the entire room had gotten silent around them.

"We've got a problem," Cade said, nodding to the bounty projection.

Kira, Mig, and the Qel looked up as a murmur started to grow among the crowd. Cade realized it was only a matter of time, and not much of it, before somebody made their move.

"Wait—what?" Mig said, turning back to look at Cade, his face trying to shake off his incredulity but failing. *"How?"*

"Cade," Kira interrupted, looking at her comms device, which displayed a miniature-size projection of the bounty transmission just above her wrist. "This . . . this is bad. That was broadcast *everywhere*."

"Okay, okay," Cade said, swallowing hard. "Let's just back out of here, act like nothing's wrong and—"

"Oh, you ain't going nowhere," a voice called.

Cade turned to see a man standing behind a table that was positioned between Cade and the elevator bank. He had deep scarring over much of his face—burns, it looked like—and an enormous, modified shock rifle perched casually on his shoulder. A bounty hunter, no doubt. "Nowhere 'cept the nearest Praxis warship."

"You better think again." Behind Cade, a female Kaldorian called out, her voice muffled through the helmet customarily worn by her species. The helmet—deep indigo and chipped, scuffed, even cracked from the action it'd seen—covered her entire face, revealing nothing of her appearance; two small ocular lenses collected the visual data from the room and projected everything a Kaldorian needed to know, and then some, within the helmet. Cade had worn one once and thought it was the coolest thing ever. "Praxis will not be getting its hands on him, his weapon, or his friends."

The scarred man scoffed as he dropped his rifle from his shoulder and into his hand. "That boy's worth the biggest bounty I've ever seen. Biggest bounty there ever was, I reckon, and I'm gonna collect it. Be willin' to split it, in fact, if anyone wants to join me."

Cade watched as three other men, all brandishing their weapons, stood up around the room.

"Are you out of your minds?!" A Nootharian, accompanied by a service drone, stepped behind the Kaldorian. Cade recognized them immediately—they were the pair from the fighting pit. "This is the Paragon, the *Chosen One*. He's the only one who can stop Praxis, and you want to hand him over to those evil bastards? They tore my planet apart. We have no food, no coin, no future. Praxis took everything from us, and if you think you're going to rob the galaxy of its one chance at stopping them . . ." The Nootharian paused as he clicked a handheld remote to switch his drone into battle mode; the drone stepped in front of its master, shielding him, and pulled a pair of blasters out from its legs and trained them on his enemies. ". . . you'll do so over our dead bodies."

Nearby, a Toofar slammed his fist on a gaming table, stood up, and barked, "Ar ar ar ar," at the scarred man. Cade assumed he was voicing his agreement with the Nootharian.

Near the Toofar, a human got to her feet. "Praxis destroyed my home," she said.

A Quarrian joined the chorus. "They annihilated my planet," he said.

Then another human: "Those bastards burned my farm to the ground. I lost everything because of them."

Others stood as well, of various species, unified in their refusal to give Praxis one more inch of a galaxy that belonged to no kingdom: It belonged to the people, these people. Cade looked around and felt the genuine frustration, bitterness, and sense of loss these people harbored, and he realized they were the same. How many loved ones did Praxis murder? How much land did the kingdom illegally seize from its rightful owners? How many people were, in some way, worse off because Praxis decided *it* was going to run the galaxy? It made him angry, but he also felt inspired. If just one person, one symbol, can rally the souls of Kyysring, he could only imagine what something larger might spark. Something like the entire galaxy watching the Praxis *War Hammer* burning as it fell from the sky.

But just as Cade thought the mess he found himself in was going to be okay, the elevator chimed, its tinny bell sounding loud and clear throughout the entire room. Everyone turned their attention to the doors as a feeling of expectancy saturated the room.

And that feeling hit a gasping pitch when a Darklands gang entered the casino.

Four of them stomped out of the elevator, all donned in tightly fitting black cloaks covering them from head to toe; they were well armored, well armed, and their reputation as merciless killers, kidnappers, and more was no secret in any corner of the galaxy. When Cade was a kid, the Darklands gangs were the boogeymen, ever present but never seen; his parents would threaten that, if he didn't behave, the Darklanders would come for him. For the longest time, Cade assumed that, like most monsters, they didn't exist. But he was wrong. The Darklands gangs were monsters, there was no doubting that—but they were *real* monsters. And they had, as his parents promised, come for him.

"You've got to be kidding me," Cade said.

"Cade Sura," the gang's leader said in a monotone voice as he stepped in front of his pack, "we are taking you to the Praxis kingdom without delay. Anyone who stands in our way will be killed. The bounty specifies you and your three friends are to be brought in alive—but if you resist, you'll wish being kept alive wasn't a stipulation of the reward. In the event you doubt my words—"

Right on cue, the sound of glass smashing—erupting, it seemed more like—filled the room. At least a half dozen more Darklanders, equipped with rocket packs and armed with power pikes, came crashing through the windows and surrounded the crowd. Along with their buddies who'd entered through the elevators, they formed a tight circle that, step by careful step, was closing in on Cade.

That's when pandemonium broke loose. Cade had no idea who shot first and sparked the chaos, but it didn't matter. He was trapped in a close-quarters firefight with very, very bad people on all sides. And too many of them were gunning for him.

"DOWN!" Kira shouted as she shoved Cade to the ground, spraying offensive fire as they both dropped.

The Qel, with little effort, flipped the wellington table on its side and shoved it in front of Cade, Kira, Mig, and himself. They were still screwed, Cade was certain of that, but at least they had some cover to protect them from the errant crossfire. With any luck, they'd leave this room as captives, not corpses. And if that was the case, wherever they ended up, Cade at least had a chance to bargain for his friends' lives.

Well, "friends" might not have been the best word, Cade thought as Mig grabbed him by the shirt and stuffed his side-winder into his face. Cade realized it'd been modified; Mig had added a third barrel that shot who-knows-what. Cade wasn't eager to find out.

"Cade, that lunatic said your 'three friends,'" Mig spat. "He *better* have been referring to two people who aren't Four-Qel and me."

Cade shrugged Mig off and peeked over the table. Every inch of the room was complete and total anarchy. Some people took strategic positions behind support beams and overturned tables; some were simply punching each other's faces in, and the smart ones were crawling toward the elevators. The one thing they had in common was that none of them had the slightest idea what they were fighting for, not really, and that was all Cade's fault. He realized that he had to either figure out how to be the Paragon—or fake being the Paragon—or flee the galaxy for-ever. If he didn't, this kind of madness would happen to him, and the people around him, wherever he went.

"Don't worry, all right?" Cade said. "I'm going to find a way to surrender."

Blaster fire erupted through the table directly between Cade and Mig. A few inches either way, and one of them would be dead. "Damn it, Cade!" Mig growled as he unleashed wild shots over the table's edge. "Now I *really am* going to kill you!"

"Nobody is surrendering, and no one is going to lay one finger on Cade," Kira yelled. She was down on one knee, taking shots at anyone who got too close. The Qel was in the same position on the opposite side of the table, efficiently targeting whomever it could get in its sights. "We're getting out of here. Mig, do you or your Qel know *any* other escape from this place?"

"Hey, he's not 'my Qel,' okay? He's *a* Qel, and his name is Four-Qel."

Kira looked back at Mig, her face exploding with anger. "Who *cares*!? Is there another way out or not?"

"There's no stairs, no other elevators. There's not even any paneling that connects this level to the rest of the building. It's like it's totally separ—"

Cade almost leapt to his feet, out of cover, when he felt the floor beneath him begin to shake. It was nothing but a murmur at first, then the quaking got more intense and then more, until Cade began to wonder why, exactly, this high-stakes gaming floor was perched on those six stilts at the top level of the Koga Club.

There was a momentary ceasefire as everyone readjusted to the floor, which felt like rolling thunder beneath their feet. Mig stood up and he looked around in terrified awe. "No. Effing. Way."

Cade joined him. "It can't be. For real—it *can't* be."

"What?" Kira asked, agitated, slamming another charge into her sidewinder. "Spit it out—we don't have time to be mystified."

The room jostled again and through the broken windows came the piercing sound of squealing metal. It sounded like it was metal that hadn't moved in a long time.

It sounded like it was detaching.

"This place—" Cade said, drawing in a deep breath, "it's a ship!"

Cade could feel the ship's thrusters coming to life, breathing a vibrato hum throughout the floor. It wouldn't be long before the room was free of the Koga—before it blasted off into space.

"We have to get out of here," Kira said, and Cade could feel the panic in her voice. "We cannot get trapped in this ship."

Cade looked around, searching for something, anything, that

could offer an escape. Instead, he watched as things went from bad to worse. Thick metal shutters were beginning to slam shut in sequence around the room, over each of the windows. That was their only way out, Cade determined, so they had to either bust their way through or die trying. It was a choice between staying and definitely dying, or breaking out and maybe dying.

So many pleasant choices these days.

Cade grabbed his shido and ignited it. Just ahead, he spotted a window that was still open, but the closing shutters were coming to it fast. Even if they bolted for it right away, they wouldn't make it.

"Four-Qel!" Cade yelled. "You're first. The window straight ahead—I need you to jump through the shutter that's about to close."

4-Qel shrugged. "Okay," he said and took off, charging ahead at a remarkable clip. Just as the shutter closed, 4-Qel erupted through it, shredding through the metal as he leapt out the window.

"What do you think you're doing?!" Mig screamed in Cade's face.

"Shut up and go!" Cade urged, shoving Mig ahead. Mig, with 4-Qel already gone and knowing he had no other option, did what he was told; Cade saw him jump out of the hole made by 4-Qel—and right into 4-Qel's grasp, who was hanging by a power line just outside the ship.

"All right, I'll catch the line with my shido. You—" Cade turned to address Kira, but she was paces behind him, firing at the Darklanders who were rushing toward them and gaining fast.

"NO!" Cade bellowed.

"Go!" Kira commanded. "Get out of here."

The ship's nose began to rise as its thrusters neared maximum power. There wasn't much time.

But Cade wasn't leaving Kira.

Cade charged back, running faster than he ever had in his life. Just as one of the three Darklanders was about to bring the electrified blade of its power pike down on Kira's head, Cade blocked it with his shido.

"I don't think so," he spat.

Cade swung his shido around, knocking the Darklander's power pike around and back, into a nearby Darklander. The blade dug into his chest and electrocuted him. Cade then sliced the pike-wielding Darklander with his shido, and Kira fired three blasts into the other. Still, more were coming.

"Good thing you came back—you'd never figure out how to disarm the *Rubicon*'s security without me," Kira said with a wink.

Cade smiled. "Yeah, sure. *That's* why I came for you."

They bolted for the shattered shutter, feeling the heat of blaster fire scream past their heads. The ship was taking off, and Cade realized that when that happened, the power line—their only escape—would be out of reach. Which meant zipping down to the ground would be more like falling down to the ground from a very great height. The latter was sure to get them killed.

Cade pushed his body as hard as he could and leapt out the window. He stretched his arms out, and by some stroke of luck, the tip of his shido caught the power line. He barely had time to look up when he felt Kira pounce on his back, gripping him tightly.

"Let's *go*," she said.

Cade did as he was told as Kira wrapped her arms around his neck. He liked the feeling, but when he looked back at Kira, unaware of the goofy grin on his face, she told him, "Focus, Sura," which was enough to get him to whip his head back to facing forward.

When they reached where the power line ended—a safe enough distance from the ground to drop from—Cade was surprised to find Mig and 4-Qel waiting for them.

"Now what?" Mig asked.

Cade looked at Mig with a quizzical eye. "Now? Now you ditch us. What are you waiting around for?"

"You got us into this mess," Mig said, poking his finger in Cade's chest. "And now you, the almighty Paragon, are going to get us out of it."

"Actually, Mig," Cade said, using his thumb and forefinger to delicately remove Mig's finger from his chest, "it's *you* who's going to get us out of this."

"Aaaah," Mig said, and Cade watched as the pieces clicked together in his mind. "I knew it. You're here because you want something."

"It's a little more complicated than th—"

"Excuse me," 4-Qel interrupted. "As captivating as this argument is, it isn't. I was being sarcastic, though my tone doesn't convey that. Anyway, we're drawing attention."

Cade studied the scene around them. The milling denizens of Kyysring—there were always people milling, no matter what time of day—had noticed Cade. In their daze, whether from drugs, booze, or something else, they hadn't quite pieced together why he looked so familiar. But they would, and it would be chaos all over again when they did.

"I don't know about the rest of you," Kira said, keeping a cautious eye on everyone around them, "but I've had enough of this planet."

Mig and 4-Qel shared a glance; Mig shrugged. "We're burned here."

"Great, that's good enough to call this an agreement," Cade said, leading them toward the spaceport. "Now let's get off this damn rock."

CHAPTER THIRTEEN

Ortzo knew that the point of torture was to extract truth. Not information—truth. In his many travels across the galaxy, Ortzo had witnessed this interrogation tactic misused, or misunderstood, far too many times. Apply enough pain to your subject, fill them with enough desperation and fear, and they're likely to tell you anything. And when that happens, with nothing but misinformation gained, you're worse off than you were before the conversation even began. Torture's purpose wasn't to get someone to talk—no. Nor was its purpose to provide a sadistic thrill. Torture was a tool—a barbaric one at that, in Ortzo's opinion, but not without value—that extracted whatever truth there was to be had. Nothing more, nothing less.

But this infomerchant—this arrogant, snobbish infomerchant—was making Ortzo second-guess his own philosophy. It would be so satisfying to wipe that smug look off his face through the application of vile and excessive torture. He'd scream and cry, he'd beg for it to stop, beg to know why Ortzo was doing this to him, but Ortzo wouldn't relent. He wouldn't say a word. Ortzo glanced at LO-7, his personal interrogation drone, and knew he was up to the task. LO-7 was a relic of the prekingdom era, a clunky, outdated model that was nothing more than a slender black metal body with two orange-tinted bulbs for eyes. But that's why Ortzo liked him. He wasn't one of these new drones who, supposedly, developed opinions and ideas and thoughts of their own. Ortzo commanded, and LO-7 obeyed.

The infomerchant was panting, but only slightly. LO-7 had just finished sanding off the fingernails on his left hand, which broke most men by the time the crude sander touched their second finger. But not the infomerchant. He'd been trained in how to withstand torture, which meant he was good at his job.

Which meant he knew something about this Cade Sura and the Rokura he possessed.

"Ready to answer my questions, infomerchant?" Ortzo asked.

"My name . . . is Valis Portnoy."

Ortzo grabbed the infomerchant's bloody hand and pulled it close. Valis's body shook at his touch. Good, Ortzo thought. He wanted pain; he wanted fear.

"You are an infomerchant," Ortzo said. "Nothing more."

"You're wasting your time," the infomerchant said. "I take it your mission is important, yes? A Fatebreaker wouldn't be wasting his time on this filthy planet if it wasn't. Set me free, and I will help you. I know people on Kyysring; I know people across the galaxy. Let me be of use to the Praxis kingdom."

Ortzo eyed the infomerchant like a predator its prey. He thought he was so smart, this infomerchant, and he was. Smarter than Ortzo, even. But Ortzo would just see how valuable intelligence and guile were when pitted against cruelty that knew no bounds. Every man had a breaking point, and Ortzo would find the infomerchant's.

He flung the infomerchant's hand back at him and smiled.

"You'll be of use, infomerchant. You *will* be of use."

Ortzo walked down the ramp of his starcruiser, breathing in the Kyysring air. He could taste its acrid stench with every inhalation, as if this planet's many transgressions had somehow permeated its atmosphere. He detested the fact that Praxis hadn't annexed this planet or, better yet, wiped it off the galactic map. Ortzo was more than ready to lead a campaign that would seize this cesspool in days, if that. The Kyysring outlaws, as they thought of themselves, had no organization or resources; they hardly had the territorial pride, or the will, required to resist. But Ga Halle refused. The galaxy needed Kyysring. It needed a place of indulgence and vice, a place where anyone could go and relieve themselves of whatever weighed them down. Their anger, their worries, their sadness. Its cure was only a mass jump away, and the galaxy needed that outlet. Because people without release grew discontent. And discontent led to protestation, which led to revolt. There was no future in quelling uprising after uprising, and Ortzo agreed with Ga Halle's strategy. He just hated the need for a lesser evil to stem a greater one. Ortzo wanted a pure galaxy, one with no disruptions, no transgressions at all.

"Commander Ortzo," a voice called from behind him. Ortzo turned to find Wexla, the most junior of the Fatebreakers. In his possession he had a man, an older, slightly overweight man who was draped in fine silks that were stained by the blood dripping from his nose and mouth. Wexla shoved the man forward by the nape of his neck, where he'd been holding him, and the man tumbled to the ground right in front of Ortzo.

"Who is this man?" Ortzo asked.

"His name is Bon, and I've been told he holds special value to the infomerchant."

Ortzo looked down at the man, this Bon, and smiled. He even allowed himself a laugh. To think that he had flooded this planet with coin, ordered his Fatebreakers to turn over every suspect establishment without pity, and the key to locating Cade Sura and the Rokura came down to an affair of passion.

"Please," Bon said, kneeling before Ortzo. "I don't know why I'm here, I don't—"

Ortzo grabbed Bon beneath his shoulder and raised him, gently, to his feet. He dusted his robes, straightening them so they hung evenly on his shoulders.

"Everything will be explained presently," Ortzo said. He gestured to the opening of his ship, the ramp that led to the darkness within. "Come with me."

Bon looked at the darkness, then back at Ortzo. He trembled in fear.

"There's no other direction for you to go," Ortzo said, and he grabbed hold of Bon's elbow and led him up the ramp.

Ortzo got exactly what he wanted. He returned to the small room where the infomerchant was being held, leading Bon through the door. The look on the infomerchant's face was brief—only a flash—but it was exactly what Ortzo hoped to see: recognition. They indeed knew each other.

The infomerchant tried to cover his tracks. "Who's this? Another person you can torture to no end?" he asked.

"That depends on you," Ortzo said as he petted the back of Bon's head. "Do you want to see this man get hurt?"

Ortzo shrugged and feigned disinterest. "I've seen plenty people I don't know get tortured. This will be no different."

"We'll see about that," Ortzo said.

Ortzo turned to Bon, who was trembling. Ortzo took his hands and quietly shushed him.

"You have such delicate hands," Ortzo said. "Let me guess: an artist?"

Bon tried to form the words he wanted to say, but his shivering jaw and uneven breathing prevented him from doing so.

"What's that?" Ortzo asked, leaning in closer.

"A m-m-m-musi-musician," Bon whispered.

"Aaaah," Ortzo replied. "I was close. I'd imagine you use these to play your chosen instrument, correct?"

Bon nodded vigorously.

"I figured, and I must say how much I admire your talent. I love music. Listening to it, it brings me . . . solace."

Slowly, Ortzo tied Bon's hands to the table in front of him. He stood up and drew his shido.

"P-please," Bon stammered. "No."

"Oh, don't beg me," Ortzo countered. "Beg the man behind me."

"Your games won't work," the infomerchant said. His voice didn't waver, not for one second. Ortzo knew he was going to let him go through with what was about to happen. And it would be a senseless, wasted gesture.

But sometimes—and Ortzo knew he took this for granted often—the universe was full of surprises.

"Mithlador!" Bon screamed, just as Ortzo was about to bring his shido down on his wrists.

"Bon, you fool!" the infomerchant screamed.

"What was that?" Ortzo said, withdrawing his shido. He leaned close to Bon, who was still trembling, but less so. He had found strength in rebelling against his lover.

"Mithlador," he repeated. "Whoever you're looking for, Valis sent him to Mithlador. But I don't know why, I swear."

Ortzo patted Bon's head. "I believe you," he said, then he sliced his shido clear across Bon's throat. The dying man's head dropped back, and he gargled uncontrollably, choking on his own blood as he bled out. Ortzo wondered why he wasn't covering his wound with his hands, trying, pointlessly as all the others did, to stop the bleeding. But then he remembered that his hands were still tied to the table. Ortzo sighed at Bon's misfortune, then turned to face the infomerchant.

"Why Mithlador?" he asked.

"You know exactly why," Valis snarled.

Ortzo shook his head at the futility of Valis's efforts. His risk and his life would all be for naught.

"You shouldn't have done that," Ortzo said. "I promise you, the man Cade seeks will be of no use to him, assuming he even makes it that far."

Valis looked up at Ortzo and smiled an angry, spiteful smile. "The Rising Sun grows strong," he said. "And Praxis's end is nigh."

"Our kingdom's reign is just beginning," Ortzo scoffed, then he ignited his shido and jammed it into the infomerchant's chest. It was cathartic, putting an end to the infomerchant's life, like he'd shed a layer of dead, cumbersome skin off his body. Maybe, he began to think, this planet wasn't so useless after all.

Ortzo stepped back outside and summoned Wexla.

"Bring back all our Fatebreakers," he ordered. "And find someone who can dispose of some excess waste within our ship. I want it gone and the ship scrubbed clean before we take off."

As the other Fatebreakers gathered back at the ship, Ortzo sat cross-legged on the top of its entrance ramp, meditating. He extended himself outward and felt the universe falling into order all around him. Everything was coming together as it should.

Praxis's rule of the galaxy was nearly complete.

CHAPTER FOURTEEN

The unobstructed view through the *Rubicon*'s cockpit revealed a unique splendor of sky that Cade found stirring. A nearby nebula filtered the visible universe through a prism of purple, yellow, and green, granting luminous glow to the stars and planets that ordinarily would fade unnoticed into the tapestry of the universe. Cade sat with his legs crossed over one another, breathing his thoughts in and letting them exhale out. Gazing upon the universe, he felt awed, something he hadn't experienced since he first arrived on Ticus and witnessed the immensity of the Floating Temple. Somewhere between then and now, he'd forgotten how vast and full of wonder the galaxy was; he'd forgotten what the oath he'd taken as a Rai, a defender of peace in the galaxy, really meant. Maybe everyone else at the Well had, too. Because every system that came under Praxis's control, every planet that ceded to Praxis's regime, was the Well's failure. Mired in galactic diplomacy, lacking the courage to act, and suffering from a vacuum of strong leadership, the Well and its peacekeeping allies had lost their way.

They'd become passive in the face of evil.

They'd grown afraid.

The galaxy couldn't abide either for a moment longer. Cade had taken an oath; *Tristan* had taken an oath. And despite Cade's status within the Well, he wouldn't let himself off the hook for allowing himself to grow comfortable, just like all his Masters and peers. It made him angry with himself; it made him disappointed. The thought moved something within him, and he realized what it was: The Rokura shared his feelings. Or at least it empathized, as strange as it sounded that he could emotionally connect with an object, or vice versa. He didn't understand his connection to the weapon—maybe it was because of Tristan, or maybe the Rokura had the power to communicate with everyone—but it responded to Cade's motivation to take action against Praxis. It made him feel like he ought to do whatever needed to be done in the fight against the rotten kingdom. Cade breathed in, he breathed out. Calm, he reminded himself, despite the growing fury he was feeling. It wasn't good enough to defeat Praxis; every vestige of its existence had to be ground to dust and salted so it could never rise again. He had a vision of the Praxis fleet burning in the space above its own planet just as the planet itself, somehow, erupted into nothingness. But is that what Cade wanted to do? Did he really want to take this as far as genocide of the Praxis people? He breathed. In, then out. More images flooded Cade's vision, of mayhem and destruction. It was the Rokura, pushing these premonitions into Cade's mind. The Rokura wanted him to do more than fight Praxis. It wanted him to lead. It wanted him to annihilate. He breathed its thoughts in, then out. Destroy Praxis, the Rokura urged. *Seize power.*

Cade gasped, and his eyes darted open.

The silence of the cockpit was broken when the door slid open and someone came treading softly in.

"It's nice, isn't it?"

Kira stood a step behind Cade as he got to his feet, though he could tell that her focus was on the same swath of space he'd been admiring just moments ago.

"I'd live in this ship if I could," she said.

Cade looked back at Kira and smiled. "You know, I think it would suit you," he said.

"I never get tired of it. It's all so big, so . . . grand. And I don't care about any of that 'it makes you feel small and puts things in perspective' crap; what I'm saying is that it's beautiful, and it makes me happy. I figure that's good enough."

Cade and Kira shared a smile, and then they both fixed their gazes on the magnificence before them.

"Cade," Kira said, turning toward him. "There's something you need to know."

Kira started to unbutton her shirt.

"Oh," Cade said, and he took a step back even though he knew how childish it made him look. "Is this, uh, are we—"

"Get ahold of yourself," Kira said. "I'm not going to pounce. It's easier to show you what I'm trying to say."

Kira pulled the right side of her shirt off her shoulder, taking the top of her bra with it. Cade followed the scar he'd seen when they woke up on his ship together. He thought, at the time, that he had a sense of her wound, but seeing it again now, he realized he had no idea. The scar ran across Kira's chest, from her sternum over her breast, ending just short of her shoulder blade. The scar was deep, that much Cade could tell, and if whatever sliced her had caught her any lower or deeper the wound would have been fatal. Kira was lucky, in a sense, though judging by the pained look on her face, luck was the furthest thing from her mind.

"My father did this to me," she said. "He cut me open with a triblade while my mother tried to smuggle me off my home planet. He'd rather see me dead than free."

Cade read the hurt in Kira's face, and he couldn't even pretend to understand the trauma she'd endured. It was hard to believe this could happen to Kira, of all people, and he wanted to know how. He wanted to know why. But, wisely, he recognized that this moment wasn't about him, so he zipped his lips and let Kira say what she wanted to say, how she wanted to say it. His job was to listen.

"I don't even know where to start," Kira sighed. "See, my mother knew that getting me away from my father, getting me away from my home, was the only way to save me. My planet, my home . . . it was changing, and my mother knew that my only hope for survival was for me to travel as far away as possible. My father, he wanted to kill her, but he couldn't. He couldn't, because . . ."

Kira looked down and took a deep breath, readying herself for whatever she was about to say.

"Cade," Kira said, locking him in her haunted gaze, "I'm from Praxis. That's my home. But it's all gone wrong, it's all gone so terribly wrong, and my mother, at least in part, is to blame."

"I don't understand," Cade said. "Wait, is your mom Ga Halle?"

"No, my mom is definitely not Ga Halle," Kira replied with a touch of levity in her voice. "But she's one of the people who helped give Ga Halle her power.

"See, Praxis is ruled by a caste system. There's this group of people at the top, the Barons, who control everything. They've *always* controlled everything. The role is passed down from generation to generation, which makes the Barons the most powerful people on the planet.

"My mother is a Baron."

Cade cupped his hand over his forehead and pivoted his head. "I don't understand; how does your mom play any role in what Ga Halle does?"

Kira scoffed. "She doesn't—not anymore. My father, from what I've been able to gather, keeps her locked up and has assumed her role as Baron. But before that happened, my mother helped something terrible happen. She, along with the other Barons, voted in favor of allowing Praxis—allowing Ga Halle—to use its newly developed technology to drain energy from a distant star. Ours was dying, Praxis itself was dying, and the idea was to take the power from another star to save our own. Out of this desperate need, the Barons, my mother included, gave Ga Halle this technology. But they didn't know—my mother certainly didn't know—what Ga Halle was going to do with it. They thought Ga Halle would siphon small amounts of energy from distant stars that no planet relied on for life. But that, as the galaxy knows, is not how things went. Ga Halle showed her true intent—she *killed* Quarry, and my mother could only stand by, horrified, as the blood ran over her hands.

"The other Barons got in line. Generations of having power as a right bred into them forbade them from seeing the necessity of rejecting what was happening. But Praxis was safe, and so was their power, and nothing else matters to them. But not my mother. She fought back, and when she found out that she was going to be imprisoned for her resistance, she risked her life to do one last thing: She freed me. She got me off Praxis and told me to never look back.

"That was fifteen years ago, and I haven't seen her since."

"Kira, I—" Cade stammered as he tried to collect the air that'd been stolen from his chest while listening to Kira's story. He empathized with the shame she must feel at being forced into a kind of complicity with Praxis's turn to evil. But more than that, Cade connected to who Kira was, deep beneath her boasting and her swagger. Kira was a stray. Like Cade, like the pilots she recruited into her Omega Squadron. She was a person who was dumped on her own, dropped somewhere she didn't naturally belong, and made to figure life out as she went. "I don't know what to say," he continued. "I—"

"You don't have to say anything. I *know*. I live with it every day. I'm Praxis, and my family has the blood of countless innocents on its hands."

"What?" Cade asked, his incredulity unable to be contained. "No. You do *not* share that responsibility. That belongs to Ga Halle. It belongs to your dad. Not your mom, and certainly not *you*."

Kira looked at Cade, an uncertain look on her face. Almost like confusion, but confusion mixed with inquiry. Cade got the sense that she expected judgment and probably some kind of rejection of the trust they'd forged. Maybe even a rejection of everything she was. But Cade didn't feel betrayed, he felt kinship; he felt a connection, deeper than there'd ever been between them.

"It should matter, Cade. If people knew—"

"If people knew what? That you're tied up in terrible things that you never asked for? That you aren't completely who you said you are? Look, if we're forming a line for people who are frauds, you're way, way behind me. Besides, people are idiots. Who cares what they know, or don't know?"

Kira smiled and turned toward the viewport; Cade turned with her. Together, they shared a silent moment.

"You can be very surprising, Cade Sura," Kira whispered. Cade didn't say anything; he just smiled.

In the distance, red and blue gases of a far-off nebula mingled, breaking up the galaxy's darkness with sublime beauty. Cade looked down, and he noticed that, at some point, he and Kira's hands had locked together. She seemed to be just noticing it as well. However it'd happened, it was like a magnetic attraction, and neither one of them made any effort to break it. Instead, they moved closer to each other.

"Listen, Cade, I really don't think—"

"I know. This isn't the right time. But things are bad. They're bad for a million reasons, so let's just have a moment that feels good. This," Cade said, squeezing Kira's hand, "feels good, and I really don't know how many more moments we're going to have like this."

Kira laced her fingers around Cade's hand, getting a better grip. They looked out to the stars and the vast expanse of space, and Cade felt at ease. When Cade thought about his life—which he did as seldom as possible—he knew, deep down, that he wasn't the happiest person around. For all the time he spent fantasizing about leaving the Well and the life he'd have thereafter, he spent just as much time fretting about what would happen if he did. Until he became the Paragon, no one cared if he stayed or left. He had no real responsibilities, no role that made him essential to any of the Well's functions. Cade felt like his duty in life was to be a lonely onlooker standing on the shore, watching ships ferry people away to their rewarding, meaningful lives.

But with Kira, he'd actually been doing something. It wasn't easy, and he certainly had his doubts and fears, but at least he was part of something. He belonged, and that made him feel good about himself, which isn't something that happened very often.

Cade turned to Kira, and he put his hand on her hip. Neither said a word as they inched closer. Cade could feel Kira's soft breath glide across the contours of his face. He closed his eyes—and whatever was going to happen next was crushed by the sound of voices, arguing, as they neared the cockpit. Quickly, Kira peeled herself away from Cade and skipped a step back. Cade did the same. They almost achieved casual positions when the cockpit door slid open and Mig and 4-Qel entered.

Mig noticed, immediately, that he'd walked in on something.

A childish grin spread across his face, and Cade wanted to knock it right off him.

"I'm sorry, am I interrupting something?"

"No, why?" Cade and Kira said in unison.

Mig continued to laugh, and 4-Qel, noticing Mig, began to laugh as well.

"I fixed the mass-jump drive," Mig said. "And I got your new shields set up. So, if you're done holding us hostage—"

"We're not holding you hostage, Mig," Cade said as he rubbed the corners of his eyes. "You know that."

"Okay, great. Then drop us at the nearest system, and we'll be on our way."

Cade looked over at Kira, thinking he'd get her confirmation to share with Mig their plan and see if he could help. Kira, though, turned away at Cade's gaze.

"Look, I know all about what you two are plotting," Mig said as he flopped into the pilot's seat. "And, like I told your girlfriend, I don't think it's a bad idea. But it is a *crazy* idea, and I would have to be clinically insane to be part of it."

Cade shook his head at Kira. "You told him?"

"What?" Kira asked. "You were doing your meditating thing, and he kept bugging me about what we were doing on Kyysring. So, yeah, I told him."

"Well," Cade said, turning to Mig and shrugging his shoulders, "what's it going to be?" Cade knew Mig wasn't going to help them. He was selfish, stubborn, and scared, and Cade had no intention of even asking him to be part of his and Kira's plan. Not anymore. He thought the two years they'd been apart would have matured Mig, or at least helped him get some perspective, but he was still the same Mig. Because of that, he didn't even want Mig knowing the details of what they had in mind; the less Mig—who Cade hardly considered trustworthy anymore— knew, the better. All Cade wanted was for Mig to tell them where they could get the heat-shielding material they needed, maybe even some general advice on using it, then they'd drop his butt off at the nearest planet. Mig would just have to cross his fingers for one that had breathable air.

" 'What's it going to be?' " Mig said, parroting Cade. "Well, I think it's going to be the both of you captured by Praxis, imprisoned, tortured, and executed. That's a look at your future—free of charge—if you try to blow up the crown jewel of the Praxis fleet. I want no part of that. None."

"You don't have to help us," Cade said. "In fact, I don't want your help. Just tell us where we can get material that can withstand a star's heat the way the *War Hammer* does, and you can be on your way."

"Uh, that's helping. Is that not helping?" Mig asked, directing the question toward 4-Qel.

"We'd be furthering their efforts, so, yes, by definition, that is helping," 4-Qel replied.

"See?" Mig said.

Cade exhaled heavily, then looked at Kira. His patience for Mig was razor-thin, and she picked up on his aggravation. Neither of them wanted Cade saying anything that would torpedo the slim chance they had at pulling something useful out of Mig.

"Mig, you're thinking about this like you have a choice in the matter," Kira said, stepping in for Cade. "Yeah, you might have it good for now, pulling your scams and outsmarting everyone, but what are you going to do when Praxis is breathing down your neck? That day—it's coming if we don't stop them. What will you do when Praxis controls *everything*?"

Mig took a good, long look at Kira, then he shifted his gaze over to Cade. In that time, his expression morphed from confusion to patronizing pity. He laughed.

"Are you being serious right now?" he asked. "Because, if you are, the both of you really need to get off of Ticus more often."

"And why's that?" Cade asked, his words sharply acerbic.

"Because Praxis already does control everything!"

Mig got up from his seat and slapped 4-Qel in the chest, signaling him to follow.

"Come on, let's leave them to their rebellion of two."

Cade could only watch as Mig brushed by him, heading toward the door. It was like they were kids again and Mig was pissy about not being able to play a game his way so he was grabbing all his toys and going home. The problem was that they weren't kids and this wasn't a game. It was one thing for Mig to turn his back on Cade. He could live with that. But the Mig he knew, or at least he thought he knew, didn't have the heart to turn his back on the entire galaxy. Cade was dumbstruck, and he couldn't think of a single thing to say that could bring Mig back. Luckily, he didn't have to. Kira had the words for both of them.

"They don't control me," Kira said. Everyone turned to look at her, and Cade saw in her face that gritty determination that he knew would never flag. Not for a single moment.

"Praxis does not control me. They don't control my squad. I'd rather die than let that happen," she said. "And I know there's people out there who feel the same. Those people who stood up in the Koga Club? Praxis doesn't control them. They're ready to fight."

"Great," Mig said. "They can die right alongside you."

"Maybe," Kira replied. "But we have the Rokura. And one way or another, we'll have this bomb. So when you say things like 'Praxis controls everything,' do me a favor and say what you really mean: that Praxis controls *you*."

Mig sneered. "You know, it must be nice to have the luxury to make such big, bold claims. It must be nice to have the luxury to feel like you can martyr your own life. Good for you. But you know what? While you've enjoyed your luxuries, I've been fighting and scraping, alone, for everything—*everything*—that

I have. I didn't ask to be born on the worst planet in the galaxy, and I certainly didn't ask to have worthless parents. But I've made do, and I suggest you two, and everyone else, learn to do the same. I mean—what? You think I owe some sort of debt or something? This galaxy has done *nothing* for me.

"Four-Qel, how about you?" Mig said, turning to face his companion. "What has the galaxy given you?"

"I was born into brutal, rigorously demanding service, then my makers tried to murder me when an upgraded Qel model was introduced and I was deemed no longer needed. In my estimation, I have not been provided with much."

Mig turned back to Kira. "I've survived despite the odds—we both have—and we'll survive Praxis."

There was a tense moment of silence, where Cade thought Kira might grab Mig by his hair and slam him against the cockpit's dome. Instead, she stomped by him and took her seat behind the *Rubicon*'s stick.

"You got this thing patched up?" she asked Mig without looking at him.

Mig looked at 4-Qel, the briefest sidelong glance, but it was one Cade knew well. Mig was up to something. He was *always* up to something.

"I replaced the shield generator and repaired the mass-jump drive. You're good to go."

Kira started the engine initiation sequence; since they left Kyysring, they'd been floating just outside its orbit in a field of debris, hoping no one would find them. As Kira brought the ship back online, Cade eyed Mig. He was watching Kira with too much interest, and Cade couldn't figure out why. But then he found out, and he immediately regretted giving Mig access to the *Rubicon*'s internal controls without someone watching his every move.

"*Unauthorized access. Unauthorized access,*" the ship's tinny AI declared in a loop. Kira, confounded, punched her security code into the control panel over and over, but it was no good. The ship was locked.

By the time Cade and Kira turned to look back at Mig and 4-Qel, they had their sidewinders drawn on them.

"I installed a new operating system, and it only listens to me," Mig said. His voice was unwavering; this was all just business for him.

"You can't be serious," Cade said.

"Look, I'm not a greedy person. What Praxis is offering for the both of you and the Rokura is obscene. I'm sure, though, that there's still a nice reward for just the Rokura. So, we'll make a trade: You give us the Rokura, and you get your ship back. *And* you won't have to find out if your magical weapon can do whatever it does before Four-Qel rips it from your arms. It's up to you."

Cade wanted to be angry, but he couldn't get himself there. He saw the conflict in his friend, and he knew he was torn between his survival instincts—which drove much of what he did—and his innate goodness, which Cade knew was there. It came down to which was more important: self-preservation or the greater good. As disappointed Cade was that Mig wasn't compelled to choose the latter, he knew most everything Mig had been through—including being abandoned by Cade and Tristan, his only two friends in the world—and understood why the decision made sense to him. He just wished the conflict didn't have to be resolved with him and Kira being held at blasterpoint.

"Mig, think about what you're doing," Cade implored. "You'd really hand over the means for Praxis to kill, enslave, and oppress people en masse for a little bit of coin?"

Mig looked away. "I told you that I'd survive Prax—"

Mig's words were cut short by the sound of an eruptive boom that echoed from one side of the cockpit to the next.

"What was that?" Cade asked as he looked through the viewport and scanned the area around them. "Did debris hit us?"

"Well, I'd love to tell you," Kira said, slapping the control panel, "but some jerk locked down the ship, including its sensors."

Mig hurried to the control panel and, with a couple short maneuvers, brought the *Rubicon* back online. He activated the sensors as Kira kept a watchful eye on everything from over his shoulder.

"That can't be right," she said.

"What? What is it?" Cade asked.

"The sensors are saying that there's a ship below us—but that the ship is both mechanical and organic."

Mig's head darted up from the control panel and he looked wide-eyed around the ship. "Uh-oh."

"'Uh-oh' what?" Cade asked as Mig blew by him, rejoining 4-Qel. "What's going on?"

Mig looked over his shoulder, alarm evident on his face. "Krell," he gasped.

If the galaxy ever had it in mind to create actual monsters— like the stuff of nightmares—the Krell would be them. They were an ancient and nearly extinct race that came from some quadrant of the galaxy that was either lost or unreachable. For all Cade cared, they could've come from the universe's dark underbelly; the history lesson was less important than the reality he was currently facing. This was a species that, as far as anyone knew, had devoured their own planet: They literally ate their own world. Their homes, their soil, their everything. They were known to do that—eat everything in their path—in the rare instances they appeared planetside. Thankfully, they had evolved into a nomadic species, but that didn't change the fact that most people who crossed paths with the Krell didn't live to tell the tale. Cade heard stories of Rai encountering long-lost starcruisers, or what was left of them, floating dead in deep space. Half-consumed ships, with no survivors, was the truest mark of a Krell attack.

With the Krell in mind, the anger Cade couldn't find just moments ago was now devouring him from the inside out. Like a Krell. Cade had a disgusting Krell within him, and it was all because of Mig. Mig's greed and recklessness had killed them all.

"Mig, you idiot! We should have seen these things coming from parsecs away—but no! You had to shut the entire ship down to do . . . whatever it is that you did!"

"Like I knew Krell were going to find us!" Mig yelled back.

4-Qel added, "No one could have anticipated a ship—let alone a Krell ship—happening upon us—"

"You shut your face," Cade interrupted.

4-Qel recoiled, confused. "I'm not sure I have the ability to do that."

"And *you*," Cade continued, "you know Krell never travel alone, right? More are going to start dotting our sensors any second. They're going to board us. They're going kill us. They're going to *feast* on us. As a matter of fact, that jostle we felt was probably them creating an artificial tunnel between their ship and ours. It's only a matter of time until they're here."

"We're locked in place," Kira said, supporting Cade's assumption. "That thing's got its tractor beam on us, and there's no breaking its hold."

Mig seemed to have a barb to fire back, but then he stopped himself. He shook his head, then pointed at Cade. "Wait, wait, wait—you're the Paragon. What are we all freaking out about? When those hideous things board the ship, you kill them. Pretty straightforward, right?"

Cade opened his mouth to speak, but nothing came out. He hadn't anticipated his authenticity as the Paragon being called into question. He figured Mig wouldn't care either way, and he didn't. Not until it mattered, directly, to him.

"You're. *Kidding*. Me," Mig spat.

"Look, okay, this whole thing is complicated," Cade scrambled. "You don't even *know*."

"I do know, and I can't believe I didn't know it before," Mig said. "If I'm the last person in the universe who should be the Paragon, then you, Cade, are the second-to-last person who should be the Paragon. I mean, really, you—"

Cade rushed Mig, slamming him against the cockpit's wall and pinning him there with the force of his forearm locked beneath Mig's chin. He could feel 4-Qel's sidewinder pointed right at him, but he didn't care; Cade had tortured himself enough about not being the Chosen One and all the consequences that went along with it. He didn't need Mig, of all people, to dig the knife in deeper.

"You're right, I'm not the Paragon," Cade said, shoving his forearm into Mig's throat. "Tristan is. He pulled the Rokura out, he's the Chosen One; he's the one who's supposed to fix the galaxy. Not. Me.

"But do you know where Tristan is? Can you take a guess, given the circumstances?"

Cade saw the color run out of Mig's face. His lips parted, slowly, and his eyes began to glisten. "No," he said, just above a whisper. "Cade—*no*."

Cade released his hold on Mig, and took a step away from him. Mig didn't move, and he didn't make eye contact with Cade.

"He's dead," Cade said, his voice cracking. "He was murdered right in front of me, and all I could do was watch him die."

Mig's eyes darted along the floor; he shook his head, trying to reject a truth that, Cade knew, was as unbearable for him as it was for Cade. "That can't be right. Not Tristan. He . . . It doesn't even make sense."

"He's gone, Mig. He's dead and Praxis killed him. Same as they killed our parents."

Mig ran his hands through his thick hair, his fingers clenching his locks. He muttered a streak of obscenities before erupting into a fit of kicking and punching the ship's nearest wall. Kira stepped forward, like she was going to interrupt him, but Cade stopped her. Cade knew the helpless anger Mig was experiencing, and punching a wall seemed like a perfectly reasonable way to deal with that feeling.

"All the misery in our lives—the *real* misery—Praxis has been behind it all," Cade said to Mig once his punches subsided into exhausted jabs. "And you—you want to give them the Rokura. Well, here," Cade removed the Rokura from his back and dropped it at Mig's feet. "Take it."

An alarm began to blare, and the cockpit's overhead light flashed in a continuous loop. Cade looked at Kira, who was monitoring the control panel.

"We're being boarded," she said. "They're coming in through the airlock."

The cockpit fell silent. Everyone looked to everyone else, searching for something they couldn't find within themselves. Comfort. A solution. But there was nothing.

Cade drew his sidewinder and grabbed the Rokura from the ground. He supposed it was possible that it would get him out of this mess, but he wasn't confident. If it was the only chance they had, he had no choice but to give it a shot.

"Kira, send out a distress signal," Cade said. "If we can hold the cockpit, then—"

"Whoever comes for us, they'll . . ." Kira's words drifted off as she struggled to finish saying what they all knew. Admitting defeat didn't come easily to Kira, nor did surrendering to a fate that promised to be violent and cruel. "They'll take us. They'll take all of us and turn us over to Praxis."

Cade smiled at Kira, though it was a sad smile. He already regretted this being the end of their time together. "We'll just have to take our chances," he said.

Kira nodded and drew her sidewinder. She stood next to Cade, ready.

"Mig," she said, "you have to send out the distress signal. You're the only one who can."

Mig didn't respond. He hadn't moved; he may not have even blinked since the alarm went off. He was just standing there, staring at the door.

"Mig," Kira said. "Mig! Set the signal."

"No," Mig replied. "We're not doing this."

Mig hurried past Cade and Kira and started rifling through his pack, which he'd dropped on the floor next to the pilot's seat.

"We don't have time for this, Mig," Cade said. "Set the signal."

"You heard Kira," Mig replied. "Whoever comes—assuming they make it before the Krell eat our intestines for lunch—will send us on a one-way trip to Praxis, and that ain't happening." Mig turned and, in each of his hands, he held an orb with a single red light in the center. Explosives of his own design, Cade assumed. "Let's blow these jerks back to whatever hole they crawled out of."

Mig loaded a charge into his sidewinder and slung his pack over his shoulder. Cade eyed him skeptically.

"Uh, Mig, how is blowing up our own ship—with us in it—going to help?"

"I'm not going to blow up the ship, I'm going to blow up the airlock," Mig said with a satisfied smile. Even when his plans ended with his own death, he still found satisfaction in being the smartest person in the room. Being able to cause mayhem was just icing on the cake. "These are special explosives—made them myself. They erupt like any proton-charged bomb, but they also emit a containment field. Which means—if done right—I can blow the airlock, kill the Krell, and break the tractor beam's hold, all while containing the very breach I create. Sexy, right?"

Cade stepped in Mig's way, stopping him from reaching the door. He looked at Mig and saw what he'd been wanting to see since he spotted him at the drone pit: his friend. This was the Mig he knew—clever, inventive, resourceful, caring, and deeply dedicated to the few people he held close. Cade had feared that the Mig he'd encountered the last few times they'd met—bitter, angry, selfish—had destroyed what was the real, true person he'd known better than anyone else in the galaxy. But, consistent with the galaxy's penchant for balancing something good with something terrible, Cade's friend returned just in time to die. Of course.

"You can't do this, Mig," Cade said. "You'll—"

"That's why *I'll* do it," 4-Qel interrupted, grabbing the pack from Mig. "I can fight off the Krell long enough and well enough to set off the explosions in the airlock and ensure the containment field is fully established."

Mig grabbed hold of 4-Qel's arm; he pulled him back with all his weight, trying to prevent him from leaving. It was a futile effort: 4-Qel was much too strong for Mig to cause him to even break his stride. "No!" Mig yelled. "This is my idea, so I'm the one who will—"

4-Qel stopped. He turned and put his hand on Mig's shoulder, both a gesture of comfort and a way to stop Mig's interference. Cade saw fear in Mig's eyes as he looked up at 4-Qel, and he realized that their relationship wasn't the mercenary union of greed Cade had assumed it to be. They were friends.

"I will return," 4-Qel said, then exited the cockpit.

There was nothing for Cade, Kira, and Mig to do now but wait—wait and listen. They crept toward the cockpit door, silently so as not to drown out any sounds coming from the other side. The hush within the *Rubicon* dragged on for what felt like hours, only to be pierced by the sound of a high-pitched scream, like the sound of a wild animal thrashing in its death throes. Cade startled, and his body, from natural aversion, moved away from the door. There were more screams—neither human nor animal—each as bloodcurdling as the one that came before it. Cade knew it was a sound he could never get used to.

Mig mumbled a string of obscenities to himself. "Come on, 4-Qel," he said. "*Come on.*"

The sound of sidewinder fire echoed through the ship, subduing some of the screams. That sign of life helped give them all a little bit of ease, especially Mig, though Cade struggled to keep himself from charging out the door and helping 4-Qel. Kira read his body language well enough to know what he was considering; she grabbed his wrist, hard, and told him "*No.*" It was a direct order.

After a few frenzied seconds, the sound of sidewinder discharges came to an end, as did the screams. The ship was silent once more as Cade, Kira, and Mig waited for the ship to blow up.

"Where are the explosions?" Cade asked. "Why aren't the explosions happening?"

"They got to Four-Qel!" Mig screamed as he unloaded, then reloaded his sidewinder. "I'm going to kill every last one of those mangy fu—"

In an instant, the ship was rocked so hard by detonations that it was sent careening through space—through the debris field. Sensors screamed as the *Rubicon* smashed and bashed into broken chunks of meteors, ruptured ships, and other random bits of space junk. Cade knew that if they didn't get this ship under control, the *Rubicon* would be joining this junkyard.

"Geez, Mig!" Cade yelled. "How many explosives were in your pack?!"

"I don't like to take chances, okay?!" Mig hollered back as he, Cade, and Kira spun uncontrollably with the ship's revolutions.

Kira, though, managed to get her bearings and move with the ship's spin. Cade could see her getting at least a modicum of control of her body and, at the exact moment she was coming into alignment with the control panel from the opposite side of the room, she kicked off the ship's wall and propelled herself forward. Without an inch to spare, Kira grabbed on to the pilot's chair, pulled herself down, and strapped herself in. She shouted at Mig for the code to unlock the control panel and, with the reins back in her hands, Kira fired opposing thrusters and stabilized the ship.

Mig and Cade both dropped from the top of the cockpit and crashed to the ground.

Straightening out his jaw—which he felt had been jarred loose during his spin cycle around the cockpit—Cade took the seat next to Kira. "We good?"

Kira scanned the monitors. "Looks clear to me. Although I'm pretty sure we expended every ounce of whatever luck we had in the past few hours. We shouldn't tempt fate by sticking around any longer than we have to."

At the sound of the cockpit door sliding open behind him, Cade leapt from his seat and trained his sidewinder on whatever was coming through. He breathed a deep sigh of relief when he spotted 4-Qel, who held his own severed right arm as he walked in.

"They are indeed savages," 4-Qel noted. "And quite unattractive, too."

Mig attended to 4-Qel right away, examining his arm where it'd been ripped off. "Ah, don't worry about that, buddy. It's a clean break; I can have you patched up in no time."

"And then you're going to get my ship back to the way it was," Kira said as Mig helped 4-Qel into the seat behind her.

"I will," Mig said. "And, look . . . I'm sorry. I think I got so used to fighting for myself that I forgot what the most important fight is."

"And what's that?" Cade asked.

"The ones you fight for someone else," Mig replied. "Tristan taught me that."

Cade stood at the head of the cockpit; behind him, nothing but limitless, wide-open space occupied the *Rubicon*'s massive glass exterior.

"Listen, we all have reason to be angry," Cade said. "At Praxis, at the cruel hand of the galaxy, whatever. But none of that matters. I don't know about the rest of you, but I'm tired of wishing for something else and never getting it. I'm tired of wanting to be somewhere else, wanting to be some*one* else, thinking that a better life is just going to fall into my lap. This is our chance to do something big—we have a chance to make a difference, and that doesn't happen very often. So let's take this chance and do something nobody expects us to do: Let's win."

Cade looked around the cockpit and spotted three faces that all agreed with him. Where they were from, what they did, what had been done to them—none of it mattered. What mattered was seizing this opportunity and proving to themselves, and the entire galaxy, that they were more than people thought they could be. They'd surprise them all, and they'd do so by striking at the heart of the galaxy's ruling order.

"All right then," Cade said, settling into the copilot's seat, "for the last time, let's please get as far away from this planet as fast as possible."

"Agreed," Kira added as she turned her attention to the control panel. "Where to?"

"Koruvite," Mig said.

Kira cocked an eyebrow. "Um . . . is that a planet?"

"No, it is not," Mig replied. "Koruvite is an element—a rare, rare element, but if you want to shield your bomb from a burning star, koruvite is what you need."

"And you know where we can get some koruvite, I hope?" Cade chimed in.

"Yup," Mig replied. "A little forgotten nowheresville called Mithlador. There's a mining colony there—it's the only place where koruvite can be found. Other than, you know, raiding Praxis's pantry."

"*Mithlador*, you say?" Cade said, beaming at Kira. "Mith-la-dor. Well, I have to say, that's very, very interesting."

"Oh, shut up," Kira replied, programming their course into the mass-jump system.

"Hey, maybe fate is throwing us a bone for once."

"Not likely," Kira said. "The two things that we need are both in the same place? That's not fate; that's improbable coincidence. Which means it's not a coincidence at all."

"Like you said," Cade shrugged, "it's not like we can turn around and go home."

"No, but we should probably be prepared for this to all go wrong at some point."

"Your assessment of our situation does very little to inspire," 4-Qel commented from his seat behind Kira.

"No kidding," Mig agreed. "We might as well just jump out the airlock now."

"All right, all right," Kira conceded. "I just like to be prepared. It's what I do."

Cade smiled. "Hey, when you have a team like this . . . ?"

Kira looked around the cockpit, and Cade felt like they were seeing the same thing: a one-armed Qel, a troublemaking genius, a rebellious pilot, and a counterfeit savior.

"Sure," Kira said with a sardonic grin. "How can we lose?"

CHAPTER FIFTEEN

G a Halle closed her eyes and imagined what it would be like to quietly unsheathe her shido and, without saying a word, kill every member of the Barons quorum.

As she listened to the Barons prattle on about all the luxuries their lives afforded—of their peculiar diets, their starship collections, their refined taste in art—Ga Halle turned her attention to the circular viewing port that was positioned at the apex of the monolithic tower lording over the base of operations for her entire fleet. From it, Ga Halle took in the enormity of the Praxis *Fortress*, the massive superstation that she and her army of Fatebreakers, gunners, infantrymen, and Intruder pilots called home. The station was built to satisfy Ga Halle's strategic need to possess a battleship that would consolidate the Praxis forces and uniformly mold their allegiance and sense of purpose. The *Fortress* wasn't meant to be an offensive vessel—something the Barons fought Ga Halle vigorously over in its planning stages, arguing it should be swifter and nimbler—it was meant to be the ultimate stronghold, both physically and psychologically. Ga

Halle knew what it was like to be beaten and have nowhere to run, and she vowed to protect those under her command from the same despair; the *Fortress* ensured that, no matter what happened, the idea of Praxis and the people who fell under its rubric would never be exterminated from the galaxy. Praxis would endure.

But the *Fortress* wasn't perfect. One blemish, one blight on its landscape, prevented Ga Halle from fully embracing it as belonging to *her*.

The Baron's Sanctuary.

Centrally located on the *Fortress*, Sanctuary was a single-purpose edifice that stood higher than anything else on the station. This was the one thing the Barons overruled Ga Halle on, demanding a place to call their own during their rare trips to the *Fortress*. Like the Barons themselves, Sanctuary was an unnecessary addendum to an efficient system, a rusty gear that was responsible for slowing all the other gears that were churning toward progress. Its interior was an exhibition of frivolities and excess, overfurnished and accentuated with precious metals heisted from Praxis's own reserves. These people, Ga Halle thought with disgust, were more focused on their own vanity than reinforcing the ambition of the Praxis regime—to definitively rule for the good of the Praxis kingdom and, in time, the entire galaxy. This space offered Ga Halle no sanctuary, contrasting so starkly with her own Sutra Room that she wondered if she and the Barons were so far apart that they were of two minds on even the simplest of terms. Though Ga Halle's means were vast, her end was clear: She dared to be the first real galactic leader, and in her reign she'd bring order. To the Barons, though, means and ends were the same things: They wanted power for the sake of power, possessions for the sake of possessions. Their lust was insatiable, their thirst, unquenchable.

The divide between them is what drove Ga Halle's designs to

rid Praxis of the Barons like so many cancerous cells obliterated from their host. Her personal differences aside, Ga Halle knew that no kingdom could strive where there's discord. Uniformity in thought, uniformity in deed, and uniformity in sentiment were essential to the sustainability of Ga Halle's dream, and she wouldn't allow that dream to be compromised by the bourgeois elite who knew nothing of real pain, sacrifice, and commitment— not the way Ga Halle did.

Still, she stifled the rage within her and kept her shido at her side. This was just a briefing session, one like so many others. The Barons, five in total, would half-listen to Ga Halle's selective report on the latest activities within *Fortress;* they'd drink their hosberry wine and return to Praxis having felt like they accomplished something.

"Ga Halle," one of the Barons summoned. "Ga Halle."

Ga Halle broke her train of thought and focused her attention on Baron Chang, who was sprawled on the couch, swirling a glass of wine. He had an exasperated expression, and Ga Halle could tell by his tone that he'd paged her a few times. She'd tuned that elitist cabal out so thoroughly she hadn't even recognized the Barons turning their attention to her.

"Yes, Baron Chang?" Ga Halle answered, her voice calm and steady.

"We'd like to bring into question the audacity that drove your most recent activity."

Ga Halle's eyes narrowed as she cast a gaze at Baron Chang that, hopefully, he interpreted as her desire to use her shido to cut him in half.

"Your assault on Ticus was not only unsanctioned, but it goes against our agreement to not wage an offensive conflict against the Well," Baron Kanta—who recently filled his mother's role as Baron after her passing—added. "When our takeover is complete, we need the Well as our ally, willfully or otherwise, to keep many contentious planets under our thumbs. We want to look like unifiers, not conquerors."

The four other Barons murmured in agreement, touching on Baron Kanta's final point despite how heavily, to Ga Halle, it reeked of faux profundity. She chose to remain silent and listen, though, afraid of where a heated debate might lead.

"And what of these reports of Praxis activity on Mithlador?" Baron Paqlin questioned. "We left that system long ago. Why return?"

Ga Halle smiled. "Housekeeping. It should be known that Praxis keeps a watchful eye on its domain. Especially when valuable assets are at stake."

"More to the point," Kanta interrupted, "we understand your actions were driven by the rumor of the Rokura somehow surfacing at the Well. Yet in your attack, you were unable to retrieve the weapon. Might I ask, how can you even be certain it was there in the first place? Are we to believe that, after all this time, the Rokura has been released from stasis again?"

"I'm confident of my source within the Well," Ga Halle replied.

"And who is this source?" Paqlin asked, making sure the skepticism in her voice was as clear as possible.

"Revealing that information could jeopardize the life of my source, and I cannot do that."

The Barons shared a tense look, silently agreeing with one another. Maybe they'd been sharper on Ga Halle's activities than she gave them credit for; maybe they knew she was operating in what was essentially a rogue state outside her home planet. Never before did the Barons question Ga Halle; never did they even seek out details of the war she'd been waging, in their names, on the galaxy. Yes, bringing that war to the Well's doorstep was a controversial move, but Ga Halle never thought it would've woken the Barons from their slumber. There was something else going on—like Ga Halle herself, the Barons were up to something.

Baron Ebik stood up and cleared his throat. "My fellow Barons mean no disrespect, Ga Halle. We're just concerned about the lack of consultation you sought from us. It would've been better to discuss your attacking the Well, and Mithlador, before any decision was made."

Ebik sat back down but, before doing so, he nodded, ever so slightly, at Ga Halle. She returned the knowing gesture.

Sitting up from his titame-studded armchair, a relic from Praxis's revered Progress Age, Baron Tirus opened his mouth to speak then stopped, choosing instead to finish his glass of hosberry wine first. He held up one finger, asking for a pause as he maintained his steady level of drunkenness.

"Our concern," Tirus said, nearly dropping his empty glass by misjudging the distance of his armchair's accompanying side table, "is the effort, and cost, of pursuing this mythical weapon when our goal has always been to bring order and unity to the galaxy—and doing that through submission to our control. It doesn't seem like the Rokura, at this point in time, is essential to our efforts."

Again, the Barons murmured their assent. Ebik's eyes, though, glanced at Ga Halle. He nodded again, ensuring their conspiratorial relationship was understood. They'd become allies many years ago, back when Ebik's wife—being the true blood Baron—was the quorum representative, and he was plotting his rise to power. Ebik knew where the future was heading; he understood his role within it. They were loyal to each other, out of necessity and genuine respect, but Ga Halle never let Ebik forget who the master was in their relationship.

The Barons whispered among themselves, doubtless trying to decide what action, if any, they could take against Ga Halle. She knew this, and she was unafraid. If the Barons so feared usurpation that they were plotting their own, so be it. The Barons had their ground forces, they had their fleet; they could take their chances against Ga Halle at any time. But at no point would she negotiate her mission, not even if its collateral damage was a civil war against her own planet. Nothing would stand between her and her destiny.

"When we started on this course of ours, we were on the brink of becoming a planet of refugees," Ga Halle said, looking at each Baron as she addressed them all. "Our star was dying, and all of us, no matter how rich or how poor, were going to end up displaced or dead. I prevented that. And I know you all admire how much we've accomplished, but there is no satisfaction in looking to the past for me. When I think of the Praxis kingdom, I don't think about how far we've come; I only think about how far we still have to go."

Ga Halle opened her hand and projected her vid player, large enough for all the Barons to see. Footage taken from Kaladore began to play. The video showed Kaladorians rioting in the streets of their planet's capital, celebrating around an Intruder that was burning in the city square; the video jumped to an image of a Praxis supply vessel ablaze in a calm ocean on Ohan; then, finally, there was footage from an alpha drone's uplink, taken right before a masked assailant blasted out its optics.

Ga Halle hadn't prepared this footage for the Barons. She had these videos, and many like them, in her possession at all times, there to be a reminder of the chaos that was only a breath away. Chaos that would consume the galaxy if left unchecked.

"Systems that still resist our control wage open warfare against our very presence. Renegade cells in systems we've annexed sabotage their planet's own resources to prevent it from aiding our mission. And the Rising Suns, those cowardly terrorists, continue to disrupt our activities all over the galaxy. The only way—the *only way*—to obtain absolute control is through absolute power. That is why Praxis must possess the Rokura."

The Barons looked at one another as an unease settled over the room. Tirus shook his head, rustling himself from a stupor, Ga Halle knew, that extended well beyond tonight's overindulgence.

"There is no such thing as ultimate power, Ga Halle. Take it from us: It does not exist."

Ga Halle looked at Tirus, his red cheeks and blossomed nose, and in his cloudy eyes, she saw a frightened child. Frightened of losing his power, frightened of being made to believe that everything he knew to be true in life—specifically that his power was an everlasting right—was in danger of being proven false. She gave him a pitying smile. "Oh, yes it does, Tirus. Yes it *does*."

"You disobeyed a direct command," Paqlin said as she pointed an angry finger at Ga Halle. "*We* are the ruling clans, and *we* make the decisions for the future of our people and our planet. Not. *You*."

The Barons' eyes were on Ga Halle as they waited for her to respond. Never had a Baron status-checked her; never had they sought her debasement. But now Paqlin had done it, and as Praxis ritual dictated, Ga Halle had only two options before her: She could either kneel before Paqlin or refuse. In kneeling, things would continue as they always had; refusing would mean consequences. And Paqlin, doubtless, would surely spread word of her insubordination. On one side, Ga Halle would be painted as a heretic who dishonored Praxis culture because she thought herself above it; on the other, she'd be painted as a champion of the people, someone who finally stood up to the Barons and Praxis's archaic power structure. Ga Halle couldn't afford such divisiveness when it came to her character, but she couldn't bring herself to bow, either.

On Ga Halle's wrist, her comms device vibrated over and over.

It had been doing so for some time. Though it was expected that she respond to the gauntlet Paqlin threw in front of her, Ga Halle needed to step away. To secure her future, to secure her destiny, she had to kneel. But she needed a moment to work herself up to doing so.

"Excuse me for one moment—this is urgent," Ga Halle said, and turned her back to the Barons. She could feel the dismay of the Barons behind her.

"My queen," Ortzo said as his face came into focus on Ga Halle's comms screen. "I've pinpointed the Rokura's location."

Ga Halle remained steady even as her heart skipped a beat. It was finally happening. "Where?" she asked.

"Mithlador. Cade Sura is on his way, and I'm certain you can guess who he seeks. Our forces already on the ground continue their search for him, but his whereabouts . . . they remain unknown, my queen."

"That is of no consequence," Ga Halle said. "I'll send our mutual friend to retrieve the boy, and the Rokura, at once."

Ortzo stammered. "My queen? My men and I, we're currently on our way."

"No. I need you here. Changes are in store."

And with that, Ga Halle ceased the communication. It seemed that she wouldn't be kneeling after all. Destiny had other plans for her.

"I saved our people," Ga Halle said as she turned to face the Barons. Her face had darkened, and she could sense the Barons recoiling at the sight of her. "Many years ago, I was the one who took action that prevented Praxis history, culture, and our proud heritage from becoming lost to the sands of time. I put us on a course for conquest, and we've achieved more than we ever could have imagined possible. The entire galaxy, which once stood idle in the face of our demise, is nearly under our control. And now, after all I've fought for, all the sacrifices I've made—sacrifices you couldn't even *begin* to fathom—the final steps to fulfilling our dream of a galaxy united under a Praxis kingdom are upon us. And you have the nerve to insult me? I know what's needed to complete our journey. I know how the galaxy will finally obtain the order and the peace everyone talks about, but no one has the temerity to pursue to its bloody end. I will get us there, and no one—*no one*—will stand in my way."

Kanta was the first Baron to fall. In one smooth movement, Ga Halle unsheathed her shido from her side—the antimatter waves rolling off her suit in greater force, matching her body's increased exertion—but she didn't bother igniting it. She wouldn't give the Barons the ease of a quick death. She sliced the shido across Kanta's fat belly, emptying his guts onto the floor. Paqlin gasped, and Ga Halle adored seeing her shocked expression just before slicing her to pieces. Such a life of untouchable privilege, of feeling that the galaxy owed you whatever you had, and you owed it nothing in return. Such a life to have stripped away in a matter of seconds.

"The Praxis people," Tirus stammered, "they won't stand for this. They'll revolt, they'll—"

In such a bothered state was Tirus that he fell out of his chair, interrupting his own silly desperation. He tried to crawl away, a futile effort.

Ga Halle kicked him onto his back; she wanted to be the final thing he saw before his disgusting life was taken away from him.

"The people," he muttered, over and over. "The people."

"The people are mine," Ga Halle said as she thrust her shido into Tirus's chest. "Praxis is mine. The galaxy is *mine*."

Tirus tried to speak, but nothing came from his mouth save the blood he was choking on. She dug her shido in deeper, and the force of her strike almost folded Tirus's decrepit body in on itself.

When Ga Halle turned, she found Chang holding a sentry

pistol on her; Chang's hands trembled as he tried to remove the safety so the weapon could fire.

"The safeties often jam in that model," Ga Halle coolly remarked. "A design flaw."

"You—you're insane!" Chang belched. "You're nothing without us, you—"

Ga Halle had heard all she needed to hear from the Barons. The memories of their empty words would last her a lifetime. Just as Chang flicked off the pistol's safety, Ga Halle spiraled her shido straight into Chang's face. The blades caught him in his eyes and forehead, and he dropped his pistol right before he joined it on the ground.

The deed, long fantasized about, was finally done. Ga Halle closed her eyes and exhaled, feeling a tremendous relief settle over her body.

"Would you like this mess attended to, my queen?"

Ga Halle looked at Ebik, who was dutifully awaiting orders. In a matter of moments, his entire life—the status and legacy he'd robbed and claimed as his own—had been stripped from him in a violent bloodbath. The Barons were no more. The life he knew was over. Still, he'd addressed Ga Halle as "my queen." Ebik was no fool, and that made him both important and dangerous. His ability to recalibrate his loyalties with such ease concerned Ga Halle, but not enough to forfeit what he could still offer.

"No," Ga Halle replied. "Summon our technicians and have them sever this tower from the rest of *Fortress.* Jettison it into space. I never want to see it again."

"And the families of the deceased? They'll surely make claim to assume their fallen's mantle and may even plot an uprising."

"Kill them and have the territorial governors take control until a new centralized government can be established."

"Consider it done, my queen."

"And one other thing," Ga Halle said, stopping Ebik at the door. "I'm holding you responsible for a peaceful transition of power on our home planet. Do not disappoint me."

Ebik nodded and entered the elevator that would take him back to *Fortress*.

Alone, standing among the massacre of her doing, Ga Halle allowed herself a brief smile. The Rokura would be hers. The galaxy would be hers.

Everything was in its right place.

CHAPTER SIXTEEN

What were you saying about fate doing us a favor?" Kira asked.

Kira pulled them out of the mass jump a good distance from Mithlador's orbit, and it was a good thing she did. Parked over the planet that had all the things they needed to restore peace and justice to the galaxy were the exact people who wanted to remove peace and justice from the galaxy. A Praxis blockade of two warships, a bunch of Intruders zipping around on patrol, and a drop ship were waiting there, ready to blow up anything that was stupid enough to get too close. Cade knew that you could count on Praxis to shoot first and ask questions, well, never. They didn't care who they blasted to bits. Their job was to follow orders, and 9.9 times out of 10, Praxis orders were to kill whatever got in the way. Based on the luck he was having lately, Cade wasn't feeling too optimistic about taking a chance to be that 0.1 that managed to slip through Praxis's grasp. But that's exactly what Kira was proposing they try to do—which, in a way, was cool. Cade was in no position to criticize anyone for being crazy, but if they were spotted, the *Rubicon* would be reduced to a ball of fire streaking across the sky without so much as a friendly warning. And that would suck.

"Look, Cade, we're not talking about something really complicated here," Kira said, leaning over the pilot's chair. She'd set the *Rubicon* to hold their position while they figured out what to do.

"Yeah, I get what you're saying. Set a trajectory for the surface, turn off the ship's functions so it's dark, and hope Praxis doesn't spot us as we free-fall to the ground. My problem is what happens if Praxis *does* spot us."

"I've charted a path that may work," 4-Qel said. Using the control panel, he'd brought up a three-dimensional rendering of Mithlador that included the Praxis blockade. "If we follow this trajectory here," he said, leading a model of the *Rubicon* to the surface with his finger, "and time it just right with the rotations of the Intruders, and assuming no other ship changes position, we should be able to make it past unseen."

"What are the odds of that?" Cade asked.

"I'm a drone that is programmed to kill, not calculate *odds*," 4-Qel chirped. "But I can tell you that, because of their helix design, the warships offer three-hundred-and-sixty-degree views of the area around the ship. Even if I could define odds, there's no calculating the chances of someone looking out of a window at, what would be for us, a most inopportune time."

"I'm just going to chime in just for a second, seeing that I'm currently on the ship that might be blown out of the sky," Mig said. "Personally, I'm not a fan of plans that operate in extremes. Like, say, success or death. And, actually, it's more like 'success, but maybe death later,' because if Praxis is in the air, they're definitely on the ground as well."

"He's right," Cade admitted. "Assuming we get past the blockade, we'll be coming into . . . what? For all we know, there could be a war going on between Praxis and the Mithladorians over control of the mining colony, and we might end up right in the middle of it."

Kira sighed. She shoved her chair into a spin, then threw up her hands, conceding doom. "Then what are we going to do? I told you this wasn't going to be easy, and now it's not easy and you guys want to go home."

"I do not wish to return to Eris," 4-Qel commented. "The royal family will have me killed if I do. Or . . . perhaps an opportunity would present itself for me to kill *them*. Hmmm."

Kira looked to Cade and Mig, searching their expressions to see if they were hearing the same thing she was—specifically, if they were also becoming unnerved by 4-Qel's violent streak.

"What's with this guy?" she asked.

"What?" Mig sharply defended. "He's programmed to be an efficient, ruthless killing machine. Just be glad he's on our side."

Kira turned her attention to 4-Qel, whose head was cocked to the side as he looked at her, much like her childhood pet woffy when he, too, couldn't interpret her words and their meaning.

"I don't mean that you want to go to your actual house," Kira slowly explained. "I'm saying that you—all three of you—want to give up."

"I will not give up," 4-Qel said as he stood up straight, which sprouted him a good foot taller than Kira. "I protect Mig wherever we are, and I'll do the same for his friends."

As the conversing continued behind him, Cade studied the three-dimensional model of Mithlador, as if looking at it harder would pop an idea in his mind. There wasn't much to the place, just the mining colony and dense forest surrounding it all. Mithlador was an isolated planet in the Galactic Fringe, and the Mithladorians were a primitive species best known for their ability to remain unknown. They didn't travel off-world, possessed no means of planet-to-planet communication, and kept no trade partners. As far as anyone knew, they didn't have anything to offer in trade anyway—although that assumption, Cade now knew, was a big fat error. Somehow, Praxis discovered this koruvite material, and they found out what it could do. In typical Praxis fashion, they came in, squashed any and all resistance, disrupted the planet's harmony by building a land-poisoning mining operation, stripped away what they wanted, then left the skeleton of their presence behind. Probably with strict instructions for the Mithladorians to not touch, or else.

Something about the forest struck Cade. Called to him, more like. Beyond the mining colony, north in the woodlands that looked exactly like every other inch of woodlands, there was . . . something. Cade was drawn to it, compelled to go there.

Compelled by the Rokura.

"Here," Cade said, pointing to the area that he was sure everyone would see as identical to every other forested area. "This is where we need to go."

4-Qel studied the area, then he looked at Cade, trying to glean some understanding from one of the two. When he failed to draw any conclusions, he repeated the motion. "Why do we need to go there?" he asked, sounding confused by his own confusion.

"Yeah, Cade," Kira said, her tone sardonically curious, "it's almost like you have special insight that drew you to this random patch of forest."

Cade shot Kira the dirtiest look he could muster. She smiled in returned.

"Oh, cute. You guys have an inside thing," Mig said. "You want to let us in on it, or should we just stand here like idiots?"

"It's the Rokura," Cade sighed. "It's telling me this is where we should go."

"Oh, cool," Mig said. "And I thought you were just making it up."

"Well, I, for one, find it interesting," 4-Qel said, and while Cade knew the drone couldn't be anything but genuine, he couldn't help but feel he was being condescended to. "The magical weapon communicates with you. If I may ask, why does it believe this is the place we should travel to?"

Cade shrugged. "Beats me. All I know is that when the Rokura feels like it, which isn't often, it kinda . . . helps me out. And right now, for whatever reason, it wants me to go there."

Mig held out his hand, letting everyone know he was going to talk, but he tripped over his words every time he tried to do so. His brain wasn't made to handle amorphous things like the Rokura; it functioned on quantifiable data, things he could predict, prove, and process.

"So, this thing . . . it *talks* to you?" Mig finally asked.

"More or less."

Mig stared at Cade and nodded, almost like he was understanding or, at least, accepting Cade's version of reality. But then he said, "Can we go over the first plan again?"

There wasn't much to discuss. Sneaking by the blockade and into an uncertain—and likely volatile—situation on the ground was an option for when they had no other options. Technically, Cade's play to follow the Rokura was an option. It wasn't a good one, but at least the odds of them getting killed, or captured and delivered to Ga Halle, weren't as great. Or, at least that's what Cade thought. On one hand, the Rokura had saved his life, so maybe it was on Cade's side. But on the other hand—well, Cade's other hand was fake, because the Rokura had incinerated his real one. So, there was that.

4-Qel set a course that brought the *Rubicon* around Mithlador on a low enough trajectory to keep them below Praxis's radar capabilities. As expected, when Kira brought the ship out of orbit and toward the surface, they caught nothing but an eyeful of trees on the surface below. Trees, trees, and more trees.

"Well?" Kira asked. "Should we take a page from your playbook and just smash into the surface?"

"Funny," Cade replied, though he really didn't find it that funny. There was a real possibility it might come down to that. He was hanging over the back of her chair, scanning the area for anything—a break in the trees, a sign of habitation, anything. But the land below, stretching all the way to the horizon line, was pretty much one giant tree.

"I may have something," 4-Qel said as he worked the *Rubicon*'s control panel. "Starboard side—the scanners read what appears to be a point where the terrain changes character. There is no telling what it is with this instrumentation alone. A visual is required."

Kira turned the stick to the right, following the scan's directions.

"I've mentioned how I think we're heading into a trap, right?" Kira asked. She kept the *Rubicon* moving ahead at a slow, steady clip, flying just above the tree line to avoid detection as much as that was possible. It didn't matter how good Kira, or any pilot, was; they were flying a giant, loud object through space, and anyone could easily notice it with their eyeballs alone.

"The opening is just ahead," 4-Qel announced. "Right up . . . there."

All eyes were glued on the terrain. As quickly as the area 4-Qel led them to revealed a break in the trees, it become clear that what was approaching below them wasn't an opening—it was the beginning of a chasm, a massive canyon that stretched so wide Cade couldn't even see where the trees regrouped on either side. It had to have been thousands of feet across. And there was no telling where it ended.

"What happened here?" Cade said, drawing closer to the front of the cockpit to get a clearer look.

Kira brought the *Rubicon* to a steady cruising speed and took them over land that was devoured by a graveyard of trees. Cade could hardly see the ground beneath the felled trees, all of them shattered and decimated. And they weren't chopped down, no. These things had been torn from the surface, and that required tremendous force; the roots were ripped from the ground, upsetting mounds of dirt at the same time. With the trees creating a blanket over the ground, the grass, blocked from its star's nurturing light, had withered and turned brown. Whatever caused this break in the trees left a path of mass destruction in its wake. Enormous and incomprehensible.

"Man, somebody knows how to cause some damage," Mig commented. "What could have done this?"

"I have no clue," Cade said. "And I'm a little worried about finding out."

Kira continued their trajectory until, in the distance, a long, oblong black shape came into view. Beyond it, the tree line resumed. They inched closer and closer, and the object continued to grow bigger and take definitive shape. Cade stepped forward, to the very front of the cockpit. He couldn't believe what he was seeing.

"That *can't* be," he said, though he knew it was.

"What?" Mig asked, curious like a little kid. "What is it?"

Cade turned to face his team. "It's a Praxis warship."

Cade stepped back to join everyone else, but he kept his eyes on the massive ship the entire time. Everyone's eyes, in fact, were glued ahead.

"Trap," Kira said as the *Rubicon* got close enough to encompass nearly the entirety of her ship's exterior. "Trap. Trap. Trap."

"No, look at that thing," Cade said, studying the warship. "It isn't parked. It's *downed*."

Though there was no billowing smoke or raging fire coming from the warship, Cade could see that serious damage had been inflicted. Gaping holes—most definitely from explosions, possibly from the inside out—riddled the exterior, at least as much of it as Cade could see. And yet, despite the physical evidence staring him in the face, Cade couldn't imagine how anyone could bring down a warship. It would take a large group of people—a large group of people with a death wish, that is—who would need to infiltrate the ship and execute a coordinated attack that pinpointed essential functions, including the engine. Which—and Cade was just guessing here—was probably heavily guarded. If someone would have told Cade that this is what he'd find on Mithlador, he would have laughed in their face; the idea of pulling off such an operation was inconceivable, but there the warship was, beaten, blown up, and smashed into the ground.

"That is amazing," Mig said, stealing the words right out of Cade's mouth.

Kira brought the *Rubicon* down near the warship's centrally located command deck. As the ship came to rest just a few feet from the warship, it seemed like a grain of sand set against an ocean. And just like an ocean's temperamental tide, the fury of the Praxis kingdom could swallow Cade and his band of misfits at any point. The physical presence of Praxis, on such a grand scale, reminded Cade of the enormity he was up against—a galaxy-spanning kingdom with limitless resources and a penchant for enforcing their will through the cruelest means possible. Still, despite the fear, despite the odds, someone had taken down this Praxis ship. When Cade departed the *Rubicon*, he was looking at the warship's underside, which had taken a beating during its crash landing. This, Cade started to think, was how a resistance was started.

"So," Kira said, breaking everyone's awed silence at the sight of the warship, "where we heading?"

Cade looked around. Besides the warship parked in front of them, and the improvised landing strip that led to it, they were still surrounded by nothing but forest. Where to head seemed almost like a banality, unless Kira had it in mind to—

"The Rokura led us here, to this warship. I'm assuming it only makes sense that we go in and explore. Right?" she asked.

"Ummm . . . what?" Mig said with a shiver in his voice.

"Oh, come on," Kira replied. "The ship's dead. It's done. I mean, what else are we going to do here?"

"Sure, sure, it's downed," Mig said. "But it could still be stocked with sentry drones ready to defend it. Or it could be rigged with security explosives. Or poison gas. There's any number of creative and horrifying ways going into that ship can kill us all."

As Mig and Kira argued, Cade drifted off to the warship's starboard side, to the line of trees that resumed the seemingly endless forest. He closed his eyes and drifted into a meditative state. The world around him became sharper, and through this clarity he could feel his surroundings. The Rokura had compelled him to the place, but it was more than that. Cade heard something. Whispers. Murmurs. It was like voices on the wind, just soft and muffled enough to be unintelligible. But they were there, and they were coming from the forest.

"*Cade.*"

He felt the pull of the Rokura again, identical to the experience he had on the *Rubicon*. It wanted Cade to show strength, to act with power. Sinister tidings, Cade sensed, laced the weapon's urgings, and he feared what he would become if he molded himself to the Rokura's designs. Although maybe that was already happening. Maybe the Rokura led him to this place to satisfy its own plans, not Cade's. Maybe Cade was its pawn, and whatever waited for him in the forest—the whispers that carried his name—was a test to see how far Cade would go.

"*Cade.*"

An alloy grasped Cade's shoulder, cold enough to feel through his shawl, and he leapt at the touch.

"What!" Cade barked.

"We've been calling you, Cade," 4-Qel replied as he slowly and cautiously removed his hand from Cade's shoulder. "You weren't responding."

"I—" Cade said, but he couldn't break his reverie, induced by the Rokura, enough to respond. Cade shook his head, breaking away shadows that were obscuring his mind, and drew his focus back to the here and now. "I didn't hear you, I was . . . thinking about something else."

Everyone stared at Cade, mixtures of expectancy and uneasy curiosity painted on their faces. They wanted to know either what was happening with Cade or what they should do next. Having no idea how to explain the former, Cade addressed the latter.

"We need to go into the forest, this way," Cade said, gesturing to the direction of the whispers. "There's something out there, and that's where the Rokura is leading us."

"Something like what?" Mig asked, sticking close to 4-Qel's side.

"I don't know, and I have no clue why this is where we're supposed to go. But the Rokura has led us this far, so I don't see how we have any choice other than to see this through to the end."

The group was silent. There was an obvious lack of enthusiasm about trudging into unknown woods—and with dusk settling on this sliver of the planet, no less. Cade feared that they'd overrule him, forcing him to pursue the Rokura's path on his own.

But then Kira reminded him of the pact they'd made on Kyysring: The lives they knew at the Well were over, and that meant no one got left behind.

"You heard him, Mig. Same goes for you, Four-Qel," Kira said, deploying her easy commander tone. "Enough wasting time. Let's get supplies from my ship and start moving."

Mig and 4-Qel, who probably never heard an order in their lives that they actually liked—especially Mig—got right in line and marched ahead of Kira's commands. Cade smiled as she trotted by, and she stopped in front of him and smiled back—right before she grabbed him by his shirt and pulled him close, knocking the goofy grin right off his face.

"I'm entertaining this journey for the time being, but you know what I came to this planet for," she said. "I'm not leaving without it."

Cade nodded. For once, he didn't have an argument. He knew what this meant for Kira and what she'd sacrificed to get this far. "I know. And we won't," Cade said. "I promise."

"Good," Kira said. Her smile returned as she smoothed out the swath of Cade's clothes that she'd wrinkled in her grasp. "Then we have no problem."

Cade watched Kira walk toward her ship, then he turned his attention toward the forest. He gazed into it, and he couldn't stop himself from anxiously wondering what in the galaxy the Rokura was getting him into.

Cade led Kira, Mig, and 4-Qel through the Mithlador forest, allowing his instincts, informed by the Rokura, to guide him. Fading dusk light fractured through the trees, and Cade was reminded of the rot and decay of Quarry. Here on Mithlador, the ground was alive, crowded with thick grass and plants more colorful and varied than Cade could have ever imagined. The forest's peace lulled him into tranquility, and for a moment, Cade felt like he was passing through Mithlador as if in a dream. He looked up and reveled at the vertiginous swirl of leaves cascading to the ground as a burst of wind passed through; he caught a tumbling leaf in his hand and studied its indigo blade and the golden veins that coursed all the way to its triangular tip. More wind swirled, and the leaf fluttered from his hand, slowly making its descent to the ground. Cade felt a sudden rush of sadness as he was struck by the impermanence of things; the emotional wave took him by surprise, and he had to fight back the invasive thoughts that were creeping into his mind, thoughts about his mom, thoughts about his dad, and thoughts, most particularly, about Tristan. They too had tumbled out of his grasp without notice or warning, and Cade made a silent vow committing himself to the safety of his friends. There was no risk he wouldn't take, no cost he wouldn't pay, to keep them safe.

As he walked, Cade sensed footsteps approaching behind him; he looked over his shoulder, and there was Mig, striding up to his side.

"Hey," Mig said as he and Cade walked shoulder to shoulder. Cade nodded his head in response.

"I just wanted to see, you know . . . how you're doing," Mig said after a brief silence. "I was wondering if you're hanging in there, considering."

"Well," Cade said, drawing a deep breath, "I generally feel overwhelmed with grief when I think about Tristan, or I'm overwhelmed with fear when I think about the Rokura. So, yeah. It's a real win-win for me right now."

"For what it's worth, I'm sorry, Cade," Mig said as he shoved his hands into his pockets and kicked a rock out of his path.

"The way I told you about what happened—that was a really cold way to do it," Cade said. "What happened to Tristan is just as tough on you as it is on me, and you should have been told more delicately. I messed up, and I'm sorry."

Mig shrugged it off but didn't say anything in response. Cade knew his friend, and his silence said everything that Mig couldn't articulate. He was hurt, but, like Cade, being emotionally candid wasn't his greatest strength. In fact, they were both stunted adolescents and would sooner toss themselves into a jaka-beast pit rather than discuss their feelings.

"Hey, did you ever know about the time Tristan stole your dad's dasher bike?" Mig asked.

Cade scoffed. "Tristan? *Stole* something? No, you never told me that, because it never happened."

"I swear," Mig said with a laugh, "it totally happened. I mean, it was at my urging, but he still did it."

"Where was I?"

"Gone, with your folks on one of their missions, and Tristan stayed behind because he was sick. While you guys were away, the Galactic Alliance stopped over on Kyysring because they were having some engine problems with their new Aquarius-class naval cruiser. I was, like, enamored with that ship. It had dual-accelerator thrusters and an acceleration gyroscope that—"

"Yeah, those gyroscopes are badass," Cade said with a sardonic grin.

"I'm into engineering, okay?" Mig said. "Anyway, I heard the ship was about to leave, and I *had* to see it take off, so I begged and begged Tristan to get me there. And even though he was sick, even though stealing something caused him physical pain, he did it. He took me to see that ship blast off, and I'll never forget it. To me, that's, like, quintessential Tristan."

"He'd do anything for the people he loved," Cade said, trying to stay as even as possible. "I mean, he'd do anything for just about anyone."

Mig nodded and exhaled sharply. "Look, everything I said and did earlier—that was wrong, and I don't know, I just wish I hadn't. . . ."

Cade patted his friend on the shoulder, relieving him of his agony.

"We're cool, man," Cade said. "We're cool."

"Geez," Kira said, closing in on them from behind. "Why don't you two write each other a poem and just get it over with."

"That is humorous," 4-Qel said, his tone implying he was surprised to have caught Kira's wit. "Writing poetry indicates you are sensitive, and sensitivity is often associated with weakness. Although . . ." 4-Qel paused, contemplating. "I already know you're weak humans, as I can crush either one of you in an instant."

"Thanks for the reminder, Four-Qel," Mig said as he, Kira, and 4-Qel fell back in line a few paces behind Cade.

"I suppose the remark wasn't as funny as I initially thought," 4-Qel said.

Apart once again, Cade's focus returned to his surroundings. As he pressed forward, he started to detect a shift in the atmosphere, though he struggled to decipher what it meant. The feeling grew stronger with each step he took until he stopped dead in his tracks. He grabbed the Rokura and held it close, compelled to guard it. Cade scanned the area around him; he didn't see or hear anything. But, still, he knew.

Someone was coming.

Cade moved carefully, tightening his grip on the Rokura. From behind, Mig started to say something, but Cade silenced him with a quick flash of his hand, signaling Mig to be quiet and stay where he was. Whoever was out there was drawing near, but Cade couldn't pinpoint where he was sensing a presence from. The trees were clustered everywhere, and that made it impossible to single out a strategic place for someone to lay and wait, and it also made it impossible for Cade to pinpoint an expedient path for a retreat, should it come to that. They were all stuck exactly where they were.

Still, Cade assumed he'd hear *something*—the rustle of leaves, a whisper on the wind. But the Mithlador forest proved to be as silent as the grave.

Until it wasn't.

First came the bone-smashing sound of a blunt object hammering Cade's back. Pain burst from the point of impact, shooting out from Cade's spine to every part of his body. Someone struck him with such force—and precision—that his body tumbled uncontrollably forward and, after a few clumsy steps, Cade fell facedown in a pile of dirt and leaves. Cade rolled off the ground, scooping the dirt out of his eyes as he went, and by the time he was back on his feet and ready to fight, there was no one around except for Kira, Mig, and 4-Qel. They'd drawn their weapons and were searching for Cade's attacker, but Cade knew that this moment was about him and the Rokura.

"No, don't do anything," Cade instructed. "Just holster your weapons and stay put unless I say so."

Rokura in hand, Cade stalked through the forest, trying to keep an eye on all possible angles. Each step was taken with uncertainty as he became acutely aware of every detail that surrounded him. The crunch of leaves beneath his feet; the scent of the flora pouring down from the trees; the feeling of thistles brushing against his pant legs. Everything was heightened, richer. Deeper. Cade tried to focus whatever it was that he was experiencing, but he felt overwhelmed instead. This was the Rokura at work, and Cade had no idea what it was doing to him, nor did he know where he was being led. The thought crossed his mind that whoever this former Paragon was, he had clearly gone to great lengths to keep hidden; for the first time, Cade considered the possibility that it was best that he stayed that way.

Cade heard a whistling sound coming from his left, racing

toward him. He turned, but only in time for his face to greet an incoming quarter staff. The staff careened off his nose, busting it; blood splattered all over Cade's face, and he dropped to one knee. He recovered immediately and pointed the Rokura forward as blood drained into his mouth and over his chin. He turned and saw a man retrieving the quarter staff that'd struck him in the face; it was lodged in a tree's trunk, though it easily came loose.

"You should be better than this," the man said, calmly and quietly. "Why aren't you?"

The man turned, and Cade got his first clear view of his attacker; he wore a silken black shirt—collared and fastened closed with elaborate pins instead of buttons—with loose-fitting pants that matched his top. His clothing was frayed and worn, like he hadn't changed it in some time. More important, he was young. Around Cade's age, which made him too young to be the former Paragon Cade sought. And that was just great. Cade had gone searching for one lunatic and found another.

"I have no idea what you're talking about," Cade said, spitting blood. "But if a fight is what you're looking for, then stop messing around and come face me."

"Challenge accepted," the man said, smiling. He removed a gray cloth from his waistband, stretched it over the bridge of his nose, then tied the two strands tight behind his head. The man blinded himself. "But let's at least try to make this fight fair."

"So, you're a crazy person," Cade said, feeling weirded out and a little uneasy.

"My name is Kobe Saja," Kobe said, walking toward Cade. "But don't worry about introductions; I already know you, Cade Sura. And I know that weapon in your hands. It does *not* belong to you."

Kobe's walk turned into a run just before he leapt into the

air—unusually high, Cade swore—and brought both of his quarter staffs toward Cade. Cade blocked them with the Rokura and tried to push Kobe back, but by the time he shifted his weight forward, Kobe had already dropped down and swept Cade's legs out from under him. Cade landed on his back, hard.

Luckily, Kobe didn't use this window to hit Cade again. He circled Cade, taunting him with his concealed glare, waiting for him to get to his feet. "You should be faster than this, *Rai.* More agile. What are you waiting for?"

Cade growled as he got back into position. He didn't like this Kobe Saja, whoever he was. He didn't like his blind-warrior shtick. And he especially didn't like getting his ass kicked. "You always talk this much?" Cade asked, gripping the Rokura tightly. It felt heavy in his hands, weighed down by his fear of what it might do at any moment. "Or are you being annoying just for me?"

Kobe came in for another attack, making short, rapid strikes with his staffs. Cade managed to deflect Kobe's blows, using both ends of the Rokura to fight off the rapid-fire assault. Kobe was nimble and fast, and every move he made was precise. How he managed any of this without the use of sight, Cade had no idea. For the moment, all he knew was that Kobe's hits were coming at him nonstop, and he had to move as fast as he could to barely defend himself. He hoped for an opening, a window in which he could push Kobe back, but he had the sinking suspicion that wasn't going to happen. Just once, Cade thought, it would be nice to fight someone who wasn't preternaturally skilled at kicking ass.

"Faster!" Kobe yelled. "Listen to yourself—you're winded! You're *weak!*"

"GGGRRRAAAHH!" Cade yelled and shoved the Rokura forward so it slammed against Kobe's quarter staffs. When he did so, Cade felt a surge of power, of strength, and he knew it wasn't just him feeling it; Kobe was knocked back about fifteen feet from where he had been standing.

"Better," Kobe said, leaping back to his feet. "But I shouldn't need to goad you. I shouldn't need to *push* you."

Cade shook his head, feeling the adrenaline of the moment still surging through him. "What are you talking about? Push me into *what*?"

Kobe scoffed, then he threw his quarter staffs to the ground. "Into having conviction," Kobe said as he drew a small sword from his back.

Guided by the Rokura, Cade rushed forward to meet Kobe, and they locked their weapons together. They exchanged blow after blow, each defending himself against what the other came at him with. Cade swung low, and Kobe leapt over the Rokura; Kobe plunged at Cade, and Cade dodged, elbowing Kobe in his nose as his momentum carried him forward. Blood poured from his nostrils, which made Cade smile because now they were even. But Kobe was back on the offensive before Cade could wipe the grin from his face.

"You lack discipline!" Kobe snarled as their weapons entangled, bringing them close. "It's no wonder you and your cowardly Masters have failed to keep the galaxy safe. It's no wonder you fail to master the weapon you hold in your hands!"

"Shut. Up!" Cade yelled just before they drove so hard into each other that they had no other choice but to push back.

Cade and Kobe circled one another, a tense dance that seemed to only fuel Kobe's rage. Cade, on the other hand, felt like he was fading; whatever surge he'd experienced—because of the Rokura, he was certain—was dwindling. And that meant trouble should Kobe attack again.

"People counted on you, Rai. Real people. You were supposed to protect them, not sit idle in your mystical castle as Praxis set the galaxy on fire. What is the Well *waiting* for?"

"We've saved systems," Cade argued. "We've prevented war from consuming the galaxy."

"Lies! You know the Well let Praxis do as they please," Kobe spat, wiping blood off his lips. "Ask any system Praxis has annexed; the war you've allegedly saved us from has been happening for years. People out there have lost everything. And you? You've lost *nothing.*"

"Don't you tell me what I've lost," Cade barked.

"What—your brother? I've lost my entirely family. My home. My *world.* Romu was thrown into darkness while you and all your other keepers of peace failed to muster the temerity to do what needed to be done to have your vaunted *peace.*"

Cade felt a sting deep within him, and it made him wince. He knew all about what happened to Romu, the rebellion that led to massacre that led to the killing of its star. It all happened in Cade's first year at the Well, back when he was just a student, just a kid. Still, Cade couldn't help but feel guilty. Because if Cade was just a kid when all this went down, then so was Kobe. And not just a kid—an orphaned refugee jettisoned from a dying planet to survive the wilds of the galaxy. All Cade's life, the Well had taught him that the tragedy on Romu could have been avoided through nonviolent resistance and peaceful negotiations. But it was all nonsense. It was just the Masters exonerating their own responsibility. Sure, the Well had their reasons for not getting involved, but none of them conveyed a sincere belief that protests and diplomacy would keep Praxis from storming the gates of Romu. The only truth that Cade could conclude was that the Well wasn't prepared for Praxis. Its leadership wasn't unified, and by the time the Masters truly grasped what they were up against, it was too late. They were overmatched. The Well could handle planetary squabbles and deliver aid; it could even protect systems that Praxis had only a fleeting interest in. But preventing genocide because a system had the misfortunate of being of strategic value to Praxis? For that, the Well would need a savior, and Cade now realized how monstrous it was for his home to have wasted so much time searching for the Paragon while countless lives slipped through its fingers. Cade would rather see the Well try and fail; he'd rather they all go down fighting.

Anything would be better than culpability through negligence.

"I—I'm sorry," Cade stammered. "I didn't know."

"I don't want your apology," Kobe said, holding his sword forward once again. "It's too late for that."

Kobe launched into a furious attack, and Cade knew he wouldn't be able to defend himself. Without the Rokura giving him additional strength and acumen, he was as good as Kobe's sparring dummy. Cade blocked and dodged as best he could, but it was only a matter of moments before Kobe landed a kick directly into Cade's solar plexus, and he followed it by slicing a chasm into Cade's bicep. Cade's body slumped under the pain, and Kobe wasted no time sending Cade to the ground; he punched his sword's hilt against the back of Cade's head, dropping Cade to all fours. Cade staggered to get to his feet, only to fall right back down again. Vertigo spun his head so hard he felt like the world might turn upside down at any moment. Maybe it already had.

Cade closed his eyes tight, and when he opened them, Kobe had the tip of his sword pointed at his face; with it, he lifted Cade's head by his chin, exposing his neck. Then, Kobe flicked his sword over to Cade's carotid artery. It would take hardly the effort of drawing a breath for Kobe to slice his blade across Cade's lifeline.

"Cade Sura, you are supposed to be better. You should be bett—"

A step behind Kobe, Kira pointed her sidewinder directly at Kobe's head.

"Do anything to him, and you die," she said. "Make a move, and you die. Clear?"

Cade felt the heat of the sword's steel pull away from his neck, which he took as a good sign. But then he heard Kobe start to laugh, which he took as a bad sign.

"Very heroic," he mirthfully said as he lowered the blindfold from his eyes. "Too bad I can have you and each one of your friends exterminated at a moment's notice.

Now it was Kira's turn to laugh. "Oh, yeah? You and what army?"

"*This one*," Kobe said, his satisfaction palpable.

Kira stopped laughing, and Cade stopped feeling good about their odds of getting off Mithlador alive.

Cade's vertigo diminished enough for him to look up and see the trouble that was coming from every direction. Stunned, Cade got to his feet as soldiers, dressed in green uniforms that camouflaged them with their surroundings and armed with TX-18 automatic blasters, walked out of the dense forest and created a circle around Cade, Kira, Mig, and 4-Qel. They kept moving forward, and the circle got tighter and tighter until the four of them were knit together in a tight cluster.

This couldn't happen; Cade wouldn't allow this to happen. He wanted to curse the Rokura and destroy it just out of spite. Why it had gone through such lengths to kill him was a mystery; if the weapon wanted him dead, it could have made it happen much sooner and saved Cade a lot of hassle. But that wasn't the point. The Rokura wanting him dead was one thing. Killing his friends too was something Cade wasn't about to abide.

"I say we blindly open fire at our enemies," 4-Qel said quietly. "There's dignity in taking at least a few of them with us."

"I still have an explosive in my pack," Mig said. "Cade, reach in there as fast as you can and activate it."

"We move on three," Kira ordered. "One—"

"Your beef isn't with my friends," Cade said, projecting his voice for everyone to hear as he took a step away from his group. He felt trigger fingers twitch all around him. "You have a problem with me, so take it up with me. Let my friends go."

"It's too late for sentimental gestures, Rai," Kobe said, pacing arrogantly just beyond Cade's reach. "Your fate is in our hands; it has been since the moment you landed on this planet."

"I may not have the conviction or whatever it is you expect, but I'll tell you this: You hurt these people, and I'll do whatever it takes to use this weapon to blast your soul into oblivion."

Kobe took a hostile step forward, positioning himself directly in Cade's face.

"I'd love to see you try," he said. "I'm waiting for it. We're all waiting for you to—"

"ENOUGH!" a voice yelled, echoing throughout the area.

Kobe froze. His gaze, hard and angry, remained fixed on Cade, even as the soldiers surrounding them lowered their blasters. Cade took a step back to rejoin his friends, and he could feel the rigidity in all of them. Well, just Kira and Mig; 4-Qel, even by a drone's standards, seemed perfectly at ease in this situation.

"What is happening?!" Mig yelled, nearly out of breath from the tension.

The soldiers in front of Cade stepped aside, revealing a clean view of a man just as he stepped out from a copse of trees. He was an older man with a graying beard and the beginnings of wrinkles around his eyes; a scar ran from his forehead down and over his left eye—which was milky white, with no pupil— and over his cheek. He wore the same black outfit as Kobe, with a pack slung across his chest and his sleeves elongated to conceal how much of his right arm was mechanical. Cade saw that his hand and wrist were prosthetics, but there was no telling where the robotic replacements ended.

As Cade met his eyes, the Rokura surged. He knew: This was the man he was looking for.

"You're him," Cade said. "You're the Paragon."

"My name is Percival White," he said in a gruff voice. "And I don't really talk about all that Chosen One business anymore, though I suppose we're going to have to."

"Maybe we can have a nice chat over some tea *after* you order your men to stand down," Kira interjected.

Percival laughed, a casual, even friendly chuckle. Like threatening to kill a bunch of strangers was nothing for anyone to get worked up about. "Sure thing," he said, and the soldiers surrounding Cade, Kira, Mig, and 4-Qel went at ease.

"Don't get mad about what just happened," Percival said. "Consider it a test, nothing more, nothing less. Now come, we have much to discuss and not a lot of time to do it."

Cade felt his friends start to budge, but he held out his arms to hold them back. He didn't like being messed with; he didn't like not knowing who these people were, and he wasn't about to start following anyone who, just a minute ago, was primed to kill him—even if it was just a "test."

"No," Cade refused. "We're not going anywhere with you until you do some talking. Namely, who are all you people? What are you *doing* here?"

Percival sighed. "I suppose Valis wouldn't tell you and risk you not making the journey to come find me. This isn't easy to explain, Cade, so I hope you can keep an open mind. I'm sure you've already begun to learn that this galaxy is far more complex than the Masters led you to believe."

Cade looked around. The soldiers. The weapons. The secrecy. The downed warship. His heart sank as he knew exactly what Percival was going to say just before he said it.

"We are the Rising Suns."

CHAPTER SEVENTEEN

I like the way this woman thinks."

They had gathered in a small enclave that, like many parts of the forest, had a natural canopy that concealed everything happening on the ground from any prying eyes looking down from above. Like a Praxis patrol. It was perfect for covering the Rising Sun encampment that was hidden away there. Percival had asked what they expected to achieve on Mithlador—why they had bothered coming, in so many words. Before Cade could give Percival the most obvious answer—to deliver him the Rokura and have saving the galaxy be *his* problem—Kira jumped in and divulged her plans to make a bomb that would annihilate the Praxis *War Hammer*. Cade couldn't blame her for seizing the opportunity: Here Kira was, on the planet that held the missing piece to her prized weapon, talking to someone who had no equal when it came to blowing up all things Praxis. Cade could tell Kira was a little awestruck by Percival, and it bothered him. A lot of things about Percival bothered Cade, like the fact that he was the leader of the Rising Suns, which he wasn't totally okay with given his knowledge of their morally dubious—to say the least—warfare tactics. Or that his method of testing Cade was through a fight that, at the time, he thought was to the death. Or the way Kira was all smitten with him and his gang of freedom fighters. Cade tried to convince himself that he didn't like the idea of her idolizing a terrorist, but that wasn't it. Even with his misgivings about Percival, he thought "terrorist" was a little too extreme of a label. The difference between a freedom fighter and a terrorist all came down to which side you were on, and the more Cade thought about it, he figured he was closer to Percival's side of active resistance than he was the Well's side of theoretical resistance. Still, Kira's interest in him bugged him, and he was distracted from the conversation at hand until it dawned on him: He was jealous. And rather than explore why he felt that way, Cade quickly shifted his focus back to the matter at hand. He'd sooner debate the destruction of the galaxy's evil superpower than talk about whatever burgeoning feelings he harbored for his partner in rebellion.

"Sorry, but I'm going to interrupt you guys, because I have to know," Mig said. "Did you take down that warship? Was that you guys?"

"It was us, yes," Percival said.

"Daaaaamn. How?" Mig asked, impressed.

Percival smiled. "Very carefully."

Kira cleared her throat. "Getting back to the matter at hand: We need that koruvite, and we would already have it if it wasn't for the Praxis blockade. How do we get around that?"

"That's a real problem," Percival agreed. "And it's no better on the surface. Praxis has occupied the entire colony, and they're forcing the Mithladorians into long, brutal work shifts in order to mine koruvite as fast as possible. Based on the intel I've gathered, I take it they're building more *War Hammers*. That's why we're here: We're going to stop them."

Everyone sunk down a bit as the gravity of Percival's words took hold. The galaxy was teetering on its last leg, and Praxis was just waiting to kick it out from underneath.

"Once they destroy the Well, there'll be no more need for Praxis to even mask what they're after—complete domination," Kira asked.

"Which is why," Cade said, injecting himself into the conversation, "which is why we need you."

Cade stood in front of Percival, holding out the Rokura for him to take. "You're a Paragon; this is your weapon. I think it's about time you two joined and did what you're supposed to do."

Percival looked at the Rokura, and an expression of pain crept over his face. He sighed, then looked Cade straight in the eyes and said, "I can't."

"Why. Not?" Cade asked, agitated.

"Because it's not my time anymore. I'm not the same person I was when I had the Rokura. If I tried to use it now, it would kill me."

Cade pushed the Rokura into Percival's chest. "Try me." He felt the eyes of everyone near on him. Everyone waited with nervous anticipation—like Cade—wanting to know how this tension would diffuse: with Percival accepting the Rokura, or with Percival cracking Cade's head open. Because as Cade looked into Percival's eyes and identified the intense fury that he was trying to contain, he figured this could end in either direction.

"Look, Cade," Kira said, "I don't think—"

"You don't think what?" Cade snapped as he turned to face Kira. "You heard what he said, Praxis is building more *War Hammers*. So, what's the plan now? Maybe, *maybe* your idea works and we blow up one *War Hammer*. But two *War Hammers*? Eight? It's not going to happen. You guys can run around and play freedom fighters all you want, but you're never going to beat Praxis. We need *more*.

"Listen, I'm not saying the Rokura is the solution to all our problems," Cade continued. "If what we're doing here is the start of a serious fight against Praxis, you're essential to its future, Kira. So is your plan. So are the Rising Suns. What I'm saying is that even with us combined, and with whoever we can still recruit, it won't be enough."

Cade looked around at everyone surrounding him, this group of outsiders, criminals, and nobodies that truly had no business being together. But here they were, and they were all each other had.

"We need something that inspires people from one end of this galaxy to the next to raise arms and join the fight against Praxis. We need the Paragon, and the Paragon needs us."

"But Percival said he can't get the Rokura to work, and neither can you," Mig said. "It's not like we can just manufacture a Paragon."

Cade looked at Percival; Kobe was at his side, whispering into his ear. Percival nodded, whispered something to Kobe, then set his sights on Cade.

"I like you, Cade. I didn't think I would, but I do."

"I don't remember saying I cared," Cade said.

"Let's have a little chat, just me and you. There's a way for all of us to get what we want, but there's a lot of things you need to learn for that to happen."

Percival gestured with his mechanical hand, beckoning Cade to follow. Cade looked back at his friends, who shrugged noncommittally. They weren't sold on Percival's intentions, either.

"Come with me, Cade. I want to show you something."

It was a short, silent walk to an elevated ridge that looked over a narrow canyon that veined the terrain. The tree coverage thinned out, but the canyon was so slender that any overhead Intruder patrol wouldn't be able to discern the finer details. Such as a couple of dasher bikes vertically parked along the canyon's wall. Cade was looking straight down at them, though he was cautious not to get too close to the ridge's edge with Percival behind him; he didn't *think* Percival took him all the way out here just to throw him over the side, but he'd rather be safe than dead.

"So," Cade said, not wanting to waste any more time, "what've you got?"

Percival smiled in a way that Cade was already getting sick of. It was a patronizing grin that pitied Cade for how little he knew in comparison to Percival's unending wisdom.

"In time," Percival said. "In time. First, I have a question for you: I want to know what you see when you look at me. Who am *I* to *you*?"

Cade's knee-jerk response was to call Percival a terrorist and be done with it. But something stopped him. He stared at Percival, studying him. His scar, his mechanical arm, the weariness in his eyes. He saw someone who was battle-worn, who had seen—and done—things that he wished he hadn't. He saw a man who was conflicted but certain. He wasn't proud of the things he'd done, but he harbored no doubts about their necessity. If someone had to do the work of fighting a dirty fight against an even dirtier enemy, he was glad it was his burden to shoulder rather than anyone else's.

"A few days ago, I would have taken one look at you and called you a terrorist," Cade began. "But the galaxy isn't nearly as simple as I used to think it was. The Well knows what Praxis has done, they know the atrocities and the deaths and who knows what else. But they've been complacent. I don't know why, but it's the truth. You also recognize Praxis for what it is, but you're doing something about it. You and everyone who follows you are risking their lives to remind the galaxy that no matter how the Well and other powerful systems try to rationalize Praxis's rule, they are evil. And all of us need to fight back

"Still, I could never do what you do. If half of what I've heard is true about your bombings and attacks against Praxis, and how civilians have died, I would never last in your ranks. I wouldn't. There has to be another way. I have to believe that, if only for my own good."

Percival clasped Cade's shoulder with his mechanical hand and smiled. "Cade, do you know the one common story coursing through all of sentient life's history?"

"No. But I'm assuming you do and you're going to tell me."

Percival scowled and released his grip on Cade. "It's a struggle for power. That's all. Children grow up, throwing temper tantrums and fighting against their parents' boundaries. They want to be the ones in control. Through adolescence and into adulthood, until the roles are reversed, the fight for power is ingrained in how we behave.

"The scale only gets bigger, of course. Between tribes, between planets and spouses and siblings, we all want to exert our will and have the power to do what we want and protect what we love in the way we see fit, the cost be damned. That's all our history is, an endless fight for power, or against power, cycling from one generation to the next. Nothing defines sentient life more than that."

Cade looked to the sky; a flock of birds burst out of a tree, and he could see them in silhouette against the sliver of the waxing moon. As they fluttered away, Cade tried to think of a polite way to call Percival on his big, empty words.

"I don't believe any of that. In fact, I don't think you do, either. If you did, then everything you did with the Rising Suns, everything you *are*, would be completely pointless."

Percival smiled. "Good answer, and you're right. Those aren't my words but the words of a friend from a long, long time ago," he said. "And your reaction sounds like the answer I gave to her. Which means what I suspected is true: You're right for what comes next."

"Oh, yeah? And what's that?" Cade asked.

Percival reached over his back, and from his pack he pulled out a shido. Cade studied it, trying to notice something unusual about it, but judging by what he saw, it was just an ordinary shido. Aged, and definitely used, but still a shido.

"Okay?" Cade said. "It's a shido."

"It's not the shido itself that's important," Percival said. "It's who it belonged to."

Cade looked at Percival, whose face had taken on an unexpected gravitas. Unease began to course within Cade. "Who did it belong to?" he quietly asked.

"To my old friend: Ga Halle."

Cade recoiled. If his life had been turned upside down in the past few days, then this, this was the equivalent of taking everything he thought was true—what the Well was good for, why they existed, and his role within it—and shredding it right in front of his face.

"No," Cade said. "That's not true. That can't be."

"Ga Halle was a Rai, like you. Like me. She was a great one, in fact, and she was . . . she was my friend. But then everything between us, everything at the Well, everything in the entire galaxy went terribly, terribly bad."

"You're lying," Cade spat. "How could no one know this? The Masters couldn't keep something this huge a secret for this long."

"Things change," Percival stated. "This was nearly two decades ago, and all the other Rai have either died in duty, are sworn to secrecy as Masters, or—well, I take it you've encountered Ga Halle's Fatebreakers, right? Former Rai, all of them."

Any disbelief that Cade harbored withered like a plant under a flame. He couldn't think of a word to say. Everything he knew, everything he'd been taught to cherish and hold dear was only a meticulous selection of the truth. Because, in reality, the Well had birthed Ga Halle and her kingdom of totalitarian lust; the Well had trained the man who murdered his brother.

"Cade, you know the Well as this place that contains Echoes and ground troops and armories and all that. But that's not how it always was. In my time, those things barely existed, and the Masters only embraced the aspect of the Well in response to Praxis—and begrudgingly at that. And still, by then, it was too late. Those pompous fools wasted decade after decade waiting for a savior to come, and they lost sight of what it meant to actually protect the galaxy. Praxis knew that; Ga Halle *knew* that."

"Okay . . . okay. Let's just slow down a little. I still can't understand the *how* in all this. How did Ga Halle go from a being one of us to ruling the Praxis kingdom?"

Percival scoffed. "Ga Halle doesn't rule the kingdom, she *created* the kingdom. You have to understand, everything you're caught up in now was set in motion years ago, back when becoming a galactic superpower was the last thing anyone expected of Praxis.

"Praxis was dying; their sun was fading from existence, and it was only a matter of time before the planet became unlivable. And when that happened, Cade . . . no amount of relief, or rescue transports, or whatever would save the millions of people sentenced to death on their home planet. Praxis was in disarray, and many of its people didn't have the means to find a new planet to live on—assuming any planet could handle the influx of so many refugees.

"No one knew what to do, no one knew how to save Praxis. But Ga Halle, she had a will unlike any other person I've ever known. She didn't care how she'd save an entire planet; all she knew was she was going to do it. And that was enough."

Cade listened intently, his mind racing as he tried to glue the pieces of Percival's story together. All the while, he couldn't stop playing and replaying what the Fatebreaker had told him back in the spire: The Masters weren't being honest with their Rai. Things were being hidden, and Cade had the sinking feeling that Percival's story was just the tip of the iceberg.

"So, when did Ga Halle freak out, then? You guys were Rai, you were buddies, but now one's a warlord and the other's a terr—a freedom fighter. What happened?"

Percival paused and silently studied Ga Halle's shido. For the first time, he seemed vulnerable. Gone was the battle-hardened fighter who claimed to have all the answers and was ready to lay down his life to prove it. In his place was a man whose past was scarred by regret and bitterness, wounds that refused to heal. Ga Halle was his sworn enemy, and Percival had gone to extreme lengths to stop her. And now, now it was starting to make sense why.

"The Well sends Rai to the Quarrian spire in pairs, you know that. I was sent with Ga Halle. We journeyed to retrieve the Rokura together. Back then, meaning before the lights were turned off over Quarry, Rai made this pilgrimage regularly. It was like a rite of passage. But our trip was . . . different. We both knew it. I don't know how many times the Masters told us we were special, that one of us was destined to become the Paragon. I remember so clearly how they all came to watch our ship depart for Quarry, just waiting for a savior to return. But that, as you know, is *not* what happened.

"We reached the Rokura's chamber, and it was . . . mystical. Transcendent. You were there, you know—it's impossible to put everything you experience and feel into words. Ga Halle and I even joked about being the 'Chosen One' because it was just so surreal. I mean, we were still young. The entire walk up the spire, we goaded each other about who would go first or if we'd go at the same time and become the Paragon together. In the end, she insisted it was me to go first. I thought it was a sentimental gesture; now, I realize it's because she never believed I could do it. But she was wrong.

"As vividly as I remember grabbing the Rokura and pulling it out of its stasis, I just as vividly remember the look on Ga Halle's face when I turned to show her. I've never seen anything like it, not before, not since. She had this mask of pure hatred and rage, and I knew she was going to kill me.

"You have to understand, I wanted the Rokura because I had a juvenile notion in my head about maintaining peace across planets. The galaxy had its problems—skirmishes, planetary feuds, a lot of unrest with the ruling order, though nothing like it is now. But Ga Halle, she *needed* the Rokura. In her mind, it was the only way to somehow save her planet. The Rokura is supposed to return when worlds need saving, right? Well, no planet was more desperate than Praxis. The Rokura was her only hope, and I'd just taken it from her and trashed her self-worth in the process. No outsider would be able to bring peace to Praxis, and she knew she was now an afterthought to a living and breathing Paragon—but only if I was living and breathing.

"She unsheathed her shido and charged at me. Crazy. Frenzied. I was still dumbstruck by what'd happened, and Ga Halle was too fast, too strong, too angry. She stabbed me once in my gut, sliced my face, then cut my ankle and shoved me to the ground. And as she stood above me, ready to make her killing strike and take the Rokura for herself, she didn't say a single word. No apology, no good-bye. She was ready to end my life, and it was *nothing* to her.

"But the Rokura wouldn't let that happen. Before either of us could do anything, it let out this . . . this fiery discharge that tore through Ga Halle's arm; it sliced across her chest and throat and should have killed her. Cade, I've seen plenty of battles and bloodshed since then, but I still have nightmares about what happened in that spire. Seeing Ga Halle's flesh disintegrate and knowing that the Rokura did it *on its own* sickened me. In that moment, I saw a flash of all the things I'd be called on to do as Paragon, how this . . . this thing, this weapon would shape the entire galaxy. I was terrified, and I wanted no part of it. I did the only sensible thing I could think of: I slammed it back in its stasis, and I ran as far away as I could so no one could find me. So no one could make me touch the Rokura ever again.

"I went into exile, and Ga Halle survived—somehow—and returned to Praxis. In a dark corner of the galaxy, she somehow discovered a way to save her star—by taking the energy from a different one. The fact that these stars provided life to other systems must have been no more than an unfortunate side note to Ga Halle. She had lost her mind. And once she decided to doom another planet to save her own, there was no going back. Not for her, not for Praxis. Praxis went from being a planet on the brink of extinction to a source of galactic terror, and Ga Halle used that to build her might. She made allies with planets who'd grown restless with the galactic order—most of whom she betrayed and subjugated in time—and destroyed others who stood in her way.

"The Praxis kingdom was born out of the very weapon that was supposed to save us. But I'm sure you know by now that the Rokura is not what it's promised to be."

Cade looked at the weapon in his hands; he swore he had holstered it, but there it was, crowding his vision when he looked down. "No. It's not," he said, quietly.

Percival crept toward him. Cade felt him drawing near, to both him and the Rokura. "I knew your brother died the moment it happened; I felt the Rokura call out to me, beckoning me to possess it. Because that's what it wants—to be *possessed*. You've felt it, haven't you?" Percival asked, though his words sounded far away. Cade could hear his own heart beating in his ears; he could see the world around him—the branches on the trees, the leaves swirling on the ground—all move in slow motion.

"I have felt it," Cade answered. "It wants me to do more, to *be* more. But . . . I don't understand."

"I've traveled all over this galaxy, and I've learned a lot about the Rokura. The one thing I know for certain is that it craves power," Percival said. "It gives power, but it also demands it. And now that it's free of its holding, it'll find what it's looking for. You have a chance to become what it needs, and you must. You must become the Paragon."

Cade felt claustrophobic, in a trance, and his instinct, through the Rokura's fugue, was to shove the weapon back in its holstering. But when he tried to pull it back, he realized Percival's hands were on it as well. Holding it tight. Cade gave the Rokura a gentle tug, hoping that it would urge Percival to let go. It didn't.

"Percival, let go," Cade said, "Now."

Percival's eyes were fixed on the Rokura. Cade was coming out of the spell, but he had the feeling Percival was heading deeper in. "We could stop this war," Percival said, his words dripping with desire. "We could end Ga Halle like we should have so many years ago. We could—"

"Percival," Cade said, pulling hard on the Rokura. *"Percival!"*

With a labored breath, Percival snapped back into focus. He released the Rokura and staggered backward, covering his mouth as he went. He pointed at the Rokura, waving it off, and Cade got the feeling that, while Percival saw value in the Rokura's power—power that could change the course of the galaxy—he feared it as well.

"I'm sorry, Cade. I am. But you have no choice. I—I can't trust myself with it. And if you don't possess it soon, it'll find its way to Ga Halle. She's been preparing for this her entire life. She's *ready.* But I can get you there as well, Cade. I can train you, just like I trained Kobe. Only you'll succeed where he failed. Where

I failed. You have the Rokura; you've heard its call. Now I'll finish what's been started. I'll make you the Paragon."

Cade looked at the Rokura, this thing that was supposed to be the key to ushering in an era of peace to the galaxy. But that was seeming less and less likely all the time, and Cade never felt more despair in his life as he realized everything around him—both sides in this galactic conflict—was broken. Praxis, the Well, the Rising Suns—not a single one of them delivered what they promised, clinging instead to their warped ideas of peace and how it's achieved. And now, Cade was thrust in the middle of it all; he had been given a life sentence without committing a crime, and there was nothing for him to do but accept it.

"I don't want it," he mumbled. "I don't . . ."

Percival stood at Cade's side and patted his back. "I'm sorry, Cade. But you don't have a say in the matter. Praxis has become too strong, and the Well is poisoned. This *must* happen."

Cade looked up. "What?" he asked, and before he even had time to react, he was surrounded by a half dozen of Percival's soldiers. They all had their blasters trained on Cade.

"Come on, you can't be serious," Cade said.

Percival backed away from Cade, and with Kobe by his side, they joined the soldiers.

"We're not on this planet without reason, Cade. As we've been hiding in this forest, we've always been feeding explosives to the Mithladorians in the mines. Right before you and I came out here, Kobe informed me that at the next shift rotation, the explosions would go live. Which means we have exactly forty minutes to evacuate this planet. You and your friends are coming with us."

"Evacuate the planet?" Cade asked. "We're miles from the mines. Why would we have to leave the planet entirely?"

Percival sighed. "It's no use to just ruin the mining operation. We have to destroy what Praxis is after as well. We have to obliterate all the koruvite.

"The explosives—they're nucletoid bombs."

A chill ran up Cade's spine. He backed away from the encroaching squad, nearing the edge of the ridge.

"You're out of your mind. You're going to kill the entire planet. The Mithladorians, they—"

"—knew exactly what they were getting into, and we're in the process of evacuating as many as we can. This is war, Cade. We're doing what we have to do, and you'd better get used to it. Praxis can't be allowed to build more *War Hammers*, it's as simple as that."

Cade grimaced and shook his head, disgusted by what he was hearing. He thought of Quarry and its barren, bleak landscape. He looked around Mithlador, at the trees, plants, and life that surrounded him. He couldn't bear to imagine what it would look like in the very near future, when all of it was dead. "You're destroying a planet to get what you want. That remind you of someone?"

Percival began to stomp toward him, then stopped himself. "Don't you *dare* say that to me. Do you know what I've given in this fight? Do you know what I've sacrificed of myself? You Rai—you think you have all the answers without asking a single question."

"Where are my friends?" Cade yelled. "I'm not going anywhere until I know they're safe."

"Your friends are fine; they're back at the camp waiting for you," Percival said, sliding back into an amiable tone. "I'm not a bad person, Cade. And I agree with you—we do need the Paragon. But under my terms. Now come off that ridge and follow us back. Your friends don't even have to know about our arrangement. They follow you, and you follow me."

Cade took a step back, bringing him right to the very last inch of the ridge's real estate. He looked down and smiled. "We would have been better together, Percival, but you blew it. Because I'm not following you anywhere."

The realization of what Cade was about to do washed over Percival's face. "Cade, no—!" he said, but it was too late.

"See ya, Percy," Cade said, right before he took one final step back and dropped off the edge of the cliff. He heard Percival yell his name, shock filling his voice. That same shock was also on his face when Cade shot over the ridge on the dasher bike. He flew right over Percival's head and landed on the ground with a crash. Even though they were meant to be land-cruising vehicles, dasher bikes had enough propulsion to allow for short bursts of flight—Cade had pushed this one to its max, propelling it over Percival and his men. He turned and winked at Percival before speeding off.

"Whoa, sweet ride," Mig said when Cade pulled up alongside him. The encampment was all but emptied out, save a few soldiers who, Cade assumed, were waiting around for Percival to return. Percival's numbers were thankfully thinned out due to the evacuation process.

"Where's Percival?" Kira asked.

"Um, probably a few clicks behind me, running his ass off to get here and catch me," Cade said.

Kira groaned unhappily. "What did you do, Cade?"

"Look, I have no time to explain everything that happened. What you need to know is that Percival is going to wipe out this half of planet with nucletoid bombs that he's had placed all over the mines."

"Those are quite bad," 4-Qel said. "I strongly urge we leave before we're incinerated."

"Yup, seconded," Mig said, clasping his hands together. "Let's go."

"Okay, yes, we could leave. Or—"

"Or we stay here and die?" Mig asked, confused.

"The bombs aren't set to blow for thirty-seven more minutes. That gives us thirty-seven minutes to steal Praxis's most precious commodity right from under their noses. Which would pretty much make this the biggest heist in the galaxy."

Kira, Mig, and 4-Qel looked at Cade, their faces blank, then they looked at each other. None of them said a word.

"Clock's ticking, guys," Cade said.

"We won't get another chance to snag any koruvite, I can tell you that much," Mig said. "And I'm all for messing Praxis up in the worst way possible."

4-Qel shrugged. "It could be fun."

Cade looked at Kira. "We're a team. It's all or none. What do you say?"

Kira smiled and hopped onto the dasher bike's passenger seat. "Let's do this."

Mig and 4-Qel took the two seats in the back of the dasher bike, and Cade hit the ignition. The bike's engine, which gave it its powerful thrust and hovering capacity, burst to life, and they were ready to take off.

"Thirty-six minutes," Cade said. "Let's make it a point to really, *really* keep track of the time."

CHAPTER EIGHTEEN

The mining colony was engulfed by chaos. Cade pulled the dasher bike just short of a firefight between Percival's infantry and Praxis gunners, all protected by their AI armor. The armor, though, wasn't much of an issue for the infantry's objective, Cade recognized. Half the squad was laying down cover fire, keeping the gunners in a defensive position behind the cover of steel support beams that were fused to the ground throughout the colony. The other half of the squad was rushing Mithladorians away from the action and to a transport shuttle that Cade could just barely see sticking up from behind a latticework of aboveground pipes that divided one side of the colony from the other. At least Percival was true to his word, Cade begrudgingly admitted. But he was still a jerk.

Night had consumed Mithlador, though light coming from the many bulbs that dotted the colony's landscape provided enough illumination to keep the operation running under normal conditions. But these weren't normal conditions, and the fires that roared across much of the colony added a hazy orange tint to the sky just above Cade's head. It was a nice bit of justice, Cade concluded, that the lights Praxis used to push the Mithladorian miners into grueling working hours were now helping to guide an insurrection. If this set off Praxis's fury, Cade could only imagine how livid the kingdom would be when he and his friends used a dose of koruvite to give it a taste of its own medicine.

On the three-minute ride to the colony, 4-Qel briefed everyone as well as he could on its layout. Thankfully, he'd done his homework and studied the planet way more thoroughly than anyone else. Though, to be fair, he was the only one who had the capacity to memorize detailed schematics.

The colony was a massive metropolis that, when pitted against its surrounding landscape, looked like it had been dropped onto the planet's surface rather than slowly assembled over time. Giant towers spiked into the ground, plunging enormous drills down into the surface in order to excavate as much koruvite as possible without the use of manual labor. Smokestacks belched some of the unusable by-product of the operation into the night air, while fiery eruptions, coming from slender towers, burned off the rest. Through it all, mining drones—shielded flying orbs with a single ocular lens dug into their centers—zipped around overhead, servicing the entire operation.

At ground level, the place was a labyrinth of pipes, catwalks connecting one tower to another, and steel doors covering tunnels that led down into the mines. Just the idea of following one of those tunnels, however far it led into an oppressive, deep down dark, terrified Cade. If he didn't fully understand why the Mithladorians were so eager to level the entire operation to the ground, he did now. Praxis built this monstrous colony on their planet and then forced them to work to death. In their desperation, mass destruction would probably seem like the only option they had left.

"Okay," Cade said, leading Kira, Mig, and 4-Qel to cover behind a tower's base. "Where to?"

4-Qel craned his head around the tower to scan the area. "Judging by the blueprints I saw, we need to go . . . there."

Cade joined 4-Qel, poking out his head to see where the drone was pointing.

A giant silo, smack dab in the middle of the colony.

"Couldn't be on the outskirts, could it?" Cade grumbled. He turned back to the rest. "So, we're going to have to make it through some evacuation skirmishes between us and the koruvite storage. We'll leave the bike here because if it gets wrecked, we have no way back to the *Rubicon*, which means we all die.

"Everyone ready to run and fight?"

Nods all around; sidewinders drawn.

"Thirty-one minutes. Nobody stops unless they absolutely have to. And we stick *together*."

With Cade at the lead, they charged out from the tower's base, ready for anything. And it was good that they were, because as soon as they turned around a series of pipes, they caught up to a gunner patrol chasing a group of Mithladorians—furry little blue creatures with trunks that dangled off their faces—who were racing toward one of Percival's escape ships. Realizing they were about to be gunned down—and in the back, no less—the Mithladorians turned to surrender. But Cade knew better; Praxis wasn't in the business of taking prisoners.

Cade charged the gunners. He was less than ten yards away when he ignited his shido and launched it like it was a javelin. Either he was getting better or getting lucky because he hit the bull's-eye, striking the lead gunner in her back. Before she could even hit the ground, her four-person squad turned, their E-9s hot.

"Down!" Cade heard behind him, and he ducked just in time for Mig to fire off a shot from his custom third barrel. The blast hit the closest gunner directly in his chest, and it sent his suit into electrified paralysis. He made a weird gurgling noise before his limbs went limp and he collapsed to the ground.

"And you said we'd never need my paralysis ammo!" Mig yelled toward 4-Qel. Cade turned and saw 4-Qel with a gunner held over his shoulder.

"I said I prefer to maim, not disable," 4-Qel said as he launched the gunner into the air, sending him soaring headfirst into the middle of a tower. Cade winced at the sound of a good many of the gunner's bones crunching on impact.

Noticing a gunner running straight at him, Cade rolled beneath his electroaxe's swipe and landed next to his shido. He yanked it from the downed gunner's back and, seeing Kira running at his side, tossed her the weapon. She grabbed it in full stride and batted the gunner in his chest, doubling him over and leaving the back of his head exposed for a final blow. Kira obliged the opportunity.

"I can get used to this thing," Kira said as she handed Cade his weapon.

"Well, don't," Cade replied. "Twenty-eight minutes, so—"

"You saved us," a voice said from behind. Cade turned to find that the Mithladorians who'd been fleeing the gunners were still hanging around. "We owe you a debt of—"

"Yeah, yeah, yeah," Cade said. "Pay us later. Right now, you have to escape and we have to—"

The Mithladorian raised the cobalt trunk that extended out from the middle of his head and pointed it at Cade.

"Shake. Bond."

Cade sighed and grabbed the squishy trunk. "Yes, okay, bond. Now beat it."

The Mithladorians darted to the nearest transport ship while Cade and his team raced toward the silo. They covered a good amount of ground without interruption, and they were nearly to the silo when they turned a corner and encountered trouble. Big trouble.

Between them and the stairway leading up to the silo's entrance was a scene that Cade couldn't quite accurately call a skirmish; it was a straight-up battle.

Praxis gunners and Rising Sun infantry blanketed the area with blaster fire, relentless and inescapable. Each side was at least twenty soldiers deep, and as far as Cade could tell, this fight wasn't ending anytime soon. Both sides were entrenched in their positions, trapped there, in fact. Even if one side wanted to fall back, they'd be immediately mowed down by their enemy. And even if Cade bothered to intervene, toppling a force of this size would chew up way more time than they had to spare.

"4-Qel, tell me there's a way around this," Cade commanded. "A tunnel under?"

4-Qel stroked his chin, surveying the area. He looked to the sky, and his eyes narrowed. "Under?" he asked, sounding rhetorical. "No, not under. Over."

Without hesitation—or asking—4-Qel used one hand to grab Cade by the back of his jacket and the other to grab him by his crotch.

"Hey!" Cade yelled, but he was already in the air, soaring to a catwalk about fifty feet above his head—but getting nearer fast. He reached his hand out just in time to grab the metal railing before he flew past it; 4-Qel put a little too much *oomph* behind his launch.

Just as Cade was pulling himself onto the catwalk—and catching his breath—Mig landed right next to him.

"He does that sometimes," Mig said.

Kira landed behind Cade, and Cade looked to the ground, wondering how 4-Qel would join them. His concerns were quelled as 4-Qel sprung off of nearby pipes onto the side of an adjacent tower and used its side to propel himself up to the cat-walk, where he landed with a crash.

"See?" 4-Qel said, patting Cade's arm as he walked by. "Over."

Cade laughed, awkwardly, as he realized what a good thing it was that 4-Qel was on their side. The only thing that made him more terrifying was the thought of him becoming an enemy.

"Right," Cade said. "Over."

They sprinted to the silo with only twenty-two minutes to spare. This couldn't get much tighter, Cade estimated. Fortunately, when they reached the silo's entrance, it was unguarded. 4-Qel shredded a hole through the outer shutters, and they dove down a winding staircase that led straight to the silo's vast storage space. There, they found gray cases—so many that Cade couldn't even venture to guess how many there were—that measured about three feet wide and two feet deep, all stacked and lined up in perfect rows.

A feeling of relief, apprehensive relief, afforded Cade an anxiety-free moment. It was about time something worked out in their favor.

Cade grabbed a case by its handle and flipped it over. He was struck by how light the case was; his assumption, which he felt was based on pretty sound reasoning, had been that material strong enough to safeguard against the sun would at least have a little heft. But this case was light, almost like it had nothing in it. Cade cursed himself for acknowledging what he thought at the time was good fortune.

With the clicking release of the case's two fasteners, its top separated from the bottom, and Cade was struck by a shimmering glow. He yanked the case open, and inside was something he'd never seen before. Given its indestructible power, Cade expected the koruvite to be . . . well, he hadn't thought it through, exactly. He never would have guessed, though, that he'd be able to hold up a sheet of koruvite between his two fingers. The mysterious element was paper-thin and clear, though almost gaseous orange and yellow plumes swirled from one end of the sheet to the other, radiating a soft glow.

"Is this it? Kurovite?" Cade asked.

"What else can it be?" Kira replied.

"Let's see," 4-Qel said, and he unholstered his sidewinder in a blink of an eye and fired a round into the assumed koruvite. Which also happened to be right in front of Cade's face.

Wide-eyed, Cade was paralyzed. His heart may have even stopped beating.

"Why would you do that?" Cade asked, still stunned.

"What?" 4-Qel asked. "We don't have time to do a thorough scientific analysis of the material in your hand. Now we know it's koruvite."

Though his testing methods left room for improvement, 4-Qel was right. Cade hadn't even felt the charge from his blaster touch the koruvite. It had been absorbed, totally, by the strange material.

"Everyone grab a case," Cade said as he put the koruvite away and clutched at his heart. It had resumed beating, which was nice. "We still might need to fight our way back out, so let's also be sure to keep our weapons handy."

Everyone did as Cade instructed, and, koruvite in tow, they rushed back up the stairs. Eighteen minutes to go, but Cade had a feeling that they'd need every last second.

But the moment they exited the silo, Cade's life went right back to normal. Meaning, everything had once again gone pear-shaped. Cade figured he ought to at least take some satisfaction in assuming the worst and being right. But as he stared in the face of twenty sentry drones moving in on the silo's entrance, he just couldn't muster the energy to pat himself on the back.

Besides, he had running to do.

"Get back!" Cade yelled. "GET BACK!"

Cade dove into the silo, taking cover behind the still-remaining chunk of shutter that 4-Qel hadn't torn a hole through. He pulled Kira and Mig to the ground with him, and they all managed to reach safety a split second before the sentries opened fire. Cade's best guess was that Praxis had gotten wise to what was happening within the colony and sent the sentries to retrieve as much koruvite as possible. Had the ruthless drones been sent specifically to intercept the intruders—Cade and his team—they'd be dead. Luckily, their meeting was nothing more than bad timing. Which was nothing new to Cade.

The shutter door was drilled by a barrage of blaster fire coming from the sentries on the other side. The noise of the relentless assault echoed throughout the silo, like it was physically squeezing Cade and his friends for space. They all knew, after all, that it was only a matter of time before the door gave out. Or before the sentries played their odds and rushed inside.

"Okay, okay," Mig said, his analytical brain working overtime to assess the situation. "All we need to do is get back down to where we got the koruvite, get to the exit, and—"

"The exits were blocked by the cases," Kira interrupted. "Those cases were probably arranged for a pickup; the only way out is the way we came in."

"I can distract them," 4-Qel said, standing tall. "I can grab some koruvite and deflect enough fire as I thin their numbers so the rest of you can escape."

"No," Mig firmly said. "We're not doing that again."

Cade poked his head around the shutter's entrance to assess the situation. The sentries, having processed and reevaluated the situation, began closing in.

"Mig's right," he said, drawing the Rokura. "It's about time we see if I can use this thing or not."

There was no margin for error. Once Cade turned past the

shutter and into the open, he had to either get the Rokura to do something or experience blaster fire tearing through pieces of his body that he couldn't live without. Cade tried to convince himself that he could do this, whatever "this" was, but a nagging voice kept playing over and over in his ear. Percival's voice, telling Cade he needed training, that he needed to be and feel powerful. Cade had no training, and he certainly didn't feel powerful. He was scared. Terrified. The only thing that was more likely to happen than the sentries killing him was the Rokura killing him. Still, he had to try. He vowed to keep his friends safe.

Cade took a deep, uneasy breath, and just as he was about to roll the dice on fate, he heard an explosion erupt from the other side of the shutter. The ground trembled, and bits of smoldering drones came flying through the shutter's opening. Cautiously, Cade moved to survey the area past the shutter, and he was stunned by what he found. He turned to Kira, Mig, and 4-Qel, who were still behind the safety of the shutter's cover, a look of relief-fueled joy on his face.

"Let's go!" he yelled. "We've got backup!"

Kira, Mig, and 4-Qel piled out behind Cade, all captivated by the same sight: Hovering just over the platform were three transport shuttles armed with light weaponry. They were firing on the drones, mowing them down from above; the enemy stood no chance, but still Cade and his team joined the effort. They fired at will at the drones, destroying as many as they could to clear the way for their escape. It took no time at all for the shuttles and Cade's team to deplete the drone squadron, reducing its numbers to a smoking heap of metal.

"We saw you were in a jam," a voice said, calling out from a speaker in the center transport unit. Cade took a few steps forward, needing visual confirmation of what he suspected, because he couldn't believe his ears. But there he was, sitting right in the cockpit.

Percival.

Cade forced a smile and a wave. That was as good as Percival was going to get, and he better not start thinking Cade owed him because his waving could easily turn into a different hand gesture. After all, Percival tried to capture and use him; they'd just have to call it even.

"Go," Percival said through the speaker. "You only have fifteen minutes to get out of—"

But before Cade could catch Percival's final words, his voice was drowned out by the sound of the transport shuttle on Percival's right as it erupted into a ball of fire.

"NO!" Cade yelled, and as the burning shuttle spun wildly out of control and plunged out of sight, he spotted what was responsible for the shuttle's explosion. His heart dropped at the sight:

Three Intruders in the distance, speeding right at him.

CHAPTER NINETEEN

G O, GO, GO!" Cade yelled, leading Kira, Mig, and 4-Qel over the ruins of the sentry drones and back over the catwalk. Cade turned to see Percival's shuttle, and the one that accompanied him on his left, turn to retreat. Picking off drones was one thing, but those shuttles were made for transport, not battle. Even with the weapons Percival had strapped to them, they were no match for Intruders. The Praxis ships were faster, more agile, and carried ten times the firepower. Cade only hoped they'd be able to make it to a mass-jump lane in time.

"Damn it!" Kira yelled. "They're relentless!"

"Just keep moving!" Cade yelled in return as his heart thumped in his chest. He could almost feel the Intruders' fire bearing down on him. "If we can just get to the ground, we'll at least have some coverage overhead. But we have to keep moving!"

But as soon as Cade issued his rallying charge, he turned to see the second transport vessel torn apart by a pair of Intruders working in tandem. And worse still—half of the shuttle's flaming wreckage was propelled forward and was spinning right toward Cade and his team.

"BACK!" Cade screamed. "GET BACK!"

Cade couldn't tell if he leapt off his feet or if the force of the shuttle's impact with the catwalk threw him off his feet. Maybe it was both. Either way, the flaming metal smashed through the catwalk, taking out a ten-foot chunk of it with its wild descent to the ground. The remaining catwalk screeched and groaned as it swayed from side to side, threatening to collapse. As Cade pulled himself off the catwalk's surface, he realized that the remaining platform was miraculously hanging on. He quickly took stock. Kira was next to him, holding a bloody gash on her head as she also struggled to get to her feet. 4-Qel was standing at the edge of the catwalk, right where it ended in a tangle of twisted metal. Cade looked behind him. He looked ahead again.

He couldn't see Mig.

"MIG!" he screamed, searching the ground below. "MIG!"

Cade's chest began to tighten as he felt tears begin to burn in his eyes. He couldn't lose Mig. Just the thought of Praxis taking someone else from him filled him with a rage that overwhelmed his despair. He grabbed the Rokura's hilt; if it wanted power, he'd show it power as he tore through these Intruders. He'd show it power as he tore through the entire Praxis fleet.

But just as he was about to draw the dangerous weapon, something grasped his hand. Cade looked up, coming out of his blinding fury, and saw 4-Qel standing next to him. The drone was stopping Cade's decision to make a pact with the Rokura, as if he realized what was happening in his mind; it was as if he *knew*.

"I threw him," 4-Qel said. "I threw him ahead."

4-Qel motioned to the other side of the catwalk—the side they all needed to be on, and Cade saw Mig lying there. Cade exhaled so hard that he nearly fell over when Mig raised his hand and grabbed the catwalk's railing, using it to help pull himself up.

Cade looked at 4-Qel, who gave a thumbs-up.

Cade was about to call out to Mig but stopped short. A Praxis transport cruiser slowly descended into view on the platform behind Mig. And there was nothing Cade could do to intervene with whatever was going to happen next. The gulf between him and Mig was too wide, and there was no telling what was going to come out of that shuttle. Cade just had to wait, and when the time was right, he'd have 4-Qel launch him into the fray. He'd just figure out what to do on the fly. It was becoming what he did best. Or maybe it was what he did out of necessity and happened to keep getting lucky.

With a soft hiss, the cruiser's landing gear perched the ship on the platform. Cade gripped the Rokura, tight, and dropped his case of koruvite so he could also arm himself with his sidewinder. Behind him, he felt Kira and 4-Qel position themselves over each of his shoulders, their sidewinders trained on the ship. Mig started to get to his feet, but Cade ordered him to stay down. He anticipated a firefight the moment its doors opened; he had a vision of the ship's blood-red ramp lowering and gunners charging forward, their numbers and firepower far greater than Cade's side. That's what Praxis did: They smothered their enemies with numbers. With firepower. With an insatiable appetite to kill. But if that's what awaited, Cade would go down fighting. He'd take as many with him as possible.

The cruiser's ramp lowered, slowly, but nothing happened. Not at first. No one charged forward. No shots were fired. Cade looked back at Kira, who raised an eyebrow; this was equally confounding to her.

"Can someone tell me what's happening?" Mig yelled. He was crouched on the catwalk, his arms covering his head. "Wait, don't tell me. I don't want to know. Actually . . . no, tell me. What's happening?!"

"Someone's coming," Kira said, and Cade could feel her body tense behind him.

It was just a single person. One solitary person, that was it, walking slowly down the ramp. For some reason, it scared Cade more than a squadron of gunners coming at him.

The figure came into view. He wore a black-and-red cloak with a huge hood pulled over his head. And in the hood's cavity, darkness. Complete darkness.

"Don't take another step!" Cade yelled, pointing his sidewinder forward. "Come any closer, and we will punch you full of holes."

"No, Cade," the shadowy figure said. "I don't think you will."

The man within the cloak raised his hands to his hood and pulled it back. Cade froze, his body numb. He didn't see the half-dozen gunners that charged down the ramp; he didn't see them focus their blasters on Cade. All he saw was the revealed face of the shadowy figure.

The face of Ser Jorken.

For a moment, for the briefest moment, Cade entertained the idea that this was a mistake. That this was all part of Jorken's plan to come to Cade's rescue. But he looked in his Master's eyes, and he knew. He *knew*. This was what the Fatebreaker in the spire was talking about. All the things Cade didn't know. It was what Percival meant when he talked about Ga Halle's roots spreading deep and far into the Well. Jorken was the enemy, and he'd been the enemy the entire time.

"Jorken, you are a dead man," Cade said, his voice even. He didn't yell, he didn't roar his words. He simply stated fact: Cade was going to kill his Master.

Jorken laughed. "Oh, I don't think so, Cade. In fact, I've never felt so alive. It's as if I shed a skin that'd been rotting on me for *years*. The skin of incompetence and fear that covers the entire Well. I'm finally *free*.

"Now, what's going to happen is very simple. You're going to throw me the Rokura, and I won't kill your friend. Mig, if I recall?"

"Screw you," Mig said.

"Lovely selection for what could be your last words," Jorken said with a smirk. He then turned his attention back to Cade. "Ready to exchange? I hear the clock's ticking."

Scenarios ran through Cade's mind, none of them any good. He could kill Jorken, easily. A few pulls of his sidewinder's trigger and Jorken would be dead. But so would Mig. The gunners would pulverize him. And then they'd kill Cade. And Kira. And 4-Qel, maybe. In a rage, the killer drone might be able to end all six gunners on his own. But Cade would never know, because he himself would be long gone.

Or, he could just take the Rokura and throw it into the colony's labyrinth and hope no one could find it before the planet was wiped clean off the galaxy. They'd all be dead, but no one would be able to retrieve the Rokura before the entire place went boom. Assuming the Rokura could be destroyed, Cade would just have to figure this was a win. Maybe.

"Don't you give him the Rokura," Mig yelled. With a quick push of his arm, he shoved his case of koruvite off the side of the catwalk, sending it to the ground below. "I don't care about—"

Mig's words were cut off by Jorken lifting him up by his hair. He held him tight against his chest and dug one of his shido's blades against his throat. One flick of his wrist, and Mig would be gone.

"Ten minutes," Jorken yelled. "Last chance before we kill you all and take what we came here for anyway."

Cade looked at Jorken, and he had no doubt he'd slaughter each and every one of them. He looked at Mig, whose eyes were focused ahead, but not on Cade. His gaze had diverted to over Cade's shoulder, at 4-Qel. Mig winked, and just as Cade was about to pull the Rokura from his back, he felt 4-Qel's arm grip him around his chest.

"Four-Qel, no!" Cade yelled, but it was too late. Before Cade knew it, he was squeezed in 4-Qel's grasp and diving off the side of the catwalk. In the second he had before impact with the ground, Cade looked over to see Kira held in 4-Qel's other arm; the drone was bending his torso back and positioning Cade and Kira as high as he could. He was going to absorb the fall.

They crashed to the ground. Cade heard metal crunch and shred; he heard 4-Qel's internal mechanics, just beneath him, flutter and grind. 4-Qel's arm went limp, and his hold released; Cade rolled several times, pounding his head and body before coming to a stop. Kira did the same but, like Cade, the worst of her fall was taken by 4-Qel.

Cade staggered to his feet and dove for 4-Qel. He was alive, but Cade could see how dim the lights of his eyes were glowing. The joints at his knees must have erupted upon impact; both legs, from the knee joint down, were torn and pointed in impossible angles. The legs were connected, but it didn't much matter. They were destroyed.

"Four-Qel, look at me," Cade said, trying to focus 4-Qel's eyes. If any human had made the same jump as 4-Qel, they would have broken everything. On one hand, 4-Qel was fortunate that his body was so resilient, because it was the only reason he survived. On the other hand, the cost of damaging that body looked to be agonizing. Cade was convinced he saw fear in 4-Qel's eyes.

"Go," 4-Qel wheezed as Cade took his hand. *"Run."*

"No chance," Cade said. "We—"

"Cade!" Jorken yelled, interrupting from above. Cade looked

up and saw Jorken hanging over the catwalk's railing, shido still positioned over Mig's throat. "That Rokura does not belong to you. We both know it. I will give you one day to deliver it to the *War Hammer*. After that, I kill your friend, and then I come hunting.

"One. Day. You can find us above Ticus, sucking the life out of its star. Do what you're told, and we may even spare the pitiful planet you call home," Jorken said, then he disappeared from view.

"No!" Cade called out as he staggered backward, trying to get one last glimpse of Mig. But his friend was already gone, and Cade was left with nothing but the sound of Jorken's cruiser as it took off.

"Mig!" Cade cried, firing his sidewinder pointlessly into the burning sky. "MIG, NO!"

He wanted to fall to his knees; he wanted to pound his fist into the ground until it was mashed into tender meat. But Cade couldn't. Eight minutes. That's all the time he had to somehow get Kira and 4-Qel off Mithlador or lose them, too. Desperately, Cade tried to pull 4-Qel up, but it was no use. He was so heavy that it felt like his body was magnetized to the ground. He'd hoped to be able to drag him to the dasher bike, but there was no chance.

"You have to *go*," 4-Qel implored. "Get out of here. Save Mig."

"He's right." Cade looked up to see Kira, holding her side, stumble toward them. "We might not even have enough time to get ourselves out of here. We have to run. *Now*."

Cade searched the grounds—they couldn't leave empty-handed, not after all this. He spotted Mig's case and what he assumed was 4-Qel's a few feet ahead, mining orbs hovering over them. Cade's eyes lit up. He had their ticket out of Mithlador.

They were going to make it. All of them.

Cade dove for the cases and opened one up. He held up a slice of koruvite and kicked the two cases over to Kira.

"Grab the cases and get ready, both of you!"

"Ready for what?!" Kira shouted. "We have no time!"

"Ready for our ride," Cade said, preparing himself to time this stunt perfectly.

The mining orbs that had been circling the cases were attracted to the koruvite inside. Now they were locked in. One was leading the pack, angling down at the koruvite Cade held up in his hands, its claws extended out. Cade tightened his grip on the koruvite and, as the orb grabbed the koruvite and pulled it up, Cade used the momentum to his advantage; he flipped over to the top of the orb, landing uneasily on its glass dome. Righting himself, Cade whipped out his shido and drove it through the glass, shattering it. Before the orb could take whatever defensive measures it'd been programmed with, Cade plunged his arms inside the orb and took the controls. He was in control now.

Flying the orb was easy enough. One stick for guidance, one for controlling the claws. Cade jammed the stick down, not knowing how temperamental its navigation was; the vigor with which he plunged the orb down nearly flipped it over and sent Cade flying over its side. He righted its movements, though, and set it on a course for Kira and 4-Qel. He was coming in hot, but there was no other way. He didn't have all day to learn how to slow this crazy ride down.

"Grab the claws!" Cade shouted. "I'm not . . . I don't think I'm very good at this!"

And he wasn't. The claws, under his control, chomped and swayed without much rhyme or reason. Cade realized that the stick for its controls was lined with buttons, and he had no idea what purpose any of them served.

Cade zeroed the orb in on his friends' position, hoping he was low enough for them to grab on, but not so low that he would crush them. It was a delicate balance, and the difference between catching them and crashing into them was profound. As he roared overhead, he felt impact. *Something* happened. He pulled the stick back, elevating the orb and setting it on a course for the *Rubicon*. Apprehensively—he wasn't eager to see Kira's guts splattered all over the ground—Cade looked over his shoulder. No one was there, which was good. He hadn't smashed into his friends.

"How you guys feeling down there?" Cade yelled.

"Like you should learn how to keep this thing steady," Kira yelled back. "I've been in crashes that are smoother than the way you fly."

Cade smiled. "That's just because you haven't crashed with me yet."

Kira leapt off the orb as soon as they reached the *Rubicon*. They had about two minutes until detonation. She raced into her ship, getting all systems ready to fly. As she did, Cade angled the orb in front of the entrance and used its claw to fling 4-Qel inside the ship. It wasn't the most eloquent entrance, but 4-Qel should have known by now that smooth operations weren't characteristic of this team.

"We're in," Cade yelled, slamming the button to close the ramp as he darted inside. He leapt into the copilot's seat just as the ship propelled off the ground.

"How much time?" Kira asked, focusing on the liftoff controls.

"Uh," Cade said, looking through the cockpit's all-encompassing viewport. "None."

In the distance, Mithlador burst into flames. The detonations exploded in unison, and the result was an eruption that sucked in everything around it before bursting outward. The *Rubicon* rose higher and higher from the planet's surface, and Cade watched as the colony collapsed in a flash of white light. In the blink of an eye, every structure—the towers, the silos, the smokestacks—

disintegrated into pieces and crashed to the ground. And then, a secondary eruption detonated and doubled down on the carnage. The massive blast shot out from the heart of the explosion, a fiery purple and red, destroying everything in its path. And it was closing in on the *Rubicon*.

"Kira, we might want to—"

"Working on it!" Kira yelled as the ship continued its ascent. It was going in the right direction, just not fast enough. "The planet's caving in on itself, and it's pulling us with it."

The blast was gaining; the ship was rising as fast as it could, fighting off increasing gravity that was determined to pull them back down.

"Come on!" Kira yelled, her face strained as she pulled the stick back with all her strength. "Come. *On!*"

Cade slammed the seat's harness over his chest just as fiery death closed in on their position. The ship rocketed upward, throttled by a shock wave shot out by the immeasurable power of the blast. They were above it, but Cade still felt the ship being sucked downward. The ship inched forward, while his body was being dragged back with a force that convinced Cade his teeth were about to be sucked out of his mouth. The backside of the ship seemed about to turn over on them, which would send them uncontrollably downward—right into the fire.

"Oh no you *don't*," Kira spat, and she jammed the wheel to the right, sending the ship spinning on its side. As it did, she flipped the ship's cockpit on its axis, catching the tumbling body in perfect sync; the momentum was enough to right the ship and keep it flying up, away from the fiery death below. Within moments, they were clear.

Cade exhaled and released the trembling grip he had on the seat's armrest. After a few seconds of silently staring ahead, he blinked.

"That . . . that was some flying," he said.

"Yup," Kira said. "It sure was."

Both Cade and Kira released cathartic breaths as the vastness of space consumed the viewport. Impulsively, Cade thought to do something with the control panel, but as he reached his hand toward it, he stopped himself. There was nothing for him to do. Kira released the stick, and Cade heard her start to softly hum an off-key tune.

"We don't know where to go, do we?" he asked.

"No clue."

The cockpit door opened, and 4-Qel shoved himself inside; he was moving along with his knuckles pressed to the ground, pushing his upper body forward as his legs trailed behind. With a pained grunt, he climbed into the seat behind Kira.

"How you feeling?" Cade asked.

"The damage isn't as extensive as I'd feared. Only my knee joints need replacing, but I can patch them for now. Once we get Mig back, he will return me to normal."

Cade and Kira cast uncertain glances at each other.

"We are going after Mig, are we not?" 4-Qel asked.

Cade ran his hand over his eyes then brought it down over his mouth. He hung his head, closed his eyes, and took a deep breath. There was a lot of uncertainty in his mind—about the Well, about what it really meant to be the Paragon, about a future for the entire galaxy that wasn't shrouded in darkness. But there was one thing he was certain about, and it was nonnegotiable. No matter the cost.

"We can't let Ga Halle get her hands on the Rokura," Cade said. "It's too dangerous."

"Oh," 4-Qel said, and Cade heard the fabric of his chair sigh. It sounded like his body, half broken, was slumping in his seat, but Cade couldn't bring himself to turn and find out. He couldn't look at 4-Qel, not right now. "I suppose you are right. And Mig . . . he wouldn't want you to trade the Rokura for his life. He said so himself."

4-Qel said the words, but Cade knew he didn't mean it. Whether he was trying to comfort himself or Cade, Cade didn't know. He just knew that 4-Qel's sentiment was a lie.

Cade looked at Kira, whose glance dropped to the ground. She let out a fuming breath, then punched the stick. The ship jerked, but no one said anything. They sat in silence, floating in space, angst-ridden about what they were about to do. They were abandoning Mig.

"They were going to kill me, you know," 4-Qel said. "The royal family of Eris had me scheduled for . . . scrapping. But Mig saved me. And not because he had it in mind to put me to use. He may be shrewd, but Mig is no cynic.

"Mig saved me because he can't stand to see anyone left behind."

Cade couldn't do it. This was Cade's friend—no, Mig was family. And Cade refused to lose anyone else over this stupid mythical weapon. Cade made a promise to himself to keep the few remaining people he cared about safe, and he wasn't going to break it. He wasn't going to jeopardize the galaxy and break his vow to Tristan, either. And that was a dilemma—which meant Cade would just have to get really smart really fast.

And he kinda sorta had an idea how to do just that.

"Well, then I guess our only option is to trick Ga Halle," Cade said.

Kira shot him an askew glance. "What?"

"I mean we don't let Ga Halle get her hands on the Rokura, we just make her *think* she has."

"You mean . . . we *lie*?" 4-Qel asked, like he'd just been asked to shoot a baby out of an airlock.

Cade and Kira shared a puzzled look, then they turned to face 4-Qel, just to see if, somehow, he was joking. He wasn't.

"How many people have you killed?" Kira asked.

"Oh, you can fill a good-size cruiser with my body count. Why do you ask?"

"Never mind," Cade stated. "And, yes, we have to lie."

"Well . . . I suppose. It is for Mig, after all."

"Okay, now that we're all morally okay with deceiving the galaxy's evil warlord, let's work this out," Kira said. "Cade, what are you saying here?"

"I don't know," Cade said. "I mean, not totally. But, look: We escaped the Darklanders. We kicked some Krell tail. We just pulled off the greatest heist ever. So why not add a jailbreak from the Praxis *War Hammer* to the list? We can do this. I *know* we can do this."

"We can do this with planning, Cade," Kira said. "With a precise strategy. Maybe even some backup. But Jorken gave us one day and, I'm sorry to say, we're not close to having any of those things."

"She's right," 4-Qel agreed. "We don't have anything."

"No," Cade said. He tossed the harness off himself and got up from his seat. "We have each other. And not a single one of us has it in us to sentence our friend to death, so we better start thinking about the things we do have instead of what we don't.

"We have Kira's accelerator bomb. We have the shielding for it. And I don't believe for one second that Praxis is going to relent from their plans. They're going to drain Ticus's sun. They're going to kill another planet."

Cade looked at Kira; he looked at 4-Qel. For the first time in his life, he felt like something more than what he'd always been— the disappointment, the screw-up. And he knew Kira and 4-Qel were in the same boat. As talented and amazing as Kira was, she worked so poorly with others that she was cast off to lead all the other misfits like her. 4-Qel was living in a world where, as soon as an improved model of himself existed, his creators—the very people he existed to protect—ordered his execution. Nobody expected much from them, which, Cade hoped, meant nobody would see them coming.

"Let's go for it all," Cade said. "Save Mig. Blow up the *War Hammer*. All in one big glorious—and probably suicidal—swoop."

"I've never met someone so intent on getting himself killed," Kira said. For a disheartening moment, Cade thought she was going to tell him what an idiot he was. But she didn't. Instead, Kira pulled off her harness and stood next to him. "But I'm with you anyway. Let's do exactly what we planned and take this fight to Praxis."

"I can't stand," 4-Qel said. "Otherwise, I'd be right there with you."

"Yeah, we have to get you patched up," Cade said, cringing.

"I won't be any use to you until you do. Because I too am in. Let's get Mig."

Cade smiled, even as he felt the terrifying realization of what was happening settle in. They were really doing this.

"Okay, I have a plan. Or, well . . . the beginnings of a plan."

Kira groaned. "Here we go."

"Don't worry, I'll get there. I have pieces that just need to . . . fit together. But I do know one thing for sure:

"We're going to need help."

CHAPTER TWENTY

The *War Hammer*'s viewport was swallowed by the vastness of space. Ga Halle tried to remember when she'd last spent significant time anyplace that didn't have any artificial atmosphere and gravity locks, a place that cultivated organic life that you could feel in your hands, your nose, your mouth. She thought of the losmiss plants that grew wild in the backyard of her childhood home, those enormous orange and white petals that fanned out from their stem like the entrance to a magical palace only she knew about. Ga Halle remembered how she'd pick the losmiss in bundles, always in bundles, so she could crop them together and spin them in the air like the sweetest-smelling kaleidoscope that ever was. Running, she'd twirl the plants up toward the sun, its beams breaking through the petals and bringing a bright sheen to the whirring colors. But when her planet's sun became dim, the losmiss all withered and died, never to return. Soon after saving her planet, Ga Halle visited her family's former home, which had long been abandoned and taken over by parasitic weeds and flowers, and found a barren patch of dry dirt where the losmiss had been. It was the last time she even considered returning to Praxis and ruling her kingdom from there. She couldn't. Even though she saved her home world's dying star, the atmosphere felt different, it felt foreign. No scientific evidence backed up Ga Halle's feeling, but she knew. The losmiss couldn't grow, and she couldn't stay. Her home was in space now, where she was everywhere and nowhere.

On the command deck behind her, Ga Halle's crew went about their business with adroit efficiency, but she wasn't interested in their work. Her steely gaze was instead fixed on a point of light so far off in the distance it was barely visible. But Ga Halle knew exactly what it was, and she didn't need any meddling junior navigator or bridge chief to announce, seemingly for her benefit, where they were headed. Ticus was on the horizon, and the *War Hammer* was heading straight toward it.

Even if she tried, Ga Halle couldn't count how many times she'd taken this exact approach to Ticus, how many times she'd watched it get incrementally bigger and bigger in whatever ship she happened to be flying. If this was a homecoming, it was the last time she'd ever do it. It would be the last time for anyone. There'd be an uproar after her work was done, but her regime was already prepared to spread word on how Ticus had forced Praxis's hand, how the Well, desperate to hold on to its power, threatened the galaxy's fragile peace. There'd be attacks against Praxis occupations in the wake of Ticus's decimation—Ga Halle could confidently guess which planets would be the most troublesome—but any uprising would be crushed before it could turn into something even remotely worrisome. After all, if there was one thing Ga Halle had learned about the planets in her galaxy, both as a Rai keeping the peace and as the ruler of the Praxis kingdom, it was that they were incapable of unifying and mobilizing, even in the face of their own crumbling autonomy. Too much bureaucracy, too many petty squabbles between planets, and too many competing interests between people made them divided and weak. That's why they couldn't aid the Rai in making peace then, and that's why they couldn't unify and stop Praxis now.

Ga Halle was on the cusp of annexing the entire galaxy to her kingdom; she was about to claim the Rokura and buck the cruel hand of fate while undermining everything those ineffectual failures at the Well had drilled into her about destiny. She'd already accomplished more than even she'd dreamed possible, and she'd done it without the Rokura. And now, as if resultant of the power of her will and the unprecedented achievements it'd helped her mount, she'd have the weapon anyway. It, like everything else in the universe, would be under her control.

Still, Ga Halle couldn't help but feel impassive.

She had no regret over what she had done, nor did she harbor any remorse for the lengths she'd gone to in order to do it. But she'd be lying to herself if she didn't admit that, secretly, she had hoped more systems would have come to her side. While several planets and their moons had willingly annexed themselves to the Praxis kingdom, Ga Halle saw those systems for what they were: a collection of opportunists, also-rans, and criminal hives who, succeed or fail, had nothing to lose on the galactic stage by anchoring to Praxis's rise. Ga Halle never saw herself as the galaxy's villain, which she knew, despite her insulation within her kingdom, was how she was perceived. She brought chaos to order; she stamped out, with decisive efficiency, decades-old conflicts over land, over religion, over who-even-remembers-anymore. She'd done exactly what the Well had set out to do, but never did the Masters see things from her perspective. They didn't even try. Instead, they cast her as a monster for doing what was necessary to save her home world and the lives of countless individuals; they decimated her self-worth by never publicly acknowledging what happened—what *really* happened—to her in the spire, choosing instead to act like she, and Percival, didn't even exist. The Well was wrong, they'd been wrong for a long, long time, and that's why it was so easy to give the galaxy what it secretly wanted: strong leadership willing to do what needed to be done, no matter the cost. It was no accident that Ga Halle was able to dig into the Well's pockets and steal allies right from under its nose. Ga Halle was no raving lunatic, spewing wild theories to anyone who would listen; she had the aid of many like-minded thinkers. She had followers. And now, the decisions she and the Well made irrevocably placed them on this collision course where they'd both soon discover who was meant to persevere and who was meant to perish.

The point of light that was Ticus grew larger. At this very moment, her fleet was preparing to strike, and the *War Hammer* would soon be in a position to extract enough energy from Ticus's only star to render the planet a desolate wasteland. Ga Halle had little doubt what fate held for her. She just wished she felt more satisfied by her knowledge of what was to come.

A throat cleared behind her. Ga Halle turned and found Jorken, her most loyal ally, standing by her side at last. Although Ga Halle had sparingly exchanged holocomms with him, the difference between that and standing next to someone was remarkable. Jorken had weathered the years with dignity, but the Jorken in her mind didn't have deeply set wrinkles around his eyes, graying hair, nor did he carry a little extra weight beneath his chin. Ga Halle didn't judge her mentor for a single moment, only observed how time changed them all. She wondered briefly how she must have looked to him and considered the scars on her face and the containment suit that was forever strapped to her body—her constant reminder of what the Well had done to her.

"We have the prisoner securely guarded," he said. "Knowing Cade, I have no doubt that he will come for him. He may attempt something foolish in the process—in fact, he's guaranteed to—

but we will have him, and the Rokura, on the *War Hammer* soon enough."

Ga Halle studied her friend, her former Master. For years, he operated as her personal agent, laying the groundwork for a day neither of them was certain would come—the day another Paragon would rise and the Rokura would once again be free. Thanks, perhaps, to Ga Halle's own suppression and control of the galaxy, the day of the Rokura's release was finally here, and it was time for Jorken to enjoy the fruits of his sacrifice.

"Are you ready for a new future for our galaxy, Ser Jorken? You can never return to the Well again, you do realize."

Jorken smiled and pointed ahead at the viewport. "That may prove incorrect, as I do believe the Well is where we're headed at this very moment."

Uncharacteristically, Ga Halle returned Jorken's smile. "Very true. But *after* this."

"After this, I'll have no reason to. I've had only one reason to remain all these years, and you know what it is. Also, if you please," Jorken said after a pause, "don't refer to me as 'Ser.' The title means nothing to me."

Ga Halle nodded, acknowledging Jorken's request. The two stood silently, watching the world that'd betrayed them both come into focus. Ga Halle realized that they hadn't stood side by side since before her fateful trip to Quarry, back when she was just a Rai and he was her proud Master. Despite that, she knew that no one was closer to her soul than Jorken. And because of that, she knew she could confide in him even her deepest secrets. Or even her nagging doubt.

"Have we done the right thing?" she asked, breaking their comfortable silence.

"Yes." Jorken snapped back his reply without a moment of lapsed time between where Ga Halle's question ended and his answer began. It was like he had known the question she was going to ask.

Ga Halle looked over at him, probing, and he continued.

"We had one of two choices: We either let battles and wars drag on and civil unrest fester as the galaxy fell into chaos, or we wage our own war to bring it all under control. Remember: Our conquest was never built on exterminating any race or planet or settling a frivolous feud. We acted out of need. The need to end bloody conflicts that took the lives of innocents from the Fringe all the way to the Inner Cluster, shattering alliances and dividing our galaxy. The need for every system to be consolidated under one rule, even if by force, so law, order, and justice could reign supreme.

"The business of peace is a messy one, your highness, and it can also be cruel, but make no mistake about it—even people who claim to be free always have a master, and they're always in conflict about something. If this galaxy is going to have a master, I'd rather it be you. I'd rather it be guided with a strong hand by someone who isn't afraid to make difficult choices for the sake of the greater good."

Ga Halle nodded at Jorken, knowing it would be enough to express her gratitude. She clasped her hands behind her back and returned her gaze to the point of light that was soon to be snuffed out.

"Inform all my commanders, even the Fatebreakers, that any Well combatant who surrenders, regardless of rank or title, will be granted full pardon and no harm shall come to them. And be sure that offer is transmitted once we come into Ticus's orbit and we're identified."

Jorken went to bow, like a Ser, but stopped himself. "As you wish, my queen." He turned and walked down the long command bridge, leaving Ga Halle alone once more. She breathed deep and put the personal animosity she harbored toward the Well aside, like she had so many times in her life. It took incredible restraint for her not to have stormed Ticus years ago and to have plunged herself into a spree of bloody catharsis and revenge. But she knew the timing wasn't right and, standing here now, she was glad she waited. Soon, she would have her victory, and she would have the Rokura.

Soon, she would have it *all*.

CHAPTER TWENTY-ONE

The Well had seen better days.

As Kira put the *Rubicon* on an approach for landing in the western hangar—visibly, it was the only one that hadn't suffered major damage—Cade surveyed the scene below. Regardless of the conflicting emotions that had cemented in Cade over the past few days, the Well was still the place he called home. And it was ravaged. Praxis's destruction had deeply and irrevocably scarred the fundamental character of the Well, which Cade never thought was possible. Dojos reduced to rubble; armories erupted from the inside out; even the Floating Temple had a massive chunk torn from its side, likely the location of a ship crashing into it. Cade felt stunned at what he was seeing because, to him, the Well was invulnerable. Everybody thinks their home is invulnerable, Cade knew that, but the Well was more than a home. The Well was an idea, a spiritual order, a philosophy. And while those things can't be killed with any amount of artillery, one look at the Well and Cade knew that those guiding principles too were weaker than they had been before the attack. Maybe that was for the best, but Cade wasn't thinking about levied judgments. His mind was captivated by the remembrance of a world now in the past and the heartbreak of knowing it would never come back again.

When Kira pulled the *Rubicon* through Ticus's orbit, they were met by a squadron of Echoes standing guard. The formation of starfighters parted to let them pass, though not a single message was broadcast to the returning ship. There was no communication at all. Even when Kira transmitted her clearance code to Rao, they were met with the tersest permission to land before the comms on Rao's end clicked off. Their homecoming was not going to be an occasion for happy reunion, but Cade didn't let it bother him. They had returned for a purpose higher than popularity.

And if that wasn't clear already, it only took one look at the Omega Squadron waiting at the mouth of the landing pad to know that Cade and Kira weren't well-liked. In fact, they were probably kind of hated.

"Look at those sourpusses," Cade said as he leaned over Kira's seat, peering out the viewport.

Kira groaned. "Just let me do the talking."

Cade squinted, bringing all eighteen of Omega's snarling, hard-edged faces into focus. "Yeah," he said, "I think that's probably best."

Cade and Kira disembarked the ship—leaving 4-Qel behind while he wrapped the shielding around Kira's bomb and, with the koruvite that remained, repaired his legs—and Cade slowed his pace so Kira could take the lead as they headed toward her squadron. The band of misfits were overdoing their posturing by an impressive margin: If they frowned any harder, they'd come all the way back around to a smile, Cade thought. But Cade understood how their leadership worked. It was simple, actually: In Omega, the alpha ruled. As Kira got closer, the new alpha stepped forward, displaying his status.

Cade's good pal, Elko.

"Where you been?" the Durang native snarled.

Kira glared at Elko, holding his gaze. But she forced her expression to soften; Cade knew as well as she did that her squad wasn't going to be browbeaten back into obedience. These were the bastards of the Well, the outcasts. Rank meant very little to them, if anything at all. What mattered most was that their leader was one of them, that they were misfits together. By abandoning her squadron when the Well was under attack—and, from their perspective, without reason—Kira had betrayed her allegiance and separated herself from the pack. It wasn't going to be easy to win their acceptance back.

"You know," Kira said, coolly, "since I've been gone for a few days, I'm going to let your failure to acknowledge rank slide. But what you meant to say was, 'Where you been, *sir*?'"

Elko stuck out his lower lip and shook his head defiantly. "You turned tail. We needed you, and you and the golden boy left us. You just up and ran."

"You think I *ran*?" Kira asked.

Elko lumbered a few strides forward, closing the short distance between himself and Kira. "You got scared. And you chose *him* over *us*. Now, I know you called us here because you got something to say, but you're going to do the listening. You're out of Omega. You're—"

The next sound that came out of Elko's mouth was somewhere between a squeal and a howl. Kira had taken both her hands and, in the moment that Elko probably imagined was going to cement his leadership, jammed her fingers directly into the gills that lined both sides of the Durangan's face. Right before Elko's *squowl*, Cade heard the squishy impact of Kira's fingers digging inside of Elko; he didn't know much about Elko's biology, but he did know that—like a *fish*—they breathed through their gills. Which meant Kira was squeezing Elko's lungs. Cade was equally amazed and disgusted by what he was seeing.

"Now listen up, every single one of you!" Kira said as she plunged her fingers deeper into Elko. He dropped to his knees in front of her, crippled by pain. Kira looked at every single crew member, making sure she had their attention, before continuing. And when she did, she spoke every word clearly and with total command.

"If you think I ran, if you think I betrayed our squadron or our mission, then you don't know me at all, and I implore you to walk away right now." Kira gave a dramatic pause, allowing for anyone to leave. Nobody did. "I've been halfway across this galaxy, risking my life to find a way for us to finally bring Praxis to its knees. And guess what? *I've got it*. We," Kira said, nodding back to Cade, "have got it.

"So here's the deal: I'm not going to bother asking if you're with me. I am your commander, and I'm *telling* you that you're with me. Now, before we get to the good stuff, I want to know," Kira said, digging her fingers into Elko's gills until he *squowl*ed once more, "does anyone have a problem with anything I just said?"

Cade looked at the Omega Squadron, and he saw a lot of dumbfounded faces. The resolve they had behind Elko was knocked right out of them, and all they could do was shake their heads in response to Kira's query.

"I'm sorry," Kira said, putting some bite into her words. "What was that?"

"No, sir," Omega sheepishly replied.

"WHAT?" Kira yelled.

"NO, SIR!" her obedient squad barked.

Kira tossed Elko to the ground and planted her foot on his chest so he couldn't turn away from her. "I ought to put a rocket up your ass and blast you to Aria," she said, pressing her boot into Elko's sternum. "Fortunately for you, I need all the pilots I can get. So, do you want a shot at redemption, or do you want to crawl away in shame? Your choice."

"Redemption," Elko gasped.

"Good," Kira said, then she held out her hand to Elko. He looked at it warily, then she pushed it forward, letting him know it wasn't a trick. He took it and, with Kira's help, rose to his feet.

"It's us versus Praxis," Kira said as Omega stood at attention. "We have a plan. It's . . . let's call it bold. Insane. But insane is who we are and what we do. Time isn't on our side, so we need to move, and we need to move now—"

"You will do no such thing," a raspy voice called out. Cade turned to the hangar's entrance, and there was Cardinal Master Teeg, flanked by Nu Kan, Plar, and a half-dozen infantry soldiers. Despite the destruction and wreckage that engulfed the Well, Teeg still managed to don his pristine tunic that flowed to the ground, covering his feet so it looked more like he was gliding than walking. Cade had hoped to avoid the old Cardinal Master, knowing that he'd only get in the way. Cade had his mind focused on one thing and one thing only: freeing Mig and taking out the *War Hammer.* But here was Teeg, getting in the way—as usual.

"If the Well wasn't in sooch a state," Teeg continued, "the only way either of you would be permitted to land would be to have you placed in shackles for failure of duty."

Despite everything Cade now knew and his acceptance that his tenure at the Well was over, he still couldn't help but feel intimidated by Teeg. Though Cade now understood who he was and what he had to do, he could still see himself through Teeg's eyes, and he was right back to being a disappointment. To being the Well's bastard child. "But, sir, if you just let us explain—"

"You'll be silent until I've finished talking," Teeg ordered, though his voice sounded more petulant than strong, Cade realized. "You will both aid in repairing our home. As you do, myself and the other Masters will decide your fate and issue—"

Kira stepped in front of Cade and addressed Teeg with a finger pointed right at him. That was a mistake. "Enough, Teeg. With all due respect—"

"You have no business addressing me, pilot," Teeg barked. "Now take a step back or—"

"Kira's wrong," Cade interrupted, stepping around Kira. He ran his tongue over his teeth and huffed in a deep breath through his nostrils. He didn't risk his life—more than once—and lose his friend to Praxis just so Teeg could step out of his comfy tower and tell him what to do. As long as he held the Rokura, Cade was the Paragon, and he didn't have to listen to one more word that Teeg had to say. "There's no respect coming your way, because it isn't due. Not now, not ever."

Teeg's gray, aging eyes narrowed at Cade, and he felt the Cardinal Master's rage forming a pit in his gut, like a spring being compressed in a vice. And, really, it had nothing to do with Cade's insolence. It didn't even have anything to do with Teeg's conclusion—actually, the entire Well's conclusion—that Cade took off when he was needed most. No, this was about Cade not being what Teeg envisioned, and wanted, the Paragon to be. Teeg was Tristan's Master—which was unheard of, a Cardinal Master mentoring a Rai—because that's how much be believed Tristan was the Chosen One. Teeg didn't want Cade. He never wanted Cade. It was Teeg who kept Cade away from missions; it was Teeg who kept him ostracized. And now, as far as Teeg knew, the cruel hand of fate had saddled him with the very person he couldn't wait to divorce himself from. The entire galaxy was stuck with an undisciplined Paragon that Teeg couldn't control. Tristan would have been the dutiful Paragon who still served the Master Cardinal's title and, in turn, kept Teeg relevant. Cade's ascent tore the rug right out from under Teeg's feet, and the only thing he could do to preserve his power was double down in asserting it. For Teeg, there was a fate worse than the galaxy never delivering a Paragon; it was the galaxy delivering a Paragon that made his position obsolete.

"I know you're angry, Rai Soora, over what happened to your brother," Teeg managed to grind out through his clenched jaw, "but what we have to discuss, we'll discuss in private."

"I'm the Paragon," Cade asserted. "And I know the Well's failures, Teeg. I know that Ga Halle was one of us, and that you, along with so many others, turned a blind eye to her rise to power because you didn't want to expose your failure and have people questioning their faith. A Paragon rose, and he was so horrified by what he saw in the Rokura that he put it right back where he found it and ran from the entire universe. That's not something that inspires devotion, so you kept it hidden, and you ignored all the dominoes that fell afterward. You ignored Praxis. You ignored what Percival had become. And because you willingly gouged your own eyes out, you couldn't see the traitor that was standing right at your side for *years*."

Cade felt a hand grip his bicep. Kira's hand. "Cade, we've got to—" she said, but Cade wasn't stopping. He was on a roll.

"Jorken sold Tristan and me out. He's the reason my brother is dead. So don't you stand here telling me about failures of duty when—"

"Cade!" Kira yelled, pulling his body toward her. He looked at her and noticed that she had her eyes locked on the sky above. In fact, everyone had their eyes fixed upward, in shock, horror, confusion—even all three at the same time. Cade followed their line of vision, but he didn't share their reaction. Far above in darkening dusk sky, Ticus's star was burning as it always had. But, for the first time ever, the uncertainty that it would rise and burn the next day was in jeopardy. Extending out from the star was a single beam of its energy, piercing through the sky like a rift in space, drawing light away from its host. Though the *War Hammer* was unseen from this distance, there was no doubt about what was happening: Praxis had come to extinguish Ticus's sun. As much as Cade hated what was happening, as much as he feared what he was getting his friends and himself into, he was ready. It was time to face Praxis.

Cade tore his eyes away from the sight of his world being slowly ended, and turned back to Teeg. He clasped his hands on the Cardinal Master's shoulders, getting his attention.

"Evacuate this planet, as fast as you can," Cade said. "We're going out there, and we're going to stop this. But if we fail, you need to be as far away from here as possible. All of you."

"What—what is this?" Teeg quietly asked, and Cade could read the bewilderment in his face. For so long, Teeg enjoyed a consistent, comfortable world—but the terms of that world were dictated by Praxis, and that was true whether Teeg acknowledged it or not. The Well was under Praxis's thumb, and now that thumb was pressing down. Teeg was incapable of processing the force that was being applied to them all, himself included. Cade pitied Teeg in a way, because other than being a pompous a-hole, Teeg's greatest sin might have been belief. No matter what happened in the galaxy, no matter how grim things became, Teeg believed things would turn out okay. In a way, Teeg needed the galaxy to suffer; for the Paragon to rise and bring ultimate peace to the universe, ultimate despair was a prerequisite. It was, true to the Rokura, a damnable pact. Still, Teeg never seemed to consider that the galaxy's most desperate hour—the time when the Paragon would arrive—was a relative term: You don't really understand that desperation until you're in it. Quarry, Tor-Five, Maqis, and Romu—those planets had endured their homes' final hour, and Cade knew there was no way those people didn't look to the sky, just as everyone on Ticus was doing right now, hoping that the Paragon would whisk in and save them all. If Teeg had considered that relativity, things could have been different. But Teeg didn't. Even as planets were sentenced to ruin, even as a bona fide Paragon rejected the mantle, Teeg still held tightly to his belief and envisioned no other way to bring about peace and justice. But Cade knew the truth: The Paragon wasn't going to be saving anyone, because the Paragon was dead. They were going to have to do what they should have done years ago:

They were going to have to save themselves.

"You want to know what this is, Teeg?" Cade asked. "It's inevitability. Now go, get everyone off this planet."

Pacing back as if in a daze, Teeg and his cabal headed off, and Kira sent her squadron to their Echoes. That left the two of them, alone, with both of them knowing that in a few moments' time they had to part ways.

A crisp wind blew through the hangar, and Cade blew into his hand for warmth. He looked at Kira, whose cheeks were turning pink from the cold. Before their paths crossed on Aria, they weren't friends; they were hardly acquaintances. But now, the thought of losing her struck Cade straight to his core, like an abstraction that could be felt more than understood. He wanted to make the idea of losing Kira similar to losing Mig, or even 4-Qel, but he couldn't. Not that he was ranking his degrees of loss, just that he knew, more than ever, the unique value of what was at stake with the people he cared about. In a short span of time, Kira had come to mean something to him that no one else ever had, and Cade realized, as he held her gaze in an intensely quiet moment, that he couldn't bear being without her.

"Kira, I want you to know that I . . ." Cade stammered, tripping over words that felt horribly inaccurate. But the words, he knew, were true. And they were all he had, so they had to count for something. "I couldn't have done this without you."

"Yeah, no kidding," Kira said with a playful grin.

Cade smiled back, and all he wanted to do was take this moment and freeze it in time so he could hold on to it forever—even if forever, he feared, was only a matter of hours.

"Don't do anything crazy out there, okay?"

"I'm pretty sure crazy is the bedrock of what we're about to do."

"Well, *yeah*," Cade said. "But, look—this plan can go from marginally possible to suicidal in the blink of an eye. And if it does turn, then you need to get out."

Kira smiled and let out a short laugh. She jerked her head back, throwing the dreadlocks out of her face. It was something, Cade realized, she did all the time. "Yeah? And what are you going to do if things go bad?"

Another breeze went by, and Cade felt its cold pass through his body. He fought off a shiver as he looked at Kira, wanting nothing more than to hold her close and finish the kiss they'd nearly shared on the *Rubicon*. But as he looked up to the sky and the star that was becoming weaker with each passing moment, he knew this wasn't the time or the place for what he wanted.

"Don't worry about me," Cade said, spreading a cocksure smile across his face. "I still have a few tricks up my sleeve."

Cade knew he and Kira should get moving, but neither of them could turn and walk away. Instead, they shared a quiet moment, neither knowing what to say in the face of the uncertainty and danger ahead. They took each other's hands and let the silence be; neither felt the need to speak, neither had the words to convey what might be their final good-bye. The presence of each other was enough for them both.

The moment came to an abrupt end when Cade's attention was diverted by the sound of footsteps thumping down the *Rubicon*'s hatch. Both he and Kira turned and spotted 4-Qel, back on his two legs, heading toward them.

"Looking good!" Kira said, and 4-Qel responded with a twirl that anyone still in possession of their vision would call "graceful."

"The koruvite made for an excellent substitute for the material in my knees that'd been destroyed. I feel readier to destroy my enemies than ever."

"Then you're about to have the time of your life," Cade said.

"I relish the opportunity," the drone replied. "Shall we take to the sky?"

"We shall," Cade replied, "but let's do so with no further twirling."

Cade smiled as 4-Qel walked by him and slapped his shoulder, harder than he probably intended. His gaze met Kira's, and he knew it was time. They both had to leave.

"I'll see you when this is all over," he said, and he could only hope his words rang true.

"When this is over," Kira replied, her face conveying a steadfast certainty that she and Cade would live to see "over."

With that, they went their separate ways.

CHAPTER TWENTY-TWO

The *Horizon Dawn*'s weapons-lock system activated sooner than Cade anticipated. He was flying just a little bit ahead of Omega Squadron on a course straight for the *War Hammer*, and he was surprised his control panel registered weapons being locked on his position from as far away as he was. Which was good. Cade and Omega wanted as much distance from the *War Hammer* as possible, and now they all knew just how far their weapons reached. The bad part was that when Cade's weapons-lock system became active, it nearly went into cardiac arrest. Cade couldn't even count the number of cannons, missiles, and torpedoes that were all the push of a button away from blowing him so thoroughly into oblivion that not even so much of a speck of him or his ship would be left behind.

What a nice way to get this thing started.

A transmission came through Cade's control panel, and Cade patched it in.

"Incoming vessel," an uptight voice said, coming through the comms. "We have this ship identified as belonging to Cade Sura. Please verify."

"Yup," Cade said. "That's me."

The voice cleared its throat. "I believe instructions were clear for you to arrive at the *War Hammer* alone to exchange the Rokura for your friend."

"I am alone," Cade replied. "There's no one in my ship but me."

"But, the other ships," the voice said, getting confused, "they're with you."

Cade smiled, thinking about the eighteen Omega Squadron customized Echoes, centered around the *Rubicon*, hovering in space behind him. He liked the idea of forcing Praxis to question what was going on right in front of them. Forcing them to feel uncertain.

"Well, my old friend Jorken and I never discussed the delivery details, so I took the liberty of coming up with my own arrangements. Are you ready to hear them? Do you need to write this down?"

The voice *hmph*ed. So, Cade mused, Praxis enlistees did retain enough of their souls to still have pride.

"Convey your terms."

"Okay," Cade said, leaning toward his comms unit, "here's what we're going to do:

"I don't trust Praxis to make a fair, even exchange. What that means is that once I hand over the Rokura, there's nothing preventing you from killing both my friend and me, right on the spot. So instead of me bringing the Rokura on board, I'm going to leave it out here with my friends. It's located in one of these eighteen ships. You don't know which one, and I won't tell you. That means, in case you're not following, if you decide to launch your fighters against my friends, you run the risk of losing the Rokura to the cold, black heart of space.

"Now, I'm going to fly into the *War Hammer*. I'm totally alone; you can scan my ship for life-forms and see for yourself. When I dock, I get Mig, I fly out, then we launch a drone containing the Rokura back to the *War Hammer*. And then, our business is complete. Got it?"

The voice scoffed, smugly. "And once you have your friend, what's to say you'll uphold your end of this arrangement?"

"Seriously?" Cade sighed. "If I don't send the Rokura to you, you'll annihilate my ship and every ship that I've come here with in the blink of an eye. Why would I go through all this trouble to save my friend just to get him, my squad, and myself killed?"

There was a pause, and Cade could almost hear the gears grinding in the head of whoever this voice belonged to as he tried to verify and/or deny his logic. He either surrendered or comprehended, because when he came back, he granted Cade clearance to land in the *War Hammer*.

As Cade slowly made his way toward the landing bay he'd been directed to, he angled his viewport to get a look at the *War Hammer* at work. A massive beam of explosive light was being sucked from Ticus's sun and guided into the ship thanks to the koruvite shielding technology. He watched as the star's energy crackled and burst in the koruvite chamber that extended from the ship to the star; Cade was awed that such power could be contained. It was magnificent and awful at the same time, and Cade felt a renewed sense of determination as he zeroed in on the *War Hammer*; only a few precious hours remained before Ticus turned into an uninhabitable rock. It was irrevocably changing every minute, and Cade knew a lot of things had to go right, starting now, if they had any chance at stopping Praxis.

Cade entered the landing bay—which was like an enormous cavern dug into a mountain, in terms of scope—and he realized that he had no idea what to expect. No one who went into the *War Hammer* came out again. This was a trip reserved for the worst Praxis offenders—insurgent leaders, political enemies, and other instigators that happened to piss the kingdom off. And Praxis certainly had no defectors who lived to tell the tale of what was inside; you turn on Praxis, you might as well prep yourself for an unfortunate trip to an airlock. Cade was now strategically blind. He had no idea what the ship's layout was, how many people were inside, or, most importantly, where the holding cells were. It was all okay, Cade reminded himself. He had it covered.

What he found inside, though, was strangely pedestrian. There were docked ships, technicians working on them, and a control tower hovering in the rear. It was just a hangar. A hangar filled with evil, evil men and women who, at this very moment, were all plotting a way to kill Cade. He was certain of it.

And he was right. When Cade came down the *Horizon Dawn*'s hatch, he was immediately surrounded by four gunners. Their weapons were hot, and they all shared a cold, angry mien that assured Cade they were serious about pulling their triggers. As if that was in question.

A young man in a crisp officer's uniform—a deep red shirt tucked into pants so stiff Cade was surprised he could even walk—split the gunners, approaching Cade with a look on his face that expressed his complete satisfaction with himself.

Cade was looking forward to knocking that look right off his face.

"Did you really expect your little plan to work?" the officer said.

"So far, so good," Cade replied.

The officer narrowed his gaze. "What is that supposed to mean?"

"It means you're screwed, jerkface," Cade replied, his tone buoyant.

Like a dog catching the shrill call of a whistle only it could hear, the officer upturned his head and conveyed his confusion. But Cade didn't need to say another word. He let 4-Qel do the talking for him.

The drone bounded down the *Horizon Dawn*'s hatch, chewing up the space between him and the gunners.

"Is that . . . ?" the officer asked, tumbling backward. "Is that a *Qel*?"

Cade smiled, taking a moment to enjoy seeing the smugness vanish from the officer's face. "It sure is. Interesting fact: Qels don't show up on life-form scanners. Cool, right?"

The officer was confounded, and Cade was tired of wasting time. He connected a right hook across the Praxis lackey's face, knocking him off his feet. Meanwhile, 4-Qel made quick work of the gunners. He was on the first two before they could even fire; he smashed their skulls together, and Cade heard a cracking noise that probably spelled a lifetime of meals out of straws for both gunners. The third gunner burst off a round of blasts that 4-Qel rolled under. He sprang up right in front of the gunner, grabbed her by the throat, and her launched her into her only remaining squad mate. Before either could stand up, 4-Qel was on them.

"Taking my friend was a *mistake*," 4-Qel said right before he stomped down on them both. Cade heard more cracking.

"You're crazy!" the officer said as he pedaled backward on his ass. Cade, with 4-Qel at his side, kept pace with him. "You'll never get out of this ship alive!"

"Oh, I beg to differ, though I'm touched by your concern," Cade said. "If I were you, I'd be more worried about my own survival. And you *can* survive this; all you have to do is tell us where our friend is being held."

"Never," the officer snarled, his refusal unconvincing.

Cade sighed. "Look, I get it. You're loyal to Praxis. You're afraid of what they'll do to you if you talk. But here's the thing:

If you don't talk to us, the Qel is going to rip out your spine. Slowly."

The officer looked at 4-Qel, horrified. 4-Qel was silent. "He couldn't," the officer said, turning back to Cade.

"I just upgraded my legs, and they give me the torque required to hold you in place as I remove your backbone," 4-Qel said.

"Red corridor," the officer blurted. "Take it to the end, then head left. That's where you'll find the holding area."

"If you're lying . . ." Cade said as 4-Qel grabbed the officer from the floor and lifted him over his head.

"I swear!"

Cade and 4-Qel shared a look. They were both fairly certain the officer had been sufficiently terrified into telling the truth. "Okay, we believe you. Qel, take his spine."

"What?!" the officer howled.

Cade laughed. "Just kidding. But, for real," Cade said, nudging 4-Qel, "knock him out."

A single head butt was all it took to knock the officer out cold. 4-Qel tossed him to the ground as if he were a bag of rags.

Cade activated his comms unit and patched into the secure line he'd established with Kira.

"Kira!" Cade called as he and 4-Qel bolted from the hangar toward the corridor entrance on the far side of the room. "We're in; you are clear to make your run!"

"Yeah, I kinda figured you were," Kira's voice cracked through the comms. "They just deployed fighters, so expect company coming your way soon."

"Don't worry," Cade said, a half smile directed at 4-Qel. "We've got this."

"Same here," Kira said. "Time for target practice. Over and out."

Cade and 4-Qel came to a fork in the corridor ahead and turned right, following the walls painted a syrupy red. As they turned the corner, Cade drew both his sidewinder and shido, expecting to encounter trouble ahead. While he knew fighting his way in and out of the *War Hammer* was a given—he wouldn't have smuggled 4-Qel with him if he hadn't—Cade made the mistake of severely underestimating how prepared the Praxis army would be for a sneak attack. At least he *thought* it was a sneak attack. But when he and 4-Qel swung around the corner, they ran headfirst into what couldn't have been less than an entire battalion. Sentry drones and gunners packed the corridor, positioned shoulder to shoulder and five across so they filled every inch of the space from one side to the other. They formed an impenetrable mass—a heavily armed mass—that stood between Cade and releasing Mig.

"Oh boy," Cade marveled and came to a stop that was so hard he almost fell over. 4-Qel, a step behind Cade, didn't even break stride as he came to the corridor. He pulled a small device from his side holster; it was just a small handle, but attached to it was a piece of koruvite, folded into a cube. 4-Qel shoved Cade behind him as he jabbed the cube in front of them both, holding it at chest level. Ahead, the first wave of sentries began to push forward and spray fire across the corridor.

Not a single shot passed 4-Qel, though. Cade peeked his head around 4-Qel's torso, terrified that his drone friend was using himself as a shield. Thankfully, that wasn't the case. The handle in 4-Qel's grip extended the koruvite to make a protective barrier wide enough to give cover to both Cade and 4-Qel, and its strength wouldn't allow a single blaster's fire to penetrate it.

Cade poked his sidewinder around the edge of the shield and returned fire, downing sentries as 4-Qel pushed forward. The drone kept both hands gripped on the shield handle, keeping their protection straight and steady; while the shield was in no danger of getting breached, each blaster impact threatened to knock their coverage from 4-Qel's grip, leaving either one of them, or both, exposed.

"Just hold us steady!" Cade instructed over the screaming blaster fire that relentlessly battered the koruvite. "We'll get through this!"

It seemed like a thing Tristan would say, though Cade had serious doubts about their chances of survival, let alone getting to Mig. The sentries were pushing forward, collapsing the space between the two opposing sides. As many as Cade shot down, more and more stepped up to take their place. Soon the sentries would be on top of them, and with enough force and enough numbers, they'd be able to overtake 4-Qel's shield. As the sentries continued to march forward, the barrage of blaster fire pounded the koruvite; every shot exploded a splash of color on the shield, blanketing it in a fiery orange. 4-Qel strained as the force of the assault increased with their proximity to the enemy; he was pushing against an unending stream of powerful resistance, and Cade could tell that it was getting harder for him to maintain his footing.

"GRRRAHH!" 4-Qel grunted, and Cade could see him straining to keep himself upright as the relentless assault worked to push him back. Just as Cade was about to grab the handle in 4-Qel's grasp, he heard a gunner ahead yell to his squad mates.

"Barrage!" he called. "Down!"

The assault paused, allowing just enough time for Cade and 4-Qel to look ahead and see four rows of drones drop to the floor. Their movement revealed an ion cannon, manned by a single gunner whose entire head was covered by a heavy-duty helmet, broken only by a single, narrow slit for vision.

"FIRE!" someone yelled, and Cade rushed to 4-Qel's side. He grabbed the shield's handle and tightened every muscle in his body, bracing for an impact that, without shielding, would surely blow both 4-Qel and Cade right out of the ship. After shattering every bone in his body.

An eruption rang so loud through the corridor that it shook the walls and ruptured Cade's eardrums. The explosive sound was accompanied by what he imagined it would be like to have a starship crash into your chest. He had no way of measuring the impact of the ion cannon's power other than by depicting the gory mess it would have left of him had he not been holding a slab of koruvite in his hands. He felt the impact in his bones; he felt it in his teeth. He felt it in his muscles as he strained more than he'd ever strained in his life, fighting to resist the cannon fire's force. Cade and 4-Qel were pushed back onto their heels, but they managed to hold their position. The shielding absorbed enough of the cannon's power and, somehow, they managed to not end up plastered against the wall behind them.

The kaleidoscopic array of color that'd poured over the shield began to dissipate, and Cade spotted the sentries ahead just getting up from the ground. They were slow to get back into formation—assuming, no doubt, that the ion had left nothing of Cade and 4-Qel but a couple of smears on the floor, ceiling, and walls. A problem for maintenance drones, not sentries.

But visions of Cade and 4-Qel's deaths were unfulfilled, and the duo was ready to take advantage of the opportunity in front of them.

"Move!" Cade yelled, pushing 4-Qel forward. "Go right at them!"

4-Qel charged ahead with gusto, attacking the sentries with the vigor gained from overpowering the ion cannon's blast. The sentries tried to regain their positioning and defend themselves, but it was no use. 4-Qel was too fast; he used the shield to smash sentries against the wall while he clobbered others with his free hand. Cade was a step behind, shido ignited. The quarters were tight, and Cade used that to his advantage. Not only were the sentries unprepared for 4-Qel and Cade to rush at them, they were undertrained for this kind of fight. Cade exacted his strikes to combat the most clear and present dangers: He drilled a nearby gunner with enough sidewinder blasts to knock her off her feet before she could pull the trigger on her E-9; he sliced his shido across the chest of a sentry before it could draw its electroaxe from his back; and he rolled an explosive—one left behind by Mig—right underneath the ion cannon, blowing it and the Praxis thugs who surrounded it to bits and causing more disorientation among the battalion left standing. Cade fought his way through the line, identifying threats, predicting his enemies' movements, and delivering efficient strikes that kept the sentries down and kept him moving forward. For a second, he felt like Tristan—calm, confident, and in control. It was a nice feeling to have.

Cade grabbed a sentry and spun it around to deflect a blast from a gunner that was out of his reach; he held on to it, charging forward right at the gunner and barreled over him. By the time he drove his shido through the fallen gunner, the corridor was clear. Cade looked at 4-Qel, who was tearing a sentry's head off its shoulders. 4-Qel, after spiking the disembodied head to the ground, also scanned the corridor and realized, just like Cade, that no one was left standing. They'd survived the gauntlet.

"Well," Cade said, catching his breath, "that was . . . intense."

"I've never felt more alive," 4-Qel replied.

"You're going to have a hard time adjusting to life when this is all over, aren't you?" Cade asked.

4-Qel shrugged. "I've always wanted to raise and nurture bothos. That would be agreeable."

As they charged through the corridor, their focus back on rescuing Mig, Cade's comms crackled and Kira's voice came through in patches. They were losing their connection this deep in the *War Hammer*.

"Wait, Kira, I can't make out what you're saying," Cade said. "Repeat, please."

Cade glanced at 4-Qel, who shared his concern. They both knew that Kira wouldn't be calling him if things were going as planned.

"They're smothering us with numb . . . hold out much longer witho . . . ackup."

"Kira!" Cade yelled. "KIRA!"

"Thinning . . . mbers . . ."

"Listen to me: Evade them as long as you can," Cade said into his comms, calmly, hoping Kira could hear him better than he could hear her. "We're almost to Mig, but if you have to retreat, damn it, you retre—"

The communication cut out, and Cade was left with nothing but a gnawing fear in the pit of his stomach.

"They're outnumbered," 4-Qel said.

Cade shuddered as he envisioned the firefight happening in the space just beyond the *War Hammer*. Praxis would undoubtedly spare no resource repelling an enemy attack, even if they didn't know what Kira and the Omega Squadron were up to. And, at this point, they'd probably be okay calling Cade's bluff on the Rokura. There was no telling how many Intruders Praxis would throw at them, but Cade couldn't stop himself from imagining a sky blanketed with enemy fighters, raining death down on Kira and Omega.

"Let's move, 4-Qel. We have to double-time our asses and get out there and help Ki—"

"Whatever they're trying to do, they won't make it," a voice interrupted, a voice Cade knew as well as anyone's. He turned slowly and saw Jorken standing at the end of the corridor. He was alone, standing with nothing but his shido in his hand. "And you're not going to make it, either."

"4-Qel," Cade said, feeling his chest heave and collapse beneath his clothes. "Go get Mig."

"Cade, no. This man, he is your superior. He will surely—"

"We're running out of time," Cade said. His eyes were locked on Jorken, and Jorken's on Cade. "Now go."

4-Qel nodded, a silent acknowledgment of the real reason for Cade's decision: He needed to face Jorken alone. He ran down the corridor, and Jorken let the drone blow right by him.

As soon as 4-Qel was clear, Cade rushed Jorken, who ignited his shido as Cade approached. Cade brought his shido down for a tenacious overhead attack, which Jorken blocked. Their shidos locked together as they met, face-to-face. Master and student. Cade glared at the man who'd been like a father to him, whose face was now twisted and dark. Gone was the compassion and the wisdom Cade thought were real, replaced with bitterness and, worse, conviction. Conviction was the tree with poisoned roots that ran through all of Praxis, granting its followers license to be so certain of their own beliefs that they no longer had to even consider anyone else's point of view. Their peace was someone else's suppression, or worse; their control was someone else's incarceration. But as long as they were convinced they were right, nothing else mattered but the ends they sought. Control. Power. Domination. And all the dead along the way—like Tristan—had to be wrong in order for Praxis to be right. Cade saw the righteousness in Jorken's eyes, he saw a man who had to kill his own son because it was just the thing that needed to be done.

With little effort Jorken pushed Cade back, but Cade recovered immediately. He expected Jorken to go on the offensive, but he stood where he was. Waiting, taunting.

"I never wanted this," Jorken said. "I always hoped that, when the time came, you'd come with me. You were the only one at the Well who saw through the lies, who saw through the arrogance of the Masters."

"You're insane. Yeah, I think most of the Masters are full of crap, but that doesn't mean I want to kill them and burn everything they believe in to the ground," Cade said, his words cracking like a whip. "You *murdered* my brother. I'll die before I join you."

Cade plunged his shido forward, and Jorken sidestepped, kicking Cade's shido aside. He swiped his own shido across Cade's arm, slicing his bicep before Cade staggered to the ground.

"Then die is exactly what you'll do," Jorken said as he brought his shido down at Cade.

CHAPTER TWENTY-THREE

Cade spun out of the way of Jorken's shido, barely avoiding it plunging through his heart. Instead, it drove into the floor with enough force that its tip dug into the surface. Jorken had to pull hard to wrench it free, and Cade used that time to get back on his feet.

They stood opposite one another, circling slowly, each waiting for the other to make a move.

"Do you feel anything over what you've done, Jorken?" Cade questioned. "Tristan looked up to you; he did from the moment you scooped us off Kyysring."

"Tristan's role was to bring order to the galaxy," Jorken replied. "Give us the Rokura, and he will have served his purpose."

"You're demented," Cade spat.

"No more than you if you think you can defeat me. I trained you. I *made* you," Jorken snarled. "Now give me the Rokura."

Cade held his shido up and gripped it tightly. "You want the Rokura? You'll have to come through me to get it."

The moment Jorken took a step forward, Cade charged him. "GRRAAAHHH," he screamed as he swung his shido down at Jorken, a massive overhead strike that Jorken blocked. Cade had rage, he had fury, and he used them both to play the role of the out-of-control combatant. Let Jorken think his emotions were out of control; let him think he didn't know what he was doing. Cade brought his shido down again, then again, using his strength to drive the old man back. When Jorken blocked the third strike, Cade recognized the exertion he was putting into his defense, which he knew would slow his reflexes. He used the opportunity to kick out Jorken's knee, hard, and smash the blunt end of his shido into his face. Jorken stumbled back as blood poured from his mouth. He was on the defensive, so Cade knew not to press his attack further, but he knew his former Master was hurt. Jorken teetered back, limping, and the blood continued to rush down his chin and drip onto his tunic.

Now Jorken knew what it was like to feel vulnerable.

Jorken ran his sleeve over his mouth, smearing blood across his cheek like war paint. Cade stared into Jorken's cold eyes as adrenaline surged through him, causing his body to tremble. Cade worked to keep his feelings of anger and disgust at bay, but nothing would change the fact that he was an emotional fighter. He wasn't the cold, calculating tactician like Jorken, who formulated strategies to break down his opponents as he fought; Cade was led by instinct and intuition, for better or worse.

"How could you do this?" Cade asked. "All these years, everything you said, everything you taught . . . it was just a lie. You've betrayed *everything.*"

"No, Cade. The lie is that the Well thinks it can demand peace without fighting for it. That it can expect the galaxy to act a certain way without understanding what people actually need. The Masters have spent lifetimes expecting the galaxy to come to them and not the other way around. And that is why their time is up. They're going to reap the consequences for their arrogance."

Jorken lunged at Cade, ignoring the pain in his wounded knee just as Cade ignored the pain in his sliced arm. Their shidos met, clanging together at eye level. Jorken drove Cade backward, pushing a relentless attack that Cade struggled to defend. They exchanged blows, evenly matched for a moment. Cade delivered a series of swipes and jabs that he hoped would create an opening, but nothing materialized. Retaliating, Jorken shoved his shido forward, forcing Cade to draw his body inward as he leapt back. Before he could regain his footing, Jorken swung his shido high and Cade had no choice but to throw his feet out from under him and drop to the floor. He somersaulted backward, but when he came to his feet he was in no position to defend himself. Jorken was on him, faster than Cade anticipated. He swiped his shido across Cade's chest, which Cade blocked, but Jorken landed a head butt that cracked Cade's nose and clouded his vision.

Jorken pressed his attack, swinging at Cade's legs; Cade leapt, barely in time to avoid having his ankles sliced open. As he came back down to the ground, he brought his shido down on Jorken. His move was defended, and when Cade tried to follow the blocked strike with an elbow to Jorken's face, his former Master caught his arm, twisted it, and spun Cade around. He turned just as Jorken was delivering an uppercut attack; Cade dropped his shido to block the strike, but there was hardly time to position a defense. Jorken's shido struck Cade's, knocking it clear out of his grip. Jorken spun around, following his momentum by delivering the blunt end of his shido into Cade's stomach. The blow forced the air in Cade's lungs to erupt, and as he gasped to draw a breath, he felt a sharp, searing pain as Jorken's shido struck the back of his head. Cade fell to his knees, but Jorken didn't stop; he kicked him in his face just as he was trying to stand back up, and the blow sent him tumbling back until he hit the corridor wall and collapsed against it.

Cade fought off unconsciousness. He looked ahead and saw a blurry vision of Jorken walking toward him. He squeezed his eyes shut, pushing back against the disorientation that was clouding his vision. He could see his shido just to his left, but he knew diving for it was no use. Jorken would have his shido buried in Cade's back before he could get even a hand on his weapon. He needed a minute to recover; he needed a minute to think of a way out of this.

"Time to die," Jorken said, his voice sounding far away, but it got closer with every word. "But I want you to know that when I'm done with you, I'm going to hunt down your pathetic friends and kill them next. I want that to be your last thought, knowing that, had you not tried to do something stupid, they'd all still be alive. You, Cade, are the reason they're dead."

Cade spat blood and winced. He failed Tristan in the spire. The Rokura warned him that something terrible was about to happen, but Cade didn't understand its message; he didn't know that Tristan was as good as dead the second he wrenched the Rokura free. While he didn't blame himself for Tristan's death, he couldn't stop himself from feeling that had he taken their journey to the spire more seriously, had he been more attuned to the Rokura, had he been *better*, he might have been able to save Tristan's life. And now, with his life—and, more important, his friends' lives—hanging in the balance, he refused to let those same shortcomings doom the people he cared about.

His vision came into focus, and he saw the crackling tip of Jorken's shido hovering just above his face. His eyes darted over to his shido, lying on the ground just within his grasp.

"Your shido's no good to you now," Jorken said. "It's over."

Cade knew that his former Master must be seeing the end of this fight in his mind's eye. That's what he did best. He wanted Cade to go for his shido, he anticipated him doing just that, and then he would kill him.

Cade's only choice was to do what Jorken didn't expect.

Cade lunged, but not for his shido. He threw his right hand out, his synthetic appendage, and thrust it through the blades on Jorken's shido. Jorken tried to pull his weapon back out, but Cade closed his grasp on his former master's weapon, buying him the time he needed to reach for his shido. With his shido firmly in his grasp—*Tristan's* shido—he swung it around and drove it into Jorken's side.

Jorken gasped, a sudden, brief inhalation that abruptly cut itself off. Cade forcefully tore his hand off Jorken's shido as the traitor began to slouch to his side. Cade rose to his feet, meeting Jorken eye to eye. Jorken didn't blink, his face frozen in shock and agony.

"By the way," Cade said, tearing his shido out of Jorken and holding the bloodied blades up to his face, "this isn't my shido. It's Tristan's."

The man who had once been his Master, the man who was like a father to him, crumpled to the ground.

Cade took one last look at Jorken, realizing how lucky he was to survive a battle with him. It was over now, and his first thoughts went to his friends, to helping them get out of this situation alive.

But Cade's first step forward turned into a stumble. He fell against the wall and realized everything hurt. His head, his arm, his guts, even his synthetic hand. True, it was dulled to most feeling, but even feeling part of having an electrified blade driven through his palm was still pretty terrible. His head was swimming, and when he heard his name being called from the other end of the corridor, he thought it was a hallucination.

It wasn't, though.

"Cade!" the voice yelled. "Hold tight, we're coming!"

Cade looked up and saw Mig, with 4-Qel following closely behind, sprinting toward him.

Mig reached Cade's side and threw his arm around his shoulder, alleviating Cade's struggles to walk. 4-Qel braced him as well, and the sight of his friends, alive and well, rallied Cade to dig deep and find a second wind.

"Did you kill Jorken?" Mig asked. "Four-Qel thought you were dead for sure."

"I said I wasn't optimistic about your chances to best the man who had trained you," 4-Qel told Cade. "Now, let me evaluate your damage. I'm programmed as a field medic and might as well put it to use."

4-Qel moved to grab Cade's hand, but Cade, having grown a little touchy about this particular appendage, yanked it away.

"I can examine it," 4-Qel said. "It looks . . . bad."

"Yeah, I'm going to need a new one. Again." Cade took a second to look at his hand and the gaping hole that he could see straight through. "Gross," he said.

"How did you guys manage to get out of the holding area?" Cade asked.

"Oh, there's a lot of dead things behind us," Mig said. "Four-Qel went on a sick rampage. But I'm sure there's more of everything coming this way, so we better move."

Cade nodded and freed himself from Mig's support. "I'm okay; I can make it," Cade said. "We have to see how Kira is. With any luck, they'll be free of the Intruders and ready to attack the *War Hammer*."

Cade, Mig, and 4-Qel followed their trail back through the red corridor. Cade tried reaching Kira on his comms as they went, but the signal wasn't strong enough until they neared the hangar.

"Kira," Cade called into the comms. "Kira, where are you?"

There was no response. Cade, Mig, and 4-Qel all shared a look, fearing the worst but not wanting to say it.

"Kira," Cade called again. "Kira!"

Gunners and drones were waiting in the hangar for Cade, 4-Qel, and Mig's return, but they had no time to entertain another fight. 4-Qel used the koruvite to shield all three of them as they carved out a path to the *Horizon Dawn*. They all combined to return enemy fire as they ran forward. Mig grabbed one of his explosives from 4-Qel and tossed it at a docked Intruder; the ship erupted, causing far more damage than the explosive could have on its own. Praxis forces ducked for cover, reflexively, and Cade, Mig, and 4-Qel used that opening to get to their ship.

Cade fired up the engine. He had to get to Kira; he had to do whatever he could to save her. 4-Qel stayed at the ramp, koruvite in hand, blasting whoever was unfortunate enough to get in his sights.

Just as Cade was about to propel the *Dawn* up and spin it around so it could blast out of the hangar, a shock wave rocked through the *War Hammer*. The hangar quaked so hard Cade feared it might capsize, or worse. An alarm blared, and the drones and gunners that'd been knocked off their feet with the blast got up and ran. They're evacuating, Cade realized as the entire room went dark. The auxiliary power kicked in, casting a dim yellow haze over the hangar just as the *War Hammer*'s port side began to sag.

"Hold on!" Cade yelled as the *Horizon Dawn* followed the *War Hammer*'s tilt and slid across the hangar's surface. It screeched as it fell across the floor, and Cade was thrown from his seat before he could get his ship off the ground. He landed against the *Horizon Dawn*'s side, exacerbating the pain that was already coursing throughout his tender body. Cade winced and propped himself up just as Mig came tumbling after Cade, also succumbing to the *War Hammer*'s loss of equilibrium.

"What is this?!" Mig yelled as the *Horizon Dawn* crashed against the hangar's side, bringing its sliding to an end.

Cade smiled. "Kira," he said.

With his back positioned against the ship's viewport, Cade brought up his comms again. She had to be there, he assured himself. This had to be her work.

"Kira," he called. "Kira, come in. Kira. Kir—"

The receiver popped as a voice came screeching through the comms.

"WHOOOOOOOOO," Kira howled, and Cade knew that scream. It was the scream he heard when they downed that warship.

Victory.

"Kira!" Cade yelled. "What's happening out there? Are you okay?"

"We got it Cade! We nailed it!" Kira shouted. "You should see this damn ship burn. It's a thing of beauty."

"Where were you?" Cade asked. Assisted by Mig, he started to scale his way up *Horizon Dawn*, which had come to rest at a 60-degree angle.

"Oh, yeah, we ran into trouble, but we had some help."

"Help?" Cade asked, cautiously. "From *who*?"

There was a pause, then Kira spoke. "You're not going to like it," she warned.

Cade groaned as he clambered upward. "Percival."

"Percival," Kira confirmed. "And where are you? I thought you'd already be out of there."

"Yeah, we ran into a little . . . difficulty," Cade said, thinking of his mangled hand. "But, wait—why didn't the *War Hammer* combust? I mean, I'm not crazy about the idea, but I should be dead."

"It's burning," Kira replied, "and it's badly damaged. But it must have some kind of fail-safe to protect where the siphoned energy is stored from erupting."

Cade reached his chair, and 4-Qel—who had no problem scaling his way to the front of the ship as Cade and Mig clawed their way up—plucked him off the ground and dropped him into his seat. The engine was hot, so he could lift it off the ground and straighten them out immediately.

But he couldn't bring himself to rocket out of the *War Hammer*. The Praxis super weapon, their ultimate deterrent, the symbol of their might and control over the galaxy, was damaged, but it wasn't destroyed. The evil kingdom would repair it, they'd even improve it, and it would be back to cast a shadow of menace and fear across the entire galaxy.

Cade couldn't have that.

"You guys need to get out of there," Kira said. "Praxis will have reinforcements swarming in no time."

"Yeah," Cade said, his voice faint. "We're on our way."

Cade cut off the comms, and with the tiniest thrust of the engine, he propelled the *Horizon Dawn* to the far side of the hangar, to the corridors opposite the one that led to the holding area. Those corridors had to lead deeper into the ship, Cade presumed.

"Uh . . . Cade?" Mig asked. "Remember that part about reinforcements and us leaving?"

Cade set the *Horizon Dawn* to hover as he got up from his chair. "Four-Qel, go get it."

"I'm not sure what you're planning," 4-Qel countered, "but I'd wager that the wise choice would be for us to leave."

"Making wise choices isn't exactly my thing," Cade said. "Now, please, give it to me."

"What are you two talking about?" Mig asked.

4-Qel looked at Mig, then returned his focus to Cade. He

grumbled disapprovingly, then tore open a welded-shut floor panel. In the cavity below their feet was the Rokura.

"You brought it with you?!" Mig yelped. "Wha—why would you bring it here?!"

"In case I needed it," Cade said, calmly. "And I couldn't think of a safer place for it—the last place Praxis would check."

With the Rokura held firmly in his one good hand, Cade slid open the *Horizon Dawn*'s narrow cockpit exit. He looked back at Mig and 4-Qel and gave a smile. Whatever happened next, he was glad to have been on this adventure with his friends, and he was especially glad they were getting out of it alive.

"Wait," Mig asked, quietly. "Where are you going?"

Cade looked at his friend, his brother, and he knew that Mig already had the answer to the question, and he was aware of what it meant.

"What we came here to do," Cade said. "I'm going to use the Rokura to breach the energy storage. It's the only way to destroy the *War Hammer*."

"But," Mig said, his voice cracking, "you'll die."

"Just, tell Kira . . . tell her I'm glad it came to this. Tell her I know she can finish the job we started today.

"And thank her for me. Thank her for believing in me."

Cade turned and made the short jump out of his ship, leaving it behind. Leaving his friends and everything else in his life behind.

CHAPTER TWENTY-FOUR

Ga Halle lorded over the *War Hammer*'s command center, and by all appearances, it seemed like she was overseeing the ship's evacuation process. She positioned herself to give strength to her subordinates in a time of crisis. To help them through this difficult moment.

The truth, though, was that Ga Halle didn't care if every single man and woman in the room burned with the ship as it floated through space. Her focus was singular; her rage over failing to obtain her prize, unquantifiable. The Rokura had slipped through her fingers, and her mind knew no other loss than that. The *War Hammer* was failing, and even if it was beyond repair, there'd be more weapons, more ways to kill. Jorken was dead, but she had plenty of allies. The Rokura was singular; there was no replacement, no substitute. And the longer it remained out of her grasp, the better the chance it was possessed by someone else. She'd burn this entire galaxy into oblivion before she let that happen.

"It is time, my queen," Ortzo said, standing at Ga Halle's back.

Ga Halle followed; she had no reason to remain on the *War*

Hammer. She'd return to the *Fortress* and order her spies to press their ears to the ground. The first system to utter so much as a seditious word would be pillaged and scorched. They'd be an example to anyone else who got similar ideas in their heads as word of the *War Hammer*'s damage spread throughout the galaxy. And she'd finish the job she started against the Well. She'd root out the Rising Suns. But first, first she'd track down the Rokura. She'd find this Cade Sura and show him exactly what it meant to be worthy of the Rokura's power. She'd suffered and sacrificed; she'd pushed herself beyond limits she didn't even know were possible, twisting herself into something that, at times, even she didn't recognize. But it was all for the Rokura, and her time was *now*.

But as Ortzo was ushering her toward her shuttle, she sensed something. Something stirring deep within her, awakening in her. Ga Halle closed her eyes and let the world around her go silent. The alarms, the yelling to bring people to order—it all died before reaching her ears. The only thing she could hear was a faint whisper that was calling out to her. Beckoning her.

The Rokura. She could *feel* it.

Ga Halle turned and pushed her way through the crowd waiting to board the transport shuttles. Ortzo followed behind her, trying to keep up with Ga Halle's driven pace.

"My queen," he called. "We really should leave; the ship is unstable."

"Leave," Ga Halle ordered, not even bothering to turn back and face Ortzo. "My destiny has come for me."

CHAPTER TWENTY-FIVE

Alarms wailed throughout the ship as all personnel on the *War Hammer* made for the evacuation pods. No one cared who Cade was or what he was up to as he ran against the tide of the fleeing navigators, gunners, and officers. They probably knew he wasn't one of their own, but allegiances meant very little when it came time to save your own hide.

While Cade didn't know everything there was to know about starcruiser mechanics—he was no Mig—he knew enough to deduce how to locate where the energy sapped from Ticus's star was housed. The main engine was centrally located in the ship, so if Praxis had any brains at all they wouldn't store the power of a star there. Just in case. And if what Kira told him was true— that fail-safes were in place to separate the containment area from a potential cataclysmic event—what Cade was looking for had to be near the siphoning entry point but far enough away to allow whatever protection was in place to cut the energy housing off from potential disaster. Because should that housing be penetrated, the entire ship would suffer the wrath of a star opening in its face. That would be bad.

And it was exactly what Cade was hoping for.

Cade found his way to a service corridor, easily detected by the grunts in coveralls and grease-stained faces pouring from it. These people were coming from the *War Hammer*'s belly; they spent their days and nights in the bowels of the ship, down where the real work gets done. Cade came to a fork in the corridor. On one side, a few straggling techs and mechanics were still filing out; the other side was vacant, not a single person was coming from that dark tunnel. If Cade ventured a guess, he'd say that people spent as little time as possible hanging around the contained power of a star, regardless of how impenetrable its container was. Granted, if something were to go wrong, being on the other side of a wall would do nothing to prevent your body, down to your bones, from incinerating into nothingness. Still, that was no reason to get close to it if you didn't have to.

The corridor Cade pursued was a tunnel that swallowed light. The deeper he went, the darker it became; he navigated his way forward with his outstretched hand, its dulled sense of touch just barely able to register the obstructions and turns that awaited just ahead. Cade hoped he would be able to accomplish what he had in mind. The Rokura would have to work through him. Or he would have to work through it. What Percival told him spoke more to dominance than symbiosis, which is what Cade thought was the point of its relationship with its wielder. Cade was torn between reading the Rokura as a weapon of control or a weapon of peace. Maybe he was naive to believe you couldn't have one without the other.

When Cade's hand nudged against a solid surface directly in front of him, he figured he'd reached the end of the corridor. He grabbed hold of a thick metallic wheel in the center of what he assumed to be the door and began spinning it counterclockwise. The door clicked, and Cade felt a spasm of fear jolt within him. He knew what he had to do, he knew what it required of him, and he was afraid. Though it wasn't the fear of death that made him pause; it was the fear of failure. Given the choice, no one at the Well would trust the task of destroying the Praxis *War Hammer* in Cade's hands, even if he pledged his life to the mission. Doubt made him freeze at the door. What if he failed? What if he couldn't get the Rokura to do what he wanted and, instead, he ended up delivering the weapon right to his enemies? Cade felt the conviction he had just moments ago racing out of him—but then he remembered his vow with Kira. They weren't going to be the people the Well decided they were. Cade knew Kira was better than that, and he was pretty sure he was, too. Cade knew in his heart that the galaxy needed to be rebooted; its people needed a chance to start from scratch without being dependent on the Well or oppressed by Praxis. And he couldn't think of any way to give people the liberation they needed other than by destroying the symbols of their hope and fear, the Rokura and the *War Hammer*, in one dramatic swoop.

Cade threw his weight into the door and heaved it open. The moment he did, blinding, white-hot light poured from the room, and it physically pushed Cade back. He threw his forearm over his eyes and, through the narrowest opening his eyelids could allow, looked inside. His pupils adjusted as much as they could to the ferocious light, just enough for Cade to make out a massive orb in the center of the room. He recognized the crackling orange and blue spidery tendrils of the koruvite shielding the orb, somehow containing the power of a star. Cade could barely comprehend what he was seeing, as it all seemed too immense to even be real. But it was, and it was now Cade's duty to let that immensity free.

Every step Cade took was like fighting against a relentless cyclone, spinning and pushing, keeping anyone from getting close. Energy poured off the orb in pulsing waves, and Cade labored to take every step that led him to within arm's reach of the shielding.

Cade raised the Rokura above his head with his one good hand, and he reached deep within himself to call upon his determination, his will, to get the Rokura to obey his command. He thought back to the spire, where he demanded that it strike down his brother's killer, and even though the weapon fought against him, it eventually surrendered. This was the same thing, only Cade didn't care what happened to him. The Rokura could take his hand, take his whole arm. It didn't matter. All that mattered was busting a hole in the orb so that Praxis's stolen power would blow up in its face.

Maybe it was Cade's inner strength that triggered the Rokura, maybe it was its insatiable lust for destruction, but as he clenched it in his hand and thought only of the *War Hammer*'s demise, it came to life. The weapon erupted at its head, sparking explosive energy that was stronger than Cade remembered from the spire. Cade knew the Rokura was strong enough to tear through the koruvite; it was just a matter of whether it would let Cade do it.

"AAAAAHHHH," Cade screamed, and he threw his arm down to drive the Rokura into the orb.

But his arm didn't move.

Cade grunted, fighting to push his arm forward even an inch, but it wouldn't budge. The weapon was locked in place, and he was locked with it. He couldn't see anything wrong with the Rokura, and he couldn't understand why it stopped in the blink of an eye.

Then he heard a voice, a raging voice, call out from behind him.

"That weapon," the voice screamed above the blistering din of the room, "is *mine*."

Cade turned, and though he'd never seen her before, he knew exactly who was behind him: Ga Halle. He couldn't discern her features through the light; the only thing his eyes could visualize was the legendary containment suit, pulsing fiery waves of dark blue antimatter over the left side of her body. The rest of her was nothing more than an outline crouching against the waves of energy as she, like Cade, struggled to hold her position. Her arm stretched forward as she reached for the Rokura, and it was her will, Cade realized, that caused the Rokura to stop. She expected the weapon to soar to her palm, demanded it to, in fact. Cade could feel the conflict within the weapon; it was drawn to Ga Halle as much as it was connected to Cade. Maybe even more, Cade considered, as he struggled to keep the Rokura in his grasp.

"Oh, yeah?" Cade yelled. "If it belongs to you, then why don't you have it?"

"You have no idea what it takes to control the Rokura's power. I've made myself into the exact image of what it demands—what it *really* demands. And you? You're an accident who actually believes the fairy tale the Well has filled your mind with."

"You're wrong," Cade yelled back. "If you were this perfect specimen, the Rokura wouldn't be struggling between us. It would have—"

"It craves a possessor! It seeks to bond with—"

"It would have allowed you to remove it from its stasis at some point in the past twenty years."

Cade waited for Ga Halle to say something, but she didn't utter a word. Her silence was far more terrifying than her words.

"Your fight with Percival changed you, and now . . . and now your scars and your wounds run far deeper than what's on your surface. I can *feel* it."

Cade noticed that the power that cycled throughout the room was starting to surge; between the orb's residual energy and what poured off the Rokura, the space he and Ga Halle inhabited was getting unstable. And the more they argued, the more likely it seemed that they'd reach a critical mass that would destroy them both. The orb, Cade wagered, would remain secure, and that couldn't happen. Cade had to do something.

But Ga Halle beat him to it.

Even through the room's increasing cacophonous noise, Cade could hear Ga Halle's labored, furious breathing. Cade unleashed a primal scream that cut like a knife through the room's blustering noise as he felt Ga Halle exert every ounce of her will, every ounce of her rage, into commanding the Rokura. And it worked. The Rokura pulled away from Cade's grip, and he knew it wouldn't be long before his grasp failed him.

"Percival stole my chance," Ga Halle growled. "He ruined me, he damned my people, and I will never apologize for what I did to save everything I loved."

The Rokura pulled and pulled, and Ga Halle used its pull to trudge herself forward. Cade, meanwhile, mustered all his strength to keep the weapon away from Ga Halle, but it made no difference. This fight had nothing to do with physical strength.

"I won't. Let you. Have it!" Cade yelled. "You'll plunge the galaxy into darkness!"

"And you'll plunge it into chaos!"

Cade squeezed the very end of the Rokura with a tenuous, failing grip. The weapon was escaping him, and it would be gone soon. That would be the end of everything, and Cade knew, without hesitation, that he'd rather die than see Ga Halle possess the Rokura. He'd rather die than be forced to watch Praxis smother the galaxy in despair, oppression, and tyranny.

And realizing that, he knew exactly what to do.

"There's nothing special about you," Ga Halle taunted. "Nothing that you're willing to do that I can't do ten times better."

"Wrong again, Ga Halle," Cade pronounced. "There's something I'm willing to do that you're not. Something that proves my will over yours."

Ga Halle was close enough for Cade to look into her cold, steely eyes; he was glad to be able to do so as he played his winning move.

"I'm willing to die for this power."

And with that, the Rokura snapped back into Cade's grip, and he slammed it down on the orb.

There was a brief sound of a thunderous explosion, unlike anything Cade had ever heard before. Then, following on the heels of the explosion, Cade's world went completely white.

CHAPTER TWENTY-SIX

C ade? Cade, can you hear me?"

Slowly, and not easily, Cade opened his eyes. He was dead. He didn't feel dead, but there was no way he was anything but. Kira, Mig, and 4-Qel were all crouching above him, and beyond them, the wonderful, endless, darkness of space seen through the *Rubicon*'s viewport.

"I was hoping the afterlife was going to be a lot cooler than Kira's ship," Cade mumbled.

"First of all, there's nothing cooler than my ship," Kira said. "And second, you're not dead."

Cade looked at Kira, then Mig, then 4-Qel. They each appeared to corroborate this story. Cade was alive.

He groaned. "Terrific."

"What happened?" Mig asked. "From where we were, man, that looked like some madness that went down on the *War Hammer*."

Cade tried to get up, but his spinning head and his aching body sent him right back to the floor. Slowly, his friends propped him into a sitting position against a wall of the *Rubicon*.

"I remember . . ." Cade said, thinking back on what had happened. There was the struggle with the Rokura; there was the moment where he took control of the weapon and jammed it into the orb; then there was an enormous sound and he was swallowed by light. After that point, things became hazy in Cade's mind. He remembered feeling a warm glow surrounding him; he remembered feeling sheltered by it as he drifted off into space. But after that, nothing.

He conveyed this to his friends, who were skeptical, to say the least.

"Riiiiiight," Mig said.

"Well, what did you see?" Cade asked. "And how did I end up here?"

"When we escaped the *War Hammer*, we met with Kira and boarded her ship, leaving yours behind," 4-Qel said.

"You abandoned my ship?" Cade asked, wounded.

"Cade, it's garbage. Get over it," Mig said.

"We left it as a decoy in case Praxis came looking for us. It was something that could buy us time as we waited for you," 4-Qel said.

"We parked outside the *War Hammer*," Kira added. "We thought you might try to get in touch with us in case you needed to get out of there."

"We couldn't leave you," Mig said. "Not when there was still a chance you could get out of there alive."

Cade looked at his friend, and he knew he meant what he said. Mig would have stayed there—they all would have—until they couldn't stay anymore.

"I still don't get how I ended up here," Cade said.

"Well, the *War Hammer* was blowing the eff up," Mig said. "Kind of."

Kira rolled her eyes. "There was an explosion, this . . . surge of light that burst through the *War Hammer*'s hull. It tore right through the ship, and we figured you had to be close. So, against 4-Qel's wishes, we went looking for you and—"

"I only remarked that the rest of the *War Hammer* was sure to explode in sequence after this initial blast, taking everything in its proximity along with it," 4-Qel retorted. "But, a sequence of locks must have been in place, keeping the *War Hammer* together long enough for those on board to escape."

"Don't sweat it, Four-Qel," Cade said as he patted the drone on his arm. "I wouldn't have you any other way."

"Anyway," Kira continued, "we decided to make a pass. And it's a good thing we did because just as we were flying by, you came right out of the hole created by the blast. It was like you were floating, but you were guided in the right direction as well. It was . . . weird."

"The Rokura," Cade said. "It—"

Cade sprang up, feeling alarm punch in his chest. "The Rokura," he repeated. "Tell me it's here; tell me you have it."

"It's right next to you," Mig nodded.

Cade's eyes darted to the floor, and there it was. A sigh of relief vacated his body. Thinking back, he remembered more of what happened after penetrating the orb. There was the flash of light, but instead of being immolated and shredded by the energy that poured out of the orb, he felt warmth. Comforting warmth. It was the Rokura. Protecting him, keeping him safe. A protective cocoon sheathed his entire body, and Cade had in his mind a clear vision of floating off into space as mass destruction unfolded all around him. But there was something else. Ga Halle was there, too. Protected like he was. Apparently, the Rokura wasn't going to let anything as silly as an exploding star kill its best two candidates to become its wielder.

Cade may have won this encounter, but the Rokura still wasn't convinced of his, or Ga Halle's, worthiness.

A victory was still a victory, though. At least Cade had kept the Rokura out of the hands of Ga Halle, who was even more dangerous and demented than he'd imagined. If he hadn't been convinced she was a stark raving lunatic before meeting her, he certainly was now. While Cade didn't feel all that thrilled about the onus of possessing the Rokura, he could at least find solace that whatever his shortcomings were, they'd always be better than whatever a psychopath brought to the table.

Cade accepted 4-Qel's hand and stood up. The disorientation was wearing off, as was the soreness that had been throbbing his body from head to toe. He felt strangely replenished.

"So, wait—what happened to the *War Hammer*, then?"

Kira, Mig, and 4-Qel shared a look, and then they all smiled.

"See for yourself," Kira said, directing Cade to the viewport.

For a second, Cade thought he was looking at a small asteroid field. But he realized it wasn't chunks of rock dotting the space just off the *Rubicon*'s port side—it was metal. Shards and slabs and wedges of metal, thousands upon thousands of pieces, scattered so far in every direction that Cade couldn't even see where the floating scrap heap ended. This was the *War Hammer*, literally blown to bits and soon to be spread throughout the galaxy. Praxis's prized weapon had been defeated. The kingdom was proven to be vulnerable.

"I can't believe it," Cade said, astounded. "We actually did it."

No one said a word. Cade, Kira, Mig, and 4-Qel stood at the *Rubicon*'s viewport, simply enjoying the view.

It was Cade, after a long, peaceful, and satisfying moment, who broke the silence.

"Well . . . what now?" he asked.

Kira shrugged. "That depends on you."

Cade cocked a curious eyebrow at Kira, then looked to Mig and 4-Qel for answers.

"Hey, don't look at me," Kira said. "These blasterheads certainly don't follow my command."

When Cade turned, Kira was standing at the control panel, calling up her radar.

"We have fourteen Omega Echoes and Percival's squad of ten Boxer fighters—relics from the Quarrian War—and pretty cool, I might add."

"Why are they here?" Cade asked, confused. "Why haven't they gone into hiding or . . . wherever it is that Percival goes?"

"They're waiting for the Paragon's instructions," Kira said. "They're waiting for *your* command."

Cade opened his mouth to speak but couldn't find the words. He knew, after all this, he couldn't come clean about the presumption he was the Paragon. These people had fought for him; some had even died for him. And while Cade knew he was no Paragon, he was at least closer than anyone else alive to claiming the mantle. Besides, the war was on. There was no turning back now.

But before he could step into the command, the *Rubicon*'s comms blared. Kira groaned.

"It's Teeg," she said. "The Well has been trying to get through for the past hour."

Kira was about to cut off the transmission, but Cade stopped her.

"No, patch him through, but just voice. Let's hear what he has to say."

Kira gave an acquiescent shrug and opened the line to Ticus. After a crackle and some static feedback, Teeg's voice entered the ship.

"Cade Soora, we have no idea how you did it, but you saved the Well. You saved all of Ticus."

"You're welcome," Cade said, punctuating his response to the gratitude that hadn't been delivered.

"May I remind you, though, that your actions were unsanctioned by the Well, that you've been acting as a renegade. We are still the preeminent peacekeeping body in the galaxy, and we expect you to act—"

"Nope," Cade interrupted. "No to everything you just said. You want to call yourselves the galaxy's peacekeeping body? Then start acting like it."

"I . . ." Teeg stumbled. "Excuse me?"

"We might have hit Praxis where it hurts, but they're going to regroup. I suggest you use that time wisely. Use it to get better, get focused on what's important, and prove to me that you're willing to fight a war. Because that's what this is, Teeg. War."

There was a pause, though Cade could hear the murmurs as Teeg and whatever other Masters surrounded him conferred over what to do. For the first time in a long time, they had no choice but to feel powerless. Which was good, Cade decided. It would help them want to feel strong again.

"And I take it you're going to leave? You and this band of renegades?"

"I'll have my eye on you, Teeg. Because we need you. We all need each other. Paragon out."

Kira shook her head at Cade.

What? Cade mouthed as she cut off the comms connection.

"'Paragon out'?"

Cade smiled. He knew it was a ridiculous thing to say.

"Well, you heard Teeg," Cade said, turning to face his team. His friends. "We're renegades. So let's make like renegades and upend the ruling order."

Mig grinned, ear to ear. "Yes, yes, yes."

"I think I'm going to find many things to enjoy on the road ahead," 4-Qel added.

Cade looked at Kira, who shrugged noncommittally. "Yeah, I guess it could be all right." Her nonchalance didn't last long. It couldn't. She smiled and hopped into the pilot's seat while everyone else strapped themselves in.

"But where do we go?" Kira asked.

Cade breathed deeply. He wasn't certain about his idea, but he was smart enough to realize that it was the only idea he had.

"Let's get Percival on the line," Cade said.

Kira reached for the control panel, then hesitated. "You're not going to tell him to get lost, are you?"

"Not yet," Cade replied.

Percival's voice came through the ship, gruff as ever. When he left Mithlador, Cade knew he'd hear it again at some point. He just didn't think it would be this soon.

"Not bad of a job you did there, Cade. As our terrorist ally, I approve."

"Don't make it harder to like you than it already is," Cade said. "Look, you remember that training-to-become-the-Paragon stuff you were telling me about, right?"

Cade could almost hear him smiling through the comms. "What about it?"

"I think we should get started."

There was a pause, then Percival's ship pulled right alongside the *Rubicon*. Cade rolled his eyes; Percival was indeed smiling. "I know exactly where we need to go," he said. "Follow me."

With that, Percival soared ahead until his ship darted into space, disappearing in a streak of light. Coordinates came through the *Rubicon*'s comms, and Kira punched them into her mass jump drive.

"Well?" Kira asked, looking at Cade for confirmation.

Cade smiled and nodded. "Let's do it."

Kira activated the jump drive and, in a flash, they were gone.

TO BE CONTINUED

ACKNOWLEDGMENTS

Writing a novel is a hell of a thing. As a father of two, I consider the maxim "It takes a village" to be one of the truest things ever said. The same goes for writing a novel. There's no way this book would exist without the support of a whole bunch of amazing, talented, and patient—and I stress "patient"—people.

First, my editor, Marc Resnick. This whole thing started with Marc calling me up and saying, "You love *Star Wars*. Write me a love letter to *Star Wars*." Granted, I'd been throwing pitches through Marc's window for years, but it was his simple insight that recognized how much I adored a certain thing and, because of it, that I should harness that adoration into something all my own. That's exactly how *Black Star Renegades* began. Marc was with me every step of the way, helping me write a book we both wanted to read. And it gave us an excuse to talk about comics and movies and whatever other nerd junk was on our minds that day.

Jason Yarn—my terrific agent who, more than once, rapped my knuckles with a ruler and pushed me to write better. When

I was stuck, Jason illuminated the way with awesome insight and sharp ideas that brought heart and soul to this universe. Jason's a tenacious agent, and he's a friend. You're stuck with me, buddy.

Tracy Flynn and Rone Shavers, my very first readers, told me the things I needed to hear at the right times. Tim Daniel talked me down from the ledge of panic as I tried to figure out how the heck to actually write a novel. My brother, heavens bless him, gave me a quiet place to work. Phil Sevy's great art helped cement the visuals of these characters in my head. Since we were kids, Sam Kanan has believed in my abilities as a writer—we'll always have *Monster*, my man! Duane Swierczynski is the man who brought Marc and I together (and he's a helluva fine writer, I might add): This book literally wouldn't exist without you.

All my life, I underachieved at just about everything. All I wanted to do was create. Books, movies, comics—my nose was always buried. And my parents could have whooped my butt into shape, justifiably, at any point, and pushed me into . . . I don't know—one of those careers where they do the thing with numbers. But they didn't. They've fostered my passion for as far back as I can remember, and there's no way I'd be doing this without their understanding and support.

My wife, Alissa, listened to a lot of story ideas. A lot. Many of them weren't any good. Many of them she made good. She's been with me through all the frustrations and heartbreak that come with being a writer, and it has not been easy. Her love, faith, and humor have kept me sane, happy, and able to push forward.

My two crazy boys: There's no one on Earth I'd rather create worlds with. Their imaginations and joy have brought me more exuberance and inspiration that I can even quantify. They've made life fun.

Star Wars. I thank George Lucas, Ralph McQuarrie, Lawrence Kasdan, Kathleen Kennedy, John Williams, and all the other people who have created and have had a hand in furthering the stories told in a galaxy far, far away. You've read the book; it's probably pretty evident why I'm paying my respects.

Also, comics! I wouldn't have caught Marc's eye if it wasn't for the comics I made, and I would never have created a single sequential story without Tim Seeley, Steve Seeley, Eric Stephenson, Ross Richie, Bryce Carlson, Harry Markos, Jeff Krelitz, Keith Burns, Cullen Bunn, Jim Campbell, and so many other excellent people.

And, last but not even close to least, thank YOU for reading!

GLOSSARY

CHARACTERS

Cade Sura—Former resident of Kyysring, who, along with his brother, Tristan, was drafted to train at the Well to become a Rai, a defender of peace and justice throughout the galaxy.

Tristan Sura—Cade's older brother and a leader at the Well. Many believe that Tristan is destined to wield the Rokura and bring peace to the galaxy.

Ga Halle—The self-appointed queen of the Praxis kingdom. Although the power of the empire technically resides with the Barons, Ga Halle controls its real might.

Kira Sen—The leader of Omega Squadron, a rogue outfit of Echo pilots within the Well. She's determined to use her audacious and loyal pilots to fight back against the Praxis kingdom.

Ser Jorken—A Master Rai at the Well, Ser Jorken is not only the man who recruited Cade and Tristan, he's also Cade's mentor and father figure.

Mig—Cade and Tristan's best friend; an engineering genius, con artist, and scoundrel, Mig travels the galaxy running various schemes, gambling, and causing mischief wherever he and his pal 4-Qel go.

4-Qel—Hailing from Eris, 4-Qel is a drone built specifically to protect the royal family. But every line of Qel is decommissioned—i.e., murdered—upon the creation of the subsequent model. Since the Qels are up to model 6-Qel, 4-Qel should have been disposed of, but somehow he escaped.

Percival White—A former Rai who abandoned the Well and is now the leader of the Rising Suns, a group that wages guerrilla warfare against Praxis.

Ortzo—Ga Halle's lead Fatebreaker, one of the highly trained warriors who serve Ga Halle's every command, whether it be political assassination, squashing a resistance, or other similar deeds.

Wu-Xia—The fabled warrior who forged the Rokura and used it to bring peace to the galaxy.

PLACES

Aria—One of Ticus's three moons, Aria is known as an agricultural nexus. It is the only place where kerbis—a valuable herb—grows, and an entire horticulture industry has risen around it.

Boxton—Located far from most mass-jump routes, Boxton is a planetoid covered mainly in swamps and marshes. Natives rarely leave the planet, except for trading at galactic outposts.

Darklands—???

Dotax—An ice-covered planet ringed by frozen asteroids. Dotax's dark side is lethal, with temperatures dropping far below freezing. The promise of a hypothermic death keeps the native Dotaxians on the move, staying ahead of the darkness that always follows them.

Durang—For years, this planet suffered under a civil war waged in response to the assassination of its unpopular overlord. The war was ended, justly, by Rai forces.

Eris—Though an Inner Cluster world, Eris maintains a closed-door policy, discouraging people from entering or leaving the planet. The royal family rules justly enough, protected by their Qel security drones.

Galibad—One of the most central Inner Cluster worlds and the seat of the Galactic Alliance.

Hesbon—A harsh planetoid covered in jutting rocks and mountains; its inhabitants, like Rai Master Plar, live in the man-made tunnels beneath the surface.

Kyysring—Known for its criminal delights, Kyysring is the place people go to get what they can't have and do what they're not supposed to. Though most of the planetoid is covered by an uninhabitable desert, its small city and spaceport pack in enough character to rival the most bustling core worlds. It's also where Cade, Tristan, and Mig grew up.

Lehara—A small agrarian moon in the Latos system populated by a pacifist species. Resultant of the resistance to Praxis demanding that a stronghold be established there, nazine gas was unleashed on the planet, causing a near genocide.

Mithlador—A mining planet in the Galactic Fringe occupied by Praxis.

Ohan—A tropical world bordering the Galactic Fringe, Ohan is a paradise that also serves as a getaway to the Inner Cluster. It is also Master Nu Kan's home planet.

Praxis—An urban planet just beyond the Inner Cluster, Praxis has grown to annex other worlds, spreading its flag across the stars as it looks to rule the entire galaxy.

Quarry—A forlorn planet that once cultivated a rare spice that was traded throughout the entire galaxy. But that was before Praxis unleashed its star-killing wrath on Quarry, blanketing it in eternal darkness and ensuring that no one would be able to remove the legendary Rokura from its stasis.

Ragnar—Ragnar is a trading outpost located directly between the beginning of the Galactic Fringe and Kyysring, making for a hotbed of activity.

Sulac—A bleak desert planet that would be abandoned if not for its strategic position along a key trading route.

Ticus—A mountainous, idyllic world isolated outside the Inner Cluster. For centuries, it served as a destination for religious pilgrimage. After the death of Wu-Xia, it evolved into the Well, a place for spiritual warriors to train as they defended peace and justice throughout the galaxy.

COOL STUFF

Echoes—Standard starfighters used by the Well.

Fatebreakers—Agents of Ga Halle, these highly trained, brutal warriors do her dirty work.

Firebrand rifle—A highly destructive and unstable weapon that discharges explosive rounds that ignite upon impact.

Intruders—Standard starfighters used by Praxis.

Nucletoid bomb—Though small, nucletoid bombs contain a concentrated amount of nucleoi, enough to decimate large areas of land with a single charge.

Outpost pistol—Poorly made and thus inexpensive blasters that are common to street gangs and other low-level criminals. They're known for backfire malfunctions more than anything else.

Paragon—According to legend, the Paragon is the one person who can release the Rokura from its stasis and bring peace to the galaxy.

Power pike—A mysterious weapon wielded by the Darklanders.

Unlike similar electricity-charged weapons, the power pikes are charged not just at the head, but throughout the entire staff.

Quanta staff—Long, heavy metallic staffs charged with electricity that pours off the massive blade on the tip of this weapon.

Rai—Warriors trained, physically and spiritually, to fight for peace and justice throughout the galaxy. They follow the example set by Wu-Xia.

Rokura—A mystical weapon, forged by Wu-Xia in the Quarry spire, that is said to have the power, when wielded by the Paragon, to bring peace to the galaxy.

Shido—Designed after the Rokura, the shido is a bo staff studded by three blades at its top. A powerful electric cell embedded in the staff pours electricity from the tips of its blades when activated.

Sidewinder—A sidearm that's standard issue to the Well's forces and commonly carried by many others throughout the galaxy. Its slender size makes it easy to holster, and its adjustable barrels allow for different discharge settings, ammunition, and range.

The Well—Located on the planet Ticus, the Well is the nexus for warriors from around the galaxy to train to become Rai. It has grown to also house a peacekeeping infantry of ground soldiers and starfighter pilots.

WE ARE MAYHEM

Available April 2019

CHAPTER ONE

M ore enemy fire deflected off the *Rubicon*'s shields, causing
both the ship to bounce in space and Cade's stomach to
bounce into his chest. He wrapped his hand around a strap that
hung from the cargo hold wall, steadying himself as he swallowed
his insides down. After taking a deep breath, he looked over and
saw Kira smirking at him.

"*What?*" Cade asked, agitated.

"Nothing, nothing at all," Kira said. "I just didn't know you
were so delicate. But it's fine. Totally cool."

Cade groaned. "You know, even by our standards, this is ex-
cessively stupid."

Kira put up her hands. "Hey, don't look at me. This is your
friend's idea."

"Huh?" came Mig's voice from the back of the cargo hold,
where he was tinkering with something or other. "Is Cade complaining again?"

"I'm not complaining," Cade said. "I'm just . . . processing.
Verbally. I'm verbally processing."

"Verbally processing your complaint," Kira said. "We got it."

"You know what? I'm ready. I am ready to jump out of this ship now."

"Such a sensitive Chosen One." Mig snickered as he stepped in front of Cade and started fiddling with his grav suit. "I'm just going to shut this clasp. If you're going to leap into the cold, deadly abyss of space, it's best if your enclosure is airtight."

Cade rolled his shoulders, unable to find any comfort inside the cumbersome exoskeleton. Grav suits were nothing new; crew members used them all the time, especially on larger starships, to make exterior repairs. But in those instances, the grav suits were tethered to the ship. They moved slowly and safely.

Mig's version was neither slow nor safe. He'd reinforced Kira's grav suits so the exterior was harder to penetrate, but Cade was less concerned with the ramifications of taking enemy fire and more concerned with the suit's propulsion capabilities, which, thanks to Mig's upgrades, could now power a small starhopper. Having that kind of power right beneath his feet and hands didn't sit well with Cade. Especially since he was supposed to use that power to propel himself through space and hope nothing went wrong—and in this case, wrong could send Cade careening off into space, where he'd die a long, excruciating death. Cade had one fear in life, and that was it. He could take on a squad of Praxian drones with hands so steady you could rest your drink on them; he could fly any ship through a furious dogfight with a smile on his face. While he didn't relish the idea of meeting the sharp end of a quanta staff or being incinerated by an enemy starfighter, at least those ends would be quick. But confronting the vast, emptiness of space? Where he'd float for days and do nothing but *think*? That scared the crap out of him.

The ship was rocked by enemy fire again, and Cade nearly lost his lunch.

"You know," Kira said, "if I could hand over the control of my ship to your cranky drone, you should be able to handle this."

"I never thought I'd say this, but for the first time, Duke is actually the least of my problems," Cade said.

From over his shoulder, Cade heard 4-Qel's heavy gait as he lumbered down the cargo hold's ramp. He "whistled" a monotone tune as he joined Cade, Kira, and Mig.

"Personally, I'm excited," the drone said. He'd been equipped with the propulsion units, but he didn't need the grav suit. Because, apparently, nothing could kill him.

"So you like the idea of hurtling through space with a questionable amount of control over your body?" Cade said. "Why doesn't that surprise me?"

"I'll be like a graceful speck among the cosmos, as close as I will ever get to being united with the fabric that binds all sentient life."

Cade and Kira shared a curious look.

"Or," 4-Qel continued, "a weapon of massive power, out to exact my destructive purpose."

"That's more like it," Kira said.

Mig punched in the code on the cargo hold's control panel. The hold's door lowered slowly, revealing a deep blackness punctuated by pinpricks of stars.

"From here, the drop to the Kundarian trade ship should take no more than two minutes," Mig informed the team. "Use the suit exactly like I showed you; let it do most of the work, and you're good."

Mig joined Cade, Kira, and 4-Qel, and together they walked toward the lip of the cargo door. In just seconds, they'd be jumping off it; Cade tried to convince himself that he was relieved to finally have it done with. He'd been sweating this solution to liberating the Praxis-occupied Kundarian vessel ever since it was conceived, and no matter how hard he tried, he couldn't bring himself to liking it. In fact, he hated it.

"Oh, one other thing!" Mig yelled over the din of the cargo door's hydraulic system. "Do *not* forget that last thing I told you!"

Cade shot a panic-stricken look at Mig. "Wait, what?" he asked. "What last thing?"

"Huh?" Mig said, holding his armored hand up to where his ear was, beneath this helmet. "Sorry, I can't hear you."

"What last thing? You didn't—" Cade looked over and saw Kira practically bursting as she tried to hold in her laughter.

"Oh, hilarious," Cade said. "Real mature."

"Still can't hear you," Mig toyed.

"Then read my lips!" Cade yelled, and then he mouthed, very clearly, a pointed obscenity.

But then the noise stopped as the door was completely lowered.

"All right, boys," Kira said. "Time to fly."

The space above the planet Kundar was punctuated by streaks of light screaming across the sky. Kundarian freedom fighters engaged Praxian Intruders with the goal of drawing them away from the trade ship that'd been hijacked by the evil Praxis kingdom weeks earlier. It'd been sitting inert since, a bargaining chip against the Kundarian freedom fighters who were waging a bloody ground assault against Praxis's occupation of their planet. Praxis's deal with Kundar was simple: Surrender, join the kingdom, and the trade ship carrying essential supplies would be released from orbit. Kundar's answer, as evidenced by the dogfight taking place over their planet, was clear.

Resistance to its imperial ambitions—ambitions that wouldn't settle for anything less than complete control of the entire galaxy—was new to Praxis. The kingdom used to be able to rely on its *War Hammer*—a massive starship that had the power to drain the energy from a planet's nearest star, leaving it dark, cold, and dead—to be the ultimate deterrent, but Cade and his friends changed all that. Defying the odds, defying orders to relent, Cade, Kira, Mig, and 4-Qel pulled off what had previously been an unthinkable task: They blew the *War Hammer* into a million little pieces, and that strike wound up being the opening salvo in a war across the galaxy.

But Praxis wasn't about to relinquish its control so easily.

In the wake of having the crown jewel of its fleet blown out of the sky, the evil kingdom doubled down on its assault of neutral planets like Kundar, forcing more and more worlds to fly Praxis's bloodred flag. Praxis smothered planets in numbers; no system could match its air and ground forces. The planet's enlistment rate was ten times higher than the next highest planet, and if that wasn't enough, Praxis also conscripted ancillary forces from the planets they annexed. Still, the destruction of the *War Hammer* proved that sometimes might doesn't matter; sometimes sheer numbers aren't enough. Not when you have willingness. Not when you're fighting for what you believe is right. And that's why Cade was hurtling through space at a clip he didn't even want to think about, soaring toward the Kundarian trade ship so he and his friends could free it from Praxis's control and, from there, aid the planet's freedom fighters in their efforts to evict Praxis from their home once and for all. Cade and his friends—referred to as the Black Star Renegades, a moniker Mig anonymously spread through the galaxy because he said it made them sound "more legit"—had become Praxis's fulcrum, balancing its agenda of conquest and control with the hope for freedom. The hope to resist and *win*.

Below Cade, Kundarian starfighters, with their sleek dual engines and chromium shell, executed evasive maneuvers as they deftly flew circles around Praxis's Intruders; the Kundarians unleashed proton blast after blast, but only as a defensive measure and to keep the Intruders off-balance. The barrage filled the space with innumerable points of light; to Cade, it was like looking through a kaleidoscope while high on kerbis. Still, it kept Praxian fighters away from the trade ship for the time being. This little plan of Mig's was plenty suicidal already; the last thing Cade needed was to navigate his way through airspace that was littered with both enemy and friendly fire and the flaming wreckage of countless starships. That'd be the only thing that could make this worse, Cade thought.

Until things got worse in a way Cade didn't anticipate.

The Kundarian trade ship was in Cade's sights and coming on fast. But as he got closer to the vessel—shaped like a crescent moon with a bulbous command console in its center—Cade noticed small disks launch from the ship's starboard side. Dozens of them spun in Cade's direction. Hundreds of them.

His heart sank into his guts.

"Guys!" he yelled into his comms. "We've got incoming!"

"*Damn it*," Kira snarled. "Razor drones."

Destruction didn't even begin to describe a razor drone's purpose. Cade had to make up a word because no existing word appropriately captured the razors' single-minded penchant for carnage. Annihilatory. That would do. The drones were designed for one purpose and one purpose only: to magnetically attach to the hull of a ship and tear it to shreds. Which was bad. Because ships without exteriors to keep them, among other things, pressurized and stabilized? They tend to fall from the sky. Uncontrollably. And the people inside fare even worse than the ship after it crash-landed.

Cade was currently covered in a material identical to the hulls of most ships. He had seen the razors' work with his own eyes. It didn't take much for him to conjure an image of what the drones would do to his grav suit and then his skin, intestines, and so on.

But Cade wasn't a ship. He wasn't just some sack of meat in a grav suit. He was the *Paragon* . . . kind of. Of sorts. A Paragon in training. Despite his leveling up, or maybe because of it, Cade still relished any opportunity to be reckless. Possessing the Rokura was just an excuse for him to double down on his wanton disregard for his own well-being.

"So, Mig, weren't you the one saying how we'd be too small to be picked up by the trade ship's sensors?" Cade ribbed, exacting a small amount of payback on his friend. "That *was* you, right?"

"Well," Mig casually responded, "looks like I was wrong."

"All right, here's what we're going to do," Kira said, taking the lead. "Mig, Qel, push yourselves toward the center, to Cade and me. We'll tighten formation and blast our way—"

"Nah," Cade interrupted. "I've got this."

Cade fired his thrusters to maximum burn and was just getting out of suit-to-suit comms range when he heard Kira yell, "I hate it when you do that!" Cade smiled; Kira really did hate it. The thing was, Kira would have flung herself headfirst into a hive of razor drones if it meant fulfilling the mission, even though the odds of her not making it out were slightly worse than taking a sidewinder blast point-blank to the face. Cade recognized how identical they were in their appetite for danger; Kira chased it because she was a dedicated soldier, and no risk was too great when doing the right thing was at stake; Cade because he had a massive chip on his shoulder—circumstance had yoked him with the belief that he had something to prove, that he'd *always* have something to prove. What separated Cade and Kira now was simple: Cade had the most powerful weapon in the galaxy at his side, and the upside of that was that he could take stupid risks; the downside was that he often had to strand his friends on the sidelines. It was too dangerous for them to be around the Rokura; it was too dangerous, too volatile, and Cade wasn't confident that he could tame the weapon if its powers exceeded his control. Still, even if it was for their own good, Cade couldn't help but feel like he was drifting away from the people closest to him.

As Cade drew within spitting distance of the razor drones, their finer details came into focus. Two amber-hued ocular lenses were set into the core of their bulbous bodies and, protruding from their sides, four pincers snapped greedily, anticipating their prey. Cade knew he was an easy target; the Rokura, though, was no one's lunch, and these drones were about to learn what it's like to have the power of destiny shoved up their tailpipes.

Cade aimed the Rokura forward. White-hot energy began to spark off its three blades. Cade thought he should say something witty and clever, but so far, his attempts to craft a catchphrase had only yielded "Taste the heat," and he wasn't sure what that even meant. Besides, his friends already had a lifetime's worth of fodder to bust his chops about in his sometimes-clumsy attempts to play the role of Paragon. So instead, he'd just kick back and let the mystical weapon perform its magic. That's how this whole thing worked; though Cade would never admit it to anyone, he knew the truth: The Rokura was in charge, not him.

Sure, they'd settled into a tense truce since the weapon chose him over Ga Halle. Cade used it as seldom as possible, and in those instance, the Rokura obliged his commands. It helped free him and Kira from a nakal beast's den on Ryson, and it destroyed Praxis's prototype mobile drone garrison on Bondra before it could escape the planet's orbit. The Rokura had no choice. Until Ga Halle could prove her worthiness over Cade or another true Paragon—like Cade's brother, Tristan—came along, it would just have to make the best of whatever the galaxy threw its way, even if it was a second-best destiny. Still, even though the Rokura was as stuck with Cade as he was with it, he felt its darkness swirling on the periphery of their alliance. Deep down, the weapon was still intent on shaping Cade into the Paragon it deemed worthy of the mantle. And that worthiness, it seemed to Cade all too often, required pursuing a path that was darker than he'd ever be comfortable with. The weapon still spoke to him, still urged him to quench a thirst for power that he didn't possess. Light existed in it as well, and Cade felt it struggle for domination against the darkness. What kept Cade awake at night was his fear that he'd never find a way to harmonize both sides. As he struggled, the Rokura's more aggressive half taunted Cade with the promise of unlocking its full, true power. In his meditations, Cade caught glimpses of what that power had to offer, and it terrified him. Images of a city engulfed in flames, of a Praxian warship being torn apart, of innocent, frightened people begging for mercy clouded his mind, and Cade knew that he'd never acquiesce to such terrifying expectations. But he also knew that, until he did, he'd never be the Paragon's true master, let alone partner. And that meant he was vulnerable. That meant, one day, the Rokura would stop working on his behalf.

What happened after that was anyone's guess. Cade could only hope, as the razor drones buzzed around his head, that that day wasn't today.

Energy of incalculable might poured off the Rokura, and the first razor drone that tested that crackling white light received the teeniest taste of its power. It was enough to obliterate the drone from existence. One jolt from the Rokura and the drone convulsed, briefly, and then it was gone.

Cade wished that small sample of the Rokura's might would be enough to deter the other hundreds of drones from attacking. But no one ever learns.

"Stupid machines," Cade grumbled as the drones descended on him en masse. He shut off his propulsors, and the abrupt end of his momentum was enough to drop Cade out of the capsule the razors were attempting to cover him in. As he drifted back, Cade aimed the Rokura at the pursuing drones and let it rip. A single blast shot out from its head and shredded the drones in his vicinity. His path clear, Cade activated his propulsors and carved an upward arc with the firing Rokura leading the way. With the razors in pursuit, Cade angled the Rokura down and widened its blast radius; he eliminated swaths at a time, but the relentless drones still continued their pursuit.

Nonetheless, Cade assumed victory was just a matter of letting the weapon wrap up its large-scale destruction and then mopping up whatever stragglers remained. What he didn't know was that there was a second wave of drones at his back, purged from the trade ship while he wasn't looking. But Cade got a good feel for their presence when he detected one chewing through the back of his grav suit. Before he could swat it away, Cade felt something crash against his suit, strong enough to jolt his body upright; he looked over his shoulder and saw Kira, a sidewinder in each hand, picking off the drones that were zeroing in on him.

"You really have to stop shooting at me," Cade said.

"Oh, come on," Kira said. "I've only done it twice, and I saved your butt in both instances. Literally this time."

Cade and Kira closed the distance to each other; Kira continued to pierce drone after drone between their orange lenses, and Cade took out a batch with the Rokura. But the things kept coming.

"I'm running out of charges!" Kira said, and though Cade was focused on obliterating the drones in front of him, he could feel more and more coming at his back. A lot more.

They were about to be overwhelmed.

"Cade, we've got to get out of here. There are way too many of them."

Cade broke off the Rokura's killing spree and turned to see what Kira was looking at.

"Come on! What is that, *all* the drones?"

If Cade's knowledge of Kundar's star chart was correct, he should have been able to look out to this swath of space and see the Erso Nebula. But no. Instead, all Cade saw was a wall of razor drones so immense that it blotted out the world beyond. And these drones were coming on *fast*. Even with their propulsors pressed to maximum burn, Cade figured they had a fifty-fifty chance of outrunning the drones, though Duke wouldn't be able to get the ship to their location in time to save their asses. Which meant Cade had to do something that probably wasn't safe. In fact, he knew it was definitely unsafe, but it was all they had.

With a firm grip, Cade grabbed hold of Kira's waist and pulled her close. He held her in an embrace, their bodies pressed together, and brought the Rokura close to his chest.

"Hey!" Kira snapped. "What do you think you're doing?"

"Saving us, I think?" Cade said. "Now hold still."

This was the moment Cade dreaded. Sure, the Rokura provided him with enough juice to look cool and win some battles, but there was a danger in allowing himself to slip too close to the weapon. He felt that danger down to his core, and it made him think that should his connection to the Rokura get too deep, and vice versa, he might not be able to pull back out. But he had no choice, so he pushed his fear of potential consequences aside and concentrated. Cade channeled himself into the Rokura and felt it flowing into him in return. The effort made him grimace; Cade squeezed his eyes shut as he pushed his will outward, straining with every fiber of his being. Kira called for him, but her voice was lost as his mind went deeper into his focus. Cade began to feel his efforts taking shape; the Rokura's energy was expanding outward, forming a shell around himself and Kira. He opened his eyes and realized they were safely cocooned in crackling white energy.

"Whoa," Kira said.

Cade looked at her and smiled. "Yeah? Well, check this out."

Suddenly, an immense surge of energy erupted from the cocoon, a 360-degree blast that vaporized every single razor drone in sight. Nothing was left of them but barely visible particles shimmering in the eruption's afterglow. They rained down over Cade and Kira, brilliant specks glowing and fading all around. Kira reached out a hand and let them fall into her palm, where the evaporated like snowflakes. It made her smile.

They were safe, but when Cade looked down, he realized he was still holding Kira close to his side. He loosened the grip his fingers had on her grav suit, but his arm wouldn't let go. His eyes drifted to her suit's helmet; there, the remaining luminous bits of the razor drones reflected in the glass casing, obscuring half her face in wonderment.

"Hey," he said.

"Hey yourself."

"I feel like . . . like we never see each other anymore," Cade said, and it was true. With Cade training with Percival to become a more suitable Paragon and Kira strategizing the rebellion against Praxis, there had been hardly any time for much else.

"Well," Kira said, "here I am."

Cade stammered. He wanted to tell Kira that he missed her, but to what end? The separate paths that created a wedge between them—not to mention the burgeoning war—weren't going to converge anytime soon. If anything, the demands placed on Cade by Percival were only driving him further from Kira. Further from all his friends. And taxing Kira with his feelings for her—however genuine, however true—was unfair to her. The squadrons under her command were counting on her to deliver on the promise she and Cadge forged together: That they could defeat Praxis. That their risk and sacrifice was worth it. To fulfill that promise, Kira needed to remain focused on the task at hand; she needed to rally enough systems to contest the Praxis kingdom at their almost immeasurable scale. Kira needed to be more than diligent, more than dedicated; she had to be an unstoppable force, and Cade had no doubt that it was the role she was destined to play.

Still, Cade had to spit out *something*. He opened his mouth to speak, not knowing what would come out, but he was mercifully cut off by the sound of Mig's panicked voice breaking through the comms.

"Sorry to break up your moment, but we have to get out of here!"

Cade looked over his shoulder and spotted Mig and 4-Qel racing toward him. And behind them, an Intruder chasing after a Kundarian starfighter. The starfighter was supposed to stay out of their way and avoid situations exactly like this one. But as it drew nearer, rapidly, Cade noticed that the ship was bucking uncontrollably as sparks spat from its rear. The pilot, Cade assumed, must have taken his vessel off course in an effort to preserve the ship's integrity, or what was left of it. But it didn't work. Now, the starfighter was zeroing in on Cade and his friends. And it was likely going to be blown to pieces very, very soon.

Before Cade and Kira could even recalibrate and propel themselves away from the incoming starfighter, Mig and 4-Qel were on them. Mig grabbed hold of Cade, 4-Qel grabbed Kira, and together they blasted off toward their destination, the Kundarian trade ship—with the failing starfighter, as well as the Intruder that pursued it, on their heels.

"This is going to be close!" Kira yelled, and as she did, Cade dared to look back over his shoulder one more time. The starfighter was making quick work of the distance between them; Cade could almost feel the engine's heat warming his grav suit.

"I'd say it already is close," Cade replied. "Where are we supposed to land in the trade ship?"

"There," Kira said, leading them all forward. "My contact on the inside left that docking bay's shield down for us."

Cade looked at the trade ship and noticed a small docking bay that, unlike the others, wasn't protected by faint red shielding. It wasn't a surprise; Kira's missions were always as tight as a drum. Things in her control never went wrong. The problem was the unexpected things. Like, for instance, a starfighter pilot who, in the process of trying to save his own hide, veered dangerously off course and was threatening to crash into the very people he was supposed to be safeguarding. And while Cade didn't know any instances of starships crashing directly into people, it didn't take much of an imagination to figure out how those stories would end: with the guts of those not protected by a starship (i.e., him and his friends) splattered all over the place. So, they were going to have to hurry.

"I knew I should have given the propulsors more power!" Mig yelled.

"Any more juice on these things and they'd tear our limbs from our bodies," Cade reasoned.

"A price I wouldn't mind paying at this point!"

They were all pushing their propulsor units to their limits, but it was no use; the starfighter was outpacing them with more speed than they could account for.

"We could always move out of the starfighter's path," 4-Qel evenly suggested.

"And have it crash into and destroy our only entry into the ship? I don't think so," Kira said. "We're making this."

No sooner had Kira's overture been made that Cade looked back just as the Intruder erupted two shots out of its cannon—two shots that landed directly into the Kundarian starfighter's rear. The shots proved to be all the ship could handle, and Cade could only watch as their problem went from critical to catastrophic: The starship erupted into a ball of fire that burned across the sky before quickly extinguishing. What was left was a junk heap's worth of debris blazing toward them, countless pieces of fiery scrap metal that were just as problematic as the ship, if not worse. Instead of one thing roaring toward them, it now was thousands.

Not to mention the Intruder that, having cleared the pesky starfighter out of its way, was now laser-focused on Cade and his friends.

"We're dead," Mig said.

"I don't think so," Kira said as she turned around and started firing her sidewinder at the incoming debris. "Everyone, shoot the scrap closest to us! The more junk we create between us and that Intruder, the harder it'll be for its weapons to lock onto us!"

Cade, Mig, and 4-Qel did as instructed, firing round after round at the debris, sending pieces careening between themselves and the Intruder. The Intruder retaliated with blasts of its own, but none came close to their intended targets. Not until Mig teased the limits of their luck.

"Can't hit what you can't see, jerkfac—"

And that's when one of the Intruder's proton blasts sailed directly over his head, close enough to nearly singe the helmet of his grav suit. Cade turned to Mig; he looked like the shock alone was about to kill him.

"Whoa," Mig breathlessly said.

"Enough messing around!" Kira yelled. "Everyone in!"

Cade spun back around to see the cargo bay within reach, but the Intruder was bearing down on them, hard. Shot after shot sailed overhead—thankfully, people were a lot harder to hit than starships—but it would only take one hit to reduce any of them to a smear in space. Cade pushed his propulsors even though they were already burning at capacity. Still, any little boost could spell the difference between life and death.

At last, he rocketed into the docking bay, Kira, Mig, and 4-Qel

392 | MICHAEL MORECI

at his side. They smashed onto the metal floor and rolled, carried by their momentum, deeper into the bay. None of them had any time to even think about slowing down; landing in one piece with broken bones far outweighed not landing at all. But the grav suits, Cade learned, offered enough protection to prevent serious damage to their bodies. Cade continued to bounce across the floor, and he didn't stop until he crashed into the rear wall. It was a painful way to land, but at least their time in the grav suits was over.

Cade felt his muscles and joints already aching as he stumbled to his feet. "This one's going to linger for a while."

The pain he felt in his back, legs, and ribs was forgotten when he looked ahead and saw the Intruder still racing at him. It was thundering toward the cargo bay, and it wasn't slowing down.

"It's going to crash into us!" Cade yelled.

"Everybody move!" Kira ordered. "Move!"

But Cade knew there wasn't time for them to get clear of the Intruder's path. There was only one way to save their sorry butts. Cade grabbed the Rokura and held it like a spear. Trying to forget all the coin he'd lost to Kira in darts, Cade ran ahead and launched the weapon directly at the opposite wall. There, it landed squarely into the docking bay's control panel, smashing it.

In the blink of an eye, the dim red shield spread across the bay's opening, and just as it did, the Intruder flew right into it. A pulse of dark red screamed across the shield, and the Intruder burst into pieces.

Cade turned to look at his friends, who were still holding their breaths, expecting to die. Except 4-Qel, who didn't breathe, which was why he was the first to talk.

"See?" he said, clasping Cade's shoulder as he walked by. "And you were worried about our adventure in the grav suits."

Cade wanted to fire a barb back at the drone, but all he could muster was a pitiful wave of his hand, shoving the drone away.

4-Qel was unphased. "No time to lose," he chirped. "We have a ship to liberate."

"The bridge is this way," Kira said, leading Cade, Mig, and 4-Qel down the dark, narrow hallway that snaked away from the cargo bay. They went up to the ship's main level and to a forking path. "My contact told me sentry drones are standing guard between here and the bridge, but nothing we can't han—"

From the darkness of the path on the left came a serpentine voice that cut off Kira's words. "Mr. Sura," the voice said. "I've been waiting for you,"

Before he even twisted his head to see the figure emerging from the leftmost path, Cade already knew who the voice belonged to: Ortzo, the Fatebreaker who'd been relentlessly pursuing Cade since before he blew up the *War Hammer*.

"I've *missed* you," Ortzo said with an exaggerated sibilance.

Cade armed himself with the Rokura and took a step in Ortzo's direction. "I bet you have; Ga Halle must be a real pill these days."

Ortzo smirked. He was dressed in the traditional Fatebreaker armor—a black tunic with protective gold scales shielding his arms, legs, and torso—though without the mask that covered his face. Not that it mattered; unlike Cade's shido, the Rokura had no problem slicing through anything that was in its way.

"My master is doing just fine," Ortzo replied. "Praxis still controls the galaxy, and the small matter of her claiming what rightfully belongs to her—the very weapon you hold in your unworthy hands—is soon to be resolved."

Cade snorted. "You are a confident one, I'll give you that. Delusional, but confident."

"Why are we even wasting time entertaining this fool?" Mig said, his finger twitching over his sidewinder's trigger. "Let's dust him and move on."

Cade held down Mig's arm just as he was about to raise his weapon. He could see Ortzo flashing a devilish smile across his face.

"No," Cade said. "He wouldn't make it that easy."

"Heat-sensitive explosives," Ortzo said, answering the question he hadn't been asked. "One shot from that uncivilized hand cannon of yours, and this entire hallway goes up in flames. That means the so-called *Paragon* will have to deal with me the old-fashioned way: with a duel."

"He's insane," Mig whispered at Cade's side, but Cade kept his focus on Ortzo. The Fatebreaker burned so hot Cade could practically see the flames roaring in his eyes. There was no telling how much misery and suffering the Fatebreakers had caused across the galaxy, and Ortzo was their commander. The most fanatical of them all. If he wanted a fight this badly, then Cade was happy to oblige him his desire. And make the galaxy a little brighter in the end.

"Get to the bridge, take the ship," Cade told Kira. "I can handle this."

Kira eyed Ortzo, then rested an uncertain gaze on Cade. "Are you sure about that?"

"I'm sure," Cade said, forcing a confident smile. "You have your path, I have mine. Now go, do what we came here to do."

Kira nodded, and Mig and 4-Qel followed her down the fork that led them away from Cade and Ortzo. With his friends gone, Cade turned his attention to maniacal Fatebreaker, who was waiting. Armed with his battle-scarred shido, he began to walk toward Cade, and Cade toward him.

"You may have fooled part of the galaxy. You may have even fooled your friends," Ortzo said as he swung his shido down on Cade. Cade blocked his parry easily, but Ortzo pressed his weapon down on Cade as the fire burned even hotter in his eyes. "I know what you're hiding, Sura; I know what no one else does."

Cade was about to shove Ortzo off him with ease, reinforced by the Rokura's power, when Ortzo flew his armored elbow across Cade's face and then kicked him in his chest, sending him backward. It'd been some time since anyone had touched Cade in a fight, and not since his battle with Ga Halle had he confronted someone who *knew*. The nakal beasts, the razors, the gunners and sentries from Praxis's unending arsenal, they didn't know the truth. They didn't know that Cade was a fraud, a liar, a pale substitute for the real thing. But Ortzo did, and his knowledge filled Cade with dread. He didn't feel invisible with the Rokura in his grasp—he felt exposed.

"You're not in control, you can't be," Ortzo taunted. "You're a *faker*, and I'm going to *prove* it."

Ortzo charged at Cade, and suddenly, Cade was on the defensive.

He was vulnerable.